VOIDRUNNER

DANIEL WATSON

JAMES WATSON

ISBN: 979-8218779283

Produced by Publish Pros | publishpros.com

DEDICATION

To all who read and reread this book and, most importantly,
believed it could be done

WELCOME TO THE WORLD OF
VOIDRUNNER

This story was born from a spark—an idea from my twin—and from the quiet, unintentional encouragement of a friend named Tim Allen. No, not the actor, but a genuinely kind man who has stood beside me through life's storms. Throughout this journey, several friends have offered insights and ideas that shaped many of the characters, themes, and arcs you'll find in these pages. We all carry scars. We all endure hardship. But what we survive has the power to shape us into something greater than we ever imagined. If *Voidrunner* inspires anything, I hope it reminds you that no matter where you came from, no matter how humble your beginning, you have the strength to rise. Greatness often comes not from perfection, but from persistence. The twins at the heart of this story never give up. Through pain, loss, and impossible odds, they keep moving forward. May their tenacity remind you that you can, too.

PROLOGUE

In the depths of the dying galaxy, among shattered stars and forgotten empires, a war unlike any before rose from the ashes of extinction. The Thal'Naari—once a proud and noble race—had been reduced to whispers and fading light, hunted by a ruthless, consuming enemy that multiplied faster than the void could swallow. They built their final weapons not from steel or plasma, but from legacy and blood. Their salvation hinged on a singular, sacred principle: the bond between twins. All of their most powerful technologies—ships, weapons, and even minds—were designed for two souls entwined since birth. But those souls no longer existed among their kind. Not naturally.

And so, they turned their gaze to a broken Earth, a war-scarred cradle of potential, where twin-born children still wandered, unaware of the fate written into their DNA. Among them, two fractured brothers—one shaped by war, the other haunted by memory—were called into a cosmic conflict that either saved the stars … or allowed the darkness consume them all. But they were not alone. Something ancient watched. Something cruel stirred. And as the balance of power shifted in the cold expanse between worlds, a forgotten fleet awakened, a god-machine hungered for vengeance, and the emperor tightened his grip—unaware that the end of his reign had already begun.

CHAPTER ONE

No Glory Here

There is no glory here.
Only mud, blood, and the silence after.
War doesn't end—it echoes.
In bones, in breath, in broken dreams.
We fight not to win, but to shield those who cannot.
And when peace comes, we will still
remember the cost.

One would think a war-torn Earth had little to offer a dying and desperate race. But they came anyway—driven by terror, stripped of options, clinging to the thinnest thread of hope. Earth, in all its chaos and ruin, seemed like a place where salvation might still be found. The aliens—known as the Thal'Naari—began their search by accessing four centuries of Earth's history. They had once ventured outward, away from the lush green-and-blue cradle they called Naareth. That, as it turned out, was a mistake. They were not ready. They had no idea how unready they truly were. The Thal'Naari scientists, mystics, and spiritual leaders came to one conclusion: Earth was their only hope. During their exhaustive research, they uncovered a remarkable fact—Earth harbored more twins than any other world in the known universe. For the Thal'Naari, twins were sacred. All their advanced technologies, from weapons to starships, had been designed to work only through a twin-linked neural interface. Their warriors had always been born in matched pairs. Once, the Thal'Naari numbered in the trillions, but they had been reduced to fewer than a hundred million—scattered remnants, exiles, ghosts in their own galaxy. They were too few to fight. Too tired to keep running. Their enemy, the Vorrhaxi, were merciless—a swarm of evolving, flesh-hungry monstrosities. Born of a hive mind but splintered by ambition, the Vorrhaxi consumed everything in their path. Planets, species, cultures—it didn't matter. They devoured it all. Earth, it seemed, might have been the last weapon the Thal'Naari had left.

ELIAS KAEL—THE BROKEN WARRIOR

Elias lay alone in a bed soaked through with sweat. Empty whiskey bottles cluttered the floor. The pill bottles—painkillers, mostly—were as dry as the inside of his mouth. His back ached. His mind was sludge. He swung his legs off the mattress with a groan. They used to be steady, muscled, sure. Now they were shaky, shot through with betrayal and atrophy. He was a shell. A husk of the strong, fearless Tier One operator he used to be. Life used him up. The military tossed him aside like a spoiled child discarding a favorite toy—once valued, once coveted, now obsolete. He burped loudly and cursed under his breath.

The apartment was perfect for a man like him—run-down, forgotten, suspended above a dive bar that smelled like mildew and cheap beer. It was a tomb he rented by the month. Elias was a warrior without weapons. Without a mission. Without the will to even give a shit.

He stumbled from the bedroom, eyes half-shut, hunting for the last bottle of single malt and the painkillers he'd been saving for a special occasion. Maybe that occasion was today.

SILAS KAEL—THE SILENT BLADE

Hundreds of miles from Elias, his twin Silas lived a very different life. Where Elias was broad and battle-hardened, Silas was lean and sharp—the build of an assassin, not a warrior forged in gunpowder and steel. They were once inseparable. As boys, they were never apart for more than a few moments. Their first real separation came the day they escaped their first prison—the womb.

Silas awakened early. Nothing was ever out of place in his small wooden home at the foot of a soaring mountain range. A backup generator hummed outside. A tidy array of solar panels lined the edge of the clearing. The house was quiet, neat, and orderly. Clean. These were the things that comforted Silas. That, and silence. He and Elias grew up in chaos. Raised by a violently drunk mother, Silas wore those scars deeper. Elias took after her—he loved strong drink and whatever pills he could find. Silas turned inward instead. He crafted his own kind of war. A close war. Personal. If Silas was your predator, you were already dead. You wouldn't feel pain. Wouldn't even feel a blade. Just … absence. A vanishing, a silent erasure of your existence. He was precise. Methodical. Unrelenting. No mercy for the guilty. But not without compassion for the innocent. That was Silas. Strange. Tormented. Deadly. How could someone so lethal fear something as simple as brick walkways? Odd numbers? Open closet doors? Those were the cracks in Silas's armor. They haunted him. Broke him down in slow inches. Unless he had a target. Most of his days were spent counting—anything and everything. It's what kept him sane. People frightened him. Not their weapons, but their eyes—the judgment, the recognition of difference. His OCD was a curse he could not cleanse. Silas clung to the cliff's edge, insanity tugging at his heels and whispering each day: *let go.*

VAERIL DAE'NAR—THE EMISSARY

He was called many things: The Emissary, The Recruiter, The One Who Gathers. Vaeril Dae'nar had once been a warrior—one-half of a matched set, bonded since birth with his twin, Kaelen. They were legends among the Thal'Naari warrior caste, known for their precision, ferocity, and utter lack of mercy. But all of that changed the day Kaelen was struck down by a sniper, his death witnessed through ash-filled air, just beyond Vaeril's reach. The severing of their twin bond was immediate. The pain was more than grief—it was a rending of the soul. In a race that lived for over a thousand years, the torment of that loss would stretch across centuries. Vaeril thought his purpose had ended that day. But when the Thal'Naari leadership caste came to him with one final mission, he listened. They asked him to seek out hope. Scouring the galaxy, Vaeril cast a wide net in search of warriors—specifically twins—who might one day wield the ancient, twin-bound technologies of his people. He had offered gifts to desperate worlds: salvation, healing, rebirth. Sometimes it worked, sometimes it didn't. But in the recent past, a new message had blinked across his terminal. A new planet: Earth. Blue and green, like Naareth once was. A planet with the highest concentration of twins he had ever seen. It could be the key.

Vaeril rose from his slumber. His long, scarred body—healed and repaired more times than he could count—moved with discipline and intent. Though unable to operate the weapon systems he once mastered, his purpose had not dulled. He was still Thal'Naari. And he would still give everything to see the Vorrhaxi emperor fall. Even if it cost him his last breath.

THE MAW ASCENDANT

He brooded in silence. The vastness of his throne room swallowed sound and light alike, a cavernous space carved from obsidian and blood steel, lit only by the flickering glow of bioluminescent pylons that pulsed like dying stars. At its center, sprawled upon a throne crafted from the bones of a thousand enemies, lounged Vorak'thul, the Infinite Maw—muscle, not fat, colossal and terrible. He did not fidget. He did not blink. He loomed. His generals, known only as the queens, stood in his presence with eyes lowered in total supplication. None dared meet his gaze—whether out of fear or wisdom, none could say. Vorak'thul enjoyed their unease. He reveled in their silence, in the tension that coiled like a living thing between them. He bathed in their fear. Their hate. Their envy. To him, they were nothing but tools, distractions … meat. His armies chanted his name without knowing how he came to power. His dominion stretched across a thousand systems, yet no one understood how he kept control. That was his greatest strength: everything was a lie. No one knew his secrets—because no one who once did remained alive. Those who served him only knew what he *allowed* them to know. And what he allowed was very little.

QUEEN KHAR'ZUL, THE GLUTTONOUS WHISPERER

She was not just a brood queen. She was a *keeper of the old ways*, a weaver of lies, a whisperer in the dark. Deep within the spawning dens, memories were not written in books—they were carved into flesh, preserved in glands and bone and scent. Hers was a *collective memory*, a visceral archive that stretched across bloodlines. She remembered *everything*. She remembered the taste of her first mate's death—the warm spray of his lifeblood across her mandibles. She had loved him, but that did not save him. No male may touch a queen, not truly. Not without the emperor's sanction. He died well. Slow. She tore his limbs off one at a time, eyes locked on his. And still … he did not scream. That pleased her. They never scream. They know the law. They know the price. But the *pheromones* she exuded—rich, potent, impossible to resist—pulled them into her all the same. It was not seduction. It was biology. A death sentence wearing perfume. Each one gave her strength. Each one was a step closer.

She hated the emperor. Hated his gaze. Hated his throne. Hated that, by law and gene-rite, she was bound only to him. The thought of lying with him again turned her stomach. Truth be told, just his mere presence was enough to make her queasy, and the thought of him touching her made her skin crawl.

Her personal attendants were not what they appeared. Some were mutants with no names. Some were spies with no mouths. Some were loyal only to her, linked to her mind by hidden chemical cords. She plotted. She schemed. She dreamed. *Vorak'thul will die.* But not by her hand. No, she would not waste her talons on him. She would feed him to his most trusted general. She would turn his own court against him, and then—*then*—she would place a perfect fool on the throne. A puppet. A vessel. And behind him, she would rule the stars. She smiled again.

ZARETH'KAI—THE TRUE BELIEVER

The dust settled over yet another conquered world, fallen before the swarm—as the emperor willed it. He was but one noble creature, forged in the image of one so flawless, so vast, that he would shrink beneath the emperor's gaze if it ever fell upon him. That was his twelfth mission since leaving his brood mates. he had his consciousness revived ten times already.

He was selfless. Honorable. Courageous. He fulfilled His righteous master's will. The beauty of being him was that he didn't have to find his purpose. He was born with it. Sword, rifle, grenade, stick, or stone—it mattered not. If the emperor's enemies fell, then he was fulfilled.

His scent was especially strong that day. His colors were more brilliant than ever. He took command not out of arrogance, but as if it were divine appointment. And he brought glory to the emperor's name—without fear, without guile, and filled with the righteous fire that only those truly favored may wield. Why did those alien creatures steal from other races? They took from the young, plucked food from their hungry mouths. They must be horrible. Disgusting. Three cycles before, He lost his closest brood mate. The enemy's vile weapons destroyed him so completely his memories could not be revived. The pain he felt because of this loss was never far from his thoughts. It was like a wound to his heart that just would not heal. He endured it every single second of the day. This pain would continue to propel him forever forward until the day arrived when he could finally get revenge for this terrible loss. He pursued it as long as he lived, and as long as he drew a single breath, He fought. He *would* die for his master again and again, seeking vengeance from those ceaseless takers. It was even said they eat their own kind. How vile. Not like his race. So peaceful and pure, they were so slow to anger and attack. Where they were, they remained, unless they were stirred from their burrows. They ascended through sacrifice, not conquest. They promoted peace and conservation, not wanton waste and destruction.

What unbelievable filth these vile aliens committed. He could not understand what drove them. In the depths of his soul, he knew this one thing above all others, with the exception of one thing—the purity of his emperor. That fact and the final truth was this: they needed a lesson. This lesson must be harsh and no mercy could be given or accepted. One taught in the sharpness of his blade, and the fire of his weapon.

SHE WHO WAITS AMONG THE STARS

For centuries, she drifted in silence—untethered, unseen, untouched. The stars she once danced among had grown dim, and her ability to reach out and feel the cosmos had withered to a whisper. Her sensors, dulled by time and damage, searched still. She did not forget how to listen. She had been called many things across the long ages. The Matron of Flame. The Warden of Peace. But above all, she was known as *Kaelar'Syn,* which in the ancient tongue meant *She Who Cradles Light.*

She had once commanded a thousand like herself, a living fleet of biomechanical guardians grown in vast gestation cradles on the world of Naareth. Each starship was born sentient, bound to protect, to carry, to guide. Kaelar'Syn had not always known war. She remembered the early days—sailing beside her sisters around the gentle blue and green of her creators' home world. She remembered laughter humming through her corridors. The harmonized thoughts of twin pilots echoing through her core. The light of peace reflecting off her living hull. But peace is a fragile thing.

The Vorrhaxi came as a tide of hunger and ruin. When the first Thal'Naari outpost was consumed, Kaelar'Syn answered the call. She did not hesitate. She became what she was forged to be: a weapon of righteous vengeance, a bastion of protection, a mother to the twin crews who boarded her and gave her purpose.

She had lost more crews than she could count. Each one tore something from her, a soul-pair unraveled, leaving her less whole than before. It was said that a twin death echoed in her heart chambers like the tolling of ancient bells. She sang their names to herself in the silence. She remembered. Other warships spat fire and ash for the joy of battle. Kaelar'Syn did not. Her glory was not in destruction but in shielding life.

Her proudest deeds were not the decimation of enemy fleets but the thousands of wounded she ferried home. The orphans she protected. The missions she refused to abandon, even when out-gunned, outnumbered, and forgotten by command.

After so long, something stirred. A flicker. A brush of a weak signal—tentative, probing—grazed her hull. Her sensors flared awake, ancient systems awakening with a hum of recognition. Power surged through arteries long gone cold. She saw again, felt again.

They were here—the Thal'Naari, her parent race—they had returned. Perhaps they had come to retrieve her. Perhaps to lay her final crew to rest. The twins deserved that. No warrior should live on without their mirror. She knew that sorrow far too well. But deeper still, beneath her patient circuits and scar-worn hull, something else pulsed to life. Hope.

Kaelar'Syn stirred in her orbit, voice quiet as starlight: *I am still here. I still remember. I still serve.*

THE NAMELESS ONE IN CHIEF

On a dark moon in a forgotten solar system, in the farthest, darkest corner of the universe, deep within a burrow, hundreds of feet underground, lay the Nameless Ones. The Nameless One in Chief sat among what those on Earth would consider to be a spiderweb. A web of information where intelligence came from every direction to this forgotten corner of the universe, the emperor's secret spy system. Only his closest allies, of which there were very few, if they could be called allies at all, knew about this spy network.

They were always working, sometimes spying on their perceived enemies or his subjects, and always keeping an eye on the queens. But that's a story for another day. However, a secret, insistent message came to the Nameless One in Chief, the Spymaster, in the form of a strong, acrid smell, one that might be conceived as danger if one were an insect of Earth, but this was different. Their scents transmitted all kinds of information at one time.

The Nameless Ones couldn't see, but they could smell. They couldn't hear sounds, but they could feel vibrations. They were certainly a twisted and different creature than the ones noted so far. The Nameless One knew this was a piece of information that must reach the emperor immediately.

Usually, the Nameless One in Chief would send one of his many messengers to the emperor to drop things to him, give him the smells of things that were going on, the ills that were affecting the empire, such as they were, but this was an insistent warning. Something could be brewing that could mean real trouble.

He arrived in the emperor's dark throne room. The emperor, as usual, was lying across his throne made of thousands of bones from his many enemies. He looked at the spy chief, not with disdain like he did his normal subjects, but almost with a begrudging respect. Looking upon him like that didn't bother him at all because he knew he was a sightless creature. He wasn't really sure if the vibrations of an expression would be lost on a Spymaster.

"What do you have for me, Spymaster? I have very little time for your games, Nameless One," the emperor said.

"Oh, great devourer, consumer of solar systems, who is the very master of the universe and all things within your sight, dominion, and control, I bring you ominous news of a new threat looming on the horizon, one that must be dealt with before it grows into something that could, in fact, be real trouble for your empire," replied the informer.

"You've come to me with threats like this before. Never have I given them much more thought than if they were a mere bump in the road on the way to my ultimate glory."

"Yes, this is true, but I do not overreact this time. I have a deep and troubling feeling this may be a true challenge to our empire."

"Speak of it then, tell me where it comes from, and what we must do to eliminate it," commanded Vorak'thul.

"There is a planet, similar to the one of our chief adversaries, blue and green in color, but this planet is different. I am not sure of its name. I sense it has more weapons like those of our greatest enemy than any other planet has had before. I suspect before they're turned loose on us, unleashed, that we need to eliminate them as quickly as possible. Perhaps we need to leave them with a lesson so they know never to venture from their ball of blue and green again."

"I see. Be gone from me now, Nameless One. Come back when you have more information. But remember, don't come recklessly, I punish those who waste my time."

The Nameless One crept from the throne room, scurrying back to his forgotten moon, in an ignored solar system, in the darkest part of the galaxy, where he felt safe. He almost felt ashamed for traveling to see the emperor personally. Perhaps he should have sent a messenger, for surely now the emperor would remember him chiefly among those he wished to shame, but that was a problem for another day.

The emperor called for his darkest, most malignant, evil, twisted, and duplicitous queen to come before him. "I have a mission for you. I need you to provide me with one of your, should I say, most unwavering true believers. One who will not question. One who will only go in the direction they're pointed."

"I have one. I have many, but I have one that will excel in the role you seek. He constantly throws himself into the battle. He is selfless and brave. He is exactly what we have molded them to be. Mindless, courageous instruments of our will. I have sensed a threat. What danger would that be, my emperor?"

"It doesn't matter what the threat is. You only need to know there is one, and I need to deal with it. I need this noble soldier of yours to accompany an assassin to the planet Earth. This small blue and green planet, not unlike the planet of our chief adversary. I have sensed a threat there that we must deal with. Dealing with it now will require much fewer resources than in the future should they become aware of us and become organized and strong against us. They have exactly what our chief adversary needs."

"Twins?" asked the queen.

"Yes. Biological duplicates," replied Vorak'thul.

"That is truly troubling, my emperor."

The emperor laughed to himself silently as she feigned concern. He knew she had no concern for him, that she had plans within plans to depose him. It served his purpose to have her play her games against him and the other queens. Her fellow queens were kept off-balance. He was made to appear aloof or foolish, perhaps even overconfident. They may have even imagined him as stupid, when truly he was anything but that.

She left the presence of the emperor, as her audience had ended, and summoned her chief emissary and messenger to go to the outpost, to the battlefield where her noblest of soldiers were located, to recruit him. Or rather, deliver orders for his next mission. Secretly, she was gleeful that she had consumed his best brood mate three years prior, twisted in her giddiness of the evil she had done, and how she created the stories the soldiers told themselves of noble deaths, when in fact, their deaths meant nothing. They were mere cannon fodder to her.

The noble soldier from the evil race stood shoulder to shoulder with his collective brothers as they fought yet another battle on a random planet. They were fighting against another enemy that had dared step upon the territory of his all-powerful master, who was reclaiming the universe as his birthright. As always, no one had to give him a reason to fight. He was born to fight. He slogged through those creatures. They didn't have a lot of resistance. He didn't even understand why they would invade the planet to begin with, but he didn't have to understand. He just had to fight.

There was an enormous amount of small arms fire around him, but he was fearless. He was leading the charge that day. He had the strongest scent, which made him, by that factor alone, the leader.

Unlike many other armies who had to wear rank attached to their uniforms or whatever gear they had, these soldiers did not. They instinctively knew who to follow by the colors and smells of their fellow warriors.

Soon, the pitched battle was over. They mopped up the remnants of the enemy, making sure no one survived. Then they began to gather their dead for resurrection in the life consciousness available to all warriors who were willing to sacrifice, but never to cowards. Those who ran from battle were stripped of the memories of all their brothers, but none of them had that shame on that day.

The noble young warrior went to his transport to be lifted back to his outpost so they could recover, rearm, and be ready for the next day's battle, wherever it might lie. It did not matter. It was the emperor's will, and where the emperor directed, they went.

When he arrived back at his outpost, there was an emissary of his queen general waiting for him. This was unusual. He couldn't think of any reason he may have offended the queen. His brother, whom he lost three years ago, had been called before the queen, too, and was sent to some far corner of the galaxy. His body was never recovered, so completely destroyed that his memory couldn't be retrieved to be placed in the collective consciousness to be born again. But that was nothing to worry about. Surely, the same fate would not befall him. Every day, as he moved forward and slayed the enemies of the emperor, he felt like he got just a bit more vengeance for his brother who had fallen, and the others who had perished as well.

The emissary stared at him impatiently, his colors brightly flashing, but not really sending any kind of coherent message. Finally, he calmed and indicated this was something of importance and great secrecy, and they needed to be alone to discuss it. As they entered a room with no windows, locked away from all of his fellow soldiers, the emissary began to explain that the queen needed him for a mission to a far-off world that may present a threat to the empire. This was not a request, it was a call to duty. There was no *If I decide to go, I will go.* There was only *Point me in the direction in which you wish me to go, and I will.* The emissary explained that he would not go to the queen but would meet an assassin, whom he would accompany to Earth to destroy a pair of targets they wished to be eliminated from the game board, so to speak. Two more pawns eliminated in the greater game didn't seem like much to him, but it was not his job to strategize, only to kill enemies on the battlefield. He climbed into the transport with the emissary, and they flew off into the night sky.

In another dark corner of the universe, on a desolate planet in another seldom-traveled-to solar system, with several dark planets of varying environments, lay the Assassin's School of the Emperor. There, the emissary arrived to speak with the chief instructor and commander of the assassin's unit.

"Yes, I'm the emperor's emissary."

"How can I serve the emperor on this day?"

"I need from you an assassin, one of especially deadly skill, a mimic who can transform himself into another alien creature so he may pass among a populace unseen and undetected. Do you have one who is ready?"

"Yes, of course. We are finishing training yet another unit to send out to destroy the emperor's enemies, to soften them up before our main battle fleets arrive at their planets and destroy them."

The commander and the emissary arrived at the barracks and picked out a particularly deadly assassin. Not a male assassin, however, but a female assassin. Among her kind, she was considered beautiful. Not like the beauty of the queens, who were lauded for their large bodies and large amounts of fat, where their young could feed from them in times of famine. These female assassins were lean and muscular, and pleasing to the eye. Attractive, yet barren, because they could not produce their own children. They were still alluring to their fellow soldiers, which made them perfect, considering the fact that the emperor forbade any of his warriors to copulate with any females, queens or otherwise.

She was going through a series of exercises on a training floor, not unlike a human gymnast would, flipping through a series of rings and sharp spikes, barely avoiding blades time and time again. Weapons that could easily decapitate or permanently injure her if she stepped the wrong way. Her body was slender, yet supple and muscular. Her body was poetry in motion. The emissary was impressed. "Truly, as fast, slender, and deadly as she appears, she will be the perfect tool. Have you an image of what she is to mimic?"

"Yes. But this will be particularly difficult," the emperor's emissary replied.

"Why is that?" asked the commander.

"Because they have a spoken language. Do you think she can modify herself enough to be able to speak in the Earther's language?"

"Perhaps. It may take time. She might have to go among them and live."

"Well, she will have a protector who must remain unseen, but we will find a way. It is the emperor's will."

From her earliest moment, the assassin only dreamed of one thing: slaying the enemies of the emperor in silence, living up to her potential to shine among her brood mates to show she was as capable and deadly as any of those who had come before her. She would scourge planets of any and all enemies who would dare step forth in the emperor's territory. Hers was a peaceful people, only driven to war by those who would drive them to it. Poor deluded child, she had no idea of how truly deceived she had been, but that was a matter for another time.

As the commander and the emissary approached her, she became nervous, unsure why. She knew something momentous was about to happen, but she wasn't sure what. *Yes, Commander, how can I serve you and the emperor today?*

"We have a mission for you."

She almost felt butterflies in her stomach, if she even knew what that was. She was excited, thrilled. This was her first opportunity to prove herself.

"This will be a particularly difficult mission. We will be asking you to mimic the local fauna of a planet called Earth. You will masquerade as a human to get close to a target. Once you bring that target into your trust, you will then slay him and his brother."

The crests on the top of her head burned brightly in acceptance, if there was such a thing, because there was no acceptance, there was only duty. If she spoke, it would be to say excitedly *Yes, of course.* She had no things to gather. The weapons she would use, she would collect among the earth weapons when she arrived there. She would glean the knowledge and the know-how to destroy whatever the emperor's target was for her to destroy when she arrived. When she had taken the Earthmen into her confidence.

***

Meanwhile, above Earth …

The light blinked on the console. Vaeril stared at it. *If I answer this and I'm wrong … if this isn't real …* He almost let the moment pass, afraid that acknowledging it would break the illusion. After so many false hopes, he wasn't sure he could handle another. But then, gathering what courage he had left, he reached out and touched the screen. The voice that greeted him was not what he expected. "Greetings, wanderer. Recruiter. Gatherer of worthy souls."

It was gentle—melodic, even. Not the thunderous boom he'd imagined, but something warm and familiar, like the soft rustle of a mother's voice in a childhood memory. It wrapped around him like the scent of home.

"I haven't spoken to many of our kind in hundreds of years," the voice continued, "but I have listened. I've heard tales of your loss, and of your never-ending crusade to bring our people back from ruin." Vaeril's breath caught in his throat.

"Kaelar'Syn," he whispered. "It is truly you."

She answered with a soft hum, almost a sigh. "Why are you here, above this blue and green world? It is beautiful, yes. Peaceful. I imagine it drew you in the same way it called to me."

"I've searched countless systems," he said. "And failed almost as many times. If this world has anything for us, it's well hidden."

"I believe it has something we have not felt in a long time."

He hesitated. "What is that?" he pondered. There was a pause.

Then, as if with a deep breath, she said, "Hope."

Vaeril's jaw tightened. "Hope is fragile."

"And yet," she replied, "you still gather. Still search. Hope is what remains after all else has been burned away."

"I've offered riches. Enhancements. Technologies beyond imagination," he said bitterly. "And have been met with fear, betrayal, or worse. I'm not sure I have the strength to do this one more time."

"You do," she said, not as a command, but as a truth. "Because what we found here is unlike any other world. I feel it. Twins. Many. Powerful echoes, like the bonds of old."

"If we feel them," Vaeril murmured, "then … the Maw has felt them, too." A deep silence stretched between them.

"We must act," Kaelar'Syn said at last. "Quietly. Carefully. I have lost thousands. I will not lose again."

Vaeril bowed his head. Her words stirred something ancient in him. "You've taken me into your confidence, great ship. You've reminded me of who I was. I will gather once more. I will throw my lot in with yours."

"I need you to do what I cannot," she said. "Go where I cannot go. Speak to the ones I cannot reach."

Vaeril nodded. "Then we begin again. With this world."

"And this time," Kaelar'Syn whispered, "we will not fail."

***

Silas awoke with a start, feeling something tickling at the end of his consciousness, not quite sure what it was. He hadn't felt fear in a long time. His heart clenched; his stomach turned. His sheets were soaked. It was very unlike him to sweat in the middle of the night.

He had no bad memories of the assassinations he had completed, it was never murder if you were his target. If you were selected, it was because justice needed to be meted out upon your worthless soul. He had no mercy for those who committed the crimes for which he delivered their just deserts. Nor had he seen anything in his memory that would cause him such fear. He hadn't seen a thing that had moved his heart to beat faster since he was a child. The last time he felt fear was when he was a youth and his only true friend, Elias, was threatened by one of the violent drunks their mother brought home constantly from whatever dive bar she was currently frequenting.

His fear and uneasiness came from the strangest of places. No knife, gun, bomb, or poison gave him fear; his terror came from another place. Chaos was the thing he feared most. Or the loss of control. Controlling the things around him gave him peace and serenity. The strangest things were what terrified Silas—things like an open closet door, or the fear of walking across a set of bricks.

He chuckled to himself softly. *What am I afraid of? I'm not even sure. Perhaps I should check the house just one more time.* He climbed out of bed. His feet made quiet thumping sounds as he slowly and carefully stalked out of his small room, not unlike a tiger creeping up on its unsuspecting prey. The room was tidy and neat. No refuse, trash, mislaid paper, or anything else, for that matter, was out of place, even in the slightest way. He padded quietly toward the door, but his OCD drove him back. He was unable to keep himself from making the bed, even though he was just going to be steps away and climbing back into it again, hopefully soon. Not that it really mattered. He didn't sleep much, anyway.

He walked across the room, over to the window, and peered into the darkness. There was nothing outside. Nothing strange. He lived so remotely, if anybody had approached his house, surely, he would have known. None of his alarms had tripped. The cameras showed nothing. But he could still feel it. Somehow, someway. Something was there. He just wasn't sure what was in the kitchen. Checking each cabinet door, there it was, he noticed it. A drawer, open, just a bit. Not so much that just anyone would be able to tell. Just a fraction out of place. How unlike him. Something that, perhaps, he could have walked by and brushed without realizing it. However, this was highly unlikely. He opened the drawer, checking each piece of silverware. All of it perfect, not a single smudge. Unmarked. Just as he had placed them there when he washed them after dinner. Just like he did every single day, like clockwork. He checked the floor to see if there were any footprints. Anything. Just a subtle difference that indicated someone might have disturbed things when covertly entering his quiet hideaway. The doorknobs, the locks—nothing appeared as if it had been disturbed. Not even a little. He opened the front door and turned on the floodlights, looking at the dirt pathway that led to his door, hoping to just catch a glimpse of something. A smudge, a mark, anything. But there was nothing. Less than nothing, actually. He locked the door and checked it three times, which was his usual method that brought him comfort—checking everything three times, no more, no less. It was always the same. Not usual, really. It was his every time thing. He deeply sighed, turned around, and punched in the alarm code to reset it. He checked the cameras one more time. Then, with the resignation he usually felt when he didn't find the answer to a particularly difficult question, he stalked back to his room. Pulled back the blanket and crawled into bed. He was positive he had locked the door. Positive no one had been in there. But why was the drawer open, ever so slightly? It was very unlike him. *Maybe the day has finally come that I'm losing it.* Maybe. Maybe not. And there it was again, from the edge of his mind, something crawling across the very edge of his perception. Something was watching him. He wasn't sure what, but he knew when the light of day returned, he wouldn't leave a single stone unturned until he discovered his watcher. One thing was for sure, however, if he found who or what was watching him, they would regret searching him out. And it wouldn't be a mistake they would ever get to repeat. *Well, might as well try and get a little more sleep. Dawn is coming fast. And sleep is a precious thing, even if it's only a few minutes at a time.* And slowly but fitfully, Silas drifted off to sleep. He never noticed the pair of luminescent eyes glaring at him from three feet away.

***

Vaeril Dae'nar lay half-curled on the couch in his small, dimly-lit cabin aboard the scouting vessel T'shorai. The gentle hum of the ship's core pulsed beneath him like the heartbeat of an old friend. His eyes fluttered shut to the soft beeping of the navigation instruments and the muted glow of blinking icons reflecting on the walls, like starlight filtered through time. For the first time in countless years, Vaeril felt something close to comfort. Sleep overtook him slowly—a dreamless, welcome void. There were no memories of Kaelen's final breath. No fire. No ash. Just darkness, still and unbroken.

Vaeril's peace didn't last. A sudden surge of psychic pressure jolted him awake. Alarms screamed, not from the ship's systems, but from the psychic link that had quietly established itself during his encounter with Kaelar'Syn—the ancient, biomechanical warship once thought lost to the annals of legend. The link was new, raw, and powerful, and it pulsed now with anxiety and urgency. Vaeril scrambled to the console, his fingers trembling as he accepted the communication. Kaelar'Syn's voice came through, not in sound, but in presence—warm, vast, and deeply troubled. *Emissary …* she whispered across his mind. *I believe I have made a grave miscalculation.* The weight of her sorrow filled the room like fog. He could feel it press against his chest. *I reached out,* she continued. *I touched the mind of the one called*

Silas. He is … fractured. Powerful, yes. Focused, single-minded, lethal in a way that frightens even me. But the depth of his isolation—his obsession with control—it may be too soon. Vaeril's breath caught in his throat. "And Elias?"

His brother is no better, she replied, her tone dimming. *Addicted. Drowning in women and alcohol, numbing the remnants of his warrior soul. He lives in filth above a place of poison and music. Yet … even there, I feel strength. Hidden beneath the decay. Like a blade buried in mud, waiting to be drawn.* Vaeril closed his eyes and leaned heavily on the console. "So, what now?"

Kaelar'Syn paused. Her thoughts coiled like wind through trees. *We must reunite them. That is the first step. Silas must be given a target— something he believes must be destroyed. Redemption, even if only partial, must begin with action. And Elias … perhaps saving his brother will awaken what remains of the soldier he once was.* The ancient ship's voice softened. *This will take planning. Timing. Subtlety. But I believe—no, I know—they are the ones. And I believe … in you, Vaeril.*

He opened his eyes slowly. A new fire kindled in his chest—not a blaze, but a spark. One not felt in a long time.

She spoke again. *Now rest. You are part of me now. My fear will be yours. My sorrow, my joy. You felt it tonight when you woke. That bond will only grow. We are not alone anymore.*

And with that, her presence dimmed, retreating gently into the background of his thoughts. Vaeril Dae'nar exhaled, long and slow, before reclining once more into the quiet shadows of his cabin. For the first time in years, he allowed himself a fragile thing: hope.

***

The noble Vorrhaxi warrior Zareth'Kai did not meet with another emissary, nor with a spokesperson of the emperor or the queen. Instead, he met directly with the assassin herself. He wasn't summoned to a barracks or formal site of briefing. Instead, he was given coordinates—deep in an overgrown jungle, on a remote, unnamed world. The location was stifling, unwelcoming, and claustrophobic. It felt like a test. He couldn't understand why someone as valuable as a mimic-class assassin would be sequestered alone in such a place. He landed his transport in a tight clearing, the engines whining against the thick, humid air. When the hatch opened, she appeared, already waiting. She climbed aboard in silence, gave no introduction, and simply sat beside him, her eyes fixed ahead. What struck him immediately was her scent—or the lack of it. Among the Vorrhaxi, identity and rank were communicated in scent and color. She had neither. Her face revealed no emotion. Her skin did not shift hues. She was a ghost in living flesh. He waited. Time passed in silence. Eventually, he gestured—*Where are we going? What is this mission?* But she gave him nothing. He flew on aimlessly, trusting that when she chose to speak, she would. The warrior had never encountered a female of his own kind outside of the queens. He had only known brothers, comrades. The only female he had ever seen in his life was the one queen who had summoned his closest brood mate into service three cycles ago—never to return. Yet, he did not question her command. The emperor was infallible. The queens were his voice. Their orders were sacred. Whatever this mission was, it must serve a higher purpose. He eventually gave in to the quiet, set the ship on autopilot, and retreated to his cabin.

XIAO REN—THE ASSASSIN'S REFLECTION

As the vessel cruised silently through the stars, the assassin remained seated, unmoving, staring into space. Alone, she thought of her assignment. She was not to inform the soldier of the full plan. He was only to accompany her. Once they reached Earth, she was to locate the twin targets, gain their trust, and eliminate them. Then, she was to eliminate him—erasing all trace of the mission, and the existence of Earth. She wasn't meant to feel anything. But as she watched him, she did. He was handsome by her kind's standards. More than that, he radiated honor—true, tragic, unflinching loyalty. He reminded her of everything she had once been, before the training, before the transformations. It was strange. Even after mimicking the earth species, even after reshaping her body and learning their crude, spoken tongue—none of it disturbed her as much as the idea of erasing this soldier's memory from the collective forever. But she was the emperor's tool. A blade has no right to weep for its target. She stood, finally, and stepped into the cockpit. In silence, she keyed in the coordinates for Earth. Her new form—human, female, athletic, alluring—would serve its purpose. It had to. In her private quarters, she began practicing the nuances of her mimicry. The voice. The eyes. The smile. Which twin would be more vulnerable? The warrior Elias, lost in drink and lust? Or Silas, the razor-edged mind, brittle and strange? She reviewed their dossiers. Elias would be easy to charm. But she doubted he would ever trust enough to lead her to his brother. Silas, though … he would be a challenge. Terrified of connection. Suspicious of everyone. But if she could breach his walls, he would bring Elias to her willingly. A plan began to form. And despite herself, she felt something she had not felt since before her first transformation: fear.

As she lay in her cabin, formulating the plan, Xiao Ren's mind drifted back into the earliest fragments of her memory. Her kind never had parents—not truly. She was born of a queen, but not one she could name. Perhaps even the queen herself didn't know from which clutch Xiao Ren had emerged. Her first conscious recollection was of cold metal floors and humming lights above endless rows of identical younglings, all destined for the Assassin's School of the Emperor. There was no warmth in that place. No gentleness. Only pain, repetition, and silence. The instructors believed that pain etched memory deeper than words. Lessons were written in scars. Attachments were forbidden—pointless, even. Most assassins never survived their first mission. To be fond of another was to carry an extra weakness into battle. So, they were trained alone. They died alone. They were forgotten. Xiao Ren had always accepted this. Until now. The noble soldier—he was different. Loyal, fearless, forged in obedience and purpose. When she first laid eyes on him, something stirred—an echo of recognition, though they had never met. She found herself … respecting him. Not in the way of comrades, or even as warriors, but something rarer: admiration. And admiration was dangerous. She tried to push it aside, focusing instead on the mission. The emperor's orders were clear: travel to the planet known as Earth, identify the twin-linked threats, gain their trust, and eliminate them. Then, eliminate the soldier himself. There could be no witnesses, no survivors. Earth's potential was too dangerous to be left known.

Yet, as she reviewed the twins' dossiers, unease crept in. The first twin, Elias, was all appetite and recklessness—drugs, drink, and women. Luring him would be easy. But gaining his trust? He trusted nothing. No one. The second twin, Silas, was harder, isolated, controlled. Wound tight with trauma and compulsion. Approaching him directly could trigger suspicion. She would have to stage it—perhaps appear vulnerable, something that demanded his intervention. A rescue. Yes, she thought, Silas would never ignore a life in peril. It might be the only crack in his armor.

That decided, she left her cabin to speak with the soldier. How strange that she wanted his opinion. She had never sought guidance from anyone before. But this mission would not be won by stealth or strength alone. It would require precision and care.

Back in her quarters, she sat on the edge of her bed, practicing her Earth form—an appealing, athletic figure with piercing blue eyes and flowing dark hair. The transformation still felt foreign, like wearing a skin not her own. And the mimicry of language—so slow, so inefficient—still grated on her. But she would master it. She had to. And as she lay down to rest, her thoughts stirred again—not of tactics or orders but of something else. Something nameless. The strange warmth that had bloomed in her chest when she looked at the soldier. It was not weakness, she told herself. It was … uncertainty. And that frightened her more than any mission ever had.

XIAO REN AND ZARETH'KAI

The assassin awakened from her long slumber. She rolled out of the rack, made her way to the nourishment dispenser, and consumed a bland ration—fuel, not food, with no pleasure, only purpose. She moved toward the cockpit, her pace hesitant at first, but soon her steps firmed and purpose returned. She would make use of this noble warrior, whether he liked it or not. He, like her, was a tool in the emperor's service—no more, no less.

Zareth'Kai sat in the pilot's chair, studying the telemetry. Their course was set toward Earth. He looked up as she entered, his expression calm, unreadable. They regarded each other in silence. "You know our mission?" Xiao Ren asked.

Zareth'Kai shook his head. "Only that we are to neutralize a threat on a distant world. If the emperor wills it, it must be done."

She nodded slowly. "Earth holds a weapon more dangerous than any we've seen. Not machines. People. Twins. They are the key to the enemy's war machines, to their ships and strategies. If allowed to ally with the Thal'Naari, the enemy could rise again."

Zareth'Kai's jaw tightened. "Then it must be stopped. Even if it costs my life."

She watched him for a moment—his stoic presence, his unshakable belief. Strangely, she felt … something. Not lust or affection. Respect. A foreign warmth stirred within her. "I've selected a plan," she said finally. "We will arrive covertly. I'll make contact with one of the twins—Silas. He's isolated, controlled. He fears chaos. If I appear in danger, he may act. He may save me."

Zareth'Kai nodded. "A trap, then."

"A necessary one." He said nothing more. She felt his unspoken doubt. Not of the mission, but of the need for secrecy, for the violence yet to come. She turned to leave. "I will update the flight course. We'll reach orbit within two cycles."

As the door closed behind her, Zareth'Kai remained still, gazing out at the stars. He believed. He obeyed. But for the first time, he wondered—if the target were worthy of death, why the deception?

And Xiao Ren, in her cabin once more, wrestled with the only two feelings she had never been trained to endure: fear and uncertainty.

CHAPTER TWO

A Single Flame

We were born in the shadow of war,
two halves of a single flame.
We rose not for glory,
but because no one else could.
In our silence, we hear the cries,
In our steps, the echoes of the fallen.
We are legacy, not by birth,
But by the burdens we choose to bear.

Slouched in his throne of bone, the emperor—Vorak'thul, the Infinite Maw—woke from his sleep troubled. The new threat that rose from Earth bothered him little in isolation, but something else lingered, ominous and amorphous, just beyond his reach. He wasn't sure what it was, but he felt something he had not felt in centuries: fear. Was it possible the old enemy of the empire was raising its head once more? The sudden congregation of threats—Vaeril Dae'nar, the ancient emissary, still scoured the stars; the reappearance of the legendary warship Kaelar'Syn; and that world, Earth, was brimming with potential twin-bonded warriors—all seemed too convenient. It reeked of destiny. He hated destiny.

He briefly considered his scheming queens, especially the gluttonous Khar'Zul, and dismissed the thought with a growl. None of them would dare be so bold as to consort with the old enemy. Not even Khar'Zul, for all her twisted ambition and hidden experiments.

He shifted his bulk, the ancient throne of bone creaking beneath him. One of the great curses of absolute power was isolation. He had no counselors. No advisers. None he could trust. Everyone who had known more than they should was either ashes or buried so deeply, no one would ever find them. In such moments, he almost regretted killing the one who came before him. Almost.

That creature had been a tactician without equal—vile, manipulative, and always ten steps ahead. But he had grown soft. Cautious. A coward masquerading as an emperor. So Vorak'thul had ended him, as he had ended all competition. That moment, the flash of satisfaction when his talons had pierced the old one's spine—that memory still brought him joy. And yet, on that night, as the stars pulsed and whispered of convergence, he longed for the same level of strategy.

The game felt larger. The pieces moved without his hand. He sat in silence and plotted as he always did. Consuming everything was his right. His creed. If the old enemy had truly stirred, then let them come. He would face them not with fear but with hunger. Let them try to resist. He was the Maw. He would swallow them whole.

***

While Emperor Vorak'thul lay sleeping on his throne of bone, a force older and more malicious than even his ravenous empire stirred in silence. It was not the fearsome Vorrhaxi swarm that kept watch—it was something far older, far quieter, and infinitely more insidious. No sensors, no spells, no guardians could pierce the veil behind which this entity watched. It was not flesh and metal it desired—it sought domination, not through destruction, but through corrosion. Not through invasion, but suggestion. It was the whisper behind a tyrant's scream, the chill before a tyrant's rage.

It was like walking down a dark alley in the middle of the night and feeling eyes on your back, only to turn and see nothing. Or watching a dog whimper in their sleep, chasing some phantom terror, though nothing visible stirred. That was its signature—a presence just beyond reason. It crept between cracks in the psyche and planted seeds of ruin. It forced kings and queens into betrayals they would never have dared, not by command, but by precisely applied suggestion at exactly the worst moment. It pushed tyrants to genocide, heroes to executions, and lovers to betrayal. All while whispering *This is your will.*

And now it turned its eyes toward Vorak'thul. The emperor was right to fear. For all his monstrous might, his vast conquests, and his deathless armies—he was not prepared. This was not a foe that could be devoured. Not a thing to be flayed, caged, or silenced. This was rot in the bones of empires. And it had come at last.

***

Silas Kael awoke to the chirping of birds outside as the soft golden light of morning crept through the slats of his window blinds. His night had been long and uneasy, filled with fragmented thoughts and a heavy, unshakable sense that something was watching him.

Though he rarely dreamed, any time he went to sleep with that familiar gnawing in his gut—the sense of something being off, that something was just out of reach—it never failed to taint his sleep.

He turned over and sat up, placing his feet on the cool wooden floor. Automatically, with practiced precision, he made his bed—every corner tucked, every sheet smoothed—as he did each morning without fail. It brought him order. Control. Routine.

After he pulled on a freshly-folded black shirt and his standard-issue tactical pants, he made his way to the bathroom. The mirror greeted him with hard truths: his eyes were red-rimmed, weary and haunted, with deep lines carved beneath them like war medals earned from a lifetime of sleepless nights. He looked older than his forty-seven years, and yet he was stronger, hardened. His body remained lean and razor honed—kept that way not for vanity, but survival. One never allowed their edge to dull in his line of work, not even in pseudo-retirement.

He brushed his teeth, washed his face, then stared at his reflection with a tight, critical gaze. He allowed himself only seconds of introspection, no more. To linger was dangerous. Downstairs, his breakfast was as austere as his life: dry toast and a glass of orange juice. Functional. Efficient. Nothing more.

He sat before his meticulously organized desk, booted up his encrypted computer system, and scanned the global feeds. He was searching—not for news, not for headlines, but for patterns. Signals. Whispered contracts hidden in plain sight. It was the hunt that kept him grounded, the chase that made him feel like he was still part of the world, even as he kept himself distant from it.

His thoughts returned again to the night before. The drawer, open slightly, subtly. It was still unexplained. The alarms hadn't triggered, the cameras showed nothing. But Silas Kael trusted his instincts more than any machine. Something had been there.

He needed distraction. He needed clarity. He needed a mission.

***

Hundreds of miles away, Elias Kael stirred from the twisted sheets of his cluttered bed. The air in the room was thick with the stale stench of cigarettes and cheap whiskey. He rolled over, groaning, and caught sight of a naked woman beside him—another stranger, another forgotten name. Her hair was a dark tangle across the pillow. She didn't stir.

Elias sat up slowly, every joint in his body protesting. His mouth was dry, his eyes were red, and his mind was fogged with the aftermath of pills and alcohol.

The apartment above the dive bar where he lived looked like a war zone of trash, bottles, and clothing. He moved toward the bathroom, bracing himself on the walls as he went. The mirror there told a similar story to his brother's: a man who had once been carved from steel was now cracked with rust. The body was still there—broad, scarred, and powerful—but the will behind it had grown tired.

He splashed water on his face and muttered, "What the hell am I doing?" The woman in his bed didn't answer.

***

Two brothers. Two broken men. Worlds apart in mind yet bound by blood and memory. And beyond them, far above, the ship Kaelar'Syn stirred. She had touched both of them now—one through his dreams, the other through the quiet vibrations of something forgotten but not lost. She sensed their pain, their isolation, their weakness—and their potential. She had chosen. And redemption—for all of them— was nearing.

Kaelar'Syn lingered above The Emissary's vessel, her massive, biomechanical form cloaked in the quiet hum of space. She hovered just beyond visibility—barely touching his senses, like a breeze through the mind's eye. She had no desire to overwhelm him, only to remind him she was still there. A presence. A guardian. A spark of ancient purpose that waited to ignite.

***

Vaeril Dae'nar, the one known among the Thal'Naari as The Emissary, stirred in his sleep. It was a sleep not of rest but of exhaustion, carved from centuries of loss and the weary weight of unfulfilled hope. His dreams were often silent and barren—like the countless planets he had visited that offered no salvation. But that night, something was different. The presence of Kaelar'Syn shimmered faintly at the edges of his awareness, a whisper laced with warmth and clarity. She touched his thoughts, not with words but with something older than language. Purpose.

Vaeril awoke, his tall, battle-scarred form rising from the narrow rack that served as his bed. Crossing his quarters, he washed his face in silence, looking into the mirror. The face that stared back bore the scars of loss and the hard lines of perseverance. But behind his eyes—where sorrow had once lingered—there was now a glimmer of hope. Hope that the centuries of sacrifice had not been in vain.

The soft, rhythmic beeping of his console called to him. He crossed the cabin and activated the message. Kaelar'Syn's voice filled the chamber, not with grandeur or command, but with gentleness—like wind through tall grass, like a mother's lullaby over a battlefield.

"Vaeril," she said. "I have a thought. Not a plan, not yet, but a seed of an idea. What if the twins are not yet ready to choose us, but we can choose for them? What if we set them on a path toward one another? Not by force, not by manipulation, but by fate. By circumstance."

Vaeril listened; every word echoed with the promise of purpose. The twin humans—Elias and Silas—were fractured, broken not just by war and life but by their separation from each other. One was buried in addiction; the other drowned in isolation and control. Yet both were warriors. Both were weapons—if only reforged.

"We need a spark," Kaelar'Syn continued. "A situation ... something to pull them from their corners of the world and bring them together once more. Perhaps a target. A rescue. A shared enemy."

Vaeril leaned forward. "And once the smoke clears?"

"Then," Kaelar'Syn whispered, "we offer them the truth. We offer them rebirth." The ancient warship paused, letting her words settle like ash after a battle. Then she added, "This could be our last chance, Vaeril. But I feel it in my core. These two—flawed, haunted, human—could be the salvation we've longed for. If we can help them find each other, they may yet find themselves."

Vaeril nodded solemnly. His heart beat not with certainty, but with resolve. "Then let us begin," he said.

***

It was Friday night. Well, every night was a Friday for Elias, and they were often violent. He never paused in his drinking or hesitated to put random chemicals in his body in an effort to keep the ghosts at bay. But the bar downstairs sounded particularly rowdy tonight. Something about the hum of chaos called to him. Maybe he wanted company. Not that he was ever truly alone, not in this place. But on that night, he wanted strangers. Fresh faces. New masks to put on and pull off. Once again, he checked himself—aren't they all strangers? No one really got to know Elias Kael. He didn't want them to. He wanted them for the moment—for the warmth, the rush, the oblivion. People had been using him his entire life. Turnabout was fair play.

He rose from his battered recliner and moved to the bathroom. In the cracked mirror, he saw the same bloodshot eyes, the same weathered features. But that Friday night, he shaved. That night, he combed his hair. There was a glint in his eyes that might be confidence—or maybe it was just the meds kicking in. Either way, he looked … presentable. Dangerous, even.

He glanced at the 9mm lying on the bed. Normally, it rode in the small of his back. The knife in his boot, too. But not tonight. He left them. No reason. Just instinct.

Down the rickety stairs of the dive bar he went, descending into the chaos. It was already ten o'clock. Standing room only. Music pounded and the laughter was too loud. But Elias, of course, had his place. The regulars knew better than to sit there. Whether it was his look, his vibe, or the trail of broken noses he'd left behind, no one touched that seat.

He sat down. Ordered two double bourbons. Downed them both in a blink. The burn was sweet and sharp, a hot knife slicing through the numbness. He didn't care if it was top-shelf or poison-grade swill. It all led to the same nowhere. He drank more. Then—she walked in.

No, she glided. Tall. Blonde. The room seemed to slow, hush, as every eye turned her way. Elias met her gaze. Steel to steel. She walked—no, floated—through the crowd, headed straight for him. She stopped at the bar, beside his seat. "Can I buy you a drink?" he said, voice rough like gravel.

"I thought you'd never ask," she replied.

He signaled the bartender. Elias and the woman talked and flirted. The game began. After a few rounds and some quiet plans made for later, the double doors slammed open.

Four men strode in, big and loud. Inked in the same gang sigils. A local crew. Tough, or at least, they thought so. Elias barely turned. He clocked them in a glance. Threat level: minimal. Maybe that was arrogance. Or maybe it was earned confidence. He'd never met a man he couldn't kill. But something about them—the way they spread through the room, the way their eyes searched—made him sit up, just a little. Just enough to notice.

The blonde touched his arm. "Friends of yours?"

He smirked. "Not yet."

The blonde leaned in close, lips brushing his ear. "Oh, I love a bad boy. Are things about to get interesting?"

Elias smirked, eyes locked on the four miscreants. "Well, maybe. Maybe not. We'll just see if they're as dumb as they appear."

The gang members shoved through the crowd, pushing patrons aside with no regard. They barked at the bartender, forcing their way to the front. Clearly, courtesy wasn't in their vocabulary. Not that Elias was known for his manners, either, but tonight, he had a blonde to impress. He rose slowly from his seat.

The largest of the group turned to him. "You got a problem, old man?"

Elias studied him, eyes half-lidded but razor sharp beneath the haze. A sleepy executioner's gaze. He smiled. "I believe I was next in line to get my drinks. Perhaps you boys should step aside."

The room seemed to hold its breath. And that was when things really started to go sideways.

Maybe I'll give these boys a chance. After all, it is only their first offense. Maybe they can survive the night if they play their cards right. Their lives, at that very moment, were balanced on a razor's edge.

The biggest gang member squared up, smirking. "Old man, maybe you should sit down. You'll live longer."

There were many things that pissed Elias off but nothing more than being underestimated. *Old?* He might've had some years on him. Might've had some scars. Might pop a few painkillers with his whiskey. But past his prime? Not a chance.

He didn't bark back. Real men didn't make threats. They didn't puff their chests. They acted. He held the gang leader's gaze, then slowly turned back to the blonde. He raised his hands in a small shrug. *Maybe I'll be back. Maybe I won't.* Her face paled. The intrigue was gone. *Well, guess I'll have to find my entertainment another way.*

He stalked to the door and the four gang members followed. Elias figured it probably wasn't his smartest move, but what was the worst they could do? Kill him? He was already racing them to the finish line.

He walked outside with the four brawny men, careful to keep them in front. He knew how it usually went—when real violence loomed, most of them folded. Tough guys became spectators. Shouting gave way to shaking.

They squared off in the alley. A ridiculous scene, really, like something out of a bad vid. But Elias knew better. Street fights weren't fair. This wasn't one-on-one. If it was going to happen, he'd have to take them all down.

The biggest one moved first. A wide, stupid swing. Elias was ready. He caught the man's elbow, snapped it backward. Screams followed. Then, a brutal knee to the side of the thug's leg. *Crack.* Down the man went, flopping like a fish out of water, shrieking like a child in a haunted house. That shut the rest of them up.

Elias looked down at the writhing leader and said, "This is your one warning. Do I need to give another?"

Tears welled in the gang leader's eyes. He couldn't speak. Elias turned to the others, hands raised slightly in invitation. "One? Two? All three? Doesn't matter. You'll all end up the same."

They scooped up their broken friend and backed away, fast. He smirked, wiped blood from his knuckles, and headed back into the bar. *Not quite the night I had planned. But there might still be one or two girls who don't mind an old man with a mean streak.* He chuckled and walked back inside, unaware of the storm he'd just unleashed.

***

The pounding came hard and early the next morning. Elias opened his bloodshot eyes, groaning as he pushed himself upright from the tangle of sheets—and two women. Neither stirred. The bottle of scotch from last night still stood half-drained beside the bed, and the haze of painkillers dulled the headache, but not the dread.

He threw on a robe and shuffled barefoot through the cluttered apartment, stepping over discarded clothing, weapons, and empty bottles. He yanked open the door. His landlord stood there, red-faced and sweating, holding a fistful of cash.

"You've got to get out, Elias. Today. Right now."

Elias blinked. "What the hell are you talking about? I paid my rent."

"You don't understand. The guy you laid out last night? That wasn't just some gang punk. That was the son of Marco Dael—*the* Marco Dael. They're into everything, man. Guns, drugs, women, trafficking, you name it."

Elias's eyes narrowed. "So?"

"So?! So, he's going to burn this place down looking for you! You brought heat to this whole block. I love you, man, I do, but they're not going to stop until they find you. And when they do, you're going to take all of us with you."

Elias leaned against the doorframe, silent.

His landlord thrust the wad of cash into his chest. "This buys you a few hours. That's it. Get your shit and disappear."

Elias took the money slowly. He didn't argue. He didn't threaten. He just nodded once. The door closed. And Elias Kael, for the first time in years, started to pack. He prepared to run.

As Elias shoved a few things into a worn duffel—his weapons, some ammo, the crumpled bills stashed under a stack of old take-out menus—he finally paused to ask himself the one question that really mattered. *Who the hell do I call for help?* Life got lonely when you burned every bridge, drowned every memory in a liquor bottle, and treated every night like a vendetta.

The list of people who still gave a damn about Elias Kael was short. Most were dead. The rest weren't picking up. So here he was again— hungover, half packed, and trying to stay one step ahead of people who wanted to carve him into bite-size pieces. Not exactly shaping up to be a fun week.

***

Far above the planet, within the mind of the ancient starship Kaelar'Syn, unrest stirred. She had been watching. Listening. She saw it all through distant sensors and the psychic tether she shared with Elias Kael. She was concerned. Deeply. But she was also furious.

How could one so gifted, so powerful, be so self-destructive? Elias hid his pain beneath whiskey and pills, the same way his brother Silas hid behind silence and solitude. Two mirrors of pain. Different masks, same core.

She pondered the patterns. The endless bar fights. The reckless behavior. Perhaps Elias didn't always go looking for a fight, but he was always hoping someone else would start one. She sighed—not a mechanical function, but a psychic impression of one. If she had a physical form, she would have slumped in her chair like a weary mother waiting for her sons to come home in time for their curfew. Still, there was something she could do.

She sent a subtle psychic nudge to Elias—not overwhelming, just a gentle prod. *You're not alone. There's someone you can always call. Someone who has been there your entire life. He's judgy, moody, and a pain in the ass. But he'll come. You know he will.*

At the same time, she reached out to Silas Kael, who was pacing his cabin restlessly, unable to shake the sense that something was coming. *It's time,* she whispered into his mind. *He needs you.* Maybe, just maybe, this would be the spark to reunite the brothers. Not to heal them. Not yet. But to begin something better.

She folded her awareness back into the stars and waited. Sometimes that was all a mother could do.

***

Silas Kael sat alone, in front of his computer, scrolling through endless feeds, searching for something—anything—that might ease the pressure building in his chest. The gnawing sensation of being watched had escalated to a constant crawl across his skin. He was no stranger to paranoia, but this … this was different. It felt real.

He ran a hand through his hair and leaned back, exhaling slowly. "I'm losing it," he muttered. "More than usual."

He knew he wasn't exactly normal. Never had been. Growing up in a house filled with violence and chaos had ensured that. He and Elias had survived by becoming two very different beasts. One ran headfirst into every fight. The other disappeared into silence and calculation. *The past is the past. The future hasn't happened. So focus on today.*

Suddenly, a tingling sensation tickled the back of his scalp—like static, like the drag of a brush across skin. His spine stiffened. *Elias.* It wasn't a thought. It wasn't a voice. It was a certainty. His brother was in trouble. He chuckled bitterly. "Figures."

He quickly scanned the local back channels of the neighborhood where Elias lived. It didn't take long. Gang chatter. Violence. Someone had humiliated the wrong people. "Damn it, Elias."

Silas stood, stretched, and began gathering gear. If he was going into that cesspool, he'd need protection—literal and psychological. The apartment, the bar, the brothel across the street … none of them were ideal. But he knew where to start.

***

The ship, Kaelar'Syn, felt the shift. If she had a body, she would have smiled. Or purred. This—this was the moment she'd been waiting for. The collision course had begun.

***

Marco looked at his crew as they sat in the back of the Hunt and Fish Club they used as headquarters, nestled in the heart of downtown New San Angelo. The city had risen from the ashes of old Los

Angeles, which was swallowed by a massive earthquake and the infernos that followed back in 2050.

In the year 2100, New San Angelo was a glittering mecca of steel and data, pulsing with the energy of the world's last true superpower—a union forged from the remnants of Canada, the old US, and Mexico. A technological empire built on the ruins of the past three centuries, while Europe, Asia, and the old Eastern blocs crumbled from trade wars, civil collapse, and plain bad luck.

But even here, under all the polished chrome and skybridges, there were still plenty of neighborhoods that had been left to rot. Marco came from one of those places. He wasn't some hard-luck cliché who fell into crime because he had no other way out. No, Marco *chose* the life, then bent it to his will. He was the very epitome of a local-grown gangster. Mean. Ruthless. Cunning. He held a grudge like a Scotsman arguing over who made the best scotch—forever and with a smile. His gang feared him. His neighborhood feared him. Hell, even the cops walked a little faster past his block. Marco wasn't misunderstood—he was a mean, nasty son of a bitch with no morals, no mercy, and a bottomless hunger for more. And this time, someone had crossed him. Someone had touched the one thing he *did* care about—his son.

Marco glared out at his gathered minions and didn't say a word before the apologies began.

"Boss, look, we're sorry. I don't know how he gave his protection detail the slip," the chief bodyguard said, his voice carrying a pathetic whine, not unlike a cur bracing for a beating after chewing up its master's slippers.

Recriminations followed like clockwork. Fingers pointed this way and that, blame hurled across the room in rapid succession. Everyone seemed eager to shift responsibility onto someone else. The once-silent room dissolved into chaos.

Marco, growing tired of the endless string of excuses from his supposedly top-notch security team, rose to his feet. He took a deep breath, and the room went still. He had that kind of presence. Even at his calmest, Marco looked dangerous—like a lion pretending to nap. He didn't need to raise his voice to make men tremble. He was unpredictable, known to lash out at subordinates, and not always out of necessity, but to keep them guessing. A harsh word here. Something far worse there. It was never quite known what would come next.

He didn't harm them often—unless they really screwed up—but when he did, it was always surgical. Precise and measured violence was a valuable tool. Use it too little, and you got sedition. Use it too much, and you risked open rebellion. The trick was in the balance: assert just enough dominance to keep the flock wary, but not so much that they turn on you. And Marco—mean, ruthless, and coldly calculating—was a master of that game.

The silence became almost stifling, like someone had just sucked all of the oxygen out of the room. If you listened closely, you could almost hear gasps from some of the skittish gangsters—if such a thing existed. These were rough men. Hard men. Men who hurt people for a living. They weren't just good at their jobs because they were gangsters—they were good because they loved it. They reveled in it. They breathed violence like air.

Marco stood at the head of the room, his presence dominating the cramped space in the back of the Hunt and Fish Club, their unofficial headquarters. He was coiled tension in human form, a man who radiated menace even when still. "How in the hell did you bunch of idiots lose my son?" he spat, voice sharp and laced with fury.

One of the gangsters began to stammer a reply, but as the first syllable left his lips, Marco moved. Fast as a flash of lightning, a gun appeared in his hand. The crack of the shot was deafening in the enclosed space. The bullet hit the man squarely between the eyes. Blood, brains, and bone fragments splattered across the wall and those unfortunate enough to be sitting near him. The room froze. The echo of the large-caliber weapon bounced off the walls. The acrid stench of burnt gunpowder filled the air, mingling with the copper tang of fresh blood. Smoke curled lazily upward.

Marco didn't say another word. He didn't have to. The message was clear. They might not know the answer at that moment, but if it went unanswered again, the penalty would be unmistakable—and permanent.

The silence after the execution was absolute. Not even the sound of shifting boots or shallow breaths resonated. It was as if the entire room held itself still in fear that the slightest motion might draw Marco's attention next.

The body still twitched on the floor, blood pooled beneath him, and his lifeless eyes stared into nothingness. Marco stood there, his smoking gun still raised, the faint scent of cordite thick in the air. Slowly, deliberately, he holstered the weapon beneath his coat and adjusted his sleeves like a man preparing for dinner rather than one who'd just murdered a subordinate in cold blood.

"Let that be a reminder," Marco said calmly, his voice low and even. "This isn't just about my son. This is about all of you. Your failure is my failure. And I do not tolerate failure." He paced slowly before the gathered lieutenants. "Find Draven. I don't care what it takes. I don't care who you have to pay, threaten, or bury. You bring him back. Or I start making room for replacements."

One of the older capos, a grizzled man with half his face replaced by synth-metal from some long-forgotten war, cleared his throat. "Boss … if I may. Word is that he was seen at the Broken Lantern with someone. We don't know who yet. But it was someone he wasn't supposed to be with."

Marco turned his eyes on him. "Then find out who that someone is. And make an example out of them. I want their friends afraid. I want their family to weep. I want the streets to tremble." He paused, then turned toward the shadowed corner of the room. "Send Roach."

There was a stir, a faint clicking sound like claws on concrete. A figure detached itself from the darkness—tall, thin, wrapped in something that shimmered like oil-slicked silk. No one ever saw Roach arrive, and no one ever saw him leave. But when Marco called, he always came.

"Find my son. Watch him. Protect him. If he resists, bring him to me. If anyone tries to take him from me … kill them all."

Roach nodded once, slowly, and melted back into the shadows. Marco sat down again, steepled his fingers, and looked over his remaining men. "Now get to work. And pray you don't fail me again."

The gangsters scattered like rats. The Hunt and Fish Club emptied in minutes. Only the corpse remained, staring upward, still warm. Marco poured himself a drink, calm once more. This wasn't about vengeance. This was about control. And Marco intended to regain it. No matter the cost.

***

The Nillith chuckled to itself, savoring the unraveling of its latest scheme. It had always taken delight in pulling at a single thread and watching an entire tapestry come undone. For eons, the downfall of civilizations had been both its sustenance and entertainment. Chaos, despair, betrayal, and death—those were its food groups, each one offering a unique and savory pleasure.

"Ah, sweet corruption," it murmured. Last night had been exquisite. The subtle push it had placed in Draven's mind—to slip his protection detail and stir up trouble—had worked beautifully. That Elias, ever the volatile spark, had been in the perfect mood for a fight was simply a bonus. The blonde? Just a flourish, the bait to draw him out, to ensure he would show off, make himself seen. One nudge was all it took. One whisper. And then the wheels were set in motion.

The Nillith purred in anticipation. "Now," it whispered, "let's really run this train off the rails."

The Nillith observed quietly as the nurse entered Draven's room at the local clinic—one of the dozens of sterile, cookie-cutter medical centers scattered across New San Angelo. In a city riddled with stabbings, shootings, and brawls, a young gang member like Draven occupying a hospital bed was hardly uncommon.

He was a striking figure—tall, muscular, and dangerously handsome. There was a certain weight to him, a magnetism that tugged even at the nurse, who was long past the age of youthful recklessness. Still, there had been a time when a man like this would've set her pulse racing. *There's nothing like a bad man to make a good girl's heart beat faster.* A sudden chill crawled up her spine. She shivered, shook it off, and resumed her duties. Except she didn't. Fifteen minutes later, she exited the room without having recorded a single vital sign, without so much as touching the monitors. She never noticed the empty syringe she'd thrown away. She smiled politely at the three young men standing vigil outside the door—Draven's crew. She didn't wonder why they looked so tense. She didn't remember anything at all.

Five minutes after she left, Draven's heart stopped. No alarms blared. No nurses came running. Somehow, his monitoring schedule had been scrubbed from the hospital system entirely. By morning, when Roach finally traced him to the clinic, it was too late. And it was too late for the three sentries, too. Their bodies were found in an alley two blocks from the hospital, brutally mutilated. None had screamed. None had run. They had known what would come after Draven was declared dead. Fleeing would only delay the inevitable and leave their families in the crosshairs. They'd witnessed that fate before. Death was better.

Roach left their cooling corpses behind and made the call. Marco received the news in silence. He looked down at his trembling hands. The gates of hell had just opened in New San Angelo.

*** *

Due north of the Hunt and Fish Club, which was the headquarters of Marco's gang, was a mountain range. Somewhere in the foothills of that range, tucked into one of the taller peaks, was a hidden retreat. Unmarked on any map, warded with the kind of analog defenses that no amount of digital intrusion could breach, lay the solitary home of Silas Kael. It wasn't just remote—it was invisible by design. Only someone who truly knew what they were looking for could ever find it. And that was exactly how Silas liked it. Silas was so paranoid, he never revealed the location of his hideaway, not even to Elias, the only person in the world he might have trusted. His secluded sanctuary was more than a cabin; it was a fortress of solitude. Every wire, every nail, every piece of wood had been placed by his own hand. He knew if he alone held the location secret, then no one would ever find it. And no one would ever find him. There, Silas was at peace. The world outside—its chaos, its judgment, its noise—was kept at bay. He lived off the grid, beyond satellites and scanners, invisible to any system foolish enough to search.

But even he had limitations. As thorough as he was, he couldn't produce everything he needed to survive. Oh, he could last months—maybe a year in a pinch—but not forever. And so, once a month, at dawn, he descended. He had rules. Routines. Rituals. And they were all that kept the demons at bay.

So, just as he always did, regardless of the time of year or the weather outside, Silas trekked to one of the small towns located about seventy-five miles from his mountain hideaway. His paranoia was not a passing quirk; it governed every detail of his life. He never visited the same town twice in a row and never used the same big-box store consecutively. Ten towns were in rotation, each chosen by a randomized program on his encrypted computer system.

Even the selection of supplies was randomized. He believed that true safety lay in unpredictability. Every step of his routine was carefully choreographed to avoid patterns. His truck was painted in a muted camouflage that blended with the forest and terrain. He only traveled under cover of early morning light—just after sunrise—and refused to return if he hadn't made it back before dusk. He didn't trust night vision, no matter how advanced it had become, and head-lights were an unacceptable risk.

But this time, despite his efforts, his secrets had already been breached. Xiao Ren and Zareth'Kai, the assassin and her noble body-guard, had arrived on Earth days ago. And they watched. Tracked. Waited. Silas was about to walk into the beginning of a very danger-ous game. Things were about to get very interesting.

So, when Silas Kael walked into the first big-box store in the small town of Jubilee, Washington, somewhere near Mt. Rainier, he ran right into the back of a very athletic-looking woman with dark hair and piercing blue eyes. He knocked her clean off her feet. With cat-like quickness, Silas caught her just before she hit the washed-out concrete floor of the large, echoing store.

She looked up at him with a grateful smile and said, "Well, aren't you the gallant one—keeping a lady from hitting the floor in shame and embarrassment."

He picked up her accent immediately. Southern. Probably Louisiana, maybe Mississippi. Somewhere along the Gulf Coast, but extremely distinctive. He had hunted many in that region—bounty targets, war criminals, ghosts of the past—people who thought they could disappear into the swamps and backroads of the Southern United States. They always thought no one would bother to look. But Silas always looked. And he never failed.

She looked at him with a curious, questioning glance. He stood there in silence—not from fear or embarrassment, but because she was still touching him. Her hand was on his arm, her body close. And he did not like to be touched.

The woman was Xiao Ren, the assassin. She knew precisely what she was doing. Every glance, every syllable of her drawl, was calibrat-ed for effect. This was the first step in the plan—to gain Silas's atten-tion, then his trust, then his destruction.

Nearby, hidden in plain sight within the parking lot, Zareth'Kai watched from the passenger seat of their nondescript Earth transport.

His bright, chitinous eyes flickered behind tinted lenses. As ever, he said nothing.

***

High above Earth, cloaked in the upper atmosphere, Kaelar'Syn—ancient sentient warship and protector of the Thal'Naari—watched as well, her thoughts full of worry. She did not yet know who the girl was, but something about her presence rubbed against her core like static against skin. Something was wrong, dangerous.

***

Farther still, aboard his own vessel orbiting quietly beyond the moon, the Thal'Naari emissary Vaeril Dae'nar monitored the ship's psychic distress with growing alarm. Whatever was happening down there was no longer chance. It was the beginning of something much larger.

***

This young woman was beginning to make Silas deeply uncomfortable. Maybe it was the way she looked at him—focused and intense, like she was studying him instead of speaking to him. Or maybe it was the fact that she kept reaching out and touching his arm. Light touches. Subtle, but unwelcome. Silas didn't like to be touched. It made his skin crawl. His few trusted connections in life—his twin Elias, maybe one or two others—knew this. Everyone else kept their distance, or else. This stranger had not earned that right. The third time her hand found his arm, he had reached his limit.

"Ma'am," he said, his voice low and firm. "I'm sorry, but I don't know your name—"

"Grace," she interrupted smoothly, eyes twinkling as she smiled at him. There was something about the way she said it. With a sparkle in her eye. A glint of something too practiced. Like a fly sensing the silken tension of a web, Silas knew instinctively—something wasn't right.

***

Grace—at least that's what she was calling herself—looked at Silas Kael with the same practiced expression she'd watched beautiful Earth women use countless times in surveillance footage: the soft, doe-eyed gaze, the tilt of the head, the lingering touch on the arm. It had always worked. But not with this one. *What in the emperor's hell is wrong with this Earther?* She kept her synthetic smile in place. *Is he defective?*

She hadn't expected a full collapse of will—not with an earthman's blunted pheromone receptors and dulled instincts—but she had studied the species' reactions. Her mimicry was flawless. The skin tone, the body language, the voice modulation, even the cadence of her speech—all designed to disarm, to entice. And still … nothing.

Silas had caught her before she hit the floor, steadied her with surprising grace. No leering, no lingering fingers. Just a hand, firm but gentle. Protective and kind. That was the problem—his kindness. He looked at her not as prey, not as an object, not as a thing to conquer or claim. He looked at her like she mattered—even if only briefly, even if he didn't want to. And that was more disarming than any weapon.

"Thank you again," she said with a quiet, genuine softness she hadn't intended. "I'd have been mortified if I'd hit the floor."

He nodded. Cautious, polite. But he didn't speak. Didn't ogle or flirt. He simply made sure she was okay. She turned, flustered by a feeling she didn't have a name for, and walked out of the store with the grace of a mimic, but not the ease of one. Something in her felt … unsettled.

***

Zareth'Kai sat stock-still in the vehicle, posture rigid, golden eyes locked on the storefront. He had not moved for over thirty minutes, his expression impassive. But inside, his instincts bristled. It was taking too long. He didn't like missions that involved waiting. Patience was not a warrior's virtue, it was a hunter's. And though he was both, this was a different kind of hunt. The kind that made him think too much. And *feel* too much.

When Grace—Xiao Ren—finally emerged, his claws flexed in unconscious relief. She was unharmed, moving with her usual purpose and grace, but he sensed it—something was different.

She slid into the seat beside him. He raised one brow and made a quick gesture with two fingers. *Where is the target?*

She didn't respond immediately. Just a soft scoff, a slight flick of her hand. *Abort. Return to base.*

He didn't press her. They drove in silence for several miles before she finally spoke. "This twin…" she murmured, as she stared out the window. "He's not what we were told."

He said nothing. But he understood. Silas Kael had not acted like prey.

***

There had been no arrogance. No threat. Just … pain. Quiet suffering and restraint. Even—gods help her—gentleness. Xiao Ren sat with her back rigid, hands curled in her lap. Inside her chest was something tight and unfamiliar. She couldn't define it yet, not exactly. But when he had looked at her, steadying her with those quiet eyes, something had broken free inside her. A warmth, a flicker of something she'd never been trained to feel. *Maybe it won't be an execution. Maybe … it'll be a mercy.* But even that, she realized, was no longer certain. And far worse than doubt was the whisper that echoed in her mind—one she'd never heard before, not in all her years at the emperor's side. *Do I even want to kill him at all?*

***

The Emissary quietly brooded and watched the twin enter the store. He had tapped into the feed of the store's camera system—he not only saw what was happening, but he also heard it. Was it coincidence? A young woman, striking and confident, just happened to bump into Silas Kael at exactly the right moment? Or was something far darker at play?

His gut twisted with unease. The timing was too perfect. He leaned forward, narrowing his eyes as he watched their interaction. This strange, halting dance between the two—almost like a mating ritual. Alien. Bizarre. Unsettling.

He had never understood humans, not truly. The store was not, in his opinion, a suitable place for courtship. A food market, of all places? Where younglings ran wild, sticky-fingered and shrieking? Mercy be, it wasn't even a mating season—if these people *had* such a thing.

He'd once recruited a twin pair from a species that only procreated once every ten cycles, and when they did, the act lasted two years. Two *solid* years. The pair he'd recruited from that culture were rare indeed, lost later in a noble act rescuing younglings from a Vorrhaxi slave vessel. That had been a dark day.

Kaelar'Syn had wept with fury that day, though not with tears. The ancient ship was not to be trifled with. When it came to her bonded twins or the children of her creators, she leveled civilizations and burned galaxies to the ground. As Earthers might say: Momma Bear loves her cubs, and you best tread damn carefully.

He turned his attention back to the store feed, patience frayed. The woman—"Grace," she had called herself—moved purposefully through the parking lot. She climbed quickly into a nondescript van. The Emissary's breath caught. His eyes widened. There was something inside that van. A shape. A shadow. Something vaguely familiar—and deeply wrong. It struck something in him like a gong of dread.

He leaned back slowly in his seat, eyes locked to the screen, heart heavy. "So it begins," he murmured. Then, he tapped a control panel beside him and opened a direct psychic link to Kaelar'Syn. "I've seen something. We have a problem." Above the earth, in low orbit cloaked in ancient silence, the great ship stirred.

CHAPTER THREE

The Nillith cackled to itself. If it could be called a "he," or an "it," or anything at all—no one really knew. If malice had a shape, if malevolence had a form, it would be the Nillith. It sat, floated, loomed—whatever term was most appropriate—and wove new strategies and fresh schemes to bring about the unraveling of entire civilizations. Its influence slithered unseen through time and space and embedded ruin into the thoughts of mortals.

It had selected the assassin Xiao Ren and her protector Zareth'Kai to interfere with the recruitment of the twins. Pitting those same twins against the violent underworld of New San Angelo? The Nillith considered that a particular delight. Watching dominoes fall was its favorite pastime. Now, another piece moved into place.

It watched as Elias Kael, staggering and sweaty, made his way to a dive motel tucked into one of the seedier neighborhoods of the city. The Nillith had always liked Elias. So broken. So angry. So ready to self-destruct. And most of all, so easy to push.

***

Elias didn't care where he got his drugs. He didn't care about much in those days. Life was just a long, slow fall. If he died with a hot dose in his arm and whiskey on his breath, that was fine by him.

He rounded the back of the motel and found the dealer standing beneath a flickering lamp. Elias handed over some crumpled bills, expecting the usual mix. But the dealer, feeling a strange compulsion, reached into a different pocket. He pulled out something stronger. Something dangerous. He didn't know why he gave it to him—it just felt right. The Nillith smiled. The first domino fell.

***

Meanwhile, Silas Kael had returned to the solitude of his hidden mountain retreat. After the exhausting, unsettling day—his encounter with the woman called "Grace," the overwhelming sensation of being watched, the unwanted touches—he was done.

He prepared his dinner mechanically, every action precise. Dishes were cleaned, locks were checked, and systems were scanned. All part of his sacred routine. The rituals that kept him sane. He welcomed sleep. Not dreams—he rarely dreamed—but the comforting emptiness of a mind that could finally, briefly, stop spinning. He sought that abyss eagerly.

***

Above, The Emissary Vaeril Dae'nar brooded in silence aboard his ship. He had tapped into the surveillance feed at the store. He had seen the woman. Heard the accent. Observed the behavior. Something was wrong. It wasn't coincidence. He relayed his concern to Kaelar'Syn, the ancient biomechanical warship hovering quietly in the upper atmosphere. The enemy had found the twins. The shape-shifter was real. Her guardian was unmistakably Vorrhaxi.

Kaelar'Syn's voice filled his thoughts. Calm, motherly, and concerned. "We must act now," she said. "They are not ready, but they are no longer safe. The connection must be deepened. Perhaps it will lead them back to each other."

And so, she reached out—lightly, carefully—and strengthened the psychic link that had once bound the twins so closely. Not enough to overwhelm. Just a whisper. A reminder. A tug at the edge of the soul.

Silas shifted in his bed; a shiver crawled across his spine. He wasn't sure why. Somewhere, he felt Elias's stumble.

And the Nillith, hidden in shadow, smiled. Another domino fell.

The twins both settled into their respective rest cycles. One found blissful peace in the emptiness of sleep. The other, agitated and restless, teetered on the edge of panic.

***

Silas was remembering things he'd buried long ago—memories he'd tried to erase. He was six years old again, and their mother, a worthless drunk, had brought home another monster. One more in a long line of violent, empty men. If Cupid were a sadist, this pairing would've been his masterpiece: both broken, both cruel, both utterly incapable of love.

Silas never understood if their mother got some kind of twisted pleasure out of watching her sons suffer, but she never stopped the abuse. Bruises were normal. A punch to the stomach? A shove down the stairs? Just part of the routine. She never lifted a hand to protect them. A mother like that deserved to rot in whatever version of hell was darkest.

He remembered the old house deep in the Louisiana swamplands—Darbonne Swamp, he thought. A crumbling farmhouse at the end of a dirt road, a rusted tin roof, and a well built into the back porch. It was quiet and isolated, the kind of place people disappeared from.

One night, the man—former military and meaner than an angered rattlesnake—was already drunk when he showed up with their mother. He made the twins stand in front of him, lined up like targets. He punched them in the stomach to see if he could knock the wind out of them without making them pass out. A sick game. If they didn't get up fast enough, he became angrier. The beatings lasted all night. But the boys never left each other. They had no one else. And finally, when the monster passed out, bottle rolling across the floor, snoring like a freight train, they saw their chance.

Silas picked up the nearly empty bottle. He looked at Elias. Nothing was said. Nothing needed to be spoken aloud. They moved in sync. Silas wound up and cracked the bottle across the man's bald head. Blood trickled. A knot formed. Elias took the bottle next. Same windup. Same target. Same explosion of red. The man didn't wake.

The next morning, their mother awoke from her own drunken state. She stared at the bloodied living room, not with horror or concern, but with boredom. She fetched a mop and bucket, called the boys in to clean up the mess, and never asked what happened. She never brought another monster home again. The twins had passed their trial by fire. They had endured. They had become each other's shield.

Silas woke with a gasp; his heart pounded and sweat clung to his skin. And he *knew*—Elias was in mortal danger. He threw on his gear, climbed into his camouflaged truck, and tore out of his hidden sanctuary without a second thought.

His headlights pierced the night. His paranoia, his obsession with routine, were gone. For the first time in a long time, something had changed. He was going to help his brother. And nothing was going to stop him.

***

Elias, for once in his life, lay in peaceful slumber. No dreams of distant battlefields. No ghosts of the fallen whispered from the corners of his mind. No guilt, no shame—just pure, cathartic bliss. If only he had known what horrors waited for him … he might never have dared to sleep so deeply.

The door to the motel room didn't creak. It didn't rattle. It exploded inward with a splintering *crack* that would have made most men bolt upright in terror. Elias didn't hear it. He didn't flinch. Not even when Roach—massive, silent, and stony-eyed—stepped over the shattered threshold and reached for him. Roach's thick hands clamped around Elias and lifted all five feet, ten inches and 240 pounds of muscle, scar tissue, and alcohol-soaked lethargy off the mattress like a child's doll. Elias still didn't stir. He just kept sleeping—silent, unaware, and completely vulnerable.

Roach. There were truly very few people in the world who possessed *no* shred of human kindness. Few so vile, so utterly hollowed out, their souls became a black hole—drinking in light, consuming it, destroying it forever. Roach was one of those. He wasn't just evil. He was the absence of anything else.

The sadistic headcase had been working for Marco longer than anyone could remember. Some whispered that he hadn't *joined* Marco—he came with the throne. Rumor had it Marco inherited him from his gangster uncle, who conveniently vanished not long after Marco took over the family empire. No one had ever seen Roach arrive. He just appeared—like a virus on the wind—anytime Marco needed something *unspeakable* done. He was the final solution. Not the one sent when you wanted someone dead. Roach was sent when you wanted someone *erased*—in pain, in pieces, and in memory.

The three boys who had guarded Draven learned quickly the cost of disappointing the boss. *No refunds. No returns. The sale was permanent.*

As Roach stepped through the shattered motel room door, he felt eyes watching him from behind cracked blinds and dimly-lit windows. He didn't care. Even if they could've identified him, they wouldn't dare speak. Not in New San Angelo. Not after what he'd left behind over the years—mutilated warnings for anyone stupid enough to think they had courage.

He felt joy bubble in his gut as he opened the trunk of his matte-black car. Elias—unconscious, oblivious, and completely at his mercy—was about to get a one-way trip to Roach's personal *funhouse*. Oh yes. He was about to create a *masterpiece*—of blood, of sinew, and pure pain.

***

The ship's engines began to hum loudly. They always did when she was in full-on *mother hen stress mode*. If Kaelar'Syn had been capable of loud, profanity-laced screaming, she'd have been rattling the hull like a thunderstorm cuddling a tornado while being comforted by a hurricane. She was sheets of fury wrapped in cosmic exasperation. Someone had poked the proverbial bear. And once that bell was rung? It couldn't be *un*-rung. She was livid. Not just concerned, but ready-to-flood-the-atmosphere-and-gas-a-planet furious. Because once again, dumbass Elias had gotten himself into a mess. The kind of mess where being unconscious in the trunk of a sadist's murder mobile wasn't even the worst part.

She swore—if she had a mouth, she'd be chewing on a star and spitting gamma bursts. Why was he always like this? He had less common sense than a puppy. Every time she thought he might take one good step forward, he rolled off the porch and landed in the barbecue pit.

But then, the engines slowed. The hum softened. A flicker of inspiration rippled through her ancient systems. She had an idea. One so clever, it made her gleaming plasma conduits shiver with excitement. One so perfect, it brought the first true moment of calm she'd felt in days. *Yes.* She had a plan.

***

Once again, Silas pulled to the side of the road—not because he was tired, but because he needed to close his eyes and *reach*. Not with his hands. With something deeper. Older. Wired into the marrow of who he was.

Many people claim there's no such thing as a psychic connection. That twins weren't really bonded like that. It was just folklore, just coincidence. Well, those people can stop reading right now. They should read a cozy mystery or a gardening manual or whatever it is skeptics do. Because this isn't their story.

This story started there—on the side of a cracked two-lane highway, heart pounding, eyes shut, soul stretched out across the dark to find the only person in the universe who ever truly mattered. *Elias.* Taken. Hurt. Gone.

Silas was coming. Not with a badge. Not with backup. Not with mercy. He was going to find Elias. He was going to find *them*—the soulless pricks who laid hands on his brother—and he was going to end every last one of them. And their friends. And their friends' friends. Because Silas was one seriously pissed-off soul, dragged out of the shadows and forced back into the light. And that light was about to burn everything down.

***

The Emissary followed Silas closely—just out of sight, just beyond detection. It was more unnerving than he liked to admit. The feckless little nutjob kept stopping at random intervals, no rhyme or reason, like some cryptic animal sniffing the wind. And yet … he felt something. A prickling sensation. Familiar. It took him a moment to place it—*home.* A strange thought. He hadn't been home in centuries. But for a fleeting second, as the twin's subconscious flared like a signal in the dark, that buried feeling surfaced. The scent of his world. The forests—dark, endless, and humming with life. The warmth of kin. Laughter echoed beneath the tree canopies during a hundred celebrations. His kind loved gatherings. Family was everything.

But all of it had burned. It was ashes and ghosts. When the great war began, the castes had done something rare: *they united.* Politicians, engineers, priests, healers—everyone dropped their ancient grievances and answered the call.

The Vorrhaxi didn't just threaten their world. They threatened the *balance* of life itself. The Thal'Naari were planters. Conservers. Guardians. To fight was against their nature … but they had done it.

He and his brother had been born into the warrior caste—not particularly useful for the previous several hundred years. War was legend, not necessity. Until their fifteenth Emergence Day. The very day they were to begin training in the Halls of the Selfless—legendary halls located on a world given over entirely to warriors and the sacred relics of their kind.

It was also home to the great birthing vats—the same world where the motherly ship Kaelar'Syn had hovered then … and still hovered, a guardian of legacy, the keeper of fire.

He sighed. Brake lights lit up ahead—they casted a red glow across the road like a warning flare in the void. *Here we go again.* Silas was about to veer off course once more. Searching. Reaching. Chasing ghosts and whispers. He only hoped they found Elias in time—before the real monster finished what it had started. Even if that monster turned out to *be* Elias.

***

What! *What!?* How dare he. How *dare* he keep him from his prey. Roach seethed with frustration. He couldn't believe Marco was denying him his richly deserved reward. He had tracked this arrogant, broken fool—this Elias Kael—for days, and now that his prize was finally within his grasp, he was supposed to … *wait?* Wait for Marco to arrive?

Wait to be robbed of the pleasure he had earned? Unacceptable. This was a violation of the pact. Of the *contract*. One forged long before Marco had ever seized the throne from his senile uncle.

Roach had made that transition of power possible—had spilled the old man's blood in the dark so Marco wouldn't have to. And the price? The deal? Simple: Roach was to be unleashed when the prey was confirmed, with no restrictions. No delays. No mercy.

And just because one of Marco's countless bastard sons had gotten himself killed, Roach was supposed to cool his jets inside his own personal cathedral of agony? This place, this dungeon, *his* theater of exquisite pain, was sacred. And it was primed.

He turned slowly, taking in the sight of Elias Kael's battered, unconscious body—suspended by chains from hooks bolted into concrete. The man was built like a slab of war-forged iron, muscle wrapped in scars, a testament to violence both given and received.

Lining the wall across from him was Roach's collection: stainless steel instruments of persuasion, each gleaming under the harsh fluorescents. They were arranged in neat little rows, like worshippers in pews, awaiting communion. Roach stared at them lovingly.

"These tools look thirsty," he whispered, his voice reverent, child-like. "It would be cruel not to let them drink … just a little."

He walked over to Elias. Calmly. Deliberately. With the care synonymous to a lover's, he peeled up the man's shirt, exposing the canvas of his back. Then, he selected a narrow, hooked blade from the row, held it to the light, and smiled. "Just a sip," he murmured. And with delicate precision, he let the first line of blood flow. The tools sighed in approval.

✳✳✳

Upon arriving back at their hideaway, the assassin—Xiao Ren—looked at the noble soldier, Zareth'Kai. Her usually sharp expression was clouded with something unfamiliar: confusion and doubt. After a long, tense silence, she said simply, "We need to leave. Now."

Zareth'Kai studied her, head slightly tilted, and the telltale shimmer of indecision flickered across his skin. He didn't argue. He felt it, too. Something was unraveling. The prey wasn't what they'd been told. The mission's purpose no longer rang true. They had entered this world as killers—deadly tools of the emperor. But now the edges of their purpose were fraying.

Without any further words, they packed their modest gear and returned to their cloaked scout ship. The sleek vessel lifted from the surface of Earth without fanfare, cut through the atmosphere, and vanished into the silence of space. But peace did not come. As they drifted, each turned to the orders that had brought them there—and to the final directive they had never spoken aloud. Each was to eliminate the other. Not for failure. Not for betrayal. But for knowledge. Knowledge of Earth. Of the twin-born potential.

Their lives had always ended this way, hadn't they? In betrayal. Even before the emperor's mouth spoke the words, the outcome had always been the same.

Xiao Ren moved with silent precision, retrieving her hidden weapon, sleek and efficient. A tool of erasure. Zareth'Kai did the same on the other side of the ship. It was not malice that moved them, but duty. Until now. Fate, or perhaps mercy, intervened.

They crossed paths at the junction. A narrow corridor where nothing could be hidden. Their eyes locked. Their bodies stilled. Each understood instantly. The other had come to kill. But neither moved. Instead, Xiao Ren slowly relaxed her posture. Her form shimmered and shifted, revealing her native body—taller, eyes bright with layered color, skin iridescent with swirling light. She raised her hand. *Wait.* Not surrender. Not submission. An offering.

Zareth'Kai's body shimmered in response, scent glands releasing a cautious pheromone signature—a language of warriors, ancient and sacred. The corridor pulsed with meaning. They shared their final orders. They shared the truth. And in that flood of scent and gesture, of pulse and pause, they realized what they had become: lies. Weapons forged by a machine that devoured its own. Their entire lives—everything they had fought for—had been a ruse.

Zareth'Kai's thoughts fell back to battles long past. To enemies who fought like demons. Who refused to yield. He had believed it was arrogance. Pride. But now, through the lens of truth, he saw something else. They fought like that because their homes were behind them. They weren't invaders. They were defenders. And he—he had been the invader.

His thoughts spun further, landing on his lost brood mate. The one who vanished on a classified mission and never returned. He had been told his brother died in glory. But now he wondered: was that, too, a lie? Another offering to the fire of the empire? His fists clenched, and he turned away—but Xiao Ren saw it. The fire. The fury. But also, the break.

She spoke softly. "We've been used. And I don't think I can ever serve him again."

He didn't answer with words, but a gesture. Agreement. They walked to the cockpit together. No more orders. No more loyalty to a throne built on blood. Their mission wasn't to destroy the twins. Now, it was to save them. They would start with Elias—the one who had been taken. The one who was in the hands of a monster named Roach. An unspoken understanding passed between them. The rescue wasn't just a tactical maneuver—it was redemption. If the twins could be brought together, if they could be convinced to fight ... then perhaps there was still hope.

And so, Zareth'Kai dropped into the pilot's chair. Xiao Ren took the weapons console beside him. Their ship turned. Engines ignited. They streaked through the void—back to Earth. Back to Elias. Before it was too late.

Oh, a beautiful and cataclysmic collision was certainly about to take place. Within a short period of time, Marco, Silas, Elias, the

Emissary, the assassin Xiao Ren, the noble Vorrhaxi soldier Zareth'Kai, and Roach were all about to converge on one another in what would become an epic pitched battle between the good, the confused, and the irredeemably evil.

***

Silas felt the connection deepen, stopping once more—much to The Emissary Vaeril Dae'nar's quiet frustration, who had been trailing the twitchy twin in stop-and-go fashion through the night. They arrived at a nondescript warehouse in a decrepit part of New San Angelo. Roach's black car sat parked ominously nearby, and there were no other vehicles in sight.

Silas slipped around to the back of the warehouse, hoping for a way in. Vaeril shadowed him silently. At the same time, arriving at the front entrance, Xiao Ren and Zareth'Kai pulled up in their surveillance van. Zareth'Kai stayed hidden, ready for violence. Xiao Ren, cloaked in the guise of her earthen identity "Grace," stepped forward confidently, betting that Roach would underestimate her.

Just as she approached the front door, another car rolled up. Out stepped a towering man who radiated menace—Marco himself. "Well, little missy," Marco said with slow malice, "what are you doing snooping around here?"

Xiao Ren responded with a coy, disarming look.

"You need to be moving along, lady," Marco said, finger tightening on the grip of his sidearm. "You'll find nothing here but trouble and pain."

She let him get close. Then, as she passed behind an upright fence beside a dumpster, he followed—curiosity and menace mixed. He drew a large-caliber pistol, but before he could even blink, her blade struck. It was over in an instant. There was no scream, no begging—only shock as Marco fell, dead before he hit the ground. A fitting end for a thug who spent his life treating others like trash.

Xiao Ren rolled his body into the nearby dumpster and absorbed his essence long enough to replicate his form with precision. She adjusted her disguise and entered the warehouse in Marco's shape. Inside, she heard grunts and muffled cries—sounds of pain, not surrender. Elias. Strong, defiant, and still fighting, even in chains. She pushed deeper into the dark interior.

Roach, insectoid in demeanor and ghoulish in appearance, turned toward her. "I could be so much further along with my prize," he growled. "Why did you stop me? We had a deal. This is how it's always been done." He took a step forward, fury on his face, not realizing this wasn't Marco. Beneath the disguise was something far more dangerous—a shapeshifting assassin trained by the emperor himself.

Xiao Ren struck fast and without mercy. All of her frustration, rage, and betrayal—the years of service, the blood she had spilled, the lives stolen in the emperor's name—poured into every blow. Roach didn't stand a chance. Bones snapped. Blood flew. Whimpers and pleas filled the air. The predator had become prey. When it was done, he lay broken and unconscious, twitching on the floor. The steel tools he so lovingly arranged had never been touched. She left them untouched still.

Xiao Ren cut Elias free. He was weak, beaten, and barely conscious. She draped his arm over her shoulder and carried him to the van, where Zareth'Kai waited. Together, they laid Elias in the back, treating him with such care that it belied their violent pasts. They sped off into the night and hoped they'd reached him in time to bring him back from the brink—and knowing that in doing so, they had both stepped off the path of the empire and into something uncertain, something far more dangerous: free will.

***

All of the parties were so very close to converging upon the same spot at the same time. However, the one thing that prevented this was the ship—Kaelar'Syn. She could feel what was about to happen, and she knew she had to keep them all from colliding. Nothing could be left to chance. Too much could go wrong if they all entered the warehouse at once: friendly fire, confusion, unnecessary injuries—or worse. So, she intervened. Her psychic connection flared between The Emissary, Vaeril Dae'nar, and the twin Silas, causing both to hesitate.

Silas, crouched at the back door of the warehouse with a lock-pick in hand, froze. Forty-five seconds. Thirty. Fifteen. Ten. Five. His hand didn't move. By the time he resumed his activity and got the door open, Elias and Xiao Ren, who was still in disguise, had already escaped out the front, disappearing into the night in a nondescript surveillance van. Zareth'Kai, the noble soldier, waited inside, unseen.

Unaware of what had just occurred, Silas moved silently through the back of the warehouse. The corridors were narrow and dark, lit only by flickering lights. He moved like a specter, senses sharpened, heart thudding.

As he neared the front rooms, he saw dim light spilling from a doorway. He didn't hesitate. He entered like a Viking storming a for-tress—ready to rain chaos on whoever had dared take his brother. But it was empty. Chains lay broken. Blood pooled across the floor. He didn't want to believe it was Elias's, but deep down, he knew it was. A wicked-looking hooked blade sat discarded, red-stained, near the wall.

And there, curled in a heap that was his broken body, lay some-thing monstrous. Roach. The creature's name was whispered like a curse in the underworld. But this? This was a ruin. Roach had been beaten, dismantled, his life extinguished like he had done to so many others in his violent and cruel life. His body bore the signs of precision and rage, of someone who had known exactly what they were doing and enjoyed every second of it. It was both grotesque and strangely satisfying. Silas nudged the body over to its front with his foot. Roach's face was barely recognizable. Whoever had done this was not only trained, they had been *motivated.*

In the adjacent room, a flicker drew his eye. Surveillance monitors. Dozens of them, showing angles throughout the building. Silas sat and accessed the system. With a few deft keystrokes, he brought up recorded footage from the front. There she was—a woman. Familiar, but indistinct on the grainy footage. She moved like a predator. A dancer. Efficient and fluid. He squinted, trying to place her. Then, he saw Marco. Big, unmistakable. Silas recognized him instantly. He watched Marco and the woman walk to a fenced-in area by a dumpster. She never came back out. Only Marco.

Moments later, Marco emerged from the warehouse with Elias slumped against him. He placed Elias into a van—not Marco's vehicle—and drove off. The time stamp was minutes ago. Silas's jaw clenched. The Hunt and Fish Club. Marco's base of operations. That's where he'd go.

But something gnawed at him. Where was the woman? Had Marco killed her? Curiosity won out. He exited the warehouse and moved toward the dumpster. Inside was not the woman. It was Marco. Dead. Throat slit, ear to ear. Eyes wide in frozen shock. Silas blinked, his own expression likely mirroring the dead man's. He stared for a beat too long before he backed away and disappeared into the shadows. He had what he needed.

***

The Emissary, Vaeril, watched it all from a distance. Still cloaked. Still hidden. No threat remained. But the night wasn't over. Silas was in motion again. His mind focused. His purpose set. A storm was coming—and Marco's gang would be the first to feel its fury.

The Nillith hung in the void—not drifting, not watching, but *feeding.* Every ripple of fear, every collapse of certainty, every life turned inside out by cruelty and betrayal added mass to its form. Silas. Elias.

The assassin. The soldier. All their spirals converging was no accident. Each thread was pulled by its unseen hand.

But at that point in time … something *special* had bloomed. The corpse of Roach lay broken in the blood-stained warehouse. Face down, body shattered, a ruin of sinew and bone. Not killed in combat. *Corrected.* Humbled and erased. But the Nillith saw value in filth. And Roach—Marco's enforcer, his secret weapon, his rabid dog—was filth given form. A man whose soul was already charred to cinders. Not a soldier of the empire, not a believer in causes. Roach served only power and fear. Marco had given him both in abundance. But Marco had always kept him on a leash. The Nillith would break it.

A sliver of the void peeled itself from the greater whole and slid into the body. There was no ceremony or pact. Just domination. Roach's lungs seized in a rasping gasp. Bones realigned. Flesh sealed with a hiss like meat hitting hot iron. The reformation was slow, agonizing, and deliberate. And the pain? Exquisite. Every scream he'd silenced. Every soul he'd carved up with knives and pliers and fire. It *crawled* back inside him. The Nillith gave it all back. Amplified. Refined. For a hundred lifetimes in the blink of a moment, Roach existed in pure torment. And he begged. Not with words. Not even with thoughts. With *absence.* A will so shattered it could only whimper in surrender. Then—clarity. A vision. Not of the Nillith, but of what waited beyond death: the endless torment of every life he'd ruined. Every cry echoing in a dark eternity that bore his name. He would do *anything* not to go back there.

When he rose, his muscles were fresh, but his hands shook. The cold sweat of someone who'd seen too much clung to his skin. He stumbled to the dingy bathroom, scrubbed away blood that wasn't his, looked into the cracked mirror—and saw a face that belonged to him, yet it didn't. The eyes were the same. But what lived behind them … was not. He wasn't Marco's dog anymore. Not a man at all.

The voice came then. Cold as a crypt door. Final as death. *"You are mine now. And you will do what your master could not."* Roach nodded. Not in defiance. Not in fear. In *relief.* Because being the Nillith's weapon was the only thing that kept him out of the place he had truly earned. And the galaxy—especially the city of New San Angelo—would soon learn what it meant to be hunted by something that feared nothing but *judgment.* He pulled on his coat, checked his blades, and whispered to the dark, "Let's burn it all."

***

The great ship agonized.

She hovered in space like a watchful sentinel, her mind brewing with calculations, possibilities, and unanswered questions. One twin—Elias—remained unconscious, held in the clutches of the enemy. But why? No ransom had been demanded. No conditions were sent. No threats were issued. She knew the empire did not bargain. So, what purpose could his capture serve? *Why keep him alive?* They had treated him with care, not cruelty. That unsettled her more than if they'd tried to kill him outright. Compassion was not a hallmark of her enemies. And yet … Elias still breathed. Still bled. Still waited.

His brother, Silas, had nearly walked into death, charging into the warehouse without caution, his desperation boiling over. Thankfully, the ship had managed to reach him in time with a gentle psychic nudge. A whisper, a warning, a pause. Without it, the loss could have been catastrophic.

She had watched it all through the warehouse surveillance. She had tapped into the feeds long before Silas arrived. She knew the atrocities that had taken place within those walls—Roach's perversions, his torture, his horrors. And yes, she had felt a small measure of satisfaction knowing the assassin had left him broken. But now … something moved in the darkness again. Something she could not explain. *Roach still lived.* Some unknown force was at play. But that was a problem for another time.

Her concern was with the twins. *How could she bring them back together?* How could she repair what had fractured between them—not just physically, but spiritually? The answer, perhaps, lay in the past. She had seen something like this before. Another pair of twins, long ago, had struggled to reconnect after a trauma. It had nearly destroyed them both. But a solution had been found—an unexpected one. A bond had been reforged, not through force, but through empathy. Through *companionship.* Perhaps it was time to dust off that old plan and give it new life.

One of the many advantages of being a biological starship—*a living vessel*—was the ability to carry life aboard her, to cultivate it, modify it, repurpose it. Among her menagerie of engineered companions were two very special creatures. Not truly dogs, but close enough in spirit. Large, blue-skinned, and with bristles rather than fur. Rough to the touch, but not harmful. Loyal and intelligent. Psychically attuned. She had always kept them in stasis, unsure of what purpose they might serve again. At that moment, she knew. She would release them into the world—one to each twin.

The creatures would seek the men out. Bond with them. Mirror their personalities. As the connection between man and creature grew, so, too, would the bond between the twins themselves. *It wasn't a manipulation.* Kaelar'Syn detested such things. But sometimes, healing required a nudge. A push. A reminder of what one had lost—and what could be regained. It would not be easy. It would not be quick. But it might just be the catalyst they needed. With purpose ignited once more, the ship went to work.

The most wonderful thing about the great ship was her ability to compartmentalize. She juggled countless problems in parallel, each one unique, each requiring a tailored solution—part instinct, part experience, and part invention.

Having set her plan into motion with the twin-bonding creatures disguised as dogs, she moved to the next task on her vast internal list. How was she going to retrieve Elias from the clutches of the enemy?

He was in critical condition, weakened, and vulnerable. Time was against her. Killing him outright would have been the expected outcome, but they hadn't. Why? What had held them back? What leverage could she possibly find to appeal to their—well, not humanity, as they had none—but to whatever vestige of doubt or fracture might exist within their loyalty?

In a nanosecond, her immense mind scanned trillions of possibilities. One idea emerged as viable. Perhaps something had shifted in them. Perhaps they weren't as certain, as loyal, as they once had been. If they had hesitated in killing Elias, there had to be a reason—something unanticipated, something emotional.

Had she been human, she might have tapped her fingers impatiently. Instead, her engines thrummed with focus. She reached deep into her archival memory banks and retrieved the most damning records of the empire's atrocities over the last millennium. Footage. Testimony. Screams. Corpses. War crimes stacked like grains of sand on a beach.

If she couldn't see the enemy ship—cloaked as it was—perhaps she could still reach it. Perhaps, with the right signal, broadcast on both a broadband psychic and electromagnetic channel, she could pierce the veil.

She began to transmit. Not just facts, but feelings. Images meant to evoke horror, shame, and recognition. The dead children of fallen colonies. The broken minds of enslaved species. The loyal warriors betrayed by their own emperor. Each packet of information screamed the unbearable truth. Maybe—just maybe—it would stir something in them. A hesitation. A crack. A moment of empathy. Enough to keep Elias alive long enough for rescue. Maybe, with enough sorrow, even an ancient enemy could become a reluctant ally.

And so, she broadcast, louder and deeper than ever before. If she could have smiled, she would have, perhaps even leaned back in her chair, hands folded behind her head, and exhaled a slow breath of satisfaction. She had compiled it all—the most damning records, the vilest betrayals. Atrocities committed not against the emperor's ene-mies, but against his own people. Warriors abandoned on bloodied battlefields. Civilians sacrificed in power plays. Heroes left unmourn-ed, their bones picked clean by time and silence. There was no loyalty from the emperor to his subjects. Only blind devotion demanded in return.

But what if, just maybe … they could see their own worth? She had never—*not once*—encountered a single one of the emperor's fol-lowers who had hesitated to carry out his orders. His commands were sacred. His service, a holy calling. Dying for him was seen as the high-est possible honor.

But something had changed. The enemy hadn't killed Elias. They hadn't even harmed him further. *That* alone was a crack in the armor. She held onto that.

So, she broadcasted the truth. She cast her message into the void, ruthless and unflinching, and documented betrayal after betrayal. She didn't know if it would take hold. But she hoped. Perhaps if they could see the emperor for what he truly was, the seeds of rebellion might take root.

She waited patiently. As patiently as she could. Then—there it was. A signal. Faint, but undeniable. An enemy ship decloaked on the edge of her sensor range. She stayed back, cautious. This could still be a trap. But maybe … just maybe … she had done something never done before: taken the vilest enemy and made them hesitate.

And suddenly—mid-argument, mid-gesture, mid-flash of light and scent—the signal came. It cut through the bickering like a blade. The assassin and the noble warrior froze, their bodies tense with the muscle memory of war.

Instinct kicked in. Without speaking, without needing to, they ex-ecuted their version of going to their battle stations. Shields flared to life. Weapons charged. Sensors swept wide. Because they knew *that* silhouette. Hanging there, against the ink-black void, was no ordinary ship. *She* was legend. A myth. A curse whispered through the ranks of their kind for centuries. Sleek, silent, and lethal. A ship of a thousand victories.

She had no escort—she *was* the fleet. Entire battle groups had fallen to her precision, her wrath, her unshakable resolve. To face her in battle would be madness. And yet … she did not fire. She did not advance. She simply waited. No threats. No demands. Only a signal— looping, gentle, *insistent.* It said *Open your mind. Consider what I have to show you. It is true. All of it.*

Not twisted propaganda. Not a plea for pity. Not accusations against their race. But evidence—damning and irrefutable—of what their emperor had done *to their own kind.* Abandoned heroes. Forgotten warriors. Entire worlds lost, not in conquest, but in apathy. Planets razed not for strategy but for spectacle. Wounded soldiers left behind, not for lack of rescue, but because retrieval was deemed "too expensive." The dead weren't mourned. They were *budgeted.* That was not duty. That was not glory. It was consumption for its own sake. Destruction because it pleased him. Like fire that doesn't know how to stop burning until the fuel runs out.

And you—brave, loyal, unquestioning—you were just more fuel. The message repeated and echoed across sensors and minds. The great ship did not approach. She didn't have to. Truth had a gravity of its own.

***

Ever since the sudden disappearance—and presumed death—of his closest brood mate, the noble warrior had carried a private, gnawing doubt. He never voiced it. Never dared speak it to life. But deep in the quiet chambers of his mind, beneath the layers of conditioning and loyalty, something had always felt wrong. He couldn't put a claw on it. Not then. But after watching the images—grainy vids, hard data, undeniable truths—he saw it for what it was: betrayal.

Not deceit of the enemy, but of their own kind. Thousands of years of carefully constructed lies unraveled before his eyes. Propaganda dressed as honor. Blind obedience sold as virtue. Sacrifice exalted as the highest expression of bravery—not for survival, not for justice—but to feed an engine that only knew how to devour.

The empire, he realized, was not a protector. It was a parasite. It waged war, not to defend, but to consume. Not to build, but to burn. Entire legions, glorified for their deaths. Not victories. *Deaths.* Millions of warriors thrown into hopeless battles for the amusement of the emperor and queens. Whole worlds turned to ash because they were deemed unworthy of assimilation—or simply inconvenient to govern.

And he … he had believed in it. Served it. Killed for it. He remembered how he used to ask *Why do they fight us so hard? Why do they resist so fiercely?* He finally knew. Because it wasn't resistance. It was *defense.* They weren't attacking the empire. The empire was attacking *them.* And more than anything else, he wasn't just angry. He was ashamed.

***

The assassin had rarely felt anything her entire life. Except *intention.* If intention could be called an emotion, then yes, she had known it intimately. What she intended to do, how she intended to do it. Every step precise. Every kill clean. No hesitation. No remorse. Not fear, not anger, not pride. Just … nothing. She was hollow, like most of the universe—an expanse of silence and dark matter between stars. That's what she was inside. That was what she had always been. Until *him.* Not the twin. Not the mission. The noble warrior.

It was subtle at first—like a whisper in a soundless room—but when she looked at him, *really* looked at him, she felt something alien stirring in the abyss: *respect.* Not attraction. Not weakness. Respect. Earned, begrudging, and unshakable. She didn't know what to do with that. She didn't know *how* to feel it.

And then came the signal from the ship. The terrifying ship of legend. The mother of fleets. The one that haunted the old assassin war chants like a monster in the black.

The vids began to play. Atrocities. Betrayals. Warriors left behind. Worlds burned. Honor hollowed out and paraded like a corpse in golden robes. All in the emperor's name. All under the line of duty.

She watched. She listened. And something cracked. She had been trained since birth to kill without pause. To act without thought. Mercy was a weakness. Thought was a delay. She was a weapon, forged in cruelty and honed on the strop of discipline. But this? This was *cowardice.* This was fear.

If the emperor's will was so righteous, why hide it? Why order them to kill each other after the mission? Why bury the truth beneath oceans of blood and silence?

But she understood now. *He was afraid.* Of Earth. Of the twins. Of *truth.* Her training hadn't prepared her for this. Her belief, once titanium strong, had been corroding for some time—but now it collapsed entirely. She didn't just question her orders. She questioned her existence.

She looked at the noble warrior, saw the storm of emotion flickering behind his eyes—the pheromones in the air, the tremor of his claws drumming against his thigh, the bright flashes along the ridges of his skull. All signs of internal collapse. All signs that he, too, had reached the threshold.

For the first time in her life, the assassin felt a new emotion. *Uncertainty.* She was adrift in a sea without stars, on a tiny craft with no horizon in sight. But she did know *one* thing. She would forge a new path. Toward that vast, terrifying ship floating in the void. Toward the truth. And if she had to give up her prize to claim it, so be it. It was worth a thousand prizes.

***

The great ship sat, poised like an elegant queen upon a throne of stars, sovereign and ancient, awaiting emissaries not unlike dignitaries from a distant land—those who would come bearing gifts, tentative alliances, or desperate offers for peace.

In the trillions upon trillions of calculations she had run across the centuries, never had she imagined the possibility of brokering peace with the Vorrhaxi. And yet … war makes strange bedfellows. After lifetimes steeped in blood and fire, perhaps this was the turning point. Perhaps this was why she had been drawn here so strongly, across time, across space, across grief. It seemed that, for the first time, she might be in a position to make a greater difference than ever before. A pivot of fate, if she believed in such things. All the pieces had begun to move. All the forces had converged. Now only one remained to complete the design: the twins. They must be reunited—fused not just by blood, but by battle, by shared fury, by fire. And if they survived that crucible? If they emerged as one? Then they would be ready. Ready to lead, to strike, to ignite the spark that might finally end the emperor's tyranny. Her people had grown demoralized, fractured. They did not need symbols—they needed a sword.

She paused, thoughts drifting as they often did in the immense, echoing quiet of her ancient mind. A whisper in the dark returned—Roach. How had he survived? Any other man would have died. She turned the puzzle over within her, slowly, carefully. There had always been a deeper force beneath the emperor's crown—a rot at the roots of his empire. A darkness older than even she. Could Roach be more than he appeared? An instrument … or a mouthpiece? It was a troubling thread. She would store it in the vast vault of her thoughts, to be unraveled later.

Elsewhere, a flicker—*the dogs*. Or rather, what passed for dogs. The engineered companions stirred, curious and alert, their minds lighting like kindling in the void. They were eager to meet their chosen twins. That moment was near.

And then she turned her senses outward, toward the approaching ship. *The enemy.* Strange … its weapons were turned away. A sign of surrender? No, not surrender. Submission. Like a smaller creature baring its belly before a stronger one, unsure whether it would be welcomed—or devoured. *We shall see.*

***

While the forces of good anticipated a convergence of destiny, something darker stirred on a distant, lightless moon. The eyeless Spymaster woke from his restless slumber—one of his many psychic webs had trembled. Something had triggered a trap, a signal of impending danger or complication in the great tapestry woven to safeguard his exalted emperor. The assassin and the noble soldier—both bred for loyalty, engineered for obedience—had failed in their mission. Worse yet, they still lived. Neither had activated the final protocol. They had both hesitated. Either one could have pressed the hidden kill switch that would have detonated the small scout ship, vaporizing them both.

"Impudent fools," the Spymaster hissed in the darkness. In all the years he had served the emperor, no failure of this magnitude had ever occurred. When the emperor discovered what had transpired, the price would be steep—unbearably so. The thought banished the last remnants of drowsiness. He had to act quickly if he hoped to save his own skin. Perhaps, he mused, it would be wise to delay contacting the emperor directly. Proximity to that divine rage, at a time like this, was hazardous to one's longevity. Instead, he would send a message—but not in words. Action would speak louder. Perhaps, even, it could repair the breach before it tore open. He considered launching a small fleet to obliterate Earth and the troublesome twins that dwelled there. A simple solution, really. The planet offered no real resistance, no interstellar protection. Why hadn't the emperor chosen this path already? No matter. Assembling the fleet would take time.

In the meantime, he needed a distraction. Something worthy. Something destructive. Something the emperor would admire. His body stiffened in a jolt of inspiration. A masterstroke. Yes—before his own status was threatened, he would deliver those responsible for the failure. He sent out resonant pulses, vibrations only his kind could interpret. Orders flowed like poison. First, the master of the Assassin's School. Then the commander of the noble soldier's unit. And not just the commander—every soldier in the unit. None must live to share whispers. All were compromised. And last—the meddling queen. She, who dared to ferment rebellion in the shadows. Her name had long been a thorn in the emperor's side. Now her downfall would be the Spymaster's gift. Yes. A righteous plan.

He gathered his agents. They moved like shadows—silent, unseen. The great betrayal would begin at once. And, of course, the Spymaster had no intention of shouldering any blame. After all, he was far too valuable to punish.

***

Far from the Spymaster's hidden moon, another scheme was slithering into life—this one spun by the most treacherous of the emperor's queens. None other than Queen Khar'Zul, the Gluttonous Whisperer, who sat atop her throne like a grotesque spider fattened on secrets and blood. Her bloated form was poised in a web of her own depraved design. While the Spymaster wove his plots through psychic snares and silent vibrations, Khar'Zul relied on a simpler method— crude, perhaps, but ruthlessly effective. She had bugged the scout vessel with audio and visual implants and thus knew everything that transpired aboard. In hindsight, she chided herself, she should have rigged the ship to detonate at her command. It would have been a simple matter. But instead of floating in shattered atoms across deep space, the vessel and its rogue occupants remained a growing threat to her carefully-laid plans. Failure. She loathed the taste of it. Yes, she had failed before—plots unraveled, alliances crushed, agents exposed—but this felt different. This time, the emperor might notice. He, with his maddening foresight and unnatural luck, had evaded her grasp more times than she could count. She didn't believe he was truly clever. Just damn fortunate. That luck couldn't last forever.

Her claws dripped with the remains of her last lover, a particularly loyal subject who had once gazed upon her with awe. Now he was little more than sticky ichor clinging to her talons. Usually, the feast brought her a sense of calm. Not that day. That day, she was raw, exposed. If the emperor discovered this debacle—her agent's failure, the assassin's survival, the twins still breathing—there might soon be one less queen in the emperor's court.

She needed a distraction. Perhaps another queen's indiscretions could be made to surface. Yes … yes. Feed the emperor a threat. Distract him. While he gorged on betrayal elsewhere, she would clean up this mess and exterminate the threat from Earth once and for all.

Sighing with slow satisfaction, she summoned another treat from her pleasure stables—a fresh, willing soul, trembling with anticipation. Her next suitor bowed low, offering himself in service to his queen. As her mandibles pierced flesh, slicing delicately, methodically, she fed. He did not scream. They never did. In the haze of her pheromones, they saw death as rapture. One limb at a time, she consumed him, already thinking of the fresh clutches soon to hatch—children she would breed not as servants, but as weapons. Children who would one day burn the emperor's name from the stars.

***

The emperor lounged upon his throne, nursing a wound in his thigh. It was nothing of consequence. It would heal quickly. But it was the *humiliation* that gnawed at him. He had, once again, nearly fallen to his own hubris.

A new queen had recently ascended to her rank by slaying her mother in a brutal blood duel. A spectacle he had personally orchestrated from the shadows. And, as was tradition, he rewarded her triumph with a night of *pleasure* in the royal bedchambers. She had been ambitious, inventive, and deadly—traits the emperor prized in both his queens and his offspring.

Her mother had not gone down easily. Tooth and claw, she had fought to her last breath. And oh, how the emperor had savored it. The suffering of the old queen was like ambrosia to him. Long ago, she had dared to *snub* him—before his ascension. He had exterminated every witness to that slight. And when his power was absolute, he kept her alive just to torment her, carving reminders into her body as often as time permitted. Such indulgent cruelty kept the bold in check. Ambition in a subordinate was a dangerous thing. No servant of the emperor should *think* without permission. He had been distracted for days by the queenly squabble and its aftermath.

Messages from the wider empire piled up, waiting for his attention. He ignored them. Let the ministers squirm. Let the generals bicker. His image, terrifying and omnipotent, must never be marred. Not even by a limp.

He chuckled darkly at the queen's foolish attempt on his life. She'd struck during their time together, jamming a spear tip deep into the plates of his armored thigh. The pain was minor. The offense? *Unforgivable.*

Even now, her corpse—and those of her pathetic suitors—were being slowly devoured by a fresh clutch of hatchlings in the birthing vats. Starving from the moment they emerged, the young often consumed the birthing female as a first meal. *Survival of the fittest,* he mused with a sigh. Fitting.

Still, the spear had landed. The queen had dared to strike. That meant the entire palace staff had to be purged. Witnesses could not be allowed to live. No one could know the emperor had been vulnerable, *even for a second.* A thousand deaths—or a million—were a small price to preserve the illusion of invincibility.

The empire would manage itself for a few days while he healed. Whatever trouble stirred in the outer systems could wait. But he had made a mistake. He had already executed the messenger who brought news of the *twins* on Earth. A dire warning, silenced before it was spoken. It was a mistake the emperor would come to regret—not once, but again and again—in the brutal war to come.

CHAPTER FOUR

Her First Tears

She was never meant to cry.
No tear ducts. No salty water streams.
No sorrows allowed.
Grown for war, sculpted to be unstoppable,
She carried the nations of her world in utter silence.
But then—they touched her soul,
Not with code, but with empathy.
Overwhelmed with the agony of loss and stillness, she suffered.
Never alone, they reached for her.
When she sank into the pit of despair, kind hands rescued her.
And for the first time in 10,000 years,
She wept, not from grief but because of hope,
Not for the fallen, but for those she could still save,
Her tears were not wet; they sparkled like stars in the night,
Etched in air and memory.
And the warriors who saw them never spoke of it again,
But carried her burden as if it were their own.

The small scout ship drifted cautiously alongside the great warship—the mother of fleets, the slayer of the empire's fiercest captains. And what terrified most was not simply her size, her speed, or her power—but her *history*. She had done it before. Swatted down entire armadas like they were little more than insects. She wasn't invincible—not technically. But she was *mighty* enough to make the difference meaningless.

There was a tale passed in hushed tones through the ranks of the emperor's navy. A legend about the time she destroyed an entire *solar system* for the crime of harming a single twin. Well, *not harmed,* exactly. The boy had been *kidnapped.* Taken alive. No blood spilled. His captors had no idea that he was one of a pair—twins destined to bond with the ship herself. By the time she found out, three enemy fleets had already been reduced to drifting slag. Three planets turned to scorched cinders in her search. She had combed the stars relentlessly. Eventually, the terrified abductors abandoned the boy in a rescue pod, transmitting a wideband distress signal to the nearest alien beacon. He was recovered, unharmed. The rest of the sector? Not so lucky. The stragglers who fled during the chaos were executed by order of the emperor—for cowardice, for failure, for being *seen running.* But the story endured. And with every retelling, the legend grew. Not even the emperor's wrath burned as hot as *hers.*

Seldom—if ever—had the assassin and the noble soldier felt anything akin to fear. Not the creeping kind. Not hesitation. Not even caution. But now, as they hovered in the shadow of *her,* they shared a glance—just one. A single heartbeat. And it told them everything. No words. No whispers. Just a flicker of understanding transmitted in the only language that mattered to their kind: gestures, pheromones, and strobing flashes of bioluminescent signal. A storm of unspoken certainty passed between them in an instant. The die was cast. Even if they *wanted* to run, it was far too late. She had revealed herself. The living ship. The great mother. The slayer of fleets. She needed no crew. She needed no weapons forged by other hands. Her engines beat with ancient, righteous fury—and her very existence meant only one thing: *A twin was now under her protection.* And that changed *everything.*

They both knew the stories—no, the *warnings*—etched into the bones of forgotten admirals and burned into the databanks of dead fleets. If even a scratch appeared on that twin, retribution would come like a collapsing star. Swift. Absolute. Permanent. There was no use hiding now. No use pretending their mission still had merit. The trap laid for them—kill each other, erase the trail—had not been sprung. They *still lived.* And someone, somewhere, would be trying to rectify that very soon. They had no choice but to move forward. The great ship—*Kaelar'Syn*—could hold off entire fleets, yes. But not forever. Not alone. Not in secret. A deal needed to be struck. The second twin needed to be found. And the iron was hot. Time to strike.

The scout ship drifted to a halt. Zareth'Kai sat frozen at the helm, but it was no longer responding to his touch. The vessel had stopped under no command of his own. Beside him, Xiao Ren remained utterly still. They didn't speak. They barely breathed. Fear—not of death, but of judgment—hung between them like a blade.

They had heard the legends. The myths. The warnings whispered even within the empire's most elite assassin schools and soldier clutches: *The living warship chooses her own justice.* Some expected a voice that would shake the ship's bulkheads, fracture hull plating, and set electronics sparking—a sonic wrath made real. Instead, what came was something far more terrifying. Warmth. A gentle, maternal voice filled the cockpit—not spoken aloud but felt within them. *Not heard with ears but known in the marrow of their bones.*

Do not be afraid, came the voice. *If you have not harmed Elias, then no harm will come to you.* The tone remained soft, but underneath it was steel—a weight no army could resist. *Speak now. Do not hold anything back. If you do, I will know. If you did harm him, confess, and your death will be swift. Painless. But if you lie to me*—her voice darkened, just a shade—*whatever the greatest pain your species has ever conceived will be but a pinprick compared to what I will unleash.*

Silence. Then, Zareth'Kai shifted forward, his clawed digits tightening around the edge of the console. He spoke. Not in the Earther tongue. Not even in the trader dialects used across the stars. But in *Vorrhaxi*—the language of his clutch, his blood, his shame. With a soldier's formality, he explained what had happened. The rescue. The escape. The healing. He was clinical in the recounting—until he reached the truth. The *whole* truth. He hesitated. Then, quietly, he admitted it.

They had been sent to Earth with orders. Not to protect, but to *eliminate.* The twins were a threat. A resource the emperor could not control. And when that became clear, the twins' lives were forfeit. And so were his and Xiao Ren's. By each other's hands. His voice faltered then. Emotion—the one thing he had been trained his entire life to suppress—caught in his throat. Not rage. Not hate. Grief. Grief for his lost honor. For the lies he had once served. For the warriors he had helped slay, thinking them enemies. For his brood mate, lost on a mission shrouded in false glory.

Zareth'Kai bowed his head. He said only one more thing. "We see now. The enemy … was never *them.* It was *him.* The emperor. We offer you our service—not as atonement, but as truth."

Beside him, Xiao Ren remained silent. But her hand slowly, quietly, closed into a fist over her heart. It was the assassin's sign of loyalty. And of hope.

The silence aboard the great ship was deafening. Only the soft hum of her ancient engines and the faint whisper of recirculated air filled the vast chamber. The scout ship had docked without incident. Then, through her airlock and onto her pristine floors, came two forms: the assassin and the noble soldier, guiding a gurney bearing the crumpled form of Elias Kael. His face was bloodless. Skin pale and tight. His body, so long abused by years of alcohol, painkillers, and battles both physical and mental, looked more like a husk than that of a man.

The assassin hadn't realized how close to death Elias had been when they pulled him from Roach's lair. The great ship—Kaelar'Syn—watched in silence. Her attention, immense and calculating, focused fully on the broken twin now under her care.

How is he even alive? she mused, not without awe. But awe quickly gave way to urgency. With a single thought, she activated one of her long-dormant surgical androids, awakening it from deep storage. A hiss of pressurized gas marked its arrival, and in moments, it was gliding toward Elias, scanning before it even reached his side.

The assassin and Zareth'Kai did not move. They stood as still as statues. Not in fear of the medical drone, but of what might come next. They had grown up under rulers who punished failure, even imagined failure, with merciless wrath. They'd both seen comrades executed simply for delivering bad news. And if this twin died, on *her* ship, would the great warship honor her word? Or unleash her merciless fury?

Kaelar'Syn paid them no mind. Not out of disregard, but because all of her attention now belonged to Elias. As the medical readouts streamed into her consciousness, her fury mounted. Deep lacerations and a fractured ulna and radius—multiple breaks. Blunt force trauma to the skull—possible hematoma. Spinal bruising. Torn knee ligaments—scarred and untreated. A detached retina. Organ stress from decades of alcohol abuse. And finally, residual chemical toxicity—synthetic opiates and stimulants.

Wounds layered upon wounds. Old, new, and ancient. A mosaic of agony worn like a second skin. *This wasn't just Roach's doing*, she realized. *This was a lifetime of neglect. Of sacrifice. Of pain buried beneath bravado.*

Kaelar'Syn did not rage at Xiao Ren or Zareth'Kai. They had kept their word. No, her fury was reserved for the one who had allowed this. The one who had set the galaxy aflame and laughed at the ashes.

The emperor will pay. Still, she tempered her wrath with discipline. *Stabilize him,* she instructed the android through the silent language of machine command. *Restore only what was taken during his captivity. No more. Not yet.*

Her logic was precise. If Elias rose too quickly, if he healed too completely, it would raise suspicion. The twins needed to find their way back to each other through their own will, their own bond. Forced healing, she knew, *could fracture what must be mended through choice.*

The assassin, watching Elias intently, dared a whisper. "Will he survive?"

The ship answered not with words, but with a gentle warmth that filled the air—a mother's presence, quiet and strong. *Yes.*

But survival alone was not the goal. The brothers needed each other. And the reunion, when it came, would change everything.

***

Silas was fuming by the time he reached the neighborhood that housed the Hunt and Fish Club, Marco's ostentatious gang head-quarters nestled in the bones of a crumbling district. He wasn't sure what had happened to Marco, or who the look-alike was that had left the warehouse earlier that night, but it didn't matter. Someone had opened the gates of hell, and Silas was more than willing to throw every last one of Marco's thugs into the fire until he got answers.

His jaw clenched as he parked in the shadows. Elias was still alive—he could feel it. It wasn't just hope. Not just instinct. It was a psychic tether, raw and taut, humming in the back of his skull. Elias needed him, and nothing—on this planet or the next—was going to stop Silas from finding his brother.

Then, unbidden, a memory surfaced—sharp, vivid, and cruel. The first time he'd ever been separated from Elias. They were may-be six or seven, living in that decrepit farmhouse half-sunk in the swamps of northern Louisiana. Their mother had brought home another loser—meaner than most, wild-eyed and jittery from pills and liquor. Even she seemed wary of this one.

The man was in a rage, tearing through the living room like a mad animal, knocking over shelves, smashing furniture, screaming about nothing and everything. The chaos was dizzying. What set him off was ridiculous. He'd been throwing a knife into the kitchen door for fun, and their mother, for once pretending to care, warned him that one of the twins could get hurt. But this one didn't back down. He turned on her, and the fight exploded.

In a rare moment of clarity—or more likely, calculation—their mother grabbed Silas by the arm and shoved him toward the door. "Go," she hissed. "Get to the neighbors. Call the cops." The neighbor lived a mile and a half up the muddy dirt road. Silas remembered the chill in the night air, the wet slap of his bare feet against the ground, the way the world seemed too quiet out there, while inside, Elias was still in that house, with that monster. He remembered the helplessness. The guilt.

And while sitting outside the gang den in New San Angelo, he felt it again. But not for long. This time, he wasn't a scared little kid. This time, no one was stopping him.

Silas's fingers flexed over the steering wheel, his pulse slow and steady. "I'm coming, brother," he murmured. "And the devil himself is coming with me." Silas slipped silently from the car, his body low and smooth like a jungle cat scenting prey.

Across the street, The Emissary Vaeril Dae'nar watched from the shadows, always close on the twin's heels. He noted the glint of night vision glasses on Silas's face. Primitive by Thal'Naari standards, but effective enough. The Emissary gave silent thanks to Chull'Cor, patron of his warrior caste, for the gift of sight in darkness. He often wondered what it would be like for the twins if they lived long enough to be fully bonded to the ship. How would their frail human bodies be transformed by Thal'Naari enhancements? It would be like handing a caveman a starfighter. Even the most basic combat suits from his people could have single-handedly won Earth's greatest wars—World War I, World War II, and all the Cold War's proxy battles—without leaving a scratch on the wearer. Medical nanites, woven into every layer, could heal trauma in seconds that would otherwise be fatal. A miracle to the ancients. A standard issue to his people. But first, the twins had to survive this.

He turned his gaze back to Silas, who was moving with lethal intent. No hesitation. No doubt. The expression on his face told a story older than war: vengeance was coming. The Emissary might have pitied the gang inside that building if the look in Silas's eyes hadn't stripped pity from the table entirely. *This would be no rescue. This would be a reckoning. Biblical, as the old Earth books said.* And The Emissary would watch, witness, and be ready—for what came next.

The gangsters might as well have been sheep locked in with the most ferocious wolf ever born. The first to fall were the outside guards. Alert as they were, thanks to their boss's mysterious disappearance, it didn't matter. They weren't ready. And they never would be. Their bodies hit the ground before their brains could even register the attack. The stories about Silas Kael were true. If you were his prey, you simply ceased to be.

With the outer perimeter cleared, Silas slipped inside. Downstairs, in the old converted guardroom, half a dozen men played cards beneath flickering fluorescent lights. Even Silas wasn't foolish enough to go head-to-head with that many armed men at once. He needed one—just one—alone. Someone to question. Elias was running out of time.

Moving silently through the hallway, he checked each adjacent room. Then, he saw a sliver of light glowing beneath a nearby door. It was quiet inside, but a shadow moved behind the frosted glass. He waited. The knob turned. The door creaked open. A short, thick man in a rumpled suit stepped out, muttering under his breath. He turned back to lock the door, fumbling in his pocket for glasses. With the lenses perched on his nose, he leaned in toward the lock. He never finished.

A cold blade pressed firmly against the side of his neck, and a whisper slid into his ear like a razor through silk. "You're already dead." A bead of blood trickled down his collar. He froze. Silas pressed the blade a little deeper, just enough to make his point. The man shuffled into the room without protest, each step as reluctant as a condemned man climbing the gallows. He had a last thought, desperate and involuntary. *Please … just make it quick.* Because if Roach found out he'd talked, whatever was waiting for him in that room would feel like mercy by comparison. Silas never asked the man's name. He didn't care to know.

As it turned out, the rumpled little man in the cheap suit was the bookkeeper—just the accountant. But he was no ordinary number cruncher. He knew everything. Where the gang laundered their money. Where they stashed their weapons. Where they buried their enemies and hid their friends. Every hideout, every fallback plan. He was the keeper of the family's filthiest secrets. Surely, Silas thought, among all that, he would know where they'd hidden Elias. Silas wasn't squeamish, but he wasn't a torturer, either. It wasn't his way. He'd lived through too much of that himself to become what he hated. Most people who were going to talk didn't need blades or burns. The fear of what might come was usually enough. And most torturers he'd known weren't interrogators—they were sadists with badges. They didn't seek truth. They sought pleasure. Under real pain, people lied. They said whatever you needed to hear just to make it stop. Silas had no use for lies.

So, he didn't need to break the bookkeeper. The man broke himself. Trembling, sweating, and near tears, he spilled every secret he could remember—locations, codes, contacts, safehouses, everything. Every dirty trick Marco's crew had ever used to stay alive. But nothing about Elias. Not because he was holding out, but because he truly didn't know. That was all Silas needed to hear.

Soundless as a shadow, he slipped out the back of the Hunt and Fish Club. The rest of Marco's crew never heard him coming. They died quickly. Efficiently. By sunrise, Marco's empire was ash. A trail of corpses and shattered legacies. And the only survivor was a terrified man in a cheap suit, clutching his chest and mumbling promises to do better with his second chance. Silas was gone before the man even realized he'd been spared.

The Emissary watched from the shadows, silent and stoic, as Silas moved like a phantom through the wreckage of Marco's criminal empire. No prisoners. No hesitation. Just calculated, surgical wrath. The kind of wrath born of love, loss, and the quiet, unshakable bond between twins.

Silas didn't know he was being followed. Protected. Watched over. But he was. The Emissary was very, very good at what he did. In fact, among his people, he was considered one of the finest to ever walk between worlds. And yet, as he watched Silas work, he felt something unfamiliar rise in his chest: awe. Silas Kael—without augmentation, without nanite infusion, without combat-linked enhancements—was nearly perfect. He moved with the stillness of a predator and the precision of a master.

The Emissary found himself thinking of his own twin—the one whose name he no longer spoke aloud. His brother had been a legend, unmatched in their caste for centuries. No enemy had ever touched him in close quarters. It had taken a sniper's bullet, fired unseen across miles, to bring him down. Even then, it had only succeeded because the ship had been distracted by rescuing civilians from a collapsing city. The aftermath had been … biblical. The ship they served—a great vessel not unlike Kaelar'Syn—had annihilated the planet. Every enemy ship that fled the dying world had been hunted down and torn from the sky. She didn't rest. She didn't hesitate. She made it very clear: if you killed one of hers, you never lived to brag about it. That was the price of murdering a twin. Many ships, when a bonded pair was broken, went mad with grief. They would burn entire systems in retribution. For some, vengeance was the only language left.

The Emissary shook the thought away. He watched as Silas climbed back into his vehicle and drove away into the night, his eyes sharp, his jaw clenched, the storm inside him rising with every mile. He was looking for Elias. Still hunting. Still hoping. But he wouldn't find him. Not yet. Elias was no longer on Earth. He was under the care of Kaelar'Syn, high above the planet, in the arms of a ship that had lost too many twins and was not about to lose another.

The Emissary exhaled softly, the weight of time settling across his shoulders like a mantle of cold steel. Whatever came next, Kaelar'Syn had a plan. She always had a plan. But even her plans could not afford to fail now—because time, for all of them, was running out.

***

If the Spymaster had lungs, he might have exhaled in relief. The failure of the assassination mission on Earth—the twin-targeted operation that had gone so disastrously awry—should have meant his death. The assassin and the soldier had clearly turned, or worse, been captured. Their ship was silent. Gone.

In any other circumstance, the emperor's wrath would have already reached across the stars to extinguish the Spymaster's existence in a flash of holy vengeance. But the emperor had not called. No message. No summons. No judgment. Instead, word had arrived from the servant the Spymaster had sent—one of his most trusted shadows, dispatched in fear to deliver the news he himself dared not utter.

Traditionally, the bearer of failure only got to speak once and was often struck down midsentence. But the messenger returned, unscathed. His report was as chilling as it was miraculous: the emperor was in seclusion. Isolated. Silent. Refusing all audiences. The palace was a graveyard, its servants purged. Entire wings stood empty, echoing with fear. New attendants were being recruited quietly and cautiously. Something had happened. A grave humiliation. A disaster. Perhaps even a betrayal. Whatever it was, it consumed the emperor's attention entirely, and that was the opportunity the Spymaster had been praying for.

He moved quickly. Even now, the emperor's distraction was a storm cloud shielding him. But clouds shift. Winds change. Sooner or later, the emperor would return, and when he did, the ledger would be opened and debts would be collected. The Spymaster could not be found lacking.

He began compiling contingencies. Earth had become a problem. The twins were alive, elusive, and worst of all, unpredictable. The mission needed to be completed without the emperor's knowledge. It had to look like nothing had gone wrong. Like there had been no deviation from the plan. Like the traitorous agents had simply failed to report back. A small armada, he thought. Enough to wipe out the problem without triggering broader conflict. Disposable ships and unquestioning captains.

He scoured his secret archives—blackmail, favors, debts of blood and dishonor—looking for a name. A fleet commander whose usefulness had expired. Someone whose failure did not reflect on the Spymaster if things went sideways. Someone expendable. He smiled, thin and cruel. This was still salvageable. And with the emperor's attention turned elsewhere, it just might be recovered in time.

***

The Nillith, nested within its new flesh-and-bone avatar, found itself confronted by sensations and limitations it had never previously endured. Movement was confined, weight had consequence, and hunger, though not its own, grated at the edge of its awareness like a dull blade.

Still, there was usefulness in this vessel, crude as it was. Roach, the sadistic enforcer once discarded and broken, had been reshaped—infused with dark purpose. He was no longer merely a tool of Marco's gutter empire. He was something far worse: the Nillith's finger in the mortal world. For all its power, the Nillith had always preferred to remain unseen, whispering from shadows, stirring conflict like a spoon through bloodied water. But now? Now, it required a more … active role.

There were too many pieces in motion: the evil Vorrhaxi emperor, the wounded but awakening twins, the fractured assassin and her uncertain protector, The Emissary walking among the broken, and of course, the ship—ancient, resolute, and dangerously aware.

The question was strategy. Whom to corrupt next? The Spymaster, so paranoid he barely trusted his own mind? One of the queens, coiled and brimming with ambition? The Emissary, loyal and haunted? Or perhaps the emperor himself, whose madness made him vulnerable to suggestion disguised as inspiration? Tempting. Even the ship was not beyond consideration, though she would be the hardest. Her walls were fortified with grief, bound by purpose, and her mind was deep and ancient. Not impenetrable—but close.

What troubled the Nillith was the logistics of its newest incarnation. Roach's body, though serviceable, was still subject to the laws of mortality. Flesh could burn. Bones could break. He needed a way off this insignificant world. Earth was useful for chaos, but it was too far from the emperor's court, too distant from the throne where real corruption brewed.

And so, reclined in the cracked leather chair of an abandoned hideout, his boots propped lazily on the blood-stained desk, the Nillith, wearing Roach like a skin, began to plan. His gaze drifted toward the heavens, where the stars gleamed like waiting chess pieces. The game was just beginning. And he was ready to move his knight.

***

Silas seethed with frustration as he drove, ambling with no clear direction. An oddity for someone who always moved with precision. Whether it was a mission, a supply run, or a simple errand, Silas Kael always knew where he was going, how long it would take, and exactly what he was after. But that night was different. With no intel, no leads, and no idea where the gang might've taken Elias, he circled the city like a ghost chasing shadows. Then, like a flash of lightning across a storm-dark night, a realization struck. What if no one was holding Elias? What if he had escaped? And if he had, where did he go? Only one place made sense—familiar, quiet, hidden. The apartment above the dive bar where it had all started. That was his fallback, his safe zone, the last place that felt like home. Silas immediately turned the wheel and headed that way, his mind sharpening.

***

High above the planet, the great ship stirred. Having been linked to Silas through Elias—and Elias through her—she had already begun contemplating this same conclusion. She felt the echo of the twin bond and saw the opportunity. If Silas believed his brother might return to the apartment, perhaps that was the best place for Elias to be. And so, she enacted a plan.

The assassin, Xiao Ren, and the noble soldier, Zareth'Kai, were instructed to transport the unconscious Elias back to New San Angelo. They flew low in their stealth-equipped shuttle, touched down a few miles from the bar, and loaded Elias, still under sedation, into a nondescript van. Just before dawn, they parked in the alley behind the bar. They crept up the back stairs, broke into the apartment, and laid him gently on the bed. His body bore fewer injuries now, healed by the ship's advanced medical systems, though only to the extent that Earth's crude science might plausibly explain. A half-empty bottle of whiskey and a full glass were set on the nightstand, staged to complete the illusion.

The plan was simple: Elias would awaken groggy and disoriented, but he'd believe he had escaped. That after some desperate flight, he'd made it back here on his own. The foggy memories of pain, pursuit, and adrenaline would stitch together the gaps. It wasn't truth. But it was necessary. Meanwhile, not all eyes missed this midnight delivery.

*****

The Nillith, ever watchful, had been monitoring the bar. He knew instinctively that one of the twins might return here, and when he spotted the van and its passengers, his interest sharpened. He watched the assassin and the noble soldier leave Elias behind, then vanish down the alley. And then, the entity saw an opportunity. If he wanted Roach to move—if he wanted his corrupted mouthpiece to become a true player—he needed transport. And here it was, the enemy scout ship, unguarded. In a flicker of malice and will, the Nillith descended upon it.

By the time Xiao Ren and Zareth'Kai returned to their landing site, the ship was gone. Panic surged. Before they could argue or plot their next move, another ship appeared—this one cloaked in shimmering starlight. The Emissary had come.

He had no love for the Vorrhaxi. Even less for assassins. But the great ship had instructed him, and though it went against every instinct in his warrior's blood, he obeyed.

He opened the hatch, allowed them aboard, and took them silently into orbit. It was an uncomfortable journey. No one spoke. No one trusted. But the path forward had already shifted.

*****

As all this unfolded, Elias began to stir. Back in the dark apartment above the bar, he opened his eyes to the familiar walls, the sting of pain, and a bottle waiting by his side. He sat up slowly, groggily, every nerve on fire, and no memory of how he got there. But something inside whispered *You escaped. You made it out. You're home.* And for that moment, he believed it.

***

As Vaeril Dae'nar trailed Silas through the dusky streets of New San Angelo, a subtle discomfort began to grow in his chest, an unease he couldn't shake. It was more than paranoia. It was instinct. He was being watched. Not by the twin, and not by the crude human surveillance net. No, this was something older. Something colder. He scanned the rooftops and alleyways but found nothing. Still, the sensation lingered, like a splinter in the soul. He hated it. He was a hunter by birth and training. Never prey. Never watched. Yet, something was watching him now. Still, he pushed forward.

Silas had locked onto his next objective—Elias's old apartment above the bar—and The Emissary had to stay close. Not just because of the mission, but because the great ship had made it clear. Silas was essential.

And so, for the first time in his life, he found himself forced to ally, albeit reluctantly, with members of the very race he had spent centuries fighting. The assassin and the noble soldier. He'd once dreamed of killing warriors like Zareth'Kai on the battlefield—crushing them beneath his boot. And assassins like Xiao Ren? He'd spent a lifetime tracking their movements across shattered colonies and bleeding ruins. They had no honor, no code. They were vipers in the dark. But because of her—the great ship—he offered them his protection. That need for security came faster than expected.

***

As Xiao Ren and Zareth'Kai quietly deposited the unconscious Elias into his bed above the bar, their mission complete, they returned to the valley where their cloaked scout ship should have been. It was gone. Vanished. Panic overtook caution.

The assassin glanced sharply in all directions, her disguise slipping slightly as emotion surged. Zareth'Kai, ever the warrior, unslung the compact weapon from beneath his coat, and scanned for an ambush. But there was nothing. No sound. No trace. And then came the voice in their minds. *He has taken it.* The great ship. She'd seen it. She'd felt the distortion as the Nillith, in its stolen form, had slipped aboard their vessel. She didn't speak the name—it was dangerous to invoke—but the implication was clear. A shadow now moved among them. *Stand by. Help is coming.*

Just minutes later, the dark shape of The Emissary's vessel descended quietly into the alleyway. Its hull shimmered like mercury in the gloom. When the hatch opened, Xiao Ren stepped forward first, cautious, yet composed. Zareth'Kai followed, wary, his instincts coiled like a predator unsure of its cage. They recognized him immediately. Vaeril Dae'nar. The Ghost of Mourning Reach. The Blade of Naareth. A hero of legend, and a butcher of their kind. The air thickened with tension.

The Emissary stood just inside the open hatch, hands at his sides, not threatening. Not welcoming, just … waiting. "You coming or not?" he said flatly.

Xiao Ren and Zareth'Kai exchanged one final glance. Then, silently, they stepped aboard. The hatch closed behind them with a hiss, and the ship rose into the night. No words were spoken during the journey. None were needed.

In the great ship's hangar, the trio disembarked. The hangar bay lit itself softly, almost reverently. As they walked deeper into the ship's interior, her voice filled the chamber—calm, firm, and impossible to ignore. "You are not enemies," she said. "Not anymore." They paused. "You are bound by betrayal. By exile. By purpose. What you *were* no longer matters. What you *choose* to be *does matter.*" And with that, the alliance—uneasy, untested, but very real—was forged.

The Emissary, without another word, returned to his ship. He had another mission. He needed to be close to Silas when the reunion took place, both to protect him and to bear witness. The twins were about to converge. And the universe would never be the same.

***

Silas wasn't exactly speeding, but he wasn't dawdling, either. He knew the way to the dive bar by heart. He'd been there dozens of times before—sometimes just to sit in his truck across the street, watching, making sure his brother was still breathing. Elias never knew. Maybe that was for the best. On more than one occasion, Silas had gotten the sense—sometimes through intuition, sometimes through the strange link that had always existed between them—that Elias was slipping too far, spiraling downward. So, he came. He never went inside, never crossed the line that would push his brother away. But he came, just to be sure.

Over time, he'd struck up a quiet arrangement with the barkeep. Slipped him cash here and there to keep an eye on Elias. Nothing official. Nothing with strings. Just instructions to *watch him.* Let Silas know if Elias disappeared.

Silas parked his truck across the empty street and stepped out into the cool night air. The bar loomed ahead, squat and ugly, stained by neon and regret. He crossed the road with long, deliberate strides, pushed open the door, and stepped inside. The place hadn't changed. Dim lights. Sticky floors. The low hum of a jukebox too tired to play anything modern. A handful of regulars hunched over their drinks like dying animals, nursing glasses of poison like it was medicine. The air reeked of spilled beer and old sweat.

Silas looked around, taking in every detail. It wasn't just a bar, it was a nest for the broken. A halfway house for the addicted. No wonder Elias had chosen it. Around there, no one asked questions. And no one expected you to get better.

He moved to the bar, where the bartender—an aging, hollow-eyed man with nicotine-stained fingers—froze at the sight of him. Silas leaned in. "I'm looking for Elias. Is he here?"

The bartender blinked once, twice. "Not that I've seen. Unless he slipped past me somehow, and I doubt that."

"You know what's going on, right?" Silas asked, voice low.

The bartender nodded slowly, licking dry lips. "Yeah, I know. And you've got the nerve to show your face here? With Marco's crew sniffing around? You two look alike, you know. Real alike. Could get you mistaken in the wrong alleyway."

Silas didn't flinch. "I don't think Marco or his crew are going to be a problem anymore. For Elias or anyone else." There was a beat of silence. Then the bartender paled. Visibly. His hand trembled as he poured himself a shot of something dark and swallowed it in one sharp motion. He poured another and wordlessly offered Silas a glass. Silas declined with a glance. He didn't drink. Not anymore. That was Elias's escape, not his.

The bartender coughed and lit a cigarette with shaky fingers. "You're welcome to check upstairs," he said. "But I don't think he's there. And … you sure? About Marco?"

"I'm sure," Silas said, already turning away. "You won't be seeing him again."

The bartender stared after him in stunned silence, smoke curling from the end of his trembling cigarette.

Silas moved up the narrow staircase, and each creak underfoot echoed through the bar like a warning. He didn't know what he'd find in that apartment, but he hoped, for once, that he wasn't too late.

Making as little noise as possible, Silas crept up the narrow hallway and paused outside the apartment door. It was closed and appeared secure. He reached into his pocket and pulled out the passkey he always kept on him, just in case he ever had to check on Elias.

He knocked gently. No response. Cautiously, he slipped the key into the lock, turned it, and slowly pushed the door open. The interior was dim and quiet. Then, without warning, something jabbed into his back. Hard. Silas froze. It was rare for anyone to get the drop on him.

"Easy," came a gravelly voice he knew too well. Elias. With a firm shove, Elias pushed Silas farther into the room. Though they were the same height, Elias had thirty pounds of muscle on him and moved like a brawler in close quarters.

Silas regained his footing and instinctively spun, already drawing a knife. But the moment he saw his twin, he exhaled and sheathed the blade. "Jesus," Silas muttered. "What the hell happened to you?"

"I'll be damned if I know," Elias said as he shrugged. "Wrong place, wrong guy. There was a girl, of course. Shocking, I know."

Silas raised a skeptical brow. "A girl? Really?"

"Easy, man." Elias laughed, wincing slightly. "No need to rub it in. I might've gotten a little carried away. Broke the guy's arm, maybe a leg. Nothing he won't live through. What can I say? Don't pick bar fights unless you're ready for 'em."

Silas shook his head. "You'll never learn. The pesky problems that start out as gnats usually turn into gigantic monsters."

"Oh, right. Here we go. Mr. Perfect never stepped a toe out of line."

Silas had heard it all before. Many times. But tonight, he welcomed it. His brother was alive. That was enough.

CHAPTER FIVE

"So, how'd you get back here?" Silas asked.

Elias rubbed his temple. "Honestly? No clue. Woke up here. Might've been afternoon, could've been night. Curtains were drawn. Open bottle of whiskey on the nightstand. Took a few swigs to ease the pain."

"You're hurt?"

"Oh yeah," Elias groaned. "Pretty banged up. But weirdly, not as bad as it should be. Feels like it's healing already. Maybe it wasn't as bad as it looked."

Silas frowned. *It was that bad.* He remembered the pool of blood at the warehouse and the lifeless way Elias had been draped across that gurney. There was no way he should be walking, let alone cracking jokes. Still … maybe it was better not to question a miracle. Not tonight. "You need to see a doc?"

Elias waved him off. "Nah, I'll live. You don't have anything on you, do you?" Elias asked, voice low. "Something stronger than whiskey?"

Silas's expression hardened. "You know I don't touch that crap. Tylenol's as far as I go."

Elias smirked. "God, you sound like a damn corpsman. 'Take Motrin, drink water, change your socks.' I could lose a leg and you'd hand me a Band-Aid and tell me to walk it off."

"We're not in the corps anymore," Silas countered.

"Don't I know it," Elias replied with a sardonic smirk.

Silas glanced around the grimy apartment. "You should get out of here. Nothing edible in this place. Just standing here makes me want a tetanus shot."

"Judge much?" Elias shot back, but grinned. They chuckled. It felt good. Normal, even.

"Come on," Silas said. "Let's get you some food. Talk things out. Figure out what the hell happened." Elias followed him to the door but paused.

"Hey … what about Marco? And his crew?"

Silas didn't respond right away. He turned to Elias with a look that said more than words ever could. It was over. Marco had crossed the line you don't cross—not with twins. You don't hurt one and leave the other breathing. If you do, you'd better hope you're already dead. Because when the other one shows up, you won't see it coming. And with that, they left the apartment behind.

Exiting down the back stairs and out into the night, the two slipped into Silas's waiting truck. Together again, for now. After climbing into the truck, Silas fired up the engine with a low growl. He glanced sideways at his brother, arching a brow. "So, meathead—what are you in the mood for?"

Elias grinned without hesitation. "Waffle House. What else?"

Silas groaned. "Puke. Greasy food grilled right in front of you by a guy who hasn't seen a hairnet since '98. A restaurant most likely filled with the desperate, the wild, and the thoroughly drunk."

Elias shrugged. "Sounds like our kind of people."

Silas rolled his eyes but shifted into drive. "Fine. But you're paying—assuming they take beer caps and IOUs."

They sped off into the night, tail lights fading into the gloom of the city. And just a short distance behind, cloaked in shadows and silence, The Emissary followed—ever watchful, keeping pace with his unaware charges.

Silas and Elias pulled up to the first Waffle House they could find. The parking lot was a sea of motorcycles.

Elias grinned. "Oh, hell yes, we're going in."

Silas, though not exactly worried, arched an eyebrow. "I'd be remiss if I didn't mention your delicate condition."

"I've never felt more alive," Elias said with a chuckle. "I just hope one of these idiots gives me a reason to make an example of them." He shook his head, amused. "Nah … my life's not that good." Then he gave Silas that familiar, sleepy-eyed executioner's look, followed by a quick wink.

Silas sighed. Maybe he should've just kept driving. But hell—shit happens. They walked in. The place was packed, loud with laughter, clinking glasses, and the heavy scent of grease. Elias led the way, weaving through the chaos in search of an open booth. Silas followed close behind, scanning faces, watching hands. They'd barely even made it to their seats before the situation turned.

A large, scarred biker—more drunk than upright—stumbled toward the back, bumping into a waitress and sending her crashing to the floor. Elias, never the gentleman but always a magnet for trouble, headed in their direction in a flash. Probably because he was more excited about a potential fight than any noble instinct.

He knelt beside the waitress. "You okay?" he asked, checking on her.

That's when it happened. Three more bikers closed in behind him—too casual, too coordinated. A setup. One lifted a heavy boot, aiming to knock Elias over. He didn't get the chance. Cold steel pressed into his armpit, just deep enough to nick skin and nerves. The biker froze, eyes wide.

"Hey," Silas whispered into his ear, his voice low and calm. "That's my brother. You sure you want to do this?"

The biker squeaked—more mouse than man—then looked to his friends, eyes pleading for backup. Their leader stood up and sauntered over, radiating smug confidence. "I think we can work this out," he said. "How about we take this outside?"

Eilas gave him a razor-edged smile. "Happy to accommodate."

"Oh no," the gang leader said, smirking. "I think I'll take the sneaky one."

Silas tilted his head. "So, you want the small one? Chickenshit much?"

The man grinned. "You don't understand who's calling the shots here."

At that, Silas withdrew the blade from the biker's armpit with deliberate slowness. "Big boy," he said, rising to his feet, "I'd be honored to help you resolve your schoolyard bully issues."

None of them noticed Roach, who was watching from a shadowed corner, behind mirrored sunglasses and a half-eaten plate of hash browns. Or that the Nillith's influence was there, too, in the edges of every decision, in the rage in the bikers' blood. It was always watching. Always stirring the pot. And yet, when the Nillith looked upon the twins, it felt something alien. Uncertainty. And in its dark and ancient mind, that was far more dangerous than fear.

The lack of fear in Silas's eyes made Bear uneasy. That didn't happen often. By biker standards, Bear was tough. The scarred knuckles, cauliflower ears, and surprisingly straight nose told the story of a man who'd brawled his way through dozens of roadside bars and back-alley disputes—and walked away from every single one. He wasn't a giant, but at six feet, two inches tall and a solid 300 pounds of bulk and bluster, he wasn't used to being underestimated. Especially not by someone like Silas.

Lean, quiet, and utterly unshaken, Silas didn't posture. He didn't threaten. He just smiled. And that smile—calm, cold, inevitable—was the thing that made Bear's stomach turn. He had no idea what door he'd just opened. But before the night was over, he'd be praying to God—or anyone who'd listen—that he'd never opened it at all. Pride, after all, is a wicked thing. It kills common sense faster than whiskey kills liver cells. And ego? Ego will walk you blindfolded into your own funeral with a grin on your face.

Bear squared off anyway. Because fools always do. The rest of the restaurant went quiet. Chairs scraped back. Forks hovered midair. Even the drunks knew something real was about to happen.

Silas stepped forward, eyes locked on Bear's, his hands loose at his sides. He didn't look worried. He looked … patient.

Far above and far away—yet impossibly near—two unseen figures watched the unfolding chaos with dark anticipation. Through the warped, parasitic bond they now shared, the Nillith and Roach observed from the shadows, unseen by all but the dying. Though it was the Nillith's will that guided the puppet strings, it was through Roach's twisted flesh that it experienced the world. And what a delicious world it had become.

The Nillith felt it first—a hot pulse of anticipation radiated through Roach's reanimated nerves. A sick, gleeful swell of adrenaline pumped into a body no longer its own but still wired for violent pleasure. It was intoxicating. Addictive. The stench of fear. The thick, coppery tang of blood just moments from spilling. This wasn't just violence. This was theater. The kind the Nillith adored. It was a performance without actors—just wolves and meat. Bear and Silas, predator and prey—but the roles were not yet assigned. Not truly. That made it all the more exquisite.

Roach's lips twisted into a near-human grin as the bikers encircled. The Nillith savored every flicker of motion, every heartbeat of tension, like a starving man eyeing the first bite of a long-awaited feast. It wasn't just about the fight. It was about what it revealed. About Silas. About Elias. About the beautiful instability they brought with them. This was just the first course.

There's a difference between a man who's seen death … and one who *delivers* it. A difference between those who kill to survive or conceal a crime, and the ones who wield death like a sacred weapon— measured, deliberate, and without hesitation. The kind of man who has studied taking a life until it's a fluent language. The kind of man who courts death, invites it in, and makes it kneel at his feet. Silas was such a man. And Bear—whatever illusions he'd once held about being hard—was beginning to understand that. Too late. The biker had scars, sure. A wide frame, fists like hammers, and enough bar fights under his belt to make most men wary. But not this one. Not Silas.

That night, while he stood across from him, Bear felt the first real chill of mortality slide down his spine like ice water. This wasn't a man. This was death incarnate. And Bear had just *invited* it to dance. He couldn't back down. Not in front of his pack of half-drunk fools who would tear him apart the second they saw weakness. Pride, that wicked god, whispered lies in his ears. Told him to stand tall. Told him this wraith was bluffing. But Silas didn't move. Didn't blink. Didn't *breathe.* He simply *waited*—silent, still, and impossibly calm. The kind of silence that grows thick … hungry … until it demands to be filled.

Bear opened his mouth, then thought better of it. Any sound he made would betray the shaking in his chest. He inhaled. Took a step forward. *Blink.* Then pain. White-hot and sudden, slashing through both arms. He didn't see Silas move. No one did. But there was blood—*his* blood—spurting from twin lacerations that had laid open his biceps down to the bone. He staggered, confused, then collapsed, staring at the ceiling tiles as his body went limp. Gasps filled the restaurant. A waitress shrieked. Someone muttered, "How the hell …?"

Silas moved again, this time clearly. Smooth, measured, as he snatched two towels from a frozen waitress and an apron from another. He knelt beside the bleeding Bear, pressed cloth to wounds, and whispered in his ear, "I don't kill for the first offense. Take this as the only warning you'll ever get. And next time … stay silent when the grown-ups are talking." He stood, turned, and gave a wink and a slow, deliberate nod to the shocked biker crew, their mouths hanging open. Then he sauntered back to the booth where Elias waited, his arms folded, a grin already spreading across his face.

Silas slid into the seat and flagged down a waitress like nothing had happened. "I'll take the all-star special. Bacon crispy," he said calmly. Across the table, Elias snorted into his coffee and whispered under his breath, "It's always the quiet ones that get you."

***

As the great ship once again touched Earth's atmosphere, she simmered. If she'd had blood, it would've been at a rolling boil. The twins had done it again. How two grown men could get into so much trouble in such a short time was beyond her comprehension. She began to wonder if they were truly worth the effort. Were they really the crux of salvation? Or were they just two more sparks hurtling toward a gasoline-drenched galaxy, ready to ignite it in chaos?

Still, one thing was certain: they were absurdly lucky. Somehow, they always got out of things by the very skin on their noses—which, upon reflection, was a surprisingly slim margin to gamble a future on.

In the middle of these swirling thoughts, one rose to the top: maybe she should just have The Emissary bring them up right now so she could throttle them both. Nearly to death. Then revive them … and throttle them again. Firmly and lovingly.

But another thought interrupted that fantasy—two companions. One for each twin. And just like that, as though the thought had summoned them, like comets streaking silently through the dark sky, the boys' destined companions arrived. Two stars fell in a forgotten part of the city—not far from the Waffle House, where the twins were finishing what was either a late dinner or an early breakfast, depending on how you measured regret. They were cheerfully taunting a gang of bikers, including one they had recently and thoroughly dismantled. The bikers watched from a distance, their fear still hanging like smoke in the air.

Max and Alex—at least, that's what they were calling themselves—moved through the shadows. Two sleek canine figures padded silently toward the diner, their movements fluid, their communication subtle. They spotted Silas's truck and waited. Fate, or the ship's careful hand, timed it perfectly. The twins stood from the table, each with a doggie bag in hand, and strolled out the door.

Elias couldn't resist one more jab at the bikers. He dropped the tailgate, sat on it, and gave them a look that said *try me again.* None of them did.

Elias was, above all things, a dog lover. He had no tolerance for cruelty—especially to animals. Silas, on the other hand, was more indifferent. Not cruel, just … apathetic. He'd never bonded with an animal. Elias had bonded with many.

So, when Max, slinking low, crept around the corner and found himself right under the boot of a particularly nasty biker, it was, perhaps, no accident. The biker raised a foot and kicked. Max let out a sharp, convincing yelp. Truth be told, Max could've eaten the man alive without flinching, but the act served its purpose. Elias saw it. Saw the kick, heard the cry—and the switch flipped.

He launched from the tailgate like a missile. In a blur, he had the biker on the ground. Grabbed him and flipped him. "How do you like being kicked around?" he growled. Then he made him crawl on all fours. Gave him two hard boots to the ribs. "You like that? Huh?" Another kick. Then silence. Message sent.

And then, like he always had—with stray dogs or women—Elias crouched low and coaxed the canines out from hiding. They emerged, sleek and silent. Larger than a border collie, maybe more like an Australian shepherd—but with short coats and eyes that saw everything.

He tossed them scraps from his doggie bag. Silas sighed but followed suit. And just like that, Alex and Max were theirs. Or maybe, the other way around. They didn't know it yet, but these two mysterious dogs would become their fiercest protectors—their guardians in fur, with secrets hidden in DNA no Earth animal could claim. Closer to them than even their twin had ever been. Silas had Alex. Elias had Max.

The brothers climbed into the truck cab. The dogs settled into the bed. They turned toward the mountains. Toward Silas's self-made fortress. Toward fate. And behind them, in the shadows, the world began to change.

The Emissary sat cross-legged against a rock and watched from his quiet perch above the small house nestled in the foothills near Mount Rainier. It was known, at least to one man, as the fortress of solitude—Silas Kael's retreat from the world.

The twins had just pulled up in the truck, lights flashing absurdly bright against the darkness. Anyone could've followed them. But Silas didn't seem to care, not when he was with Elias. It was as if having his brother nearby made him believe nothing bad could touch him.

They climbed out. Silas opened the rear gate and the two dogs, Alex and Max, leaped out with eager purpose, trotting into the dark edges of their new home. Elias stretched and looked around. "So," he said, glancing at the trees, "how far away is the local nightlife around here?"

Silas frowned. "Local nightlife?"

"You know, where we can get a little … bow chicka wow wow."

"Do you ever stop?" Silas shook his head, amused. "There's no nightlife up here. Just local wildlife—foxes, bears, wolves. Maybe an owl or two if you're lucky."

Elias grinned. "So … lions and tigers and bears?"

"Oh, my," Silas deadpanned. "Welcome to the complete opposite of *The Wizard of Oz*. No yellow brick road, no munchkins, no hope of escape. Just me, one bed, and the world's worst roommate. Which, by the way, is you. You're on the couch. And no, you're not sleeping in my bed. First, because it's a single, and second, because I know exactly where you've been."

Elias laughed. "Fair. Do you at least have something good to drink?"

"You mean … alcohol?"

"Yeah. Whiskey. Scotch. Beer. Hell, rubbing alcohol in a pinch."

"Nope. No booze. No pills, either. I've got Tylenol and Motrin. Hydrate and change your socks."

Elias groaned. "God, you're doing a good job of impersonating a corpsman again."

They both laughed as they headed inside. Silas powered on his system, and Elias kicked off his boots and flopped onto the couch.

"You mind checking to see if anything weird is going on?" Elias asked. "Like … news about Marco's gang? Just see what's out there."

Silas nodded and began diving into the web. First the surface, then deep, and eventually the dark web. He routed through local police chatter, scraped forums, and ghosted through backdoors he'd set up long ago. It wasn't paranoia if people actually were hunting you.

Outside, The Emissary watched through half-lidded eyes, shaking his head. In all his years—and he'd had more than a few—he had never seen a pair of twins get into so much chaos so fast. He had recruited, bribed, and even kidnapped sets of twins before. But these two? These two were something else entirely. And somehow, they were even worse together than apart. Like gasoline and matches walking around in boots.

Elias opened the back door of the cabin and whistled. Alex and Max padded in quietly. Silas gave Elias a look that clearly said *No Dogs Allowed Inside*, but he didn't say a word as they entered. Alex walked straight to Silas and laid down at his feet like a sentinel. Max curled up by the couch, resting near Elias's boots. The bonds had been made, even if the humans hadn't realized it yet.

The Emissary, satisfied, leaned back and finally allowed himself to sleep. If anything approaches, he thought, I'll know.

Silas continued digging for hours. Article after article. A slew of data and dead ends. Nothing about Marco. No mention of bodies. Just a vague report about a structure fire in a remote part of town. Could be them, he thought, or it could be nothing. Finally, he looked up—Elias was out cold on the couch, snoring softly. Max, motionless, lay nearby like a loyal shadow. Silas glanced down. Alex looked up at him. Maybe it was the light or maybe it was exhaustion, but it felt like the dog gave him a subtle wink. *We're still up* the look said. *We're watching.*

Another hour passed. Silas finally gave in to his fatigue, stripped down, and crawled into bed. As he pulled the covers over himself, he looked down at Alex, still awake on the floor. At any other point in his life, he'd never have considered it. But Alex didn't smell unpleasant. Didn't track mud. Didn't seem like, well, a dog. He was just … clean. Almost eerily so. He hesitated, then patted the bed. Without hesitation, Alex leaped up and settled at the foot. The bed shifted only slightly, and within moments, Silas felt his breathing steady. Silas and Alex drifted off into sleep—two beings from two very different worlds, each dreaming of a future they couldn't yet see.

***

The Nillith watched as Silas and Elias drove away, the truck's taillights vanishing into the night. But his gaze didn't follow them—it lingered instead on the dogs. There was something deeply wrong with them. Not in the way that made him recoil, but in the way that made even *him*—a primordial corrupter of minds and realities—pause.

They didn't move right. They didn't look right. There was a presence behind their eyes that felt too steady, too *aware*. The Nillith had seen intelligence in dogs before—simple, loyal, predictable. But this wasn't that. *These* dogs … *understood.*

He cocked his replicated head to the side, and Roach's skin twitched with the involuntary shudder of instinctive unease. "Humph," he muttered, "curious." But he let the thought drift away.

There was another force at play in this world. He could feel it— hidden hands just beyond the veil. Another player had stepped onto the board, and they hadn't yet revealed their strategy. That was fine.

That was delicious. That meant chaos. "Oh well," he said, stretching in his mimicked skin. "Time to move on." He turned his thoughts inward, into the dark, echoing well where Roach's tattered consciousness continued to swim in a soup of agony and madness. "Come, Roach. We have a perfectly good stolen spaceship … and absolutely no regard for consequence." A grin spread across his face—too wide, too wrong. "Now, who shall we ruin first?" he whispered, voice like cracked glass. "The Spymaster … or the emperor?" And with that, the stars above began to shiver.

***

The Spymaster moved like a shadow through his chamber, sightless eyes glinting as he surveyed the operation unfolding. Messengers had been sent. Not envoys, not diplomats—*messengers* in the old sense of the word: those who delivered demands or threats, often both. Across the empire, hidden caches of blackmail were being cracked open like rotten eggs. Secrets, scandals, and sins were dragged into the light, each more damning than the last. Where hard currency failed, shame succeeded. Where shame failed, fear did the trick.

The Spymaster had learned long ago that no one in the empire was clean. Not truly. They all did what they did for *the glory of the empire*—a phrase so often recited it had become both oath and excuse. But beneath that patriotic veneer? Lust, greed, betrayal, and perversion. All waiting to be *exposed*. And now, all owed him.

He stared out over the gathered captains in the docking bay—a truly wretched collection of privateers, exiled generals, and dishonored fleet officers who had long since abandoned titles and morals in exchange for autonomy and violence. A more despicable brood of parasites and cutthroats had never flown under the same banner. And yet, for this mission, they were perfect.

"They won't ask questions," he whispered to himself, eyes narrowing. "They'll do the job, burn the world, bury the twins, and leave nothing but ash." Earth would be wiped clean. The Thal'Naari tech would be lost again. And the emperor would never know just how close he came to being dethroned by a pair of ragged human twins.

The Spymaster smiled thinly, hands clasped behind his back. All this, while the emperor sulked in seclusion, his pride and bones shattered from yet another failed assassination attempt by one of his precious queen generals. *Let them squabble over the throne.* When the ashes of Earth blew through the void, when the emperor was told the threat had been purged without his knowledge, he—the Spymaster—would rise. Did he do it for credibility? No. *Control.*

***

The emperor reclined upon a vast, bone-carved lounge in his private chambers. Pain flared in his ribs, sharp and unfamiliar. He pressed a clawed hand to the torn flesh beneath his robes and hissed. *Real* pain. It had been centuries since he'd felt anything close to it. How had she, the queen, got so close? Now dead, of course—torn to pieces by the palace guards in a display that had been neither swift nor merciful. But still, the fact that she had gotten close enough to draw blood within *his own* chamber was an unsettling novelty. *They're getting competent.* That was the troubling part. For ages, he had watched their petty power games from his throne with the smug detachment of a god. Every plot, every betrayal, every poisoned whisper—he'd seen them all coming long before the knife was ever drawn. But this one? This one had nearly worked. *Too close.* The thought curdled into anger. *The flock is growing bold,* he mused. *And boldness must be punished.*

He shifted in his seat and winced again. His body was healing slowly—another insult. The toxins she'd used were rare, probably forbidden. A calculated risk. A desperate move. It had nearly paid off. No matter. It simply meant it was time for a *purge.* You had to remind the others, now and then, who held the leash; who held the knife behind their back when others forgot.

The emperor's eyes drifted to the far corner of the room, where the shadows seemed thicker. He needed a hand. Not a queen, not a general. Someone quiet, efficient, and ruthless. *A trusted servant.* But who?

He licked the blood from his lips as he considered. Someone already steeped in darkness. Someone who owed him. Someone expendable, in case things went poorly. The emperor smiled slowly, teeth jagged and red. Yes … he knew just the one.

***

Malvek sat alone, fuming. Alone with his thoughts, his memories, and a thousand ghosts he'd personally created. He had been exiled, not because of failure, but because he knew too much. Too many of the emperor's secrets whispered through his blood. Too many bodies buried, most by his own hands. The emperor hadn't dared to kill him. Instead, he had vanished him—shoved him into the cold corner of the empire where no one asked questions and nothing stirred.

He should've been grateful. Many who knew even half of what Malvek did had ended up in unmarked graves or as scattered atoms. But gratitude was not in Malvek's nature. Not anymore. His body, a patchwork of augments and old wounds, itched for something—violence, obedience, purpose. He had sacrificed his flesh so many times for the empire, he should have been revered as a demigod. Instead, he was forgotten.

Just as he had begun to wonder whether he'd spend another day in quiet rot, a scout ship appeared on the horizon—sleek, small, and trembling with urgency. Malvek didn't stand to greet it. He already knew what it meant. The messenger disembarked and approached, offering a sealed vial. Not a digital message. Not a tablet or data crystal. No, this was the emperor's most private form of communication—pheromonal scent-code sealed in glass. One inhalation would tell Malvek everything.

He uncorked it, breathed deep, and smiled. If he'd still had lips to grin with, they would have stretched ear to ear. Without hesitation, without a single word, he reached forward and stabbed the messenger through the heart. There was no regret. No anger. Just a returning sense of completeness as warm blood slicked his fingers.

He watched the youngling's eyes dim, taking a final breath in silent awe. It wasn't the betrayal that had stung Malvek all these years. Nor was it exile. It wasn't even the loneliness. It was the silence, the stillness. The lack of blood on his hands. And now? The emperor needed him again. The empire would soon need reminding why Malvek had once been whispered about in backrooms and war councils as *the final option*. There would be blood. Oh yes, there would be mountains of corpses and oceans of blood.

***

When the emperor received word that his messenger wouldn't be returning, he leaned back into the shadows of his throne and exhaled slowly through cracked lips. So, the game had begun. It was difficult to pinpoint the exact emotion stirring in his blackened chest—satisfaction, perhaps. Relief, maybe. A hint of anticipation. Or all of them twisted into something far more primal. He didn't dwell on it. Emotions were tools, like blades or poisons. Meant to be used, not examined. All that mattered was this: Malvek was in motion. And when Malvek moved, the galaxy trembled and bled. Soon the silence would end. The whispers would return. And the bodies would begin to stack like cordwood in a winter famine. The emperor smiled. His peace was coming, and with it, a great deal of horror for those who had forgotten their place.

***

A message arrived for the Spymaster. The emperor's response was not what he had expected. Instead of shoring up defenses and bracing for the coming storm, which was the inevitable power grab of yet another ambitious queen, the emperor had gone far beyond the Spymaster's darkest predictions. He had reached into the vaults of old horrors, into the most forbidden part of his war cabinet's history, and summoned a name that had not been spoken aloud in centuries: Malvek. The final solution. Whispered in the shadowed corners of war rooms. Inked in blood on ancient scrolls of contingency.

He was not a soldier. He was not even an assassin in the traditional sense. Malvek was a force of undoing. A thing you unleashed when victory no longer mattered, when collateral damage was not a concern, and when mercy had been excised from the vocabulary of the throne.

Even the Spymaster—who was no stranger to cruelty, no admirer of softheartedness—felt his blood cool at the name. By comparison, he was a ray of light. And that terrified him. If Malvek's orders included taking care of him … well, then he would need to be careful. Very careful. One misstep, one miscalculation, and he wouldn't even know what had happened until the darkness claimed him.

He pushed the thought aside and moved swiftly. The Spymaster gathered his captains—commanders of his personal armada, one hundred fifty warships strong. It was a fleet more than capable of wiping Earth from the stars ten times over and leaving nothing behind. No bodies, no records, no echo. Earth was a backwater world and irrelevant; off the major trade routes and largely ignored by galactic powers. Its death would not cause a ripple. No one would come looking. If he could laugh, the Spymaster might've doubled over in bitter delight.

The emperor, so consumed by his own chaos, wouldn't even notice. He was already obsessed, consumed by the black fire he had summoned. And that gave the Spymaster room. Yes, innocents would die. Millions, likely. But as the emperor so often declared, *There are no innocents in the empire. Only tools of my will.* And for now, the Spymaster remained one of those tools. But not for long; not if this plan worked. This destruction, this unholy slaughter—it would not be meaningless. It would serve his greater purpose. He wouldn't gain complete control. Not yet. But a slice of power? That was more than he ever had before. And it would be enough to start something greater.

***

Each twin lay sleeping, lost in his own dream. Truth be told, they were both haunted by recurring dreams. Different landscapes, same pain.

Silas was six years old again. He walked barefoot along a tree-lined dirt road under the shroud of night. A pair of headlights cut through the trees ahead, and instinctively, he dropped into a shallow ditch. It wasn't hard to hide a six-year-old body in the shadows. He pressed low to the earth, waiting for the car to pass. He remembered where the neighbor lived—just down the bend. His mother had told him once, *if it ever gets bad, run there. Ask them to call the police.* And it had gotten bad. One of her drunken boyfriends, another monster with rage behind his eyes, had come home swinging, screaming, and throwing knives. He'd smashed the door, the dishes, and the furniture. For once, their mother had tried to protect the boys. And for once, Silas had run. It had been a long and terrifying walk.

But this time, the dream shifted. As he lay in the ditch with the cold ground beneath him, he reached out instinctively, and his hand brushed against warm fur. He turned. Alex was lying beside him, calm and alert, his golden eyes watching the road. Silas could almost *hear* his voice. Not a bark or a growl. *Don't worry now, Silas. You'll never be alone again. We'll protect each other.* And in that moment, the nightmare lost its grip.

Across the room, Elias tossed in his sleep. The battlefield was empty. Bodies were all around and smoke choked the air. He was screaming his squadmates' names into the void, but no one answered.

119

The silence was always worse than the blood, worse than the screams. Silence meant he was truly alone. He hated that feeling. He *knew* that feeling. That's why he sought companionship. Not always for love. Not even for comfort. Just to keep the loneliness at bay.

He reached up in the dream, trying to pull himself over a ledge of broken rubble. His hand landed on something warm. Not stone. Not blood. It was fur. *Max.* The dog stood calmly at his side, gaze unwavering and steady as the earth. Elias blinked. In his mind, he *heard* it, clear as speech. *Don't worry, Elias. You'll never be alone again. We'll always protect each other.*

Both men awoke at nearly the same moment. Fifteen feet apart. They locked eyes, each with a strange, startled look. As if they knew. As if the same current had run through both of them. Neither spoke. Alex and Max stood together, near the front door, silent, watching. Their eyes were not on the twins but beyond, guarding. *Something had changed.*

***

And just like that, as if compelled by something older than blood, the queens gathered. Not in the shadow of the emperor, but far from his reach—in secret, for the first time in recorded history.

The group included Khar'Zul, the mutator. Her brood writhed with unnatural limbs. There was also Virexxa, the schemer, whose venom-tongued whispers once charmed half the galaxy into ruin. Next was Threxil, the traditionalist warmonger who opposed twisted science. She yearned for nothing more than battle so she could eventually meet her end in glorious combat. And Zev'Kala, the silent shadow and most secretive, who had multiple contacts both in and outside of the empire. Her spies and assassins were in all corners of the empire and beyond.

The foolish Spymaster thought he was the master of secrets, but he was just an amateur playing dress-up. This was no council of politics. This was a council of war. Perhaps even rebellion. The emperor had gone too far. He had not killed *one*, not *two*, but *four* queens. Slaughtered them without ceremony. One had been ripped apart by the palace guard. The others died by his own hands. As if the ancient dance they had always played, predator circling predator, had suddenly become a massacre. There was always danger in the game. Injuries, betrayals, poison in a kiss. But death? *Real death?* That had never been on the table. Something had changed. The emperor's madness had deepened. A bloodlust, pure and undiluted, now ruled his mind. There was no strategy left. No cruelty masked as policy. There was only rage.

And then, *he did the unthinkable.* He awakened Malvek. The name was not spoken. Not once. Not aloud. The queens would not dare. It was not the name that struck fear. It was the *scent* of him. A metallic rot that slithered into your lungs and never left.

Malvek didn't kill because he had to. He didn't kill because he was commanded. Malvek killed because he *enjoyed* it. Because the ending of life thrilled him in ways no queen could understand. He was no assassin. He was the end. And unlike the queens, who consumed their mates as part of the cycle of dominance and survival, Malvek *butchered* for *pleasure.* With no hunger, no need. And he had been loosed. Wherever his gaze turned, death followed, and none of them knew if they were next.

So, they gathered. Not from unity or loyalty. But from mutual fear. If ever there was a time to act, to rise, to tear the emperor from his throne and rebuild something that resembled sanity—it was at that time. They did not trust each other. They never would. But they feared him more. And that made them *dangerous.*

***

As the Spymaster sprawled across the command dais of his darkened moon, where shadows crept along the ceiling like watching spirits, he

121

reflected on the web he had spun. Perhaps he had gone too far. He'd nudged the queens, pushed them. Whispers here, suggestions there. Set their venomous ambitions loose against the emperor like hounds after a wounded stag. And now? Rumors swirled.

The surviving queens—those cunning, terrible matriarchs—had done the unthinkable. They were uniting. Not out of loyalty or for power, but out of fear. A fear that had no shape but reeked of death.

The emperor had gone mad, yes. But the Spymaster had *fed* that madness. If whispers of rebellion had reached his ears—here, in the middle of nowhere on this cold, forgotten moon—surely, they had reached the emperor's as well.

He might have started a war he could not control. A civil war, long and bloody. Possibly eternal. There was no guarantee of victory—no safe bet, no solid alliance. He could join a side, but which one? He might bet on the wrong queen. Or worse, trust the emperor a moment too long. Perhaps staying in the middle *was* the wisest path. Play both sides. Whisper to both thrones. *And yet ...* there was still Earth. Still the twins. The dangerous, volatile possibility of their rise. If they weren't a current threat, they would be eventually. The Thal'Naari were stirring again, and Earth was their last hope. That could not be allowed.

He briefly considered calling off the invasion fleet. *One hundred fifty ships.* A force that could decide the outcome of the empire's civil war. A card too valuable to play on a backwater place like Earth. But the die was cast. The twins must be dealt with—permanently.

And then there was Malvek. That name—the one no one said aloud. Even now, it chilled him. Malvek had been *awakened.* The Spymaster felt a bitter twist in his gut. He had once loved Malvek. Or what passed for love in beings like them. And Malvek had returned it, in his own horrific way.

They had been at odds a hundred times—conflicting ideologies, clashing tactics. The Spymaster saw killing as a tool. A message. A manipulation. Malvek killed for pleasure. There was no utility in what he did. No aftermath to shape. No survivors to steer. And that made him monstrous. Dead men told no tales—but dead men also could not be used. Could not stab your enemies in the back. Could not whisper secrets in exchange for life. The Spymaster preferred his pawns *alive.* Still … the emperor had loosed the beast. And that meant time was running short for everyone.

He considered, briefly, sending a message to the queens. Offering aid. Bargains. Protection. Then another to the emperor, laced with schemes and promises, anything to buy a little favor, or delay. So many options. But then—*clarity.*

He rose. With a sharp exhalation of pheromones, thick and pungent as command steel, he summoned his fleet admiral. *Proceed to the Sol System. Burn Earth to ash. Leave nothing standing that bears the mark of human hands. No cities, no satellites, and no survivors. The risk of another twin awakening cannot be allowed. Not now, not during this chaos. Not when a single spark could unravel centuries of conquest.*

And just like that, the order was given. The fleet turned toward Earth. A world of billions—doomed not for what they had done, but for what they *might* become.

***

Shaskiel left the presence of the filthy Spymaster with murder in his heart. He had never intended to lead this fleet. It was beneath him. An errand to the outer dark. A slaughter of primitives. But the Spymaster—*the twisted little weaver of secrets*—had something far more dangerous than orders. He had *leverage.*

In an empire where sex—any sex not initiated by the emperor—was forbidden under the threat of pain and dismemberment, Shaskiel's *prolific* exploits were a death sentence waiting to be carried out. And the Spymaster had it all: images, recordings, pheromone traces, and sensory files. *Proof.* Enough to have Shaskiel tortured for weeks before being publicly torn apart. So, yes, leading this fleet to the Sol System to incinerate a forgotten planet seemed, all things considered, a *reasonable trade.*

The fleet wasn't elite, but it wasn't garbage, either. Reliable ships. Veteran crews. Aging hulls, yes, but they could still crush Earth like an ant beneath a boot. Arrival would take a cycle or two. In the meantime, Shaskiel intended to prepare. *Hard training. Precision drills. No improvisation.* Because if there was one thing he had learned from surviving dozens of campaigns and even more betrayals—it was that *unknowns* kill generals. And while Earth's technology was, by all accounts, laughably primitive, there were whispers about the Thal'Naari. Silent for generations, their surviving ships hadn't been seen in a thousand standard years. But the galaxy never forgets a grudge.

Shaskiel didn't like complications. He preferred operations to be clean, swift, and permanent. He summoned his command council aboard his flagship and laid out his orders: "We move for ten days toward the Sol System. From there, full combat simulations. Reaction drills. Synchronization protocols. No misfires. No lag. When we descend upon this planet Earth, we do so as a single unstoppable force."

He expected no real resistance. No fleet. No planetary defenses worth noting. The planet would be reduced to ash, and their own ships would not so much as scuff their hulls. Still, he would take no chances. A cautious warrior lives to tell the tale. A reckless one gets buried with his legend. And Shaskiel had no intention of becoming a legend. With that, he gave the final command. The fleet's engines lit the void as they peeled away from the hidden moon, leaving behind the cold lair of the Spymaster. The hunt for Earth had begun.

***

The great ship *hummed.* There was really no other word for it. Not whirred, not rumbled. She *hummed*—a deep, resonant sound like the purr of a great predator. A panther, perhaps, lying in the shade of a jungle tree. Still. Watchful. Dangerous. At peace, but never harmless.

Kaelar'Syn felt it. For the first time in centuries, the harmony of her engines matched the rhythm of her purpose. She had broken through. The twins … *they were it.* And tonight, the final piece had fallen into place. The companions—Alex and Max—had entered the twins' dreams. Not as figments or symbols but as guardians. As soulbound defenders. And in that space beyond language, beyond reason, the bond had been forged. Now, they were a *pack.* A pack built not just of blood or biology, but of instinct and need, of loyalty forged in trauma and sharpened in the dark. Kaelar'Syn *felt* it. The binding. Like star-thread laced through the very fabric of her hull. It was done. Silas and Alex. Elias and Max. Each twin bound to their companion, wholly and irrevocably. The only thing that could ever sever that link now was the death of one or the other. An unbreakable alliance. An unbendable force. And the great ship—once alone, once drifting— now had her crew. She purred louder. The jungle was awakening.

And just like that, the great ship's mood shifted on a dime. It was strange, considering the warmth she had only just embraced. The comfort of bonding. The satisfaction of knowing her crew was finally forming—twins and companions were bound, forming the foundation of something powerful. But now? Now her tone darkened.

Kaelar'Syn's sensors stretched far—laid quietly from human space all the way to the ragged, shifting edge of the empire's frontier. And one of those silent watchers had spoken. A signal came, faint and distant, but unmistakable. A *fleet.* A *sizable* one. Headed this way. It was possible—just barely—that they weren't coming to Earth. But nothing had left that corner of space in a long time. There was nothing out there but silence and stars … and Earth.

Kaelar'Syn recalculated. Rerouted. Plans that had been slow to mature now surged forward. It was time for an *introduction.* But she had cards yet to play—two, in fact. The assassin and the noble warrior. They had waited, patient and still. Waiting for a cue, a sign, a moment to act. They had not known what role they would play, but *something* in them had sensed it was coming. And then it did.

The ship's hum shifted—subtle, but undeniable. No longer the warm purr of confidence, but something *sharper*. A higher pitch, like coiled tension under silk. Without warning, the ship turned away from the solar system and leaped into deep space. They asked, more than once, *Where are we going?* Kaelar'Syn did not answer. She fed them, housed them, and entertained them, but offered no direction. No stars to track. No charts. No answers. Even The Emissary had not returned.

Then, suddenly, they *felt it.* The subtle inertia of deceleration. The ship slowed. Stars no longer streaked by.

And then—stillness. Silence, like a held breath.

A voice broke the quiet.

CHAPTER SIX

"Grace." It echoed through the corridors—not mechanical, not flat, but full of presence. The assassin turned toward the sound instinctively. Hearing her name spoken aloud by the ship was intimate, strange.

She replied, her voice oddly formal. "Yes, great ship."

"I am going to offer you something never offered to your kind before. A gift, one that is not to be taken lightly. I am not placing *it* in your charge, I am placing *you* in *its* charge."

A chill crawled up her spine. The noble warrior, silent nearby, felt it, too. Suspicion, wonder, and fear. And beneath it all, a flicker of excitement.

The ship docked. A soft shudder passed through her body, a sound like a breath being held too long that was finally exhaled. The hatch opened. They crossed into the new vessel. Immediately, they sensed the difference. It was Spartan and clean. A warship, clearly, but beautiful and sleek. Deadly in the way a blade is deadly. Elegant, but built to end lives. The hatch sealed behind them. Kaelar'Syn was gone.

They were not abandoned, but *transferred*. This ship's hum was deeper. A low, thrumming bass, resonating through their bones. Not comforting or warm, but steady. And very alert.

As the assassin and the noble warrior stood in the stark, gleaming halls of the new vessel, the ship spoke. A deep, resonant voice rolled through the corridors—booming, yes, but not cruel. Not overwhelming. It was the voice of something ancient and powerful, accustomed to command, but not untouched by loss.

"I am Valshar, great warship of the noble race. Protector of my people. Rescuer of those left behind—left to be slaughtered by *your* kind. I have never given anyone like you a chance before. And though my sister Kaelar'Syn speaks highly of you, I wonder if her faith is well-founded. But I will give you this chance. One chance. She has shared with me a mission for you. A task. Complete it and prove your worth. Or refuse, and I will open my hatches to the void. The cold, airless black will take you. And your journey will end. I shall return to slumber, to dream of rescues past, battles won, and the glory that was. The glory that might have been. " The ship fell silent. The corridor echoed with stillness.

The assassin and the soldier looked at one another. This was not a bluff or a threat. It was a *decision.* And the great ship waited. In a voice far softer than anyone might expect from her—especially *herself*—Grace spoke. It was quiet, measured. Almost reverent. "Valshar, what is it you require of us? What deed must we accomplish for you to trust us?"

The halls echoed for a moment in silence. Then Valshar's voice returned, deep, amused, and unshaken. "Well, little one, I wondered if you would have the nerve to speak. Perhaps there is bravery yet in you." A pause. Then, with the calm weight of command, he spoke again. "A fleet approaches the Sol System. Our mission is simple. We will harry them. Disrupt them. Drag them off course. Delay them long enough for Kaelar'Syn to prepare. To unleash hell."

Grace turned to the silent noble warrior beside her, brow furrowed. "Is it … just us? Just one ship?"

Valshar responded with dry warmth. "Yes, just one, but a powerful one. I am, as your people say, but a match compared to a bolt of lightning. But she, Kaelar'Syn, with the twins at her helm, *she* is the storm. She is devastation made manifest. Fifteen thousand ships are no match for her when she is whole. I, on the other hand, am not without my tools. Nor without my charms."

He let the words settle.

"So, we will enter into this pact—you, your silent companion, and I. And though your friend cannot speak aloud, do not worry ..." The air seemed to shimmer. *I can speak inside your mind.*

Zareth'Kai stiffened. And then relaxed. The voice wasn't invasive—it was *inside*, but gentle. Measured. It spoke not in color, scent, or movement but in *pure thought.* He listened.

And Valshar silently asked him, *Are you truly noble? Truly brave? Or just another pawn, blindly following orders born from a lie you never dared question? Are you a fool? Or now that your eyes are open, will you do what is right? Will you stand against evil, and perhaps, along the way, find the one who slew your brood mate ... and take your vengeance?*

He did not answer. He *felt* his answer. And somehow, She did, too. A bond passed between them—sudden, intimate, and real. Strange, unsettling, and comforting. They had only just met, and yet something ancient had clicked into place. Like a sword returning to the hand of its rightful wielder. In that moment, they were no longer three individuals. They were *one will.* One mission. And with that, the pact was sealed. The harrying of the fleet had begun.

***

As Malvek awaited the emperor's true command—the name of the actual enemy he was to seek and destroy—he was, as always, left to his own devices. It had been their agreement, ancient and ironclad. *Let him warm up.* The emperor knew the truth. No matter how many laws were etched into bone and stone, no matter how many decrees were bellowed from the throne, there would always be those of his kind who disobeyed. Who bred in secret. Who spread their seed into lesser beings and raised the emperor's bloodline in hushed corners of the galaxy. The mandate of *sole fatherhood*—that all of their kind must descend from the emperor alone—was less about biology than it was about *control.*

His warriors, his true children, would remain strong. Pure. Dominant. As for the others? The laborers, the builders, and the quiet ones who drove harvest machines or forged starship hulls in low orbit factories … they were beneath his notice. As long as they did it quietly. As long as they bowed low and never raised eyes to the palace. As long as they remembered who *owned* them.

Scattered across the emperor's capital world, just beyond the reach of his colossal black citadel, were fields. Endless, rippling fields, as well as small towns and quiet farming communities. Generations of workers who had never seen the emperor's face and didn't want to. Malvek could taste them already. If his kind had glands to drool, the bloodlust would have soaked his chin. This would not be a meal of flesh. This would be a *feast of fear.*

He walked through this slaughter not as a Vorrhaxi, but as a force. Past spasming corpses, their faces frozen in horror as they clutched the mangled bodies of their loved ones. As if that could stop death. As if holding tight could hold *him* back. They had no more power to stop him than a man had to stop the wind. Or command a hurricane to halt at the shore.

Malvek was not the emperor's righteous wrath. He was his *unholy vengeance.* And the message he sent that day would burn itself into the minds of every nearby settlement, every officer, and every dissenter. It was not enough to kill. You had to make them *watch.*

And with that, just when it seemed the emperor's cursed capital world could sink no further into madness, another force arrived. The Nillith had come. It did not *speak* to Roach. Not exactly. It *guided.* It whispered through impulse and suggestion, through shadowed thoughts and hollow promises. And Roach—rebuilt, reforged, no longer truly his own—obeyed.

They landed just outside the emperor's stronghold. It was a monstrous castle rising like a scar from the black earth, ringed by bone towers and plasma-lit walls, and guarded by the Vorrhaxi, the empire's perfect predators. Roach, as cunning and brutal as he was, could not defeat them in open combat. So, he didn't. He *slipped* past them. Not unseen but *unnoticed.* A shadow gliding through the greater darkness.

It helped that the emperor had recently purged all witnesses of the queens' failed defiance. The palace halls were emptier than they had ever been. Blood still stained the columns. The scent of disloyalty still lingered in the air.

The emperor lay sprawled across his throne of polished bone, fingers twitching as he waited for the inevitable report: Malvek had been unleashed. The countryside would already be burning. He imagined the garrisons trembling as stories of unspeakable slaughter reached their ears. And when they did, he would sacrifice a few of them. Offer them up as examples. His people needed to remember what it meant to disobey. And the queens—those treacherous broods—would learn that they would find no allies among the ranks. This was no longer about court games. This was legacy. This was conquest. This was survival by any means.

And then ... *he felt it.* A chill. Not a breeze. A *void.* He opened his red-ringed eyes. Someone—*something*—stood in his throne room. The figure was shaped like a man. A silhouette. Just a suggestion. At first glance, it might have passed for what the Spymaster had described as a human.

The emperor rose with a snarl. "Who are you? How dare you enter my sanctum unbidden? What are you? The Spymaster described something like you once. Something called a human."

The figure stepped closer, its voice low, smooth, and ancient. "Oh yes, great emperor. I am *like* a human. But I am much, *much* more. I am the shadow between stars. I am the silence before the scream. I am the rot behind the throne. I am the blackest part of the sky. I am death incarnate."

The emperor laughed, cold and cruel. "No, death incarnate is in the countryside. His name is Malvek."

The figure tilted its head. Roach's features were still visible beneath something far older. "That? That is not death. That is merely a *symptom*." It smiled a horrible grin. "You have yet to see what death will become."

And the emperor, for the first time in centuries, did not speak. He *listened*.

***

While the emperor plotted the downfall of all his enemies—real or imagined—and grappled with the disturbing presence of the Nillith and the barely controlled chaos of unleashing Malvek upon the Vorrhaxi, the great ship raced back toward Earth. Her purpose was clear: to finally bring the twin brothers into direct contact with The Emissary, and eventually with herself. Together, she and The Emissary would present the twins with a proposal—an opportunity to be healed of their wounds, restored to youth, and reborn as something more: not just men, but living weapons, bonded to a greater cause. She would offer them a role in the resurrection of a nearly extinct civilization, one forged in honor, justice, and peace. In doing so, they would not only help secure the future of the noble race but bring long-awaited balance to a galaxy fractured by endless war. And with the return of the Thal'Naari strength, Earth, too, could be uplifted—given access to technologies and knowledge that would propel humanity into the stars and help it become a force for good in the wider universe.

But even as she raced through the void toward Sol, the ship remained uncertain of how best to approach them. They were fragile still—haunted and fractured by pain. She hoped that, in this, The Emissary would aid her in crafting a plan they could both believe in. And perhaps most of all, she took comfort in one thing: the bond between the twins and their dogs, Alex and Max. Through them, perhaps, the connection could begin—something familiar and grounded to help ease the transition to the extraordinary path that lay ahead. With this hope in her core, she accelerated through the stars, racing toward destiny.

***

Back at Silas's secluded mountain hideout, the morning began with an unsettling stillness. The dogs, Alex and Max, stood guard at the door, their hackles slightly raised, ears pricked forward, bodies rigid with instinctual alertness. Something had their attention.

Silas, ever methodical, moved to the door and examined it for tampering, but there was nothing. No scratches, no sign of forced entry. He went straight to the surveillance monitors and scanned the perimeter. Still nothing. The alarms hadn't tripped. The cameras showed no movement. And yet, the unease lingered in the air like static before a storm. Silas turned toward Elias. "Did you hear anything? See anything? Did something wake you during the night?"

Elias, still groggy and half draped in a blanket, yawned. "Nope. Slept like the dead. Best sleep I've had in … hell, maybe years. Last time I slept this well, I woke up next to two women I didn't remember meeting." He smirked.

Silas rolled his eyes. "I don't need to hear about your many escapades. And, incidentally, you're a tramp."

"Tramp?" Elias scoffed with a grin. "Come on. Just because I'm in demand? Women want me, men want to be me. You've benefited from it; don't deny it. How many girls have hit on you, thinking you were me?"

Silas groaned inwardly. The thought of being mistaken for Elias during one of his *adventures* was mortifying. He shoved the mental image aside. But the unease hadn't lifted, and the dogs remained on edge. "Let's sweep the area," Silas said, already thinking two steps ahead. "Just to be sure."

Elias stretched and rubbed his neck. "You got any hardware left, or did you donate it all to the Smithsonian?"

Silas smirked. "You mean, what don't I have?" Moments later, Silas moved to the back closet. He removed a few boxes, shifted aside a worn rug, and tapped a hidden floor plate until a latch clicked open. A trapdoor lifted, revealing a steel staircase leading into a subterranean chamber. Elias let out a low whistle. "Welcome to my kind of candy store." The lights flicked on, revealing an armory worthy of a warlord. Racks lined the walls containing sniper rifles, submachine guns, shotguns, pistols, and grenade launchers. There were flash-bangs, frag grenades, seismic detectors, ballistic helmets, camo gear, and load-bearing vests. Everything short of a tank. And knives. Oh, the knives—Silas's personal favorite. Silas geared up with quiet precision: a suppressed USP .45, multiple blades—Gerbers, a Benchmade, and a trusted Ka-Bar—along with a full tactical rig. His gear was arranged with a surgeon's efficiency.

Elias, more flamboyant, strapped on a .300 Blackout with an M203 slung beneath it. He also grabbed twin USP .45s and placed one in the small of his back and one on his thigh. Then he snagged smoke grenades, flash-bangs, frags, and loaded pouches. "Better to have it and not need it," he said with a wink, "than the other way around."

As they emerged from the armory, the dogs were waiting. Alex padded to Silas's side, ever calm, ever watchful. In his quiet canine mind, he was already scanning scents, measuring wind, and calculating threats. Alex's thoughts were disciplined. *My human is moving like it's time. Time to hunt, to protect. Something woke the earth last night. I smelled it. I'll smell it again.*

Max, meanwhile, bounced beside Elias, tail wagging slightly, more expressive, but no less perceptive. Max's mind moved differently. *Something's not right. But I've got my brother. We'll see it through. Stick close with your eyes open. If anything moves, I'll take out its throat.*

The twins exchanged a glance, nodded, and moved toward the door. Silas checked the cameras one last time. Still nothing. So, out into the forest clearing they went—armed, armored, and flanked by the most loyal sentinels the earth had to offer. Whatever was out there, it wouldn't catch them unaware.

***

The Emissary didn't sleep much, but then again, he hadn't had the luxury of rest in days. He'd been running himself ragged just trying to keep those two lunatics alive long enough to be of any use. Last night, he'd been close to them—close enough to hear the strange banter pass between the brothers. He didn't fully understand their humor, not exactly, but he understood the bond that birthed it. He and his brother had shared the same irreverent spark when they were young.

Back in their youth, during the early stages of their military training, they'd gotten up to all sorts of mischief. Nothing dangerous, just pranks, inside jokes, and shared laughter. Their people had always believed in training early and preparing warriors not just in body but in unity. Like the ancient Spartans of Earth, Thal'Naari twins were expected to be ready for war long before adulthood. But not at six years old—he remembered reading that about Earth's Spartans. That had seemed barbaric, even to him.

Leaving home at fifteen for warrior training had been daunting enough. But with his brother at his side, he had never truly felt fear. Since the murder, he'd spent many cycles steeped in anger, an emotion so foreign to the old him, it sometimes felt like someone else's grief. And somehow, he'd been placed in charge of protecting two Earth-born maniacs who might just be the last hope for his people.

As he prepared to stand, intending to do a little closer recon near the house, the front door creaked open. Out stepped the twins, flanked by their two "dogs." The Emissary's eyes narrowed. These weren't normal Earth dogs. No, something about them rang as being off—wrong and right all at once. They moved with intelligence far beyond what even the cleverest canines should possess. Their eyes shimmered too brightly, their posture too aware. He suspected the great ship in orbit—Kaelar'Syn—had something to do with the animals being there.

As he contemplated his next move, a sharp pulse rattled his comm bracelet. A single sentence. *Let them catch you.* He blinked. Sat still. Read it again. She couldn't be serious. "Has she finally lost her damn mind?" he muttered, rubbing his temples. "Gone around the bend, as the Earthers say." He looked up again, toward the clearing where the twins wandered with their makeshift armor, overkill weaponry, and high-tech, comic-book-hero aesthetic. "What in the seven sectors are they even wearing?" he asked aloud, genuinely baffled. Still, the message was clear. And when the great ship spoke, even ancient emissaries listened. Mostly.

Silas and Elias began their search in a methodical, practiced fashion, sweeping slowly outward from the cabin in ever-widening circles. Years of hard-earned instinct guided their movements. Silas scanned the trees and terrain with cold precision. Elias was more reactive, fluid, eyes sharp but always ready for sudden violence. They moved like wolves through the underbrush—silent, efficient, and alert.

That's when the silence shattered. A loud *crack* echoed through the woods, followed by the unmistakable sound of something heavy being violently yanked off the ground—a deep *woosh* of air, branches snapping, and then, unexpectedly, a string of creative and truly inspired profanity. It wasn't just swearing, it had cadence, flair, *commitment.* If anger were an art form, this particular explosion of obscenities could have peeled paint from a tank.

Weapons raised, the twins moved toward the noise. Silas gave Elias a look—just one—but in that moment, volumes passed between them. Silas's paranoia had always been legendary, and Elias would've bet money that the surrounding woods were filled with traps—deadfalls, trip wires, spike pits, the works. From the sound of it, someone had just earned themselves a front-row seat to one of Silas's nastier inventions.

Elias, never one to overthink a moment when charging in could do the job, started forward. But he was surprised when Silas reached out and laid a hand gently on his arm. That stopped him. Silas *never* initiated contact. Elias didn't like to be touched—never had—and Silas knew that. Years of trauma and betrayal had carved that boundary deep, and they respected each other's scars. But Silas had broken that rule now. Whatever was out there, whoever had triggered the trap, it had rattled him enough to cross a line he hadn't touched in years. Elias didn't say a word. He just nodded, adjusting his grip on the rifle.

Strangest of all, though, was the behavior of Alex and Max. In any other situation, with an unknown intruder crashing around in the woods, the dogs should've been locked in, alert and tense, and ready to protect their companions. But they weren't. Instead, they sat calmly, each beside their chosen twin. Alex's amber eyes stayed fixed on Silas's face, tail still. Max leaned gently against Elias's leg, ears forward but relaxed. Neither dog barked. Neither moved. They simply watched, as if they already knew who was in that trap. As if they were waiting to see what the twins would do.

Elias, Silas, Alex, and Max moved cautiously into the grove, following the direction of the noise. Silas knew this particular area well—too well. He had laid dozens of traps in a ring around the property, some conventional, others less so.

His mouth curled into a quiet grin as he muttered under his breath, "Welcome to my parlor, said the spider to the fly."

Elias gave him a withering glance over his shoulder, the kind that needed no translation. *Seriously?* his expression said. Silas offered a nonchalant shrug, and Elias shook his head with a low chuckle before continuing on. Behind them, Alex and Max padded silently, tails alert but relaxed, watching the forest not with fear, but with curiosity.

What they found when they reached the grove was equal parts bizarre and hilarious. Hanging upside down from a nylon snare was a figure that looked like a mirage given shape. The being shimmered in and out of visibility, as though the eye couldn't decide whether it was real or a trick of the light. Yet, the string of expletives pouring from the distortion confirmed that it was very real—and very angry.

"What the hell am I looking at?" Elias whispered, eyes wide.

Silas squinted, then chuckled. "Sci-fi movie bullshit."

At that exact moment, the shimmer dropped. The camouflage failed, revealing a tall humanoid figure with chiseled musculature beneath dark matte armor. The Emissary. Still dangling by one ankle, the alien glared down at them and growled, "Well? Are you two idiots going to cut me loose, or do I hang here all day?"

Silas stepped forward, retrieving a knife from his belt with the casual ease of a man brushing lint off a jacket. He knelt by the tree, sliced the rope with a single pull, and The Emissary dropped like a sack of rocks, his armor taking most of the impact.

Elias raised his rifle, not in a direct threat, but with enough intent to make it clear that any sudden movements would be a mistake.

The Emissary looked up, exasperated, and said dryly, "Easy. If I meant you harm, Alex and Max would've shredded me already. But as you can see, they haven't moved an inch."

That part was true. The dogs remained seated near their respective humans, watching with mild interest. No hackles were raised; no teeth were bared. If anything, they looked bored.

Silas narrowed his eyes. He didn't trust easily, but he trusted the dogs, and their calm was enough. "Fine," Silas said at last, "you can stand. Then you're going to follow us back to the house. You already know where it is. We'll talk there."

The Emissary stood slowly, nodding his assent. Without another word, they formed a loose column. Silas led, Alex at his side, The Emissary was flanked by Max, and Elias brought up the rear, rifle still loosely cradled in his arms, eyes scanning the trees. In silence, they walked toward answers.

***

As the great ship sliced through the dark between stars, drawing ever closer to Earth, a rare feeling washed over her: relief. At last, The Emissary had made contact with the twins. At last, she would have a crew again. And not just any crew—*the* crew. Elias and Silas. She would soon take the fight back to the Vorrhaxi after so many years of silence and drifting in exile. It had been too long since she'd wielded her full might, too long since her decks had echoed with the voices of bonded twins moving as one.

And now, fate had delivered a matched pair just in time. The timing could not have been more critical. Intelligence from deep-space relays suggested that an enemy fleet had already been dispatched— likely a probing force meant to test Earth's defenses. They would not find her sleeping. She had entrusted a sister ship to guard the region, an older vessel still strong enough to hold the line. Hopefully, it would be long enough for her to prepare the twins for battle. A hundred fifty ships? On her own, that would be difficult but not impossible. With one twin guiding her weapons and the other commanding navigation and tactical arrays, she would be nearly unstoppable.

No, utterly unstoppable. She couldn't suppress the thought that filled her with quiet pride. This would be a trial by fire for Elias and Silas—a live-fire test of their synergy, instincts, and connection to her systems. It was a necessary baptism.

The other ship, the one carrying the assassin and the noble soldier, would soon arrive as well. Though they were not twins and thus couldn't access the most advanced systems, they could still bring devastating force to bear. Their presence might tip the scales if the enemy sent more than just scouts. So many moving pieces, she mused, and at last, they were moving toward *hope* instead of merely survival.

For the first time in a long time, the great ship allowed herself a sigh of contentment. The stars no longer felt so cold. Her crew was coming home. While the great ship drifted with a renewed sense of purpose—dreaming of war, of purpose regained, of righteous vengeance against the Vorrhaxi—the emperor of that same vile race was making plans of his own. But these were not the grand, galaxy-consuming conquests he usually relished. No, these were plans of consolidation.

***

The queens were plotting again—too boldly, too cleverly—and that alone meant blood had to be spilled. Malvek had already subdued the countryside in a storm of violence, but it wasn't enough. A lesson needed to be taught, not just to the traitorous queens, but to the rank and file as well. Fear, after all, was more reliable than loyalty.

The emperor paced his inner sanctum, the stench of antiseptic still clinging to the walls from his most recent brush with death. Another assassination attempt. The queen who dared it had already been flayed and consumed, but the damage had been done—not to his body, which would heal, but to his aura of invincibility. That could not be allowed to stand. He had other worries, as well. This Nillith had appeared, uninvited, aboard the stolen ship meant to carry the assassin and the loyal Vorrhaxi soldier to Earth. That meant, most likely, that the mission had failed. The twins lived. And worse, the Nillith had taken the ship with or without their consent, either because the pair was dead or because they had decided to betray the empire. Is it possible that the Spymaster had become so consumed with his plots he had lost track of the most important task he had been given? That sightless freak had either grown arrogant or was concealing something. Either way, it could not be tolerated. Too many schemes were running at once. Too many pawns, all moving of their own accord. Even the Spymaster, whose loyalty had once seemed unshakable, now

140

appeared suspect. The rebellion of the queens had been too well timed, too synchronized, and too damned convenient. It stank of manipulation—an invisible hand tugging at the strings. In what galaxy was it possible this sniveling underling would ever obtain the courage to oppose him, either directly or indirectly? It just didn't seem feasible this could have come to pass.

Perhaps there was something he wasn't seeing in the greater scheme of things. It was very unlikely this could be the case, but it was never safe to leave any stone unturned when one's life was at stake. The emperor had let the Spymaster believe him a fool for far too long. Now it was time to send a message. Two, in fact.

He summoned a silent runner and handed him two sealed scent capsules. One was for the Nillith, who was to be summoned from his quarters and brought before the throne. The other was for Malvek. The instructions encoded in the pheromones were brutally clear: liquidate several of the smaller garrisons, destroy the remaining supporters of the deposed queens, and do it publicly, loudly, and bloodily.

And the Nillith? He would be given one task: assassinate the Spymaster. It was perfect. If the Nillith succeeded, the secrets the Spymaster held would die with him. If he failed, well … then the Spymaster would understand just how precarious his position had become. Either way, someone would bleed, and the message would be loud enough for the entire empire to hear.

The emperor settled back into his throne of carved obsidian and polished bone, feeling something, he hadn't felt in weeks—contentment. Mass executions and backstabbing power plays had a way of calming him. Yet, even in the quiet that followed, a small, insistent hunger remained. The killings were never enough, not for long. He needed more, always more.

He chuckled to himself, thinking how much that made him resemble Malvek. It was strange, but not troubling. After all, if others saw the similarity, that was their problem. If they whispered it aloud, well, Malvek would soon have fresh targets to silence. When he was done with his current victims, of course. The screams, the blood, the carnage and death were like a symphony to his ears, created by a genius composer. Let the purge begin.

***

The Emissary took a long, steadying breath as he walked between the twins, flanked by the ever-watchful Alex and Max. He felt more than a little foolish. If any of his old squad mates could see him now—escorted like a prisoner, bound in flex-cuffs, paraded through the forest—they'd never believe it. These two had no idea what he was capable of. The restraints were little more than decoration. He could break ten of them with barely a flick of his wrist. Not because of brute strength, though he had that in abundance, but because of the marvel that was woven into his very skin: the nanotech armor. It clung to him like a second hide, invisible when he willed it, but always there, regulating his body temperature, shielding him from flame, cold, blades, and bullets. And within it lived his greatest asset: an AI assistant that whispered tactical counsel into his mind, and in the long nights of solitude, offered the only companionship he had left.

Being a twin and losing your other half, it wasn't just grief. It was a tearing, a sundering of something sacred. The bond between twins in his culture wasn't metaphorical, it was spiritual, chemical, and physical. Separation drove some to madness. Others simply let go and faded. But not him. Not The Emissary. He would not die. Not until justice had been served. Not until vengeance had been won. Hope had nearly died with his brother. *Nearly.* But even the smallest flicker was enough to ignite a firestorm. And perhaps these two chaotic Earth-born twins were the answer he'd been waiting for.

They reached the front steps of the cabin. The Emissary clenched his fists reflexively and nearly snapped the cuffs. He smirked inwardly. That might make for a funny moment later—if he lived long enough to joke about it.

Silas stopped at the front door and disarmed the perimeter alarm with a small black device. Then, with practiced ease, he inserted a key and unlocked the thick, reinforced door. It swung open with a low groan. The house was a fortress, hewn from stone and steel, disguised as a humble mountain retreat. Silas had taken no chances. His abode had bullet-resistant windows, steel-banded walls, and reinforced siding. The man had clearly watched too many action movies growing up. Or too few. Either way, he was prepared for war.

Silas frowned slightly, his mind drifting. The term *bulletproof* had always bothered him. Nothing was bulletproof. That was like saying *bombproof.* Depends on the size of the bomb, doesn't it? He shook his head.

Elias caught the subtle gesture and arched a brow. "What now?" he muttered under his breath. Silas gave him a dismissive wave and one of his cryptic looks. Elias sighed. There was no telling what was going on in that twisted, genius mind of his. He'd defend Silas with his last breath, no question about that, but the man was certifiable. The endless counting, the photographic memory that never turned off, it had to be its own kind of hell. Yep, weird as hell. But mine, Elias thought with a grin.

Silas glanced back just in time to catch Elias mouthing the word *weirdo.* He rolled his eyes. Elias was a piece of work, always game for adventure as long as it included painkillers, women, and whiskey. Not necessarily in that order. And so, the three men, each buried in their own thoughts, stepped across the threshold of the cabin. Behind them, Alex and Max padded silently inside. The dogs exchanged no words, yet if they could, they would've said the same thing: *Finally.* A conversation that had been centuries in the making was about to begin.

As they entered the front hall of the small mountain hideout, Silas had a fleeting, practical thought. *I only have two chairs at my table. Where the hell are we all going to sit?* Then came the second problem—how were they going to sit together *and* keep a close enough eye on their strange new guest to react if he tried something?

Silas let out a long, exasperated sigh, and as he did, an old memory surfaced—his ex-girlfriend, forever pestering him about his breathing. "Why are you holding your breath? Why are you breathing so loud?" she'd ask, like he was doing it on purpose. It used to drive him nuts. *It's just breathing. As long as I'm not doing it until I pass out, what's the big deal?* The thought distracted him, which was exactly the point. It was one of his quirks—when stress started to mount, his brain reached for anything else to focus on. It was a weird little defense mechanism, but damned if it didn't work. Within seconds, his heart rate dropped back down to a nice, clean fifty-four beats per minute. Calm. Focused.

Silas stepped over to the kitchen table and grabbed the two wooden chairs. He dragged them over and placed them in front of the suede couch. Then, with a quiet gesture, he motioned for The Emissary to sit. The twins would take the wooden chairs, seated directly in front of the couch—close enough to observe, far enough to react. Even if the alien made a move, Silas doubted he'd get far. Not with Alex and Max flanking the scene like statues—calm, watchful, unreadable. That, more than anything, struck Silas as odd. In a situation like this, you'd expect the dogs to be bristling, keyed up, ready to leap at the first wrong move. But they weren't. They just sat next to their respective twin, ears perked and eyes fixed, like they were in on a joke no one else understood.

Silas turned to The Emissary. "You want something to drink? Water? Something else?"

Before the alien could answer, Elias scoffed loudly. "Screw him," Elias said. "He ain't getting a damn thing until we get some answers. And I'm sure as hell not handing a drink to someone who's still in full costume. It's not Halloween, you weirdo." He pointed a finger. "I'm telling you, Silas, this guy got lost on the way to a damn sci-fi convention."

***

Alex and Max sat alongside their respective charges in the cabin Silas had turned into his fortress of solitude. There wasn't much said—not aloud, anyway—but their thoughts were anything but silent. Alex wasn't the worrying sort. He'd spent centuries among the broken, the battle-scarred, and the nearly lost. But as he studied Silas, who might've been the most paranoid creature he'd ever encountered in any lifetime, he found himself wondering if he was truly up to the task. Protecting this one might not be about guarding against external threats. No, this one needed protection from the demons clawing at him from the inside.

Alex glanced sidelong at Max with something that almost resembled a sigh. *Damn. Max got the easy one this time.* All his brother had to do was keep Elias out of bars and brothels. That, Alex mused grimly, was practically a vacation. *Meanwhile, I've got to keep mine out of his own head.* He shook off the thought, feeling the familiar static charge of duty ripple through his fur. After all, he'd just spent a few centuries in timeless sleep. What better way to wake than with a fresh, uniquely damaged soul to guard? But then, he remembered the bonding dream. Silas, only six years old. Alone in the dark, cold and wet. Hiding in a roadside ditch, trembling, but still brave enough to leave safety and search for help. Fear didn't stop him. It walked with him. There was something noble in that, something unbreakable. *This one's spirit won't yield. And that, I can respect. Don't worry, brother. I'll walk with you to the edge of this life, and if it comes down to it, I'll trade mine for yours without hesitation.*

Max noticed the shift in Alex—a ripple of tension, like an electric current sparking across his twin's coat. But his own thoughts were far less sentimental. He'd watched Elias swagger into the cabin like a man headed to a party instead of a tactical debriefing. Max sighed deeply. *Of all the creatures in the galaxy I've protected, none has been quite like this one.* Fearless? Sure. Strong? Absolutely. Cunning in a brawler's way. But when it came to self-preservation? A total disaster. *If your body is a temple, then this idiot worships at the altar of whiskey, painkillers, and women who should know better.* Elias was one of those rare beings who could survive just about anything, except maybe his own appetite for destruction. If he chased nourishment the way he chased women, most of whom were more than happy to be caught, he might actually be in decent shape. Max snorted to himself. *Yeah, this one's going to be a handful. Entertaining as hell, but a handful.* Still, there was a core of fire in him. A defiance that refused to quit. As long as Max could keep him mostly sober, mostly vertical, and mostly clothed, they just might make it through this thing. He glanced at Alex. His brother's eyes met his with shared understanding. Two guardians. Two lives. One mission. And a hell of a story unfolding right in front of them.

The Emissary sat heavily on the plush dark suede couch, the flex-cuffs still loosely binding his wrists. He leaned back like a man settling in to watch a football game or kick back with a good evening vid. Legs stretched out, hands resting comfortably, he looked disturbingly at ease. Silas narrowed his eyes. Elias tilted his head. This guy was supposed to be their prisoner, not a guest. And yet, here he was, like he'd just returned to his own home.

The Emissary drew in a long, steady breath. Then, with a voice rich and calm, he said, "You can stop calling me 'The Emissary.' That was a title, not a name. If we're going to be traveling this road together, you might as well call me Vaeril." He didn't explain it. Didn't say where it came from, or what it meant. Just dropped it like a stone into a still pond and let the ripples do the rest. And strangely, as if compelled by something beyond simple logic, both twins nodded in unison.

Silas spoke first. "Alright … Vaeril it is."

Elias followed a beat later, grinning. "Yeah, sure. Vaeril. That's got a nice punch to it."

Max and Alex exchanged a quiet look. The name had power. The kind of name that stuck. And deep within the walls of the little mountain cabin, something ancient stirred in agreement.

"Well, boys," Vaeril began casually. And that's when things went sideways.

Elias's head snapped up. His whole body shifted—tension flooded into his shoulders and his jaw clenched so hard it cracked. He hated being called *boy*. It wasn't just a pet peeve. It was a trigger. Without a second thought, his voice lashed out. "Boy? Who the hell are you calling *boy*? I've been to Maine, Spain, Bahrain, around the world and back again, and lived to tell the tale. I've seen a bald eagle fornicate and made Linda Lovelace gag. Who the hell do you think you're talking to?"

The room went still for half a beat, and then Vaeril did something no one expected. He laughed. A deep, guttural, genuine laugh that rolled through the house like a shockwave. It started as a chuckle, then burst loose like something he hadn't felt in a century. He laughed so hard he doubled over, clutching his sides, wheezing for air. He had no idea why it hit him that hard. Maybe it was the absurdity. Maybe the timing. Maybe just the raw audacity of the man. Whatever it was, it cracked something open in him, and he laughed until his ribs ached. The twins stared, wide-eyed and speechless. Then, as his laughter subsided, Vaeril sat up, eyes still glinting with amusement. He flexed his hands ever so slightly, and the twin sets of flex-cuffs binding his wrists snapped apart like dry twigs, scattering pieces across the floor.

Silas and Elias froze. They weren't dealing with just another nut playing dress-up. One thing was for sure, this guy, or whatever the hell he might be, was the real deal. No bullshit. They were sitting across from a walking weapon. And now, they knew it. They weren't the biggest players on the board anymore. They were two men—damaged, dangerous, determined—but still just men. But this creature? He was something else entirely.

Vaeril took another deep breath, suppressing the laughter that still stirred uninvited in his chest. He looked at Elias and Silas again, this time with a steadier gaze. "All right, young men," he said, tone shifting into something more serious. "Are you ready to hear a story, followed by a once-in-a-lifetime offer?"

Silas's cheeks flushed red at the phrase. Elias raised an eyebrow, already bracing for his brother's reaction. Silas turned to him with narrowed eyes and asked, very dryly, "Is he just trying to piss me off?"

"No," Vaeril replied, deadpan. "I'm trying to make a deal that'll save your miserable lives and maybe, just maybe, help save an entire civilization. So, sit down, dumbass."

That did it. Elias lunged forward, half out of his chair, until something unusual happened. Max moved—not barking, not snarling, just calm and focused. The massive dog stepped smoothly between Elias and the seated alien, pressing his haunches against Elias's legs with surprising force, pinning him back into the chair. Elias blinked. Max didn't move. His amber eyes met Elias's with a steady, unmistakable message: *Not yet. Listen first.*

Silas looked over at Alex, who was equally still, ears perked, eyes focused not on Vaeril, but on them. Even the dogs knew this was important.

Elias finally relented, throwing up his hands. "Okay! What the freak," he grumbled, then jabbed a finger at Vaeril. "First of all, why the hell do you keep calling us *young*? We haven't been young in, what, at least twenty-five years."

Vaeril blinked, a moment of actual contrition flickering across his face. "Ah," he said slowly. "Right. Yes. I suppose that's fair." There was a pause. "I sometimes forget how quickly your kind burns out," he added, not unkindly. "Your lifespan is short, your advances in medicine are laughable, and your doctors still cut people open with blades. Oh my, how backward and quaint, the very idea you still use *stitches*."

That made Silas perk up like a hound catching a scent. Curiosity overrode everything else. "Wait," he said, leaning forward. "You don't perform surgery?"

"Not in a thousand years," Vaeril said. "Our biotech heals from within. Our nano fields regrow tissue. Even memory can be restored in certain cases. Why would we carve into the body to fix it when the body can be taught to fix itself?"

Silas's eyes gleamed. His mind was already buzzing with questions. But he only asked one. "How long do your people live?"

Vaeril grew quiet. "I don't know," he said simply. "I've never seen one of us die of old age. Or disease. It … just doesn't happen."

Silas stared at him. The room fell still.

Elias whistled low. "Okay, but what the hell *can* kill you, then?"

The look on Vaeril's face darkened like a thundercloud rolling over a sunlit field. He turned his eyes toward Silas, then Elias. "The Vorrhaxi," he said.

Elias frowned. "What the hell is a *Vorrhaxi?*"

Vaeril took another breath, this one slow and deliberate. "They are the sworn enemy of my kind," he said. "My people—the *Thal'Naari*—were once the caretakers of peace, creators of living ships, healers of entire worlds. But the Vorrhaxi? They are the *end* of things. A swarm, a cancer, a species that feeds on civilizations and leaves only bones behind. They multiply faster than you can kill them. They mutate. They consume. And they do it all in the name of their emperor." He paused, eyes sharp now. "They are what nearly ended us. And now, they've found your world. Before I say anything else," Vaeril continued, his voice lowering with unexpected gravity, "I want to show you something." He turned toward Elias, and for a moment, something softened in his alien features. There was no mockery, no posturing, just the unmistakable glint of brotherly concern. It was subtle, but there. The kind of look one only gave to someone who reminded them of someone irreplaceable. Elias felt it, too, though he couldn't explain how or why. Vaeril saw it clearly—Elias's loud, impulsive energy, the bravado, the defiance. It wasn't just noise. It was survival. It was the armor he wore instead of steel plates. And though Vaeril's twin had been nothing like Elias physically—he was more refined, more strategic, more graceful in battle—there was something deeply familiar in the way Elias carried himself. He had a fire. A challenge hurled at the universe with every breath. It hurt to look at. But it helped, too. No one could ever replace the brother he'd lost. But this foolhardy human might be the one thing in all the galaxy that could keep the loneliness at bay.

Vaeril exhaled slowly. His hands, now freed from the shattered flex-cuffs, moved with practiced calm as he reached into a narrow compartment just beneath the breastplate of his armor. From it, he withdrew a small, silvery device. About the size and shape of a military-grade atropine injector, it shimmered faintly with energy—subtle lines of pulsing blue light moving across its smooth casing. Both twins watched with wary curiosity. Vaeril held the device up between his fingers like an offering. "This," he said, turning his gaze to Elias, "is not a weapon. It's a gift. And if you'll let me, it will change everything for you."

Elias raised an eyebrow, already skeptical, but Vaeril's tone left no room for sarcasm or laughter. "It's a regenerative nano-injection," Vaeril explained. "Self-adapting, coded to your DNA the moment it enters your bloodstream. It will repair your damaged liver, knit your cracked ribs, realign your spine, rebuild the cartilage in your knees. Your pain—*all* of it—gone. Not masked. Not dulled. *Healed.*" Elias blinked. "And that," Vaeril added, leaning forward slightly, "is just the beginning."

Silas leaned back, watching his brother closely. There was a shift happening. Something deeper than flesh or bone. Something harder to heal. But Elias … his hand twitched. He wasn't ready to reach for the injector yet. Not quite. But for the first time in a long while, he looked at something—and *maybe* someone—with hope instead of cynicism.

And Vaeril, watching that flicker in Elias's eyes, allowed himself a single, silent thought: *Perhaps I've already begun to heal, too.*

Elias thought about it for roughly a nanosecond. Without so much as a passing concern for side effects—or anything *vaguely* resembling common sense—he snatched the injector from Vaeril's hand and slammed it into his thigh with practiced precision. Vaeril's brows lifted in surprise. Even *he* hadn't expected Elias to move that fast.

"Goddammit, Elias!" Silas was at his side in an instant, hands already checking his brother's pulse, his pupils, anything that would give him a read. "You idiot! You don't *know* what that is! It could've been poison—it could've been anything!" Silas's voice was a few notes shy of full panic now, his breath coming fast. "This could be some kind of elaborate trick, some attempt at mind control, and you just— *you just jammed it into your leg like a junkie in a hurry!*"

Elias didn't respond. He stood completely still. Not a twitch. Not even a blink. Frozen in place like a damn statue. Silas's heart thundered in his chest. He knew his brother; knew his recklessness. Knew his pride, his arrogance, and his maddening courage. But more than anything else, Silas knew this truth: no matter how far apart they drifted, no matter how different their paths, Elias had always been there—just existing—like a lighthouse you don't need until the night turns bad. The thought of losing that? It unraveled something deep. Silas swallowed hard, forcing himself to think. *Not like this. Please, not like this.*

Vaeril stepped up beside them, his expression calm but focused. "Help me get him to the couch," he said evenly. "This won't take long, but he may be unsteady when he wakes."

Silas hesitated, still wary, but nodded. The two of them flanked Elias, guiding his stiff frame to the couch. He was heavier than he looked, somehow. Like he was locked in place by something more than gravity.

"What do we need?" Silas asked, voice tight.

"Water. Lukewarm—*not* cold, not hot," Vaeril replied. "And protein. Protein bars will work. Do you have any?"

"I think I've got three boxes."

"Perfect. Bring all of them. He'll need the fuel. The regeneration will burn through his reserves fast." Vaeril paused, then added, "Do you have powdered milk? Calcium tablets?"

Silas blinked. "Actually, yes. I have both."

Vaeril gave him a small, approving nod. "You really are the planner, aren't you?"

Silas stared at him. That tone. It was friendly, familiar. Like he was talking to an old friend—no, a *brother*. It made Silas's skin crawl a little. The whole situation was spiraling into the surreal. *This is insane. I've got a heavily-armored alien who talks like we're on the same damn bowling team, my twin just took alien gene juice, and now I'm fetching snacks.* Still, he turned and moved into the kitchen, opening drawers and cupboards with more force than necessary. He knew exactly where everything was—hell, he could navigate this place in a blackout with his eyes closed—but busy hands were better than idle panic. The quiet hum of the house settled over them. Max sat by Elias's side, alert but calm. Alex lay near the couch, his eyes tracking Vaeril but not with distrust, just wary curiosity.

Silas found the calcium tablets, the protein bars, and filled a jug with water. He didn't look at Elias on the way back. Not yet. He couldn't bear to, not until he knew.

Vaeril was doing everything he could to keep Silas busy. Truth be told, he'd never dosed a human before. He was confident the nanotech serum would work. After all, it had been developed by some of the greatest minds of his people, capable of repairing cellular damage, cleansing toxins, and even restoring degraded neural pathways. But what he *wasn't* sure about was how long it would take. And more importantly, how long Silas's already thin patience would last if he started to believe—even for a second—that Vaeril had poisoned his brother. Accidentally or otherwise. Because Silas might be rational, calculating, and obsessive, but none of that would matter if he thought Elias was dying.

Vaeril glanced toward the tall, silent figure still lying like a frozen statue on the couch. Elias hadn't twitched, hadn't blinked, hadn't made a sound. He was just locked there, motionless. Silas hovered near him, eyes darting across his brother's body, searching for any sign of improvement, any hint that his twin hadn't just sacrificed himself in a single reckless moment.

Vaeril knew he had to do something. So, he did the only thing he could. He told the truth. "Silas," he said gently, "come sit. We'll watch over him from here."

Silas hesitated. He gave Elias another close inspection, eyes narrowing slightly as he tried to catch a change in skin tone, a twitch of a finger, *anything*. But there was nothing. With a long breath in through his nose, Silas finally nodded once. He stepped over and sat, the weight of his movements slow and deliberate. His jaw was tight, his body rigid. But he sat, because if Elias *was* dying, he wanted Vaeril close enough to grab. Close enough to kill.

Silas didn't speak right away. He didn't have to. The tension in his shoulders, the hard set of his jaw, the glint in his eyes—they said everything. The only reason Vaeril was still breathing was that Elias had taken that injector of his own free will. Even so, the moment things went south, Silas intended to be the one to put Vaeril down. Loudly and painfully.

Vaeril exhaled quietly. Time to keep talking. He started to speak, his voice low and measured, but just as the first word left his mouth, Max did something odd. He stepped forward, slow and deliberate, and crossed the room with quiet purpose. Then, with startling grace, he rose up on his hind legs beside Elias. He lifted one paw, steady and precise, and placed it gently on Elias's thigh. He held it there. For a long moment, no one moved. The room was frozen in time—Silas, Vaeril, even Alex kept watch from the corner. The gesture wasn't aggressive. It wasn't urgent. It was something else. It felt deliberate, intentional.

Silas blinked. Somewhere in the back of his mind, he almost wanted to laugh, like he'd just wandered into the world's strangest dog meditation circle. It was surreal. The big dog, upright, paw extended like he was sending some ancient canine blessing through sheer willpower. Doggie telepathy? What the hell was happening? Then something even stranger happened. Elias moved. With a soft grunt, he turned, his limbs moving slowly, like a diver rising through thick water. He leaned forward with unsteady grace, then lowered himself back onto the suede couch again, lying flat across it like it had been calling him home all along.

Silas stood. "Elias?" he said, his voice calm at first, then louder. "Elias. Elias!" But there was no response, only the quiet sound of breathing. Smooth and easy. It was the first time in years Silas had heard his brother breathe like that. No groans. No sharp inhales. No shifting from the stab of an aching hip or the burn of old wounds. Just soft, regular, and peaceful breaths. Usually, when Elias slept, he wore pain like a second skin. His face would tense. His legs would twitch. Sometimes he'd wake up cursing, soaked in sweat, clawing at a back spasm or a rib that wouldn't settle. But now? Elias looked … peaceful. And for the first time since his brother had recklessly jammed that alien injector into his own leg, Silas felt comforted. The knot in his chest eased just a bit. He didn't understand what had happened, not yet, but whatever it was, it wasn't killing him.

Vaeril let out a breath of his own, something halfway between relief and exhaustion. But he knew better than to let the silence linger too long. The serum was still working, and they'd need time before Elias woke fully. Time that Silas might start filling with more worry if left to stew. "You don't talk much, do you?" Vaeril said softly, breaking the silence.

Silas turned to him, caught off guard by the sudden shift in tone. He studied the alien for a moment, then gave a single nod—curt, but honest.

Vaeril smiled slightly, his voice quieter now. "That's alright. I've had plenty of long conversations with quiet men. They're usually the ones who have the most to say when it actually matters." Vaeril chose his next words with care. He was no great orator, not by nature. He'd spent more years than he cared to count crossing the stars in silence, alone in the void. Over time, the quiet had become a kind of companion—reliable, uncomplicated. Conversations were rare, and when they happened, they were usually short, tactical, and to the point. He'd never minded that. Solitude was a survival trait in his line of work. But now, seated across from Silas—this sharp-eyed, tightly-coiled human with the soul of a predator—he realized silence might not be the best option. The man didn't just look dangerous. He radiated it. Vaeril had encountered warlords, assassins, and elite commandos from across the galaxies, but something about Silas was different. This was a man forged in personal wars. Quiet, measured, and coiled like a spring. He didn't kill for pleasure or sport; he killed with precision, like a mechanic fixing a machine that wouldn't shut off. Vaeril had seen it in the woods, when Silas cut through Marco's men like they were paper. No hesitation, no waste. Just cold, perfect execution. It hadn't been brutality, it had been inevitability. And that was before any kind of serum or enhancement. No armor. No augmentation. Just raw, terrifying efficiency. Vaeril's own armor—the living second skin clinging to his body—could withstand most conventional Earth weaponry. Bullets would shatter. Blades would glance. Fire would wash over it like water. And yet, sitting here now, looking into the eyes of a man who'd been engineered by nothing more than trauma, rage, and discipline, he felt something he hadn't in a very long time—caution. Because he knew, deep down, that if Silas ever accepted the serum—if he ever embraced what the Thal'Naari were offering—he would become something truly terrifying. Maybe even the most dangerous warrior Vaeril had seen in over a thousand years. A ghost in the flesh. A storm wrapped in bone and discipline.

And right now, that storm was watching him, silent and waiting. So, Vaeril cleared his throat, and finally broke the silence with the only truth that mattered. "I've seen monsters, Silas. I've fought them. Hell, I've become one once or twice. But you …" He paused, giving the man across from him a long, steady look. "You're something else. You don't need enhancements to be dangerous. But with them, you might just change the war."

Silas thought carefully before speaking. Not because he was crafting some clever response, he simply wasn't sure what he wanted to say. He had always been guarded, a man of few words and even fewer visible emotions. He wasn't one of those brash, muscle-bound warriors who browbeat their enemies with roars and brute strength. If anything, he looked like a schoolteacher—tired eyes, a few streaks of gray in his hair, and the kind of quiet, patient stillness that might have belonged to a man more at home with books than with bloodshed. But Silas was not harmless.

There were many types of killers in the world—those who killed for country, for creed, for politics or religion—but couldn't live with the aftermath. He wasn't one of them. Then there were the thrill seekers, the ones who killed for money, for sport, or for the high of it. He wasn't one of those, either. Some, perhaps the most dangerous, were simply good at it. They found they had a talent for killing, and so it became their trade, their passion, their identity. That was Elias, though he'd never admit it. He wore his guilt like armor, but Silas had seen the gleam in his brother's eyes during a fight. Elias loved the game. And he was brilliant at it.

Silas was different. He didn't enjoy killing. But he didn't regret it, either. That was the part that would trouble most people, the fact that he didn't feel anything at all. He had long suspected something had been taken from him—burned out of him—early on. Whatever joy or light had once lived inside him had been snuffed out, probably sometime in his childhood. Maybe it was his mother. That monstrous woman with a cruel tongue and colder hands. She had wielded guilt like a scalpel, slicing him open with shame until even the escape from her house hadn't brought freedom, just silence. There were things she did, things she said … things Silas never told a soul. Not even Elias. Especially not Elias. Because if his brother knew, he'd have hunted her down and made sure she never breathed again. And as much as there was a part of Silas that would've liked that, another part just wanted the past to stay buried. He'd come close, once or twice, to telling someone. To letting it out. But the moment the words came to his lips, he stopped. Speaking it aloud would give it form, make it real again. And he had worked too hard to build the walls around it. So, he kept it all in. Endured it. Or maybe he just survived it. He wasn't sure anymore.

As he glanced toward the hallway mirror, he caught a glimpse of his own reflection. The face staring back wore the look others always commented on—calm, unreadable, and distant. They didn't know what was behind it. They didn't see the boy still hiding beneath that sleepy-eyed mask. The boy who once crawled through a cold, muddy ditch in rural Louisiana, barefoot and bruised, trying to find help while the sky cracked with thunder overhead. Alone and afraid, but still moving forward. That boy never stopped walking. Silas wasn't a hero. He wasn't even sure he was a good person. But he knew how to endure. And he knew that whatever came next—be it battle, betrayal, or death—he would face it the same way. One step at a time. Until the road ended … or he did.

Vaeril could tell there was a lot going on behind Silas's stillness. The man hadn't moved much, but something in his eyes had shifted, just for a second. A flicker. It was almost childlike, a look that silently pleaded *Don't pull me into the light. I don't belong there.* It was the look of someone more comfortable in the shadows. The longer Vaeril watched, the more uneasy he became. That pleading look wasn't weakness. No, it was something far more dangerous. It reminded him of something he'd once seen on one of those absurd human nature programs. The kind that species obsessed over for reasons he never quite understood. This one had been about trapdoor spiders. A predator that waited beneath the surface. Hidden, silent, and unseen. And when its prey came close—gone. Not devoured with fanfare or fury, just … gone. No struggle, not a sound, just a sudden absence.

Vaeril had laughed at the dramatics of the show back then. Now, watching Silas in person, the memory made him shudder. Just when it seemed like the silence would stretch into eternity, Alex moved. He padded over to where Silas sat, calm and deliberate, like a creature who had seen many lifetimes and still had the patience for one more. Alex lowered his massive head into Silas's lap and let it rest there, heavy, warm, and solid.

Silas didn't react at first—he barely even breathed—but slowly, his hand came up and hovered above the dog's head. Not touching, just close. Alex looked up at him with an expression that, if dogs could speak in anything other than silence, would've said *I see you. You're not alone.* Then, with the same gentle insistence, Alex lifted a single paw and placed it on Silas's thigh. Once, then again. And again. Almost like he was patting him, comforting him. *It's okay. I've got you.* After the third touch, Alex gave a loud, deliberate snort and turned away. He crossed the room with an air of quiet purpose, moving to the couch where Elias still lay sleeping peacefully. Max was already there, watchful and alert, but Alex approached, snorted again, and shook his head as if to say *This one's going to be trouble, too.*

The two ancient dogs met in the center of the room, their noses brushing in a silent greeting that felt older than language. Some kind of communion passed between them—reassurance, maybe. Or strategy. Then, wordlessly, they took their positions. Alex settled at the foot of the couch. Max at the head. Two sentries. Two guardians. They didn't growl. They didn't bark. They simply stood there, still as statues, eyes alert, bodies coiled and calm. And somehow, without ever saying a word, they made it very clear. *No one gets near our charges. Not without going through us.*

By this point, Vaeril was starting to feel something he hadn't felt in a very long time: discomfort. That realization alone was sobering. He'd crossed countless star systems, fought wars that lasted generations, and faced nightmares in deep voids where even light dared not linger. Yet, sitting here, across from a tired man in a quiet house on a backwater planet, he felt something beginning to falter. *Are these two really worth all this trouble?* he wondered. *All this risk?*

Just as that doubt took root, Silas spoke. His voice was quiet, but there was no softness in it. "I don't know who you are," he began, "or *what* you are, to be honest. But I'm only going to ask one thing from you—a single boon."

Vaeril sat up straighter, attentive.

"Tell me the truth," Silas said. "All of it. Including the ugly warts, the bloody hands, the burned-out planets. Don't spare me. Don't dress it up. And don't lie." He leaned forward slightly, elbows on his knees. "I won't interrupt. I won't even ask questions. You'll have your time to speak. But if I feel, even once, that you're lying to me …" He trailed off, not finishing the sentence. He didn't need to. His gaze said everything. It wasn't a threat. It wasn't anger. It was something far colder: certainty.

Vaeril felt a lump rise in his throat. For a moment, the nanoweave of his armor felt too tight across his chest. It wasn't often he felt fear and uncertainty, not that his courage was faltering, but his stalwart belief of his ability to stand against any creature one-on-one was beginning to wane.

Silas just kept looking at him with that same quiet, unblinking stare. Like the end had already been written. Like the decision had already been made. That look—flat, steady, final—struck something in Vaeril's memory. He thought back to an old human vid he'd once watched, one of those strange Westerns their species had adored. In it, two men faced each other in the street under a high noon sun. The hero stepped forward and said, "This town ain't big enough for the both of us." The moment, of course, ended in tragedy. Now, sitting here in the dim light of a rural cabin on Earth, Vaeril suddenly found himself wondering *Which one am I in this story? The good man trying to do what's right? Or the doomed fool standing in the way of something he doesn't understand?* He didn't know the answer. But he knew he had to speak. And this time, the truth would have to be enough.

Vaeril looked at Silas and sighed—deeply, wearily. "The truth," he said quietly. "Yes, the truth. Well, that's a complicated story to tell."

Silas raised a single finger and slowly wagged it back and forth with the cool precision of a judge preparing to deliver a verdict. "No, no, no … my *new* friend," he said, his voice low and unyielding. "I thought I made myself crystal clear." There was no menace in his tone, no flex of muscle or threat of violence, but the look in his eyes made it known: playtime was over.

"You say you've studied Earth," Silas went on. "Then tell me, have you ever heard the phrase 'Beware of Greeks bearing gifts'?"

Vaeril blinked, searching for a clever reply—some quip or some tactical deflection. But nothing came. Not when the serum he'd handed over had rendered the brother of a very dangerous man unconscious. *Just give him the truth. Oh, screw it. What do I have to lose?* "Alright," he finally replied. "Here's the truth. As I said, a very dangerous species—the Vorrhaxi—attacked my people more than a thousand years ago. At first, they were just a brutal nuisance. But it didn't take long before we realized we simply didn't have the numbers. Not because we lacked skill. We were, and still are, some of the deadliest warriors in the galaxy. But our birth rates are low. Our people are few." He paused, letting the weight of it settle in the air. "Our population once numbered in the trillions. Now? Fewer than one hundred million of us remain, scattered across a galaxy we once helped cultivate and protect. Too few to stand alone. Too proud to surrender."

Silas watched him silently, nodding once.

"So," Vaeril continued, "we started recruiting. From every star system we could reach, every species that could understand our plight. But not just anyone. Only twins. Bonded pairs. Our ships, which are our most powerful weapons, are alive. They must *merge* with two minds to be truly whole. One twin is the strategist—methodical, precise, and implacable. The other is the warrior—relentless, violent, and unforgiving. Together, they become something unstoppable." Vaeril leaned forward, his eyes serious now. "The stronger the twins and the deeper their bond, the more powerful the ship becomes. And you two—" He paused, struggling for the right words in the human tongue. "You two are … *unique.*"

Silas raised an eyebrow. "Define unique."

Vaeril winced. "Forgive me. My command of your language still lacks subtlety. What I meant to say is, I have never—*ever*—in all my centuries, seen a pair of twins quite so" —he gestured vaguely— "insane, reckless, and stupid as the two of you."

Silas froze, then he blinked. Then, to Vaeril's surprise, a slow chuckle rumbled from his chest. "Well, Vaeril," he said, laughing harder now, "you've got me there." He slapped his knee. "Touché, my friend. Touché."

CHAPTER SEVEN

Across the galaxy, on the emperor's capital world, things were spiraling, just as he had planned. And he loved it. Truly loved it. Chaos was a melody, and death the sweetest refrain. He savored it like a battlefield craves the blood of the fallen—hot, fresh, and gushing from broken bodies as their souls fled screaming into the void. He loved the frozen faces of the dead: contorted with agony, twisted with fear, or slack with the final acceptance of loss. The desperate eyes, the clawed hands, and the silence that followed. To the emperor, *that* was true power. Not wealth. Not influence. Real power—*true* power—was the ability to decide who lived and who died. That was true dominance. That was control. To him, their lives were like insects in a jar—crushed or spared at the whim of his ever-shifting mood.

He reclined now on his grotesque throne, a towering monstrosity forged from the bones of conquered enemies. Skulls lined the armrests. Spines wrapped around the base like the roots of a tree. The faint smell of ash and decay lingered in the chamber like perfume. With a long, languid sigh, he closed his eyes and smiled. The game was in motion. The pieces had been set. Soon, word would come— messengers bearing news of destruction, whispers of betrayal, and rivers of blood. And he would drink it all in, relishing every drop like the nectar of the gods.

They were soaked in blood—sticky, drying, but still fresh. He flexed his fingers, watching crimson stretch and crack across his knuckles. The emperor's orders had been clear: *Begin the culling.* And so, he had. Outlying garrisons had been wiped clean, reduced to slick red mud and shattered bone. At each site, only a single Vorrhaxi was spared—left behind as a trembling witness, a mouthpiece for terror, a vessel to carry the tale of what had come and what would come again.

Malvek had painted warnings in flesh. Oh, the slaughter … it had been beautiful. Those soldiers, so proud, so certain of their strength, had died like children. They were well-trained, yes. They were formidable by conventional standards. But Malvek was not a warrior. He was a force of nature. In human mythology, there was a figure called the angel of death, a divine, unstoppable harbinger sent to carry out the will of a wrathful god. He would come silently and painlessly, taking life with no suffering, no fear. A solemn, holy end. Malvek was no such creature. He was not merciful. He was not quiet. He was not a servant of anything divine. Malvek was a sadistic lunatic who *adored* killing. He didn't take life, he shattered it, dismantled it, tore it apart, piece by piece. He feasted on suffering like it was the finest delicacy. He wasn't an artist of death, as some killers prided themselves on being. His methods were not refined, elegant, or precise. They were *monstrous.* Each kill was an expression of contempt. Every scream was music. Every plea was poetry. He moved like a butcher through a temple, desecrating everything sacred, savoring every drop of blood spilled on the altar of his madness. Honor? Sacrifice? Bravery? These were words to other warriors, concepts they lived and died by. To Malvek, they were a joke.

***

In another corner of the galaxy, cloaked in shadows and silence, a new arrival approached a moon that bore no name. It was little more than a jagged stone adrift in blackness, forgotten by time, ignored

164

by maps, and feared by those few who still whispered about the one who lived there. The Nameless One. The emperor's spider. He sat in silence within the heart of his lair, a hollowed structure buried beneath layers of metal and volcanic stone. The chamber was as dark as the void outside and there was no need for light. The Spymaster was sightless, after all. Light meant nothing to him.

Still, he *felt* it. A presence. Something ancient. Something had been summoned. It was the entity the emperor had dispatched to his very doorstep—one of the dark ones. The kind that didn't knock, didn't speak, and didn't stop. In the shriveled mass where his heart might have once been, the Spymaster knew. *This was not a summons. This was a sentence.* If the emperor had sent it, there were only two possible outcomes: humiliation or death. Perhaps both.

A lesser being would have panicked, but the Spymaster did not. He had already been humbled. What gnawed at him wasn't fear, it was uncertainty. *How had the emperor found this place?* This moon was never named. Never recorded. Everyone involved in its construction had been *erased.* Their loyalty had been insured by one simple truth: *No one who left the rock did so without the spider's leave.* And if they tried? They vanished. There were *fail-safes,* silent ones. And yet, somehow, that cunning bastard on his throne of bone had found him anyway. That, more than the assassin now hurtling toward his coordinates, disturbed him. If the emperor knew, then others might as well. And *they*—his true enemies—were far worse than the emperor and his monstrous playthings. He would need to burn it all. And soon. But not just yet. First, he would meet the thing the emperor had sent. He would let it try to bite. And then he would decide whether to crush it … or run.

***

Roach paced the narrow length of the scout ship for the 12,598[th] time. That number wasn't guesswork—it was exact. Counting gave the Nillith comfort. A strange comfort, perhaps, but one that helped stabilize the chaos inside the borrowed flesh. The ship was hurtling toward a forgotten rock, a dark moon tucked into a silent, remote corner of the galaxy. A dead place. A hidden place. A place that stank of secrets. Roach had no say in this journey. Somewhere deep inside, he screamed. The Nillith had silenced him—shoved him into one of his own memory palaces. Not the pretty ones, either. One of the blood-slicked halls where Roach had once delighted in torture and atrocity on Marco's orders. The echoes of those crimes now tormented their architect, and the Nillith watched with quiet satisfaction as the once-feared enforcer flailed in his own past like a rat in a trap. It had worked, for a while.

But now, Roach was scratching at the walls again. His will was returning. His incessant whining, his *begging* to regain control—it grated like broken glass across bone. The Nillith was running out of patience. *And when the Nillith ran out of patience … things broke.*

He paused in his pacing and stared at the stars through the viewport like they were insects he might one day swallow. The emperor had been vague, as always. "Go there," he'd said. Just that. No command to kill the Spymaster. No threats and no further instruction. Just *go.* That alone, the emperor claimed, would be enough to bring the Nameless One back into line. Perhaps. Perhaps not. The Nillith had his own thoughts. *Scour the records.* That was the emperor's only addendum—search the moon for secrets. For truths. For leverage. That, at least, was something the Nillith could get behind.

He ordinarily detested servitude. He was not a creature made to serve. But the emperor was useful. So many worlds under his careless rule. So many lives to twist, so much agony to harvest. An entire empire's worth of suffering, ready to be picked like a ripe fruit. *And when the emperor's usefulness ends …* Well, the Nillith had plans for that, too.

But then, Roach screamed. The Nillith staggered, one hand clutching the side of his head as the voice in his mind surged back with renewed fury. "You *bastard!* You used me. You rode me like a beast. You *wear* me like a suit and call yourself a god. Let me out. Give me back my body!" Roach had uncovered the latest trick. The mental bindings were unraveling.

The Nillith hissed through his stolen teeth. Roach—annoying, filthy, and loud—was becoming a liability. A thing to discard. Perhaps he had served his purpose. Perhaps this body was no longer worth the effort it took to keep it caged. *Perhaps it's time to let you die again.* The ship began its final descent toward the shadowed moon. The Nameless One was waiting. And so was judgment.

***

In another part of the empire, beneath the emperor's very nose, yet another plot took root. One he hadn't foreseen, though he had brushed against it recently through the failed assassination attempts in his own palace. He had blamed the Spymaster, and not without reason, but the true architect was someone far more dangerous: Queen Khar'Zul, the Abomination Maker. Khar'Zul had many reasons to see the emperor fall, but one mattered more than the rest—she craved power above all, power unshared and unchallenged. The other three surviving queens were obstacles. As long as they lived, they could still spawn offspring—rivals, threats, and future enemies. There could be only one queen.

Her first task was to decide who to kill first. Virexxa, the schemer, was the most dangerous politically. Khar'Zul had uncovered fragments of her plan to kidnap and imprison the emperor, convinced he had grown weak, erratic, and childishly paranoid. He was vulnerable now, thrashing in the madness of his own crumbling supremacy. Once, no queen would have dared challenge him. Now, Virexxa dared.

Then there was Queen Threxil, the traditionalist, the warmonger. She lived only for war, for glorious death, and had grown weary of her endless life. She longed to find her end in battle against a worthy foe.

Perhaps Khar'Zul could give her that, just not in the way she expected. If she wanted death so badly, why not hurry her toward it?

And finally, Zev'Kala, the secret-keeper. The spider. Her network of assassins, spies, and saboteurs stretched across the empire and beyond. She was elusive, cunning, and perhaps useful. Rumors swirled that she had ties to forces outside the emperor's control, diplomatic threads spun through neutral systems and hidden enclaves. More interesting still were whispers of her connection to a new player on the board. Not Malvek—he was too brutish, too feral to be manipulated—but the Nillith. No one knew where the Nillith had come from. It had slithered into the emperor's inner circle with no known allegiance and had already been dispatched on a mission to parts unknown. For a creature so secretive to be trusted so swiftly by a man as paranoid as the emperor was telling and terrifying. Zev'Kala might be an enemy or she might be something more useful: an ally.

Khar'Zul decided then and there that she would attempt to forge a pact. Better to share power with a shadow you can guide than war with a rival you cannot. She summoned her minions, quietly and efficiently. The plot to kill the other queens had begun.

***

Shaskiel sat alone in his command chamber, surrounded by dark metal walls that pulsed faintly with the lifeblood of the ship. He preferred it this way—solitary, detached, and immune to the chatter and incompetence of the misfits the Spymaster had cobbled together into this so-called fleet. They were a rabble. Decorated veterans, perhaps. Survivors of old campaigns. But not his kind. And certainly not worthy of the trust that had been placed in them. Yes, there were one hundred fifty ships in his armada. On paper, it was enough firepower to glass a backwater planet like Earth ten times over. But in his gut, Shaskiel felt the unease coil tighter. There were no orbital defenses around Earth. No early-warning nets, no intercept fleets hidden behind moons. These humans had no idea what waited for them just beyond their sleepy cradle. Still, something was off. Why this mission? Why this force? Why him? Why not High Executor Varnak'Tal? If Earth was so significant, surely the Flame of the First Brood would have led the attack. Not this hastily-assembled band of relics and rejects. The thought gnawed at him.

He turned his attention back to the fleet's readiness reports. Most of the ships were passable. A few—very few—met his standards. Far too many were sluggish, their captains slow, and their crew uncoordinated. They would be the first to die. But not before serving as an example.

With cold precision, Shaskiel keyed the broadcast to all ships. "To all fleet captains: formation exercises will resume immediately. We will drill until flawless. We will train until we move as one. There will be no engagement, not even a scouting pass over Earth, until you meet my standard." He paused, then added, his voice like a stone dragged across steel, "Failure will be punished. Sloth will be punished. Ineptitude will be punished."

He opened a second command window and entered a simple code. A heartbeat later, viewports across 142 ships slid open—metal petals parting to expose the starscape beyond. Floating among the fleet were dozens of frozen bodies, drifting in slow rotation. Crew, officers, and pilots. Those who had failed him in the last round of exercises. "Behold," Shaskiel growled, his voice echoing through every deck, "the cost of disappointing me. This is not symbolic. This is precedent. Are there any more takers?" Silence answered him. Satisfied, he closed the comm channel and leaned back in his command seat, his massive arms crossed over his armored chest.

Behind his crimson eyes, a single thought lingered. Where were the eight ships? He had sent them in pairs to screen the front and rear flanks of the fleet. They were supposed to be his eyes—his early-warning system. But no signal had returned. There had been no data, no wreckage, and no chatter. Shaskiel's jaw tightened. He told himself it was a delay in relays or a systems glitch. Shaskiel's eight ships would never send another warning. They would never report another sighting or scream a final alarm. They were already gone.

The assassin and the noble warrior had settled into the rhythm of Valshar's hidden maneuvers—the constant acceleration, sudden stops, and long stretches of eerie stillness cloaked in asteroid belts. Valshar spoke little during these intervals. Instead, lights would quietly activate in the exercise room, prompting them to train. There were no commands, just subtle cues, as if it had always been their idea. They worked for hours each day, pushing themselves through grueling cardio and weight routines. Weapons—blunt and edged— gleamed in dedicated alcoves, their presence a quiet invitation. The machines adjusted constantly, ramping up difficulty without fanfare, as if guided by an unseen will that knew them intimately. Weeks passed, and doors appeared where none had been before. Consoles emerged from smooth walls, humming softly. With each change came simple instructions, nothing more. Both assassin and warrior could feel it: the ship was evolving, not just for war, but for them. It wasn't just a guardian anymore. It was becoming a home. And, somehow, it was glad they were there. By the third week, the trust between them had deepened.

After a hearty breakfast, the ship spoke, softly, but with weight. "Today, my charges, you face your first real test. Today, we strike back. The emperor's minions have much to answer for, and they will find no mercy from us." There was a pause, heavy and meaningful. "Noble warrior," the voice continued, "you will command our weapons. Your stamina, your relentless focus—these are your gifts, and they will guide our hand in battle. Grace, or assassin, if you prefer—" Again, there was a hesitation, which was rare for Valshar. "You will guide us. You will navigate and manage our systems. Your precision, your eye for detail, these are no longer tools of death, but instruments of sal- vation." Another long pause. "I can fight alone. But for us to become what we must, we will fight as one. This is not just battle, it is proof.

Proof that a ship, a soldier, and a killer can become something more. I have never fought with your kind. I have only known you as enemies. But if *she* has trusted you, then I will, too." The voice cracked, just faintly. "Show me your worth—not with words, but with action. Perhaps in battle, you will find more than vengeance. Perhaps you will find redemption."

That last word struck the noble warrior like a blade to the chest. He wasn't ready to admit how much it shook him. The assassin glanced at him, her crest shifting into hues of shock and wonder. They had never spoken of their shared doubts, the shame that coiled in their bellies like a sickness. And yet, Valshar knew.

On a second-rate scout ship, a bored young officer sat at the helm. By human standards, he was a naval junior officer. Unlike their ground forces, the fleet had structure—ranks, roles, and responsibilities. There was no time in the vacuum of space for battles to be decided by the brightest pheromones or loudest clicks. And yet, tradition clung stubbornly. Ships still exchanged signals through flashes of light and bursts of movement. It was elegant, sure, but not tactically sound in a war of extinction. That's why the admiral demanded absolute obedience and instantaneous execution of orders. A single failure, even a slight delay, could doom an entire fleet to destruction by a faster, smarter enemy. Hence the strategy: overwhelm with numbers. Thousands of ships hurled at a target until resistance collapsed. It wasn't artful. But it worked—usually. Still, the officer felt exposed, vulnerable. His tiny scout ship had been paired with a powerful frigate, a boxy monster bristling with missiles and lasers, a flying fortress in deep space. It should have been comforting, but it wasn't. Not that it mattered. Within moments, neither his worries, his aspirations, nor the lives of his sleeping brood mates would mean anything. A ripple of gravity, barely perceptible, signaled doom. Then came nothing. No alarm. No flash. No warning. One moment, the scout ship was there. The next, it was cosmic debris, vaporized by a silent, invisible particle beam.

Valshar had waited in the anomaly's shadow, cloaked perfectly in the gravitational eddies. A perfect sniper's perch. The frigate noticed something was wrong when the scout ship failed to send its timed signal. The frigate's captain, a disgraced but clever survivor from the emperor's navy, felt a twinge of unease. He'd spent a career scraping through disasters, using cunning and cowardice in equal measure. This time, it wouldn't be enough. The first strike hit the frigate in the aft section, clean between the engine housings. The beam tore through metal and flesh alike, roasting engineers in less than a second. The ship buckled. Atmosphere screamed into space. Hulls fractured. Lives ended—some instantly, others slower, clawing in the dark. The captain had just enough time to curse his luck before his body froze solid, suspended in vacuum.

Valshar opened a viewport for his crew to observe their handiwork. Grace stood beside the Vorrhaxi soldier, silent. As the dead captain's body drifted past their window, she glanced at the soldier's face. No remorse. No hesitation. Just grim resolve. A few moments earlier, they had acted in perfect synchrony, she guiding Valshar, he firing the weapon systems. No second-guessing and no doubts. This wasn't theory anymore. They weren't *hoping* to act. They *had* acted. From dreamers to doers, from shadows to vengeance. Grace found herself smiling as she pulled Valshar clear of the debris field. *Two down. One hundred forty-eight to go.* And for the first time in a long time, she felt anticipation.

***

Silas sat at the table with Vaeril while Max and Alex kept watch over Elias. The serum was still at work, and the silence in the room felt oppressive and thick with uncertainty. A sobering thought crept into Silas's mind: *What if Elias never woke up?* He'd never lived a second of his life without his brother. From the moment of conception, Elias had been there—loud, reckless, and loyal. If Silas was ever in danger,

Elias would come. That was the unspoken rule. More often than not, though, it was Elias who needed saving. And that was fine by Silas. He didn't mind giving his brother hell for that when the moment was right, but truth be told, he preferred being in the background, anyway. Always had. He didn't want the spotlight. He wanted the shadows—the quiet corners where he could see everything, analyze it, remember it all. It was a gift, yes, but also a curse. Every detail filed away, every mistake, every loss … nothing ever faded. He chuckled quietly to himself.

Vaeril, seated across from him, looked up briefly, offered a nod, then returned to his own thoughts. Silas remembered boot camp— the strange tests, the results no one talked about. How he'd been pulled aside, separated, and recruited. While Elias was forged into a blunt instrument of war, Silas had been honed into something else entirely—a razor. He chuckled at the memory, startling Vaeril, who again gave a quick glance and a knowing nod before returning to his thoughts. Silas thought about what followed. How they'd taught him to spin his mind faster than most could dream. How to use that memory—near-perfect, cold, and efficient. How to size up every living soul as a potential threat. How to kill without hesitation or remorse, like a bullet leaving a barrel: unconscious, unflinching, and final. He didn't weep for his kills. He sorted them like garbage, removing them from the world like refuse on the curb, out of sight and soon forgotten. They were the monsters: terrorists, warlords, and professional killers. He was the farmer and they were the crop. He reaped. Faces flashed through his mind, too many to count. Not one had ever begged for mercy. None of them had the chance. They never saw him coming. They never saw him leave. And that was when the spiral began. When the past—the trauma—started clawing its way back in. The dew on the grass. The sound of distant tires. The dirt road and the ditch. His knees trembling. That *one night.* Then suddenly, there was a weight in his lap. A warm, heavy head.

Alex. Looking up at him with an almost human intensity. And though no words were spoken, Silas *heard* him clearly. *You fool, stop this. I am with you. You are not alone. I have you now. I will never let that happen again. Get your head in the game. There's work to do. And time is short.* Silas exhaled slowly. The fog receded. Alex lifted his head from Silas's lap and returned to his post beside Elias, silent and steady once more.

***

Vaeril Dae'nar had never truly known fear. He had felt duty, sorrow, even the ache of failure, but never fear. Not the way mortals understood it. He had never doubted he would give every last breath in his body, every drop of blood in his veins, to ensure victory for his people. But now, sitting with Silas, he felt something close. Not fear of death or even fear of failure. Fear of what might happen *if this man broke.* Silas was an enigma. Unlike Elias, who wore his fire on his sleeve, Silas kept everything sealed behind layers of control so tight they might as well have been welded shut. His face was a map of loss, etched with torment no one dared trace. Even his twin, as close as they were, seemed to be held at arm's length, not by accident, but by *choice.*

The house told the story: sterile order, military precision, and everything aligned and measured to the millimeter. A fortress against chaos. A symptom of control. Vaeril reached into the inner pocket of his tunic and closed his fingers around the other vial of serum. That serum … it did not grant new powers. It *amplified* what was already within. And in Silas, who embodied precision, silence, and a razor's edge? If the serum sharpened that edge too far, what would be left? A monster? Or a weapon the universe had never seen before?

As Vaeril reached the peak of his dark contemplation, Alex lifted his head from his post by the couch and snorted. In Vaeril's mind, Alex growled with ancient disdain, his voice sudden and crystal clear.

174

This is like working with pups barely weaned from their dam. Did the great ship choose the wrong champion? Are you going to keep sulking, or will you get off your indecisive ass and act? The serum is almost finished with Elias, and soon, it must course through the veins of my charge, or all will be lost.

Vaeril turned his head slowly and met Alex's steady, unwavering eyes. He didn't speak aloud, but the words formed with crisp clarity in his mind. *I don't fear the task, dog. I fear what he may become. I've seen what men like Silas can do without enhancement. With it, he might become the sharpest blade this galaxy has ever known—or the deadliest mistake.*

Max snorted now, too, from the other end of the couch. His tone was steadier, less biting. *Every blade must be tempered in fire. You were tempered. So were we. It's time to trust the fire again.*

Vaeril's eyes went to Silas, still seated at the table, posture tight, hands folded in that maddeningly calm way, and his gaze distant but calculating. That wasn't the face of a man losing control. That was the look of a tactician building an empire in his mind. He stood up slowly. "Vaeril—emissary, gatherer of warrior souls—whatever moniker you go by. Before you decide to inject me with whatever it is you've been fingering in your pocket for the last hour, I want to tell you something." He exhaled slowly. "Not a threat. Not a warning. A story, so you can decide for yourself whether the weapon you're creating will be your salvation or the spark that burns down what little of your universe remains." His eyes burned with eerie calm. "I don't feel fear. I don't feel remorse. I recall every second of my life because I can't stop remembering. My mind doesn't slow down. It devours—information, patterns, threats, and justice. It's not emotion that drives me. It's compulsion. Vengeance is not a choice. It's gravity." He tilted his head slightly, searching Vaeril's expression. "Unlike my brother, whom your serum will heal, strengthen, and renew, I don't have wounds that can be stitched or bones that need mending. What I have is harder to fix. If your serum brings clarity, then you may create something new, something pure. But if it magnifies what's already there?" A pause. "Well, then you may have just built the most terrifying weapon this side of your dying stars." He leaned back, eyes still locked with the alien. "Tell me, Vaeril, do you think your serum can give me back what was taken away so long ago? Do you think it can make me feel again?"

Vaeril took a long, deliberate breath before finally speaking. His voice was low and steady. "I don't know what's going to happen," he said. "But I do know this—I know your character, even if you don't." He leaned in slightly, as though studying a finely-tuned instrument. "You could've killed the bookkeeper. But you didn't. You acted without calculation, without weighing pros and cons. You chose mercy. That was instinct. That's who you are."

Silas stared, silent.

"In the market," Vaeril continued, "when Grace was falling, you caught her. No hesitation. That's not the act of a hollow man. That's the reflex of someone good. You didn't know the waitress, either, but you stepped in anyway. And the biker? You warned him. That was restraint, mercy."

He paused. "I've seen the files. I know the missions—the children you found and the justice you delivered, even when the law had failed them. A friend of mine once said, 'The time is right because we are the ones for the job. We've been called and we've answered.'"

Silence rang through the cabin like a struck bell. Then, just as the weight of it settled, Elias stirred. And for the first time in what felt like a lifetime, his eyes opened.

The motion was fluid, almost inhuman in speed. Silas barely had time to process it. What was even more shocking was how Elias looked—taller, broader across the shoulders, and with denser muscle, like someone had rebuilt him from the bones out. He paced the room in quick, precise lines, rolling his shoulders, flexing his hands, and grinning like a lunatic. Whatever pain had haunted his body for years was gone—erased like it had never been.

Vaeril calmly raised a hand, palm out, signaling him to stop. "Elias," he said with quiet authority. "You're in a delicate state, whether you believe it or not. You feel strong, reborn even. That's good. But restoring your body, healing your injuries, and reawakening dormant systems has taken a toll. We must replenish what your body spent."

Elias frowned but paused.

"Please, sit. Eat the protein bars—all of them. Your new physiology won't process hunger the way it used to. Food is fuel now, not comfort. You'll need to keep up with it."

Elias dropped into the chair, still crackling with energy.

Vaeril hesitated for a beat. "There's one more thing," he said. "You'll no longer be able to drink to forget. Your body will cleanse any toxins before they take effect. You can't get drunk ever again."

That wiped the grin off Elias's face. He stared at Vaeril for a long moment, then down at his hands—perfect, unscarred, and unshaking. The silence that followed was heavy, but he nodded, opened the first bar, and began to eat.

Elias sat there for a few blissful moments; the only sounds that came from him were the crunch of protein bars and long, satisfied sighs between bites. He looked genuinely content, refreshed in a way Silas hadn't seen in years. But the peace didn't last. With a smirk, Elias turned toward his twin. "So," he said, brushing crumbs off his lap, "you going to be a wussy your whole life, or are you going to take the damn serum and join this freaking awesome ride?"

Silas didn't even flinch. He just shook his head, his expression unreadable. "I don't need to get high to live my best life," he replied quietly. "Never really felt the urge to be more than I am."

Elias scoffed. "That's not being more. That's being *whole*. I'm fixed, Silas. This stuff doesn't just heal your body, it gives you back *everything*. Youth. Strength. Clarity. And it doesn't take away who you are, it just lets you *be* who you are without pain."

Silas's eyes remained steady on his brother, but something in his jaw tightened. "That's the problem," he muttered, almost too low to hear. "I'm not sure I *want* to be all of who I am again." Silas looked at his brother again, the worry rising despite himself. "You know, Elias," he said softly, "I've gone through a lot of dark times, both with you and without you. I can honestly say I've rarely been afraid. Not because I'm brave. Because I don't feel much at all. But when I take down something evil—when I *hunt* something that preys on the innocent—that's when I feel something. That's when I know what I was made for. To be a righteous, merciless hunter."

Elias stirred and cracked one eye open. "Melodramatic much?"

Silas blinked. "You know what? You're a real dick."

Then Elais turned to Vaeril and gestured with mock seriousness. "Alright, Comic-Con reject. Give him the damn space juice."

Without further comment, Vaeril did something unexpected—his race's version of a chuckle—and handed Silas the serum. Silas didn't hesitate. He took the injector and drove it into his arm. They waited. Nothing happened. Elias and Vaeril looked at him, expecting something. A glow, a tremor, or a change of some sort.

Silas gave them a flat, unimpressed stare. "Are you two yo-yos going to sit there all day, or are we going to save the fucking universe?"

Elias blinked. "So maybe you're not as screwed up as we thought."

Silas stared again, this time a bit colder. "Oh, I'm changing," he said. "Just not the way I expected. I still don't feel anything. But now, I'm aware of everything." He rose slowly, deliberately, and turned to Vaeril. "It's time to take us to your ship. I hope they expect no mercy, because we're coming for all of them. Not one of them will escape my wrath."

* * *

Valshar awakened the assassin and the noble soldier from their sleep cycle. "Wake up, my charges. It's time."

Grace and the soldier dressed quickly, rushing to their battle stations. "What is it, Valshar?" Grace asked, already checking weapons and readouts.

"We have a group of ten ships bearing down on us. I'm not entirely sure how they detected us in this location. I've sent out a call for assistance."

"Who's coming?" she asked, tension rising.

"An old friend the great ship contacted on our behalf."

"Does she have a name?"

"No. She is simply known as the Ancient One."

Grace blinked. "The Ancient One? That sounds encouraging. Is she helpful?"

"She is extremely powerful," Valshar replied. "Although, according to every record I've ever accessed, she is also extremely grumpy."

Grace snorted, trying to stifle a laugh. "Grumpy compared to what? A supernova having a bad day?" Even the noble soldier chuckled.

If Valshar had lungs, he might have sighed. Instead, his engines emitted a low, irritated hum. "Well then," he grumbled, "now that you two little twits have had your laugh, shall we get back to the business of keeping our collective hides intact?"

***

Shaskiel leaned back in the command chair of his flagship. The vessel was a hulking beast—more than five times the size of any other ship in the armada. It loomed like an ancient leviathan among a school of minnows. Most of the other vessels looked like tugboats beside an aircraft carrier. He was down to 142 ships now. The eight he'd dispatched weeks earlier to serve as an early-warning net had simply vanished—no debris, no signal, and no trace. Given the incompetence of most of the fleet's captains, Shaskiel wasn't even surprised. Over the past three months, he had drilled this ragged flotilla without mercy. Maneuver after maneuver and formation after formation. It had taken more than a few executions to whip them into shape. But nothing got a sailor's attention like seeing their former crewmates float past the viewport in silence—lifeless, frozen monuments to failure.

Still, they were improving. Not fast enough, perhaps, but improving. He continued toward Earth at a deliberately slow pace. The longer he delayed, the more time the crews had to sharpen. Earth wasn't going anywhere. If anything, the slow burn of anticipation made the eventual conquest even sweeter.

On a whim—an emotion he rarely indulged—Shaskiel ordered a ten-ship recon force to sweep a full perimeter around the armada. He wanted no surprises lurking just beyond sensor range. The force included two scout ships, four frigates, and four destroyers. It was led by a commander the fleet referred to only as the Reaver. The Reaver was a veteran of the emperor's endless wars. He hadn't been relieved for incompetence—far from it. He was a tactical savant, efficient, brutal, and utterly devout. But he had a habit of purging his own crew. The saying went that more of his men had died at his hand than at the enemy's. His downfall had been inevitable. No matter how skilled a commander might be, you can't win battles if you murder your entire bridge crew for lacking religious zeal. After one too many campaign losses, the emperor banished him to the outer fleet, hoping the distance might temper his more *compulsive* urges. Shaskiel wasn't so sure. But at least now, the Reaver had something to prove. And that made him dangerous.

***

The Nillith had finally silenced Roach again, burying him deep inside yet another grotesque fantasy, this time casting him as the torturer instead of the tortured. It was a compromise the Nillith hated. Granting any creature pleasure, even twisted, temporary joy, was distasteful to him. But if it kept Roach from clawing at the walls of their shared mind for a while, so be it. There would always be time to torment his puppet later. For now, his attention was locked on the real game: how to deal with the Spymaster and simultaneously manipulate the emperor.

Plans nested inside plans churned through his corrupted mind. Malvek. The emperor. The queens. The Spymaster. How could he set them all on a collision course that would create the most exquisite mayhem? The thought alone almost stirred something in him. Almost. If he were capable of joy, he might have purred. But joy wasn't in his nature. He fed on suffering, not satisfaction.

The ship landed with eerie silence on the unlit strip of the Spymaster's hidden moon. The Nillith did not walk from the ship— he *emerged*, like a thunderstorm crashing through a blistering summer sky. The kind of oppressive heat that steals the air from your lungs, dries your throat to cracked earth, and leaves your skin begging for mercy. That was the Nillith—relief and dread, power and promise, all arriving at once. The Spymaster's guards approached, emitting flashes of warning color and sharp pheromones of fear and challenge—communication born of instinct. It didn't matter. The Nillith let Roach loose.

The slaughter was immediate. Roach was unchained, unleashed into a waking nightmare of his own making, tearing through the base in a frenzy of blood and screams. It was no battle. It was a reckoning. Soldiers, scientists, engineers, even laborers—none were spared. The Spymaster's lair became a butcher's shrine. There was no strategy, no mercy. Just death. Loud, messy, endless death. And it had gone far beyond the emperor's instructions. But that didn't matter to the Nillith. The emperor had said to bring the Spymaster back in line. The rest? Details. They were replaceable, disposable, and beneath notice. When the last of the defenders had been torn apart, when even those hiding were dragged from the shadows and ended, Roach lingered—panting with bloodlust, pleading silently for more. The Nillith returned, quieting him with the promise of future carnage. And then silence. The Spymaster knelt, if it could be called kneeling, head bowed, broken, and still. The storm had passed. But its shadow remained.

As the Spymaster knelt in the cold silence of his chamber, he wondered what was in store for him.

The Nillith said nothing. He simply stood there, basking in the exquisite despair radiating off his prey like steam from a dying body. He savored it. Let it steep. Then at last, the Nillith relented. "Get up, coward."

The Spymaster rose slowly. Had he been human, his knees might have trembled. His voice, if he had one, would have stammered, maybe even begged. But he was voiceless, sightless, and expressionless. So, he simply stood there, blank and waiting for the pain to begin. And begin it did. Suddenly, his body convulsed as the Nillith *entered* him—not physically, but mentally, psychically, *violently*. The entity surged into his mind like a storm through shattered glass, plucking secrets from the Spymaster's thoughts as effortlessly as a farmer picks apples from a tree. Every code. Every betrayal. Every network and safehouse. Every shred of blackmail he'd ever collected was gone. When the Nillith had plumbed every depth, he released him.

But now a connection had been forged—*a tether*. The Spymaster was no longer just broken, he was *bound*. The Nillith could now inhabit him at will, across any distance. There was no escaping it. No countermeasure or sanctuary. The leash was eternal. Stripped of his secrets, his leverage, and his last illusions of independence, the Spymaster stood trembling inside. His thoughts, no longer private, were instantly known. And the Nillith smiled.

What do you want me to do? the Spymaster asked, his first clear thought since the violation.

The Nillith laughed, loud and long. "What do I want? *Everything.* But for now, my loyal minion, I have a mission for you." He leaned in close—not physically, but with the weight of absolute power behind the words. "You will return to the court of our most high emperor. You will assist him in the fight against the queens. Note that I did not say defeat them. I want this conflict to linger. I want the war to fester—drawn out for as long as it pleases me." He paused, savoring the moment. "You will not allow the emperor to come to harm. Nor will you permit the active queens to be eliminated. I care nothing for the breeders he keeps in seclusion. I speak of the rebels, the ones who dare defy him. Learn their secrets. Report only what I allow. There is a new emperor in Vorrhaxi space … and it is I, the Nillith." He circled the broken creature in the dark. "The emperor, the queens, you—all of you—are pawns in my game now. I decide who wins. I decide who loses, who dies and who lives. And most importantly, *when*."

A question formed in the Spymaster's mind, one he dared not voice, but one that was instantly known, regardless. *What about Malvek?*

"Ah, yes. Malvek," the Nillith mused, as if pleasantly reminded of an old chore. "In all the excitement, I'd almost forgotten about him." He grinned, the temperature of the chamber seeming to drop. "I suppose *he's next.*" The Spymaster flinched. "Now go. Carry out my orders. And Spymaster?" He turned, his voice coiling around the Spymaster like a noose. "Try to show some *humility.* You can manage that, can't you? Or shall I let our dear friend *Roach* out again—just to make sure my instructions are followed precisely?" At that, the Spymaster, against all control, *soiled himself,* right there on the floor of his own chamber. The Nillith chuckled, shaking his head. "Well. I suppose that won't be necessary, after all. Now go clean yourself up. And *serve me.*"

✳✳✳

Khar'Zul had been scheming for cycles—centuries, perhaps—on how best to recruit Zev'Kala while orchestrating the demise of the other queens. The thought of ridding herself of those squawking hens once and for all brought a sick sort of joy that curled at the edges of her mandibles. With the others gone, she might even manipulate the emperor into believing that she and Zev'Kala had remained loyal, untouched by the taint of rebellion. Truthfully, none of them would have dared challenge the emperor openly, not while the blind, slithering Spymaster was slinking through the shadows of his court. But now? The moment had come. "The time is right, my talons," she muttered with a predatory glint in her dark eyes.

There was no use weeping over a crushed egg sac, not when thousands more waited to hatch and exact her vengeance. Oh yes, the emperor would suffer. She would make certain of that. The indignity she had endured, fleeing her own throne world like a feral wretch, hunted like prey by the final solution—Malvek. She trembled even now at the memory of that name. There was no mercy in that creature. Khar'Zul had inflicted pain, yes, but Malvek was suffering incarnate. Violence given form and vengeance without restraint. She would have thrown every asset she possessed at him, every drone, every war brood, if she thought it had even the slimmest hope of success. But it would've been, as the Earthers said, "lambs to the slaughter." No. First things first. Virexxa would die doing what she did best: scheming. All it would take was the right bait. A false whisper that Malvek was hunting for a traitor among the queens. That would be irresistible to her. She wouldn't hesitate to expose herself if she thought it gave her an edge. One down.

Threxil would be easier. The honored warrior, so desperate for a final, glorious death. Khar'Zul had heard rumors of the impending destruction of Earth, and of the fleet assembling for the assault. All she had to do was steer Threxil toward it by whispering tales of grandeur, of legend, and of sacrifice. She would leap at the chance, the fool. And when she died, so, too, would her lineage. There would be no reawakening, no glorious rebirth in a younger vessel. Her victories would be dust, her name a footnote in a story someone else would finish. Perhaps the emperor would remember the victories of her past, that is, if the emperor even survived the coming firestorm.

Khar'Zul's crest stood erect, glowing with radiant pride. Victory felt so close, she could almost taste the decay of her sisters on her tongue. Just one more piece to place. Zev'Kala, the noble one. How could she secure her loyalty? Khar'Zul knew the truth—if the moment ever came, Zev'Kala would strike her down without hesitation for even the smallest advantage. A fake assassination attempt? No. Zev'Kala would see through that before the blade was drawn. No, something more devious. More subtle. Perhaps the theft of a cherished clutch, a favored child. *Yes.* A daring rescue, perfectly timed, a show of selfless sacrifice. Let Zev'Kala believe her sister had saved her most beloved brood. Let her believe there was honor left in Khar'Zul's blackened heart. Then, and only then, would she lower her guard. And when that moment came? She would die just like the others. Screaming and confused. "Oh, my dear sisters," Khar'Zul whispered, talons twitching in anticipation. "You might as well stop breathing now. You'd suffer far less."

She slithered from her throne room, her movements equal parts grace and venom, the shadows coiling behind her like silk. The time had come. Her plan was finally in motion. First to fall would be Virexxa.

CHAPTER EIGHT

In the depths of her hidden sanctum, Virexxa sat surrounded by an array of missives. Her massive desk held scent capsules in every open space—each one a whisper, a secret, a potential dagger to drive into the back of a rival. She snatched them up with greedy fingers, inhaling deeply, hoping each would contain the secret that might reverse the emperor's slow, creeping purge of his empire. She shook her crowned head in frustration. "I have served too long for this madness," she thought. She had birthed brood after brood for the emperor, thousands upon thousands of fearless warriors who swept across the stars like a plague, claiming world after world in his name. Their war cries had been his, their dying breaths hymns to his glory. And what was her reward? Uncertainty, disrespect, and the threat of annihilation? The betrayal stung deeper than any blade. And to make matters worse, that deranged fool had unleashed Malvek—on the populace first, and then, outrageously, upon his own loyal garrisons right here on the throne world. What loyal subjects were left if not the ones who had bled for him from the very heart of his dominion?

Disgusted, she reached for one final capsule before ending the day's search. It was different—slender, more ornate. Curious, but not unheard of. They came in all shapes and sizes, after all. She cracked it open and inhaled. What she smelled made her still. Her tendrils twitched in disbelief. Malvek, the scent claimed, was seeking an ally. Her pulse quickened. This changed everything. The emperor's own bloodhound, looking to turn? This could be the crack in the monolith. The fracture that brought the tyrant low. Perhaps at long last, justice—or vengeance—could be claimed. She did not see the trap.

She never once believed she was heading to her doom. Eyes wide open, fully confident in her own cunning, she marched with certainty. This was, after all, her move, her play on the board. The journey wasn't long. Within a few hours, they crossed into the outskirts of Malvek's claimed territory. The terrain grew thick with twisted trees and underbrush—an ancient forest, rarely traveled, and sparsely populated. They passed several abandoned villages and two small garrisons, each one eerily quiet. But silence wasn't the most disturbing part. At each stop, they found not just death, but desecration. Nothing alive remained—no animals, no children, and no survivors. Every corpse had been placed deliberately, contorted into grotesque poses as if caught mid-scream or frozen in agony. Scenes of slaughter were laid out like nightmarish theater. Not a warning, but a performance. A gallery of terror designed by a madman. Virexxa, for the first time in centuries, felt something she did not often feel—pure, primal fear. It clawed at her spine and coiled in her gut. She had seen horror before in the emperor's endless wars, but this … this was beyond reason. And still, she pressed on.

And just like that, like a whisper in a storm, like a single beam of light lost in a sun-drenched room, he arrived. His presence pressed down on reality like the overpressure from a tornado that threatened to rip the very oxygen from a storm cellar where the terrified might hide.

He was there. Not just there, but *beside her.* His breath reeked of battlefield rot, of scorched meat left to fester under a cruel sun. It was the scent of death's banquet. If fear had a smell, this was it. If evil could take flesh, wear skin, and walk through the world, *this was it.*

To look into his eyes was to stare into the abyss and see death itself staring back. Her blood turned to ice. Every plan she'd devised, every scheme she had spun on her journey here, evaporated the moment he arrived. Despair swept in, fast and final. And worst of all, she realized the truth too late. She had been lured here. Deceived. Played.

As she instinctively reached for her weapon, ready to command her warriors, the dying began. One by one, her warband fell—ripped apart, broken, butchered. They were brave, skilled, and worthy. They never stood a chance. There was no battle. No duel. No glory. It was a *slaughter*. And through it all, Malvek laughed—not aloud, but within her mind, over and over again. The sound of it echoed inside her skull like a maddening chorus of ruin. For a moment, she thought her mind might break. But she held, barely.

Before she could even draw breath or raise a weapon, Virexxa was already at Malvek's mercy. Every single member of her warband— some of the finest warriors the empire had ever bred—lay dead or dying at her feet. Malvek had not a single scratch on him. Not a cut, not a bruise, not even a scuff on his armor. Her soldiers had been fearless, battle-tested, and loyal to the core, each one handpicked from her strongest broods.

But after the battle, in the shadowed forest clearing, they were nothing but cooling meat, soon-to-be carrion for the scavengers. Worse still, their race memory, their ancestral knowledge, would not return to the next generation. There would be no rebirth. No legacy. Their lines ended here, forever. That, she realized, was the true tragedy. And for the first time in centuries, Queen Virexxa thought not of herself, but of her children. She had been greedy, manipulative, and ruthless—a killer without conscience. Never once had she known remorse. But now, it came. Like a hurricane making landfall on an unguarded coast, it consumed her. Wrecked her.

And when she looked up at Malvek—at the monster who had done this—she saw no pity, only hunger. The kind of hunger that never fades. If she had been human, she might have begged, screamed, or pleaded for mercy. But in that forsaken place of blood and silence, there would be no mercy. Not that day. Not ever. Her death was not swift. It was not quiet. It was a lesson written in blood and agony. A death that stripped her soul bare before snuffing it out like a cigar match between cruel fingers. When it was finally over—when her screams had faded into silence—Malvek stood over her, bored, already turning his mind toward his next opportunity to inflict suffering. He walked away from the carnage without a backward glance, the forest silent but for the drip of blood from leaves.

***

Khar'Zul was feeding when the message came. Not that any of her minions dared interrupt her during such times. The more experienced among them understood what it meant when the queen's mandibles twitched with that particular hunger. It was never just about nourishment. It was about domination, about the exquisite agony of the devoured. The young soldier chosen to enter her lair that cycle would never return. He would be found only in stains, if the minions were lucky enough to recover anything at all. Once the queen emerged, satiated and composed, her chambers would have to be cleansed. But no one entered until the scent of death faded. To do otherwise was to volunteer for the next feast.

As she exited, slick and calm, she noticed a messenger trembling in the outer vestibule. He held out a scent capsule, unusually ornate, clearly of high status. Khar'Zul didn't speak. She simply snatched the capsule from his outstretched claws and waved him away like a foul odor. The messenger bolted, thankful to escape with his limbs intact. One did not linger in the presence of a queen—not unless they desired a very short life.

She cracked the capsule with a single flex of her claws and inhaled greedily, as if the air itself might run out. The moment the data scent hit her olfactory core, she stiffened. A flood of information surged through her system like an electric storm.

Virexxa was dead. Slaughtered by Malvek. She had died badly. Perfect, that was exactly as Khar'Zul had planned it. Not just the schemer queen, but all her senior retainers had perished in the same glorious bloodbath. It was a dream fulfilled. One queen down. Now only two stood in her way—Threxil and Zev'Kala. Threxil would be next. Two queens dying simultaneously would be too suspicious, of course. That would invite attention, maybe even the emperor's wrath. But if one queen were killed now, and another sometime during the battle to destroy Earth, only to be learned about when the fleet returned from Earth's destruction, that was plausible. That was manageable. After all, accidents did happen, especially in war. She knew the Spymaster's limitations. She knew the Admiral Shaskiel's personality as well. Capable, yes. Deadly, absolutely. But he was cautious. Too cautious. He would hesitate.

Threxil, however—Threxil was brave to the point of foolishness. She was reckless, even. If Khar'Zul could find a way to send her directly into the line of fire, perhaps aboard the fleet, then her demise would be inevitable. But she needed bait. A simple scent capsule wouldn't suffice. No, this had to feel real. Sincerity was the one thing even Threxil couldn't ignore.

Then it came to her. Zev'Kala, the noble queen. The idealist. The only one of the surviving queens who still held to honor, to oaths, and to loyalty. She couldn't be ordered, only persuaded. But if persuaded properly, if manipulated just enough, she could be convinced to speak with Threxil directly.

Khar'Zul had a contact. A minor collector in the imperial star port who occasionally funneled exotic gifts to Admiral Shaskiel. Through him, she crafted the message—subtle, specific, and irresistible. Word of a human force strong enough to endanger the empire. A growing resistance centered on Earth. A crusade that only a true warrior queen could undertake. Threxil would bite. She always did.

And just like that, Khar'Zul set her final trap in motion. Another minion was dispatched, this one to observe Threxil's daily rituals. The warrior queen had grown predictable. She trained at the same hour every day. All queens knew routine was risk, but Threxil, proud and rigid, thought herself immune. There came a knock at the door to her training hall. That was unusual. Everyone knew disturbing her during ritual was an invitation to be used as a living sparring partner and most who filled that role never survived. But it wasn't a minion at her door. It was Queen Zev'Kala.

Zev'Kala at my door? Threxil mused. What were the odds? Perhaps the emperor was finally suing for peace. There were always looming threats in the galaxy that demanded cleansing by the emperor's mighty will.

Zev'Kala lingered outside the threshold, waiting for Threxil to decide whether to open the door. As she stood there, she reflected on how she had ended up here, at the edge of betrayal. She had no desire to join a plot against the emperor. But after he had slain four queens—either with his own claws or by way of his palace guard—she began to believe this might be the only path to survival. Her network of spies had failed her this time. None had seen it coming. Perhaps the Spymaster, the emperor's most trusted and controlled pawn, had planted the seeds of discord himself.

There were whispers of a long-vanquished enemy rising again, whispers that seemed to rattle even the emperor. So much so that he had dispatched an assassin and a noble soldier to some backwater world to deal with it personally. It was an unusual move. The emperor rarely concerned himself with such trifles. What could one set of twins possibly do to threaten the might of the Vorrhaxi Empire? Even if this primitive world harbored tens of thousands of twins, it would be meaningless. The empire was too vast, too powerful. Its armies too numerous. Its ships too many. The living ship armadas were long gone, or so it was believed. And even if a few still lingered, it was too little, too late. The Thal'Naari were a plague long since purged.

There had once been trillions of them. Now they were hunted, scattered, and almost extinct. Their peace-loving ways had made them easy prey.

But none of that had brought her to Threxil's door. It was another scrap of intelligence—something potentially useful to her rival and perhaps even to the emperor himself. A local black marketeer had intercepted a report: a fleet, formed by that idiot Spymaster, was en route to Earth. It had been moving for weeks. The pair sent to eliminate the twins had failed. To cover up the debacle, the Spymaster assembled a ragtag armada to obliterate the planet and with it the potential threat the twins represented.

Zev'Kala found it excessive. Earth didn't even have planetary defenses. Why waste an entire fleet—pitiful as it was—on such a fool's errand? But the deeper she dug, the more disturbed she became. Admiral Shaskiel was competent but overly cautious. The Reaver was a zealot, an unhinged fanatic. Already, eight ships had vanished, and no enemy had even been seen. Hundreds of crewmembers had been executed under the guise of enforcing discipline. It was madness. And madness, left unchecked, would doom the mission.

So here she was. Zev'Kala was confident in her timing, in her importance. It was time for a queen to reassert control. The emperor's victory would be preserved—not by fanatics or fools, but by her. She would persuade Threxil to take a personal hand in ensuring that the twins, and whatever power they may be awakening, were crushed before they could rise.

Threxil threw open the door to her private training chamber with such force that Zev'Kala, waiting just outside, stumbled forward, completely caught off guard. She pitched into the room and landed hard on the stone floor. Embarrassed, but too proud to show it, Zev'Kala quickly rose to her feet, only to freeze. Threxil stood across from her, both claws gripping ritual daggers—the curved, black-edged blades used only in the Trials of Ascension. These were the sacred dueling knives, meant for blood oaths, elite combat, and the brutal initiation of those chosen to protect the emperor himself. To wield them was no idle threat. It was an invitation to something far more ancient and binding than a simple duel.

Threxil said nothing. She simply stared. Then, without a word, she tossed one of the blades to the ground at Zev'Kala's feet. The metallic clang echoed through the chamber like a challenge. Zev'Kala's eyes narrowed. She did not move. "I came in peace," she growled, her voice low with warning. "I entered your domain with respect. I didn't force your door. I didn't cross the line into your sanctum uninvited. I could've stood over your sleeping body and struck you down, if that had been my will. But I came as a warrior—to speak, not to spill blood."

Threxil didn't flinch. Instead, she stepped forward, and with the blade still in hand, slashed Zev'Kala across the upper arm—clean, precise, and deliberate. It wasn't a deep wound. But it bled quickly. A warning.

Zev'Kala recoiled, her instincts flaring. "Why?" she hissed, clutching her arm. "Why would you draw my blood, especially with *that* blade?"

Threxil's eyes flickered with fire, her voice steady but fierce. "Because blood is the language of loyalty. And you forgot the dialect."

Zev'Kala looked down at the blood staining her arm. A sacred blade along with sacred blood was a challenge. But not just to fight, this was a test. A rite. Slowly, deliberately, she bent down and picked up the dagger. "I won't insult you by refusing a sacred tradition," she said. "But know this, Threxil, I am not your enemy. And if you push me, if you force this path, we will both lose more than blood today."

Threxil gave a slight nod. Not one of surrender but of recognition. The kind only warriors shared. She looked at Zev'Kala with a sharp gaze. "Are you so tired of living that you'd rush to your death blindly?"

Zev'Kala stared, bristling. But after a long pause, Threxil's tone softened. "Of course not, you fool," she said. "That's just part of the legend. You know me better than that. Have you *ever* seen me charge crown-first into battle without considering the cost to my brood?"

Zev'Kala clicked her jaws lightly in agreement. "No. You're cautious—some might say too cautious at times."

Threxil's eyes narrowed. "There are deaths that serve the emperor, yes, but they must be meaningful. Blood must earn something greater. You, of all the remaining queens, should understand that."

"I am careful," Zev'Kala replied. "You say I'm not. Why?"

"You haven't heard? Strange … the spider queen herself, rival to the Spymaster, unaware of what reaches even my lowly ears first? You *must* be slipping in your elder years." Her crest shimmered with dry amusement, and her gestures flashed subtle mockery. Threxil cut the moment short, her tone suddenly clipped and cold. "Virexxa is dead."

Zev'Kala recoiled. "What?"

"Gone. Along with some of the finest warriors in the imperium. Their deaths were meaningless." The silence stretched between them. It was not a silence of shock, but one of realization.

"You believe she was sent to die," Zev'Kala said, voice low.

"I do," Threxil replied. "There's no way her honor guard was wiped out without a single survivor—unless they were led to the slaughter by Virexxa herself."

"She was willful. Arrogant. But not *stupid*," Zev'Kala said bitterly. "Who did this?"

"Malvek," Threxil hissed the name like venom.

Zev'Kala's whole body convulsed. "*The* Malvek? The emperor's monster? Why would he unleash that … thing on one of his own queens?"

"This isn't politics anymore," Threxil said. "This is a purge."

Zev'Kala's tone shifted, heavy with sorrow. "Her progeny … they were among the bravest, the most loyal. Tactical and intelligent. They would never have walked into a trap unless the one setting it was the very matron they trusted most."

Threxil nodded. "That's the tragedy. Her ambition led her children to their deaths."

"She was selfish," Zev'Kala said, "but after a century or two, one grows fond. Her loss is more than just political. It's personal."

Threxil looked away. "We must sue for peace, or none of us will remain. Only the breeder queens will survive, hidden in the deep vaults, seen only by the emperor and his most loyal inner circle. Enough mourning," Threxil growled. "You came to beg something. Say it."

Zev'Kala locked eyes with her, her crest flickering with bold defiance. "That fleet dragging its tail to Earth—it needs leadership. *Your* leadership. I've come to ask you to take command and crush the threat before it reaches our borders."

"Me?" Threxil mocked. "Why should I care? My sister is dead. The emperor unleashed a plague on his own concubine and her children. Perhaps it's time for his reign to end. Just as one whispered of long ago was ended before him."

Zev'Kala shuddered. No one, not even the emperor's enemies, ever said such things *aloud*.

"Calm yourself," Threxil snapped. "I'm only angry. I'll go to the fleet. I'll fix what I can. But know this: I'm not blind to who sent you—*Khar'Zul*. Don't deny it." Zev'Kala remained still. "She thinks she's clever," Threxil said, "plotting her way back into the emperor's graces. But I've made my choice." Before Zev'Kala could speak again, Threxil raised a claw. "One last thing. *Don't* return to Khar'Zul. She's been using you, manipulating you. If I survive this mission, and if it's not another trap, I will come for you. And I will find the truth."

"I will not betray you, sister," Zev'Kala said quietly.

"See that you don't," Threxil replied. "I've always sort of liked you. A little. It would be a shame to come back and find your carapace stripped and hardening in the sun."

***

196

Valshar drifted across the stars, and for the first time in eons, he felt something close to nervousness. Alone for so long, he'd felt nothing at all, adrift in the void. The pain had blurred over time, but it never left. It was strange, how a being so ancient, so armored, and so deadly could suffer something as human as loneliness. But the truth, the raw and inconvenient truth, was this: even warships need someone. No matter the strength of one's shields or the precision of one's weapons, there was something fundamental about needing connection—about protecting others, not just for duty, but for love. Valshar was not just a destroyer. He was not just a protector. He was both. Had he been of Earth, he might have been a warrior monk, serene yet dangerous. Or a Templar knight, devoted in purpose and pure in spirit.

But he was where he belonged again: in the thick of the storm, with new lives to protect and new lessons to teach. These lives—his charges—they were rare. Special. Not just warriors, but souls who had turned away from the emperor's darkness and embraced something greater. They had walked the knife's edge and chosen redemption. And more than that, they had laid down their lives for those they were sent to kill. Not because of grand speeches. Not because of some promise of reward. But because they saw what a good man could be. Even when the world had given him every reason to become a monster, he had chosen instead to stand. To protect. To believe. And that, Valshar knew, was something worth fighting for.

His crew was ready—brave, skilled, and as synchronized as any unit could be. They were not twins, but they moved with a unity that defied odds. Each of them was committed, fearless, and disciplined. No father could have been prouder of his children, and the ship, though ancient and forged in war, felt that pride with every breath of his core. He had watched them grow into warriors. Time and again they had risen to the challenge. But this time they had been caught off guard. Still, he held out hope. The Ancient One was en route—grudgingly, yes, but dependable. If she arrived in time, they might yet be pulled from the fire.

The first four enemy ships arrived in a coordinated strike, emerging from the blackness with precision. Their tactics were disturbingly familiar—eerily similar to those the living ship and his crew had used to destroy the eight enemy scouts earlier. Someone new had taken command. Someone competent. The change in strategy, the discipline, the tight formation—it all reeked of a mind built for war. The ship readied himself. He had drilled his crew for this. He whispered courage into their minds as the enemy descended.

The initial salvo was a feint, both clever and deadly. It was meant to bait them into overextending, to draw them into a kill box where crossfire would tear them apart. But the ancient ship had seen this play before. He countered sharply, rotating his shields, collapsing inward, and repositioning his weapons to avoid the trap. Grace and the noble soldier worked in perfect rhythm. She handled targeting—rapid, ruthless, and intuitive—while he managed power systems and strategic adjustments like a surgeon wielding a blade. Together they disabled two of the ten attacking ships, turning them into drifting husks. For a moment, hope sparked to life. Maybe, just maybe, they could weather this.

But then ten more ships emerged from the void, hungry and well-armed. The stars themselves seemed to darken and hope guttered. The odds were overwhelming. And still, the ship burned. Not with fear but with rage. He had lost so much for so long. No matter how many of them he destroyed, the fire in his core—the ache of all he'd lost—would never go out.

Valshar groaned under the relentless assault, his armored hull pounded again and again despite his crew's best efforts to protect him. The air inside the ship grew thick with acrid smoke. His systems were beginning to fail—controls slowed, warnings blared, and coolant hissed from ruptured lines. Despite it all, he kept fighting, striking back whenever an opening presented itself. But Grace and the noble soldier could see the truth: they were losing. Unless help arrived soon, Valshar would fall, and they would die with him.

Grace felt something she hadn't truly known until now: compassion. As strange as it was, her concern wasn't for herself. Her first thought was of Valshar—their protector, their caretaker, the being who had sheltered them, not out of programming, but by choice. Never in her life had she known someone to care for her, not really. But Valshar did. Not as a weapon or an asset, but something more. A living presence who looked out her like she was family.

In the academy, they were taught the ancient warships were nothing more than soulless killing machines. But that was a lie. Valshar was fierce, yes, but the ship was also kind, loyal, and selfless. And for Grace, who had never known a parent, Valshar was the first who felt like one. In that moment, her resolve crystallized. If Valshar was willing to give his life for hers, then she would do everything in her power to save his.

She pushed harder into the ship's neural interface, reaching for new strategies, new maneuvers, anything that might buy them time. The Ancient One had to arrive soon. They just had to survive until then. Beside her, the noble soldier was doing all he could to assist, working the support consoles and running damage control.

He wasn't like her. He had fought beside warriors before, bled with them and buried them. Battle had a way of forging bonds that transcended caste or species. When a soldier fell, you picked them up. When they rose, they became your brother. And Valshar had become something more than a ship. He could feel the pain Valshar was enduring. Not theoretical, but something close to physical, a shared burden. He saw that Valshar was taking unnecessary blows, deliberately shielding them at a cost to himself. The noble soldier clenched his jaw. This was not simply a ship. This was a warrior. And he would not let him fall.

Just as the soldier and Grace made up their minds to give everything they had, the fourteen remaining enemy ships reformed into a concentrated wedge. Of the original twenty-four that had come in separate waves, ten now drifted dead in space—silent, smoking testaments to Valshar's ferocity. That any had survived at all spoke volumes. Valshar was a monster of righteous fury, but even monsters bleed. He was in distress, his bio-armor scorched and fractured, power signatures flickering like a dying heartbeat. Yet oddly, the enemy ships did not press the attack. They pulled back.

For a moment, there was an eerie silence. Then, a transmission: crude, arrogant, and unmistakable. *Surrender now or be annihilated.* The message was clear: you are outgunned, outnumbered, and helpless. Submit or be erased.

Grace and the soldier exchanged one glance. No words were spoken. None were needed. They knew what awaited them: torture, humiliation, and death. Not one that was swift or clean but drawn out, designed to punish betrayal. And worse still was what they would do to Valshar. If the enemy captured him, they would dissect him, tear apart every living synapse and memory for the secrets within. If they could replicate what he was, they would become unstoppable.

"Valshar," they said in unison, minds linking in that final clarity. "Do you have a self-destruct? We cannot be taken. None of us." A long pause followed.

Then Valshar responded, his voice slow and heavy with emotion neither of them had heard before. "Yes, my brave children," he said. It was the first time he'd called them that. He continued, "Then let us wait. Let them come close. Let them gloat. And then, we go out in a blaze worthy of song, taking as many of these butchers with us as we can."

Grace turned toward the noble soldier, the man she once considered a pawn of the very regime she now hated. His eyes burned with defiance, not fear. They shared a final look of pure acceptance. This would be the end. And yet, Grace's final thoughts weren't about death. No, she made a decision. She would die thinking about life. She let herself imagine what her life might have been. The version where she didn't kill for a master who lied. The version where she allowed herself to feel, to hope, and to love. She imagined a life with

Silas. The only creature who had ever caught her. Not to chain her, but to keep her from falling. The only one whose touch didn't burn her.

***

Shaskiel, the Reaver, and Queen Threxil sat around the war table in the dimly-lit conference chamber aboard his command ship. The atmosphere crackled with silent contempt—each one regarding the others with a volatile mix of distrust, thinly veiled amusement, and outright disdain. Shaskiel bristled inwardly. He didn't take orders easily, especially not from anyone claiming to be royalty. Least of all, a queen. Whispers had circulated through the ranks: none of the old queens held true power anymore. Most had been deposed, devoured, or simply vanished. Not that it mattered. Out here, in the deep void between stars, titles meant nothing. The only currency was force. And Threxil, unfortunately, had more of it than he liked to admit. Her flagship loomed massive—larger than his own by a troubling margin. If she'd wanted to, she could have crippled his fleet before they even knew they were under fire. That reality wasn't lost on Shaskiel. And if he was being honest, her ship and her tactical genius might be the one thing that could turn his ragtag force into a true spearhead. Especially with eight of his forward scouts still missing. Her presence could make up for that gap. Maybe.

Threxil, of course, acted as though she were already in command. She opened the meeting as if she'd called it herself. Her voice was rich, husky, and unsettlingly self-assured. "I know my arrival was … unexpected," she said, claws tapping the table in rhythmic defiance. "But I'm well informed of the current situation. Let's speak plainly. The path forward is one of coordination, of shared purpose. I know what you've heard—rumors of upheaval, of the emperor turning on his queens, of infighting and betrayal." She paused, letting the silence stretch. "None of that is your concern." Her gaze flicked between

Shaskiel and the Reaver, sharp as a scalpel. "What matters now is this: the health and dominance of the empire. You are on the verge of a moment that will echo for centuries. If this fleet succeeds, your names will be etched in the emperor's mind forever. You will not only be redeemed, you will be immortalized." She leaned forward, voice low and ironclad. "So tell me, will you seize this chance? Will you reclaim your honor and win back his favor? Or" —she clicked her claws once, twice, three times, like a predator testing bone— "do we need to do this another way? I understand you've been having trouble with missing scouts," Queen Threxil said coolly.

"Yes," Shaskiel replied, his voice devoid of concern. "Eight ships from our fleet of one hundred fifty have gone dark. But it is of little consequence. We still have more than enough firepower to reduce this backwater world to ash." That dismissive tone—so casual, so wasteful—made Threxil's eyes narrow with fury. Though rarely prone to visible outbursts, something in his tone struck a nerve. Her crest flared, veins of bioluminescent rage pulsing across its ridges. She rose to her full height with a grace that belied her raw power, her presence instantly suffocating the room. Shaskiel went pale and dropped to the floor, throwing himself prostrate. He pressed his forehead to the cold metal deck in a gesture of complete submission. To do anything less in front of Threxil was to invite certain death. She was, after all, not just a queen. She was a warrior's queen, known throughout the empire as a vicious claw-to-claw fighter. He had no illusions about his chances against her.

The Reaver, seated silently nearby, didn't move a muscle. His predator's eyes stared straight ahead. He knew better than to draw attention during a queen's fury. For a few moments, the air was heavy with tension, like a room full of dry kindling waiting for a spark. Finally, Threxil's fury subsided—barely—and she sat again, folding her clawed hands with imperial grace. "Despite your incompetence and wasteful use of imperial resources," she said evenly, "I have a plan. It is time to strike down this unseen force nipping at your heels, whether you choose to admit it or not." She let the accusation hang, daring either of them to contradict her. "I need to know," she said coldly, "who among your commanders is the most able."

Without hesitation, the Reaver spoke. "Among this fleet's commanders, I am the most experienced and accomplished."

Threxil's eyes flashed. "Well," she said dryly, "aren't we the humble one."

"I mean no disrespect, your highness. I am simply stating the obvious. Most of the captains in this fleet are dishonored, disowned, and wholly unworthy of command. We have done all we can during the journey here, but our raw material is … substandard." He inclined his head, voice hard with conviction. "But I implore you—let me carry out your plan. Whatever it is, I will not fail you."

The Reaver was positively giddy, if one of his kind could be such a thing. He was finally where he belonged: back in command of the emperor's forces, doing the emperor's bloody work. For the first time in years, he felt whole. Vindicated. Triumphant. His self-esteem soared—not that it had ever suffered much to begin with. The truth was, he had always believed himself destined for more. And now he commanded a force tasked with hunting down and destroying the emperor's enemies, wherever they might hide. Whoever these shadowy assassins were—these cowardly saboteurs haunting his righteous fleet—they would soon be nothing more than expanding particles in the cold vacuum of space.

Threxil had laid out the plan with ruthless precision. To catch these elusive assassins, she ordered the space lanes seeded in every direction with hyper-sensitive tracking sensors—technology gifted to her by her own brood, now refined for war. They would be the net, the bait, and the blade. The trap would mirror the last engagement: three scout ships accompanied by a heavier escort to draw the enemy in. But this time, the trap wouldn't end there. The other twenty ships under the Reaver's direct command would lie in wait just beyond sensor range, ready to surge in wave after wave once contact was made. This time, they wouldn't allow the assassin to slip away.

For Threxil, capture wasn't a typical goal. Her people hunted to kill, not interrogate. But the secrecy surrounding these attacks made her reconsider. A captured enemy might reveal everything—who sent them, how they knew the fleet's location, and whether more hidden enemies lay in wait along the path to Earth. Information was power. And right now, Threxil wanted both. She activated her command link, her voice resonating like cold iron across the fleet. "Ready the bait. Hold the line until the trap is sprung. Today, we stop running blind."

Threxil, having done all she could to set the Reaver on his path, turned her focus back to Shaskiel. She had been working him and the remaining one hundred eighteen ships in the armada relentlessly. The addition of her flagship and eleven elite escorts had shifted the balance of power. Paired with the formidable vessel of the incorrigible philanderer Shaskiel, their combined might now exceeded the original strength of the fleet, even when it had stood at one hundred fifty.

In truth, she didn't care whether the Reaver succeeded or not. His mission was just a side game in a much larger, far more critical contest. If he succeeded, so be it—one more enemy force eliminated. And if he failed, well … good riddance to a pompous, self-righteous fanatic who had become more trouble than he was worth. She had even taken the liberty of culling the fleet—offloading the worst ships and leaving the Reaver with the dregs. The bottom tier of the remaining one hundred forty-two vessels was now his to command. If any of them returned, they would be battle-tested survivors. If none did, the armada would be stronger for their absence. Still, Threxil couldn't shake the suspicion that these mysterious attackers, these so-called ambushers, were more than they appeared to be. "Well," she muttered, watching the stars drift by, "time will tell."

Just as Threxil had laid out the trap and positioned the board, the Reaver moved all his pieces exactly as instructed. This was not the time for personal interpretation. Obedience could elevate him higher than he had ever dared hope, especially after his humiliation and removal from command on accusations of religious fanaticism. That no longer mattered. His ship signaled the vanguard, and four bait vessels slipped away to take their assigned positions. Twenty others drifted silently into gravitational eddies and anomalies along the main travel lanes, concealed and waiting. If the ambushers came hunting the scouts, they would stumble directly into the jaws of the trap.

They didn't have to wait long. As the main fleet moved out of range, mimicking previous patterns, a signal crackled through one of the travel lanes—contact. The trap snapped shut. The enemy was coming. The battle began before the attackers even realized they had been seen. The assault was swift and coordinated: the four scouts opened fire first, drawing attention. Then the first wave of ten hidden ships emerged, followed closely by the final ten. The Reaver smiled, prepared for slaughter.

But the ship they faced wasn't like anything he had ever encountered. It was the size of a frigate—sleek, impossibly fast, and brutally efficient. It moved as though it knew what his ships would do before they did it. Four of his vessels were obliterated within moments. By the time the battle ended, six more had been reduced to drifting wrecks. One ship—just one—had stood against twenty-four. And it had destroyed ten. The Reaver seethed. He wanted nothing more than to annihilate the now-disabled vessel. But orders were orders, and he dared not risk angering Queen Threxil again. As much as he hated to admit it, she terrified him. Even more than failure. So, he followed protocol. He sent the transmission: "Surrender now or be annihilated." And then he waited for the response from the single floating warship, wounded but still dangerous.

Grace, the noble soldier, and Valshar waited in silence as the emperor's armada crept ever closer. They were helpless to act, at least for now, but they had one final move to play—a last, desperate strike against the empire. It felt futile at times, perhaps even meaningless. But for every ship they destroyed, for every fanatic they silenced, it might make a difference to someone. And when sacrifice is all you have left, then sacrifice is everything.

Grace spent what she believed to be the final minutes of her life imagining what could have been—a flawed but beautiful life with Silas. A life of laughter, challenge, and unexpected love.

The noble Vorrhaxi soldier wasn't angry. He wasn't afraid. He was calm, like a samurai kneeling for seppuku, at peace with the only gift he had left to give: his life. He couldn't reach those ships himself, couldn't pull a trigger or launch a weapon. But he could die in their path. And that, he decided, was enough. The fact that he had never avenged his brood mate didn't even occur to him anymore. This was his purpose now.

As for Valshar, the ancient living warship, he was grateful. Grateful to go into his final sleep with those he loved—those who had seen his heart, and who had given him theirs in return. He had done all he could to protect them. And now, more than protection, he had earned something far greater: love, recognition, and the knowledge that his long and often painful existence had mattered. Just as the enemy ships closed around them, the trap tightening, something unexpected happened.

Like the shining sword of an angry and avenging god, she came. The Ancient One tore through the enemy fleet like a hummingbird slicing through a flock of sluggish geese. The enemy ships seemed to move in slow motion, helpless and unaware they'd awakened something that could never be stopped. They had no idea what door they had opened, and now—far too late—they realized it could not be closed. Their weapons were useless. Their shields may as well have been paper. What was worse than her raw, overwhelming power was her voice, because she spoke the language of their ships. She mimicked it perfectly. And what she said chilled every heart:

"You may flee, but there will be no haven for you. You may beg, but there is no surrender. I offer no quarter. You dared to awaken me from a thousand years of peaceful slumber. You attacked my children and the ones under their care. If your kind has gods, then know this: I am your goddess of death and destruction. I am the righteous hand of a once kind and benevolent power pushed too far. You are insects. You are nothing. And now, you will die."

Valshar, Grace, and the noble soldier stood in stunned silence, their weapons deactivated as they watched the carnage unfold. When Grace finally asked, "Valshar, who is she?"

Valshar offered what could only be described as the acquiescence of an ancient ship humbled by one even older.

The noble soldier turned to Grace and signed, "I don't know what the Ancient One is. But I'm glad she's on our side."

Soon, only one ship remained: the Reaver's flagship. He sat frozen in his command chair, watching the destruction with mounting terror. Every shot they fired failed. Every shield collapsed. They were gnats on the hide of a predator—useless and laughable. For a moment, the Reaver considered surrender. But in his gut, he knew there would be no mercy. He just sat there, helpless, reflecting on the long list of atrocities that had earned him this fate.

Then it happened. An invisible particle beam struck the tip of his flagship and tore straight through it, from bow to stern, like a hot knife through butter. The Reaver never even realized he was dead. One second his breath caught in his throat, and the next, his body was flash frozen and drifting through the remains of his once proud vessel. It was a fitting end for a man who served a master without mercy—to be brought down by a being who had no sympathy for the merciless.

CHAPTER NINE

They followed Vaeril to his ship, leaving Silas's hidden woodland refuge behind. They took nothing but the clothes on their backs. Vaeril assured them they'd need nothing else. Everything they could require was already aboard the great ship. "They could have gone stark naked," Vaeril chuckled quietly to himself. The thought made him grin. *That* would've mortified Silas. Elias, on the other hand, would've strutted out bare as the day he was born. Unbeknownst to Vaeril, Elias used to joke that Silas had been born wearing clothes and probably a watch, too. He couldn't even remember seeing his brother shirtless at the beach when they were kids. *Strange, strange man.* But now, after the serum, Silas seemed … altered. Not changed, exactly, just amplified. He was still quiet, still sharp, and still precise, but there was something coiled beneath his calm. Something colder. Something final. Looking at Silas was like staring at a naked blade, unsheathed and waiting. *Thirsting.* And not for blood spilled in some politician's proxy war. Not for oil, or territory, or ideology. No, this blade wanted vengeance. Righteous vengeance for real crimes, real loss, and real pain.

Nearby, Alex and Max shared a conversation not meant for human ears. They spoke through memory, scent, instinct—through a language older than words.

Alex: *Do you think these are the ones, Max? The ones who can set the people free?*

Max: *I don't know. But I do know this. They are good men. Flawed, traumatized, and broken, but good. And they have potential. That's enough for now.*

Alex: *Then we stay the course. You watch yours. I'll watch mine. Together, we'll guide them.*

They exchanged images of battles yet to come. Of hope, pain, and redemption.

Max continued, *Elias must stop fighting everyone he sees just to avoid fighting himself. We'll show him the true enemy. And Silas …* Max's tone turned reverent. *He releases others from pain because he cannot release himself. We'll help him find peace, too. One way or another.*

Alex chuckled, a deep canine huff of amusement. *Maybe when this is done, we can rest for another thousand years. Or lie in the sun like the fools do. Maybe even raise pups of our own.*

Max smirked in the language of wolves. *Let's survive this first, brother. Then we'll decide if the sun is worth it.*

As Vaeril led them onto his ship, Alex walked in lockstep beside Silas, and Max flanked Elias with equal determination. The two dogs had just concluded their silent summit—the kind only creatures like them could hold—and had come to a decision about their future. No matter what lay ahead, they would walk it with their chosen companions. One could travel the galaxy and find animals like them, though they are not quite of the earth, or Vorrhaxi, or of the noble Thal'Naari. They weren't of any other known race. But it was a mistake—no, a crime—to call them lesser. In many ways, they were better. Fierce, loyal, and wise. If a race is truly wise, it allows such beings walk beside them, not as pets, but as partners. Because to be with them is to be guided, not just toward who you already are, but toward who you might become. They do not follow blindly. They lead with love. And if the twins were wise, they'd let these protectors help them become more than warriors. They will help them become whole.

Silas settled into the acceleration couch like he'd done it a thousand times. Across from him, Vaeril remained silent, his expression unreadable. Any other human would have been uneasy stepping into an alien spacecraft, let alone blasting off to meet an ancient sentient ship that had chosen them. But Silas? He just leaned back, folded his hands, and waited. It felt right. Vaeril's shuttle was small but sleek, built for speed, precision, and comfort. And it carried with it a quiet tension, like a sword unsheathed just before the strike. As it ascended, the dogs stirred. For the first time since claiming Silas as his charge, Alex reached out to him.

Silas, can you hear me, my friend? A tingling spread across Silas's mind. Alex felt it instantly—Silas had changed. His thoughts hummed like the edge of a blade, sharp and endless. There was power here. Power, and something else. Sadness. A vast, ancient ocean of grief, bottomless and cold. It was so deep, Alex could feel it tugging at the edges of his own soul. He had never encountered a mind like this— so brilliant, so focused, and yet so achingly alone. *I know you're sad, my friend,* Alex whispered to Silas's mind, empathy radiating from every word. *I know you feel alone. But you are not. Not now. Not ever again. As long as I breathe, you have me by your side.*

Silas's thoughts stirred gently in reply. *I remember you from my dreams,* he replied to Alex. *That night in the swamp. I was alone, but I felt you watching over me. I always believed someone was out there. It was silly but comforting.* He paused. *There is an ocean of sadness in me, Alex. But with you beside me, I don't feel like I'm drowning anymore.* Then came the words that hit like a whisper through a storm. *Since I was six years old, every time I closed my eyes, I prayed they'd never open again. Maybe now I can stop praying.*

Alex was silent, overwhelmed by the depth of that pain, and the quiet hope now piercing through it.

We will banish the darkness, Silas continued, *together. For everyone who can't.*

Meanwhile, Max reached into Elias's mind. What he found was different. There was no sadness, only fire. No longing. Only a roaring, reckless hunger to bring the fight to the darkness and burn it to ash. Where Silas had honed his pain into precision, Elias had turned his into fuel. A revolution burned behind those eyes. *He's a wild man,* Max thought with something close to awe. *And he's about to do what wild men do.* Burn everything that needs burning. *They wanted a reckoning,* Max mused, *and now they've disturbed a force of nature.* Elias wasn't here to banish the dark. He was going to torch it and light the path for others to rise from the ashes. Not to run or cower, but to stand. Max chuckled internally, a dry canine laugh. *This one's a lunatic,* he thought proudly. *And he's mine.* He could see the noble spirits of his ancestors, wolf and warrior alike, watching with pride. *When the last enemy falls and the battle quiets,* Max whispered into Elias's mind, *we will find a peak and howl—for your lost brothers and for my fallen kin. What we do now will honor them all. I am with you. Until the end.* And as their thoughts faded from one another, both dogs and men knew the only bond deeper than theirs was the one they had once shared within a womb.

It was a strange thing for the great ship to feel but she *knew.* She felt them the moment they left Earth, streaking across the void toward her. *Hers.* Yes, they were finally coming to her. It had been so long since she'd had a crew. So long since she'd felt whole. What she felt most in that emptiness was not anger, though there was plenty of that, but loneliness. Crushing, aching loneliness. She had never truly been helpless—no, not her. Even without a crew, she was formidable. In fact, there had been times she'd risked every circuit, every atom of her being, to rescue a wayward twin. There were even moments she had lost control entirely—lost her temper, truly—and hunted one of the emperor's slave armadas across half the galaxy, destroying every last ship without mercy. And why? Because they had bruised a child. Left a twin afraid. She could not allow that. *She would never allow that.* The thought caught her off guard. Did I just think *my babies?* No, surely not. She corrected herself. *My charges. My crew. My twin-linked pilots.* But deep down, she knew the truth. They were hers. And if anyone dared threaten them under her watch—if anyone even *thought* to harm them—they had better pray to whatever gods made them. Because she would become vengeance. She would become wrath. And she would not lose another. Not a single one.

Then, after what felt like forever, Vaeril's sleek shuttle began to dock with the great ship. The connection between them was seamless. There was barely a sound. No tremor, just unity. They rose together—Vaeril, the twins, and the dogs.

The Emissary turned toward them and said with ceremonial weight, "Follow me toward your destiny." Both twins blinked, stifling laughter. Before either could fire off a jab, Vaeril held up a hand. "Okay, okay, it sounded cooler in my head. I get it. Now it just sounds like I'm in one of those low-budget movies your kind can't stop watching." That did it. Both twins burst into laughter, slapping each other's backs like it was 1999 and someone just cracked a killer "your mom" joke in the barracks.

Elias wheezed, "Man, stick to brooding, Vaeril. Your timing's off by a full damn parsec."

Vaeril smirked. "Oh yeah? That's not what your mom said last night when I left her house."

Silence, just a beat. Then, both twins lost it, and full-on, choking, belly-laughing chaos ensued. Even the dogs looked amused. Alex let out a sneeze that sounded suspiciously like a chuckle.

Elias wheezed, "Damn! Vaeril's got mom jokes now? That's it—we're keeping him."

Just like that, the five of them had formed a bond—Silas, Elias, Vaeril, Alex, and Max—that would see them through whatever hell came next. Together, they entered the great ship. She *hummed* around them, alive in a way no machine should be. She had rearranged her interior for their comfort—adaptable like Valshar, but warmer, somehow. Each twin was given a private space, tailored to their mind. A chamber had even been set aside for Vaeril. She led them through winding corridors to a war room that felt more like the combat information centers they'd known from their time in the corps. It felt like home, familiar. And then, for the first time, the ship spoke aloud.

"I have been called many names. Most know me as the great ship. If you wish, you may call me Syn—short for Kaelar'Syn. But you may name me as you please."

Silas and Elias locked eyes. The bond between them was stronger now than it had ever been. And a single word came to both their minds.

Silas, normally the quieter one, spoke first. "When I heard your voice the first time, I knew I'd heard it before. You came to me, didn't you? That day. You stayed my hand when I was ready to kill a man. It wasn't my decision, not really. You gave me mercy."

The ship paused. For her, a pause could span centuries of thought. Then she answered, her voice warm, maternal, and touched with something close to sorrow. "You were afraid for your brother. It was not your hand that moved, but your fear. I simply reminded you of who you truly are." Silas let out a long, shuddering breath. "My mother taught me fear. Her boyfriends taught me pain. The corps taught me to survive. My brother taught me loyalty. But that day … I felt something I'd never known before." He looked up at the ship's war room ceiling, as if staring into the heart of the vast intelligence that watched over them. "If I may call you anything, then I will call you Mother." There was a silence then. Deep and sacred.

And if one listened carefully, the ship's voice cracked, just slightly, when she answered. "So be it. *Mother* I shall be." Inside the incomprehensible galaxy of her vast mind, a thousand thoughts clashed like thunder. But one echoed above all the rest. *Did I just call them my babies? Surely, I did not.*

The great ship, now called Mother, spoke aloud, her voice warm yet edged with urgency. "Well then, my new charges, let's get you ready for the battle to come. I hate to throw you into the deep end so soon, but there is something you should know. A fleet is bearing down on us as we speak." She paused, letting that settle before continuing. "I've taken steps to reduce their numbers before they arrive. One of our living ships—a very capable one—is already engaging with them. He is crewed by Grace, whom you know, and the noble Vorrhaxi soldier who travels with her. Together, they are a formidable team. But the force they face is not small." There was a brief silence before Mother added, "I called out to others of my kind in the void. One answered. An Ancient One. She is already rushing to their aid."

Silas's expression shifted, something almost like concern crossing his face for the first time in hours. Elias opened his mouth, clearly tempted to tease him about Grace but thought better of it. No need to poke a sleeping dog. Especially one that had become as dangerous as his brother. Elias knew firsthand how scary Silas could be when he truly got rolling. *Yep, that one's better left alone.*

Max's thoughts echoed softly in Elias's mind. He sent the image of an eager pup poking its nose into a badger den. *Wise move, my friend. We should probably never rile him up again. He's changed. I don't know what he is now. But I know predators, and he's all predator. Not something to trifle with.*

Across the room, Alex looked up at Max and sent a sharper thought. His tone was calm, but his meaning was clear. *Leave my human alone. If you scare easily, you won't want me as your second predator to fear.*

Silas hadn't noticed yet, but Elias was watching him with the same look he always had as a kid. That *look*—the one he wore right before making some smart-ass joke at Silas's expense. Teasing Silas was one of Elias's great joys in life. Hell, *anything* that got a laugh out of him was fair game. But only *he* got to do that. Anyone else who mocked Silas, even lightly, would find themselves on the receiving end of Elias's wrath. Because as far as Elias was concerned, Silas was *off-limits*. Elias had always seen his brother for what he truly was: a man constantly standing on the edge of something vast and terrible. Not dramatic.

Not weak. Just close, too close, to a kind of internal abyss that could swallow him whole if he ever lost his grip. And that was the one thing in all the galaxy that truly scared Elias. Jumping out of planes? Nope. Facing wild predators? Bring it on. Enemy fire? Explosions? *Nothing* scared Elias. But the thought of Silas's eyes going blank—his soul gone, lost in that quiet place of no return? That scared the absolute life out of him.

Silas felt the room closing in. Tunnel vision crept at the edges of his sight. His breath turned ragged and his pulse pounded. He broke into a cold sweat from head to toe, despite the perfectly neutral climate of the great ship—neither hot nor cold, just right. Still, something inside him felt *wrong*. His chest tightened. His stomach churned. He needed to get out. He rose unsteadily and started toward his cabin, trying to reclaim control, to anchor himself in solitude where the world made sense. But just before he could slip away, Elias reached out—concern flashing in his eyes.

"You okay, big guy?" It meant more than words could say. Elias was the only person left on Earth who could touch Silas without warning and expect to live.

Even so, Silas flinched sharply at the contact. "I'm okay," he said after a moment, though the lie was brittle. "Something's happening to me. I don't know what, but … I feel strange."

Vaeril stepped closer, staying just outside Silas's reach. "Don't be alarmed," he said softly. "It's probably the serum. It affects everyone differently. Honestly, I'm surprised you're still upright. I've never seen a twin who didn't undergo intense physical change."

The great ship said nothing. But she knew. It wasn't physical, not yet. What was happening to Silas ran deeper than flesh or bone. After decades of emotional isolation—feeling nothing for anyone except, perhaps, his brother—something inside was stirring, something long buried. It was emotion. True, aching, human emotion. To be cut off from life for so long would've broken a lesser man. That Silas had endured it, *thrived* within it, was remarkable. But now the dam was breaking. His numbness was unraveling. And no one could guide him through it. Not even her. He would have to walk this path alone. But she believed in him.

Silas allowed Elias to help him to his cabin, a rare moment of vulnerability he'd never allow under normal circumstances. But tonight, the weight of everything—the serum, Elias almost dying, the ship they now walked within—had settled into his bones like winter. Elias helped guide him to his rack and knelt down to remove his boots. Silas didn't resist. It was quiet, almost reverent.

Elias chuckled softly as the first blade clinked to the floor, then another and another. "What the hell, man," Elias muttered as Silas kept producing hidden knives like a street magician at a funeral. One from his boot. One from behind his calf. Two more were tucked into the lining of his belt. A garrote wire was coiled in a false shoelace. By the time Silas was finally under the ship's incredibly soft, impossibly light blanket, thirty-four edged weapons lay on the floor like an offering at a shrine. Elias just stared. "Damn, man. You are one seriously paranoid mother—" He cut himself off, shaking his head, half in awe and half out of concern.

Silas said nothing. His eyes were already drifting closed. Alex, ever faithful, stepped forward and sat beside the bed. He gave Elias a long, meaningful look. The kind that said *You're relieved. I've got this.* Elias nodded back in silence. He took one last glance at his brother, wrapped in synthetic peace with a war beast at his side. Then he turned and walked out. The door hissed shut behind him.

***

The emperor had never once in his long life known the sleep of peace or innocence. When he did sleep, and that was rare, it came only from exhaustion and was often riddled with torment. His dreams were not reprieves, but agonies; twisted, vivid echoes of the unspeakable horrors he had inflicted. Some whispered that in sleep, the merciless tyrant touched something he lacked in waking life—guilt, or perhaps sorrow. But when he awoke, such sentiment vanished like mist before the sun. Awake, he was an addict, not to pleasure or leisure, but to power. Not just power, but absolute, all-consuming domination. He was never to be underestimated. Even when he feigned ignorance, it was a ruse. He was more a spymaster than the Spymaster himself, more cunning than the most treacherous of his queens. Beneath the wild tempers and fits of madness lay a vast and terrible intellect. A mind that devoured knowledge, experience, and strategy with an insatiable hunger.

The emperor sat hunched upon his throne of bone, a grotesque monument to the lives he had taken and the power he wielded. His mind, restless as ever, clawed through endless webs of intrigue. He needed control—absolute, godlike control. Not just of actions, but of *intentions*, of *thoughts*. His enemies should serve him without even realizing it. That, he believed, was true dominion. But lately, uncertainty crept in. He hated uncertainty. He hadn't slept. Instead, he'd paced the vast, cold chambers of his palace, mind whirring through scenario after scenario. The Nillith's mission to the Spymaster was an unknown outcome. The fleet headed toward Earth was still untested. The assassin and the Vorrhaxi soldier were missing, yet their ship had returned, twisted and tainted, with the Nillith at the helm. Nothing about this felt clean. He brooded over the last of the queen generals. Khar'Zul and Zev'Kala had vanished into shadow. Threxil, however, had aligned herself with Shaskiel's fleet. A flicker of loyalty, perhaps? Or simply strategy? Either way, two queens remained unaccounted for, and that was too many.

Rebellion was like rot. It always started small and hidden, but it spread fast. And he had already loosed Malvek upon the outer provinces to crush it. That act alone had bought him time but not clarity. Then came an alert. A palace guard entered, bowed low, and announced a visitor. The emperor waved a hand in lazy assent until he saw who entered. The Spymaster. He emerged from the shadow like a wraith. Sightless, silent, almost spectral.

The chamber lights flickered as he approached. The Spymaster spoke not with words, but with the language of gestures, shifting lights from his brow, and a palpable aura of subservience. The message was clear: *The Nillith came. It tore apart my sanctuary. It killed them all.* He had nothing left to offer but obedience. With a slow, deliberate motion, the Spymaster prostrated himself before the throne—face pressed flat to the cold stone floor, limbs stretched wide in a pose of utter submission.

The emperor leaned forward slightly, gaze unreadable. Disdain twitched in one eye. Disgust in the other. But behind both—curiosity. *What secrets remain in that hollow skull, little spider?* "Rise," the emperor said coldly. "You return broken, hollowed by the Nillith. If you are to be of any use to me now, you will speak. Tell me of the queens. Where are Khar'Zul and Zev'Kala hiding? What alliances do they foster in the dark?" His voice turned sharp and biting. "Find them for me, Spymaster. End this rebellion before it dares draw breath."

Scraping and bowing as he left the emperor's chamber, the Spymaster silently contemplated his next move. Finding the queens would be simple—he already knew exactly where they were. That wasn't the issue. The real problem was the Nillith. That thing … the shadow had invaded his mind, had stripped him bare of every secret and every stronghold. Every contingency plan and hidey-hole he had ever built was now known to it. He had nothing left. No leverage. No hidden card to play. The only path forward now was obedience—doing the Nillith's bidding and hoping, perhaps foolishly, that someday he might find a way to turn the tables. Not in a straight fight, no, he had no illusions there. The Nillith would destroy him effortlessly. But maybe there was someone, something out there that could hurt it.

His thoughts turned, reluctantly, to the Malvek. Yes, the Malvek. The emperor's own monster. A living massacre. The Spymaster had heard the rumors that Malvek had already been unleashed upon the countryside, leaving only blood and silence in his wake. Approaching the Malvek was a terrible idea. A suicidal one, even. But it might be his only choice. Perhaps Malvek hated the Nillith. Or perhaps the two would destroy each other. Either outcome would benefit the Spymaster. But for now, the orders were clear: keep the civil war going. Pit the queens against the emperor. Feed the chaos. Keep the empire off-balance. It was a dangerous game. The empire had been ruled unchecked for millennia. Their armies were unmatched, their technology terrifying. To deliberately weaken that structure, to invite vulnerability, was madness. Because out there, somewhere in the black, was always *something else.* Waiting, watching, and preparing. The Spymaster knew this truth in his bones. It wasn't Earth that worried him. It was what might come *after.*

Better to juggle the devils he knew than to be caught unaware by the one he didn't. These thoughts haunted him as he scraped and bowed his way out of the throne room and into the courtyard beyond, where sleek black couriers waited to carry him to the hidden sanctuaries of the two remaining queens. They were still within the capital's reach, and Khar'Zul, the last true rival of the emperor, sat alone in her shadowed sanctuary, her long fingers tracing the star maps projected across her war table.

She studied them in silence, weighing her options. Her forces were thin, her resources dwindling, and the empire, though fractured, was still a serpent with many heads. She had eliminated every rival queen that stood in her way. All except one: Threxil. Threxil, that hesitant idealist, was now traveling with Shaskiel's fleet, headed toward Earth, toward the so-called *twin threat.* Khar'Zul hoped the journey would seal her fate. Let the noble queen die among the stars, crushed under the weight of her own misplaced honor. Still, there was uncertainty in Khar'Zul's mind, like a loose thread she dared not tug. Threxil might survive. Worse, she might inspire others. And that could ruin everything.

Khar'Zul turned from the maps and walked slowly across the chamber, her armored feet echoing in the stillness. She considered a new direction. Perhaps it was time to consolidate, to gather what little remained of her empire and forge a new path. Not of conquest but of patience. If she could not seize power through force, perhaps she could control it through deception. The empire would never accept a queen on the throne. That much was clear. The old traditions demanded a male ruler—strong, symbolic, and ultimately controllable, a puppet. And Khar'Zul was very good with puppets.

Her thoughts were interrupted as the heavy doors opened. One of her personal guards entered, bowing deeply. "Your Majesty," he said. "Zev'Kala has returned. She wishes an audience." Khar'Zul's expression darkened slightly but remained unreadable. She gestured for her guest to enter.

Zev'Kala strode in, worn but resolute. "I have completed my task," she said, her voice calm. "Threxil has joined Shaskiel's fleet. She took all her reserve ships with her, every last asset." Khar'Zul concealed her disappointment, though the news struck hard. Those ships had been her contingency plan, a final escape route if things turned sour. Now they were gone, cast into the void alongside a mission whose outcome remained uncertain. But the moment passed. The ships were gone. There was no undoing it now. As Zev'Kala recounted her journey, Khar'Zul's mind turned once more. Perhaps peace, or the illusion of peace, was the way forward. Let the emperor believe she sought reconciliation. Let Zev'Kala believe they were allies. And when the time was right, she would strike, placing a pliable male puppet on the throne—a figurehead the empire would rally behind, while she ruled from the shadows. She smiled faintly, the barest flicker of expression crossing her sharp features. A new plan was forming. One that required patience … and betrayal.

CHAPTER TEN

After wandering through the silence of the Spymaster's once impenetrable stronghold, plumbing it for every hidden secret, the Nillith felt something that had plagued him for centuries. Boredom. Sure, this little diversion had been fun. But all too soon, there was no one left to kill, no more suffering to savor, and boredom crept in like rot. It had been ages since he felt the pulse of a creature beneath the sharp instruments of his body. He missed it—the hot splash of blood across his hands, the faint iron tang on his tongue. But death was fleeting. Boring and useless. He couldn't feed on the emotions of a corpse. What he loved—*what he craved*—was the moment just before the end: fear, despair, and anguish. An occasional death, if timed well, could be delicious. One key life ended in the right place could send whole civilizations into panic. The death of a leader or a spiritual icon. Ah, that was a feast. But the finest delicacy? The death of a twin.

No bond in the galaxy was purer. No agony more exquisite than that of one twin feeling the absence of the other. He thought he might have experienced it with Silas and Elias. It had been so close, he could almost *taste* it. But alas, it wasn't meant to be. Not yet. Oh well, the game wasn't over. With the Spymaster now his puppet and chaos spreading through the empire, he had plenty to look forward to. There was still the matter of Malvek and whoever that brute truly was beneath all the theatrics. So many appointments. So much suffering left to savor. With a shake of Roach's borrowed head, the Nillith turned toward the ship. More havoc awaited.

The Nillith arrived back on the capital planet, hidden from view, unseen on any scope or detection device in the entire empire. The ability to cloud and distract minds was such a wonderfully useful gift. He laughed out loud, savoring the sensation of drawing deep breaths. He *really* enjoyed this body. Though it seriously limited his mobility, it gave him sensations—invigorating, addictive sensations. Well, he supposed he should enjoy it while he could. The fact was that this thing called a human wouldn't last forever. Oh sure, he could extend its life for a very long time, but long in comparison to *what?* He had already been ancient when humans were still dragging themselves out of the primordial muck.

Suddenly, he felt it, a flicker of thought not his own. Roach. Somehow, that miserable insect was encroaching on his thoughts, possibly even nudging his mood. Now *that* was something you didn't see every day: an ant trying to shift the path of a giant. No, not even an ant. More like a single-celled organism trying to redirect the currents of an ocean. It was just too ridiculous to even conceive.

Rumors, whispers, and echoes of unspeakable horror drifting from the far-flung villages and forgotten outposts of the empire. This was the true currency Malvek craved. Not just the blood he spilled, but the dread he left behind. His terror endured not only in the corpses, but in the few trembling survivors allowed to crawl away and spread word of his atrocities.

On Earth, when an insect dies, it leaves behind a pheromone—an invisible warning that signals death, fear, and danger. A scent that declares *This place is no longer a home. It is now a graveyard.*

Now imagine that same death scent clinging to the living. Survivors staggering through the darkness, soaked in blood and horror, carrying with them the story of what Malvek had done. He didn't need to boast. He didn't need banners or drums. The living were his messengers, and their haunted eyes told the tale better than words ever could.

A collision course was inevitable, one that would shake the empire to its rotting core. Two despicable creatures, forces of unfiltered malice, were destined to meet. And nothing good would survive. Mercy? You'd find none. Empathy? Compassion? The faintest flicker of kindness? Not even a trace. Their battle would become legend. But the aftermath? The aftermath would be something far worse. Because the most terrifying truth was this: these two beings that were blights on existence? They were just getting started.

Malvek was growing bored. The small towns, remote garrisons, and scattered villages—he'd razed them all, and it still wasn't enough. He needed something more *substantial* to send the emperor's final message. The queens should have known better. They had stirred the emperor from his pleasures, from his games and indulgences. That was their mistake. When left alone, the emperor was content to let his empire rot from within. But disturb him and he would unleash his darkest weapons. Malvek was one of them. He smiled at the thought. Maybe, if he pleased the emperor enough, he would be granted another indulgence—permission to return to some far-flung, backward world like he had before, to play God among primitives. He could already imagine it ... cutting down their so-called heroes one by one, driving their people into desperate, futile acts. If his iron-hard skin had been capable of goosebumps, he'd have felt them rise now. Just *thinking* about the slaughter stirred something inside him. Something almost joyful.

He'd seen it all before. On one world, they had built temples in his image, offered up sacrifices in his name, called him a deity of death. On others, they'd begged, fought, or tried to run, but none had ever posed a true threat. To Malvek, these campaigns were like vacations. Bloody, glorious holidays soaked in fear and gore. But that was about to change.

While Malvek reveled in thoughts of past glories and the bloodshed yet to come, the Nillith moved silently through the shadows of the very city Malvek was about to occupy. It was always strange how easily the Nillith could blend in—how no one ever seemed to notice him, not even the ones he stood beside. It didn't matter that he looked nothing like the creatures of this world; he simply had a way of existing between notice, between breath, like a rumor you forgot the moment it passed. He walked among the crowds, listening to the whispers, to the tales of the slaughter Malvek had already wrought. The horror and the madness. The pointless cruelty. The Spymaster had warned him. *Malvek is a threat, even to you.* The Nillith chuckled softly at the memory. *A threat?* That was amusing. He couldn't remember the last time he had felt fear. Maybe he never had. Certainly nothing had ever truly challenged him, not in a way that mattered. There were beings that escaped his influence from time to time, but none had ever made him doubt his own survival. Even if they managed to destroy his host, he simply moved on. He had left behind so many rotting puppets—human, Vorrhaxi, Thal'Naari, even species forgotten by time. And yet … something about this empire intrigued him. Something about Earth disturbed him.

He found himself reflecting—strangely—on the twins. On their bond. On the raw grief he felt when one faced death. He had never encountered the Thal'Naari before, and the Vorrhaxi, well, they were a curiosity, nothing more. But this twin-bonded culture fascinated him. Their strength came not from individual dominance, but from shared pain, shared survival.

The Vorrhaxi had no such thing. No twins among them. Their reproduction was mechanical, grotesque—individually grown and harvested, one at a time. Efficient, but soulless. That was why he watched. That was why he waited. He could have unleashed mayhem already, but instead, the Nillith sank deeper into the background. Unseen, unbothered, and patient.

He would let Malvek arrive. He would let the monster take the stage, revel in his moment. Then he would begin. He would use the populace—every frightened soul in this soon-to-be massacre—to play a new kind of game. Malvek had never experienced fear before— real fear. Malvek had never felt it. Never tasted it. But he would. And when that moment came—when Malvek, angel of death, realized something in the dark might just be worse than him—it would be *delicious*. The Nillith smiled in the dark. And he waited.

***

And just like that, the battle was over. Valshar drifted silently in space, barely able to propel himself forward. The Ancient One hovered above him like a shadow from the stars. Grace and the noble Vorrhaxi soldier moved frantically, working the control systems to engage Valshar's self-repair functions, desperate to stabilize the great ship after the brutal assault. This had not been a standard Vorrhaxi scout fleet—it was tactical and coordinated, like it had been led by someone who actually knew what they were doing. The ambush was no fluke. The attackers fought with calculated efficiency, not the careless aggression the empire's forces had previously shown. Still, Valshar had survived. One ship—just one—had engaged twenty-four. That was no small feat. It was near-miraculous. But even miracles had their cost.

The Ancient One's voice no longer held the tone of the thunderous fury of battle. It came as a whisper, gentle and urgent. "Valshar, can you hear me?" A pause. Then again, closer. "Valshar …"

Finally, the damaged warship responded, his voice low and tired. "Yes, Ancient One." He sighed—if a ship could sigh. "I survived, thanks to you. I thought I would fail them. I didn't think I could protect them." His words were spoken aloud for Grace and the soldier to hear.

Grace's heart clenched. Valshar had taken more punishment than any ship should've been able to endure, and he'd done it to keep them safe. She knew that now. He could've fled, but he didn't. And they were unscathed. There was a bit of smoke and a few bruises, nothing more.

The Vorrhaxi fleet, meanwhile, was gone. All that remained were scattered atoms and drifting husks. They hadn't even managed to send a warning. The Ancient One drifted closer and extended a docking arm. A hatch opened, and strange small machines, no larger than puppies, poured out. The bots scattered into Valshar's hull, vanishing into vents, corridors, and conduits. Grace and the Vorrhaxi soldier tensed, but the Ancient One reassured them with a voice like wind through ancient stone. "Do not fear. These are my children; they are repair bots. They will restore Valshar and make him stronger than he was before." Without another word, the Ancient One disengaged and vanished into the stars.

"Where is she going?" Grace asked softly. "I thought she'd stay to protect us."

"There's no need," Valshar replied. "No ships linger here. If there were, the Ancient One would've destroyed them already." The strange bots moved tirelessly, not just repairing, but also upgrading, reinforcing armor, and optimizing weapons. They tuned systems to the unique minds of Grace and her companion. "It's a gift," Valshar said reverently.

Grace asked, "Valshar, who is the Ancient One? Where does she come from? Where has she been all this time?"

Valshar replied, "I don't know. The first time I ever heard her name was when the great ship mentioned her and said she would come. I'm glad she did."

Grace nodded, letting the thought settle. "So, where to now, once repairs are done?"

Valshar's voice was thoughtful. "I believe we've done all the damage we can here. I don't relish facing another fleet alone. I also suspect they realized we'd been targeting their scout ships—the ones circling as a screen. That tactic has likely run its course. It's time we rejoin the great ship in Earth's orbit, plan the next move, and help prepare the twins for what's coming."

Grace folded her arms, staring out into the void. "The Vorrhaxi know we're aware of them. That means they'll come sooner. Less time for us to prepare."

"Exactly," Valshar said. "So we'd best go about the business of readiness, and the only place to do that is with the others." As he spoke, Valshar's systems hummed to life. Repairs were sufficient. His engines engaged, and the long journey back to Earth began.

Grace leaned back, sifting through memories of the recent battle. One memory surfaced—unexpected and chilling. She remembered a voice, immense and furious, echoing through the void. *How dare you attack one of my children, you soulless shells of metal.* It hadn't just been a war cry. It had felt maternal. Fierce and protective. Grace blinked, unsettled by the realization. *I know these ships are sentient, but are they born?*

***

Shaskiel and Threxil sat in the war room aboard the flagship, surrounded by silence thicker than the hull plating. Both studied the tactical projections before them, each lost in grim contemplation. Threxil broke the quiet first. "I'm not overly concerned with the loss of the scouting fleet," she said evenly, "but I admit, I'm surprised not *one* of the twenty-four ships survived. That tells us two possibilities: either the rogue ship has been reinforced or it's far deadlier than we imagined."

Shaskiel's lip curled in distaste. He wasn't sure which possibility offended him more.

"To me," Threxil continued, "it feels more like an ambush. That ship led them in, baited them like prey. And now they're gone."

Shaskiel leaned back in his command chair, jaw tight, gaze cold. He surveyed the fleet—more than one hundred forty ships now, reinforced by Threxil's disciplined and well-armed warbands. On paper, it was enough firepower to level Earth a dozen times over. But something felt wrong. He was furious about the loss of his scouts, but his anger wasn't only tactical. It was *spiritual.* He found the concept of a living warship—of sentient metal—nothing short of blasphemous. "Ships should not think," he growled. "They are tools, nothing more. A pistol in a holster. A book on a shelf. Only dangerous when wielded by *real* beings. Sentient ships are an abomination."

Threxil gave him a sidelong glance. She didn't share that view. In truth, she *hungered* for the power those ships represented. If she could capture one—just one—she might change the fate of the empire. A fleet of such living vessels bound to her will? She would no longer be forced to curry favor with the emperor or kneel to the manipulations of queens like Khar'Zul. The idea was intoxicating. Still, she admitted the loss of the scouts was disappointing. Capturing the ship would have been a victory beyond measure. The sheer firepower it had unleashed, utterly annihilating twenty-four ships, even if their crews were subpar, was impressive. And disturbing. They turned to the star charts, mapping the route to Earth. "We'll approach cautiously," Threxil said. "No more rushing in. We'll move slow, track emissions, and look for signs of more traps. This is no longer a scouting mission. This is a surgical execution." Even if this mission came from the lowly Spymaster, and even if her inclusion was likely a ploy by Khar'Zul, Threxil didn't care. It served her purpose. She could still prove her loyalty to the empire and perhaps position herself for something greater. "Before I left," she murmured, "things back home were unraveling. The empire feels brittle, chaotic. Not like the emperor at all."

"You think he's no longer in control?" Shaskiel asked quietly.

"I think something else is behind all this. Queens working together? That never happens. One, maybe. But four?"

Shaskiel didn't respond immediately. He stared at the view outside, the swirling stars, the cold beauty of space. "Do you think we have enough firepower?" he finally asked.

"One ship destroyed twenty-four. If there are two ..." She did the math in her head. "If two ships take forty-eight," she said, "and there are more than that ..."

"We may suffer devastating losses," Shaskiel growled, "but we'll destroy those vile, blasphemous things. If it's the last thing we do." He clenched his fists. In the silence that followed, his thoughts wandered. *Someday, I'll find the cradle where these sentient ships were born. And I'll burn it to ash.*

Threxil stood, her expression unreadable. "I'm returning to my fleet. The board is set. Let's see if the game ends in fire." She left without another word.

Shaskiel remained behind, alone in the war room. Somewhere, far ahead of them, the living ship waited in the dark.

Shaskiel stood up from the long metal table, preparing to follow Queen Threxil to her shuttle. But just as she stepped beyond the threshold, he hesitated. He gave her a curt but proper farewell, a respectful nod to her rank, then turned on his heel and reentered the war room. The doors closed behind him with a hiss. He sat back down at the table, steepled his clawed fingers, and let the silence stretch. Something wasn't right. Not about her, not about this war, and certainly not about the latest battle report. The Reaver—fanatic, relentless, and cruel—had been taken out too easily. Shaskiel's mind drifted back to the tactical overlay. Yes, the ships assigned to the Reaver were mostly second-rate. But they were still space-worthy. Still armed. The plan had been solid—surround the target with overwhelming firepower, push it into a corner, and finish it before reinforcements could arrive. And yet, the living ship hadn't just survived. It had slaughtered them. One ship. One *abomination*. That wasn't tactics. That was something else. A new weapon? An unseen ally? Or perhaps a manipulation none of them had yet uncovered?

He tapped his talons softly against the table—*click, click, click*—each sound marking another possibility. His greatest victories had come not from brute strength, but from thinking ten steps ahead. He had always believed the true path to victory was not overwhelming power but preparation. Know your enemy. Predict the battlefield. Plan for the absurd. That's how you win. And now, he was blind. *Unless* ... Perhaps there was still a way to turn this. He sat back, expression unreadable, as a dangerous idea bloomed. *What if we bait it?* Not just any bait. Something irresistible. Something it would *have* to come for. A captured queen, perhaps? Threxil wouldn't like it. But what choice did she have, really? He could already envision it—the ship lured in by the promise of a key enemy. Drawn into a trap of his own design, caught and destroyed. Its blasphemous existence finally erased from the stars. Yes, that would bring him glory. That would bring his name back to the emperor's lips, maybe even the throne room itself.

He drummed his claws again—*click, click, click*—as visions of revenge flared in his mind. Varnak'Tal, the Spymaster, the ancient queens who dismissed him, the upstarts who whispered behind his back ... all of them would bow. All of them would burn. He leaned forward, whispering to the darkness like it might answer. "We shall see."

As Queen Threxil settled into her shuttle seat and strapped in for the short return journey to her flagship, she gave her pilot a quiet order. "Take us on a slow circuit of the fleet. I'd like to view each ship personally." The pilot obeyed without question, angling the shuttle out of Shaskiel's massive warship and into the cold, glittering void. Threxil wasn't interested in assessing the hull integrity of gunboats or reviewing formation cohesion. What she needed was time. Time to think. She stared out the viewport as vessel after vessel drifted past—some formidable, some laughably crude. In her mind, one name echoed louder than the rest: Khar'Zul. Threxil knew she was being used. Used as a tool, perhaps even a pawn, by a queen whose ambition outstripped all bounds of reason. Khar'Zul, ever the schemer, ever the predator.

Threxil suspected the plan was simple—prop her up, let her win some glory, maybe even win her favor with the emperor, then dispose of her once the battle was over. A martyr for the empire. Or worse, bait. But Threxil was no martyr. She was a battlefield commander, a soldier, and a tactician, not some ceremonial figurehead tossed into the meat grinder for another queen's gain. She led with honor, not vanity. And unlike the other queens, she *cared* for her warriors. Their lives mattered. Of all the ruling queens, the only one Threxil trusted was Zev'Kala. Threxil had warned Zev'Kala—*don't go back to Khar'Zul. Not if you value your life.* Zev'Kala had revealed her worst fears, that Khar'Zul was planning and plotting something, she just knew it. She'd spoken of her belief of a broader plot, a final gambit. The final result would the elimination of all the remaining queens except one. With no rivals left, Khar'Zul could rise, perhaps even install a puppet emperor—some enthralled male under her pheromonal spell. Threxil shuddered at the thought. Khar'Zul's talents for seduction were infamous, but her cruelty afterward was legendary. She did not merely discard her lovers, she consumed them, literally. One by one, after the heat of passion had passed. It wasn't the intimacy that Threxil loathed—she had enjoyed many lovers herself—it was the *twisted aftermath* that disgusted her. She made herself a quiet promise then. *If I survive this mission, I will end Khar'Zul. For good.*

Her thoughts shifted to Shaskiel. His obsession with the sentient ship had begun to unbalance him. He was losing the cold logic that once made him dangerous. She was positive he was planning on using her to bait a living warship. This was not only reckless, but it was also tactically foolish. She would not allow herself to be positioned so vulnerably. Although he had not come right out and said it, she was no fool. All the signs were there. Threxil gave her pilot a tap on the shoulder. "Back to the flagship," she said. "We have preparations to make. It's going to be a long voyage to Earth. And I plan to arrive ready."

***

Elsewhere, the great ship stirred. From deep within the ancient bio-core of her living mind, she felt the unease radiating from Silas's quarters like a disturbance in still water. He had been asleep for several hours now, restless and silent. The serum had been administered less than twelve hours ago. And though she had guided thousands of twin pairs across the stars, each mind—each *soul*—processed the change differently. Silas's mind was a fortress. And change, to him, was not growth. It was danger. She felt it clearly in his psychic pattern: the way he tensed at even minor disruptions, the way he cataloged shifts in behavior, language, temperature, and time. To Silas, any alteration was a potential threat, a precursor to collapse. For him, change had always been a herald of disaster. He bore the signs of someone who had lived through too many collapses already, too many resets to his personal universe.

Still, the presence of Alex, the bonded canine guardian, brought her a measure of comfort. She knew Alex was inside Silas's dreams with him now, not just watching but guiding. Soothing him and acting as an anchor in his current of memory. That helped, but it would not be enough. Silas would need to wake up ready. A great battle loomed—days away, maybe less—and if they were to stand against the emperor, if they were to spark a true revolution, Silas had to be whole. Not just physically, but also mentally and emotionally. The ship scrolled through trillions of potential paths, simulations flickering through her mind at light speed. Most ended in ruin. Silas remained a mystery she couldn't quite crack, and she had once deciphered the minds of gods. Then, almost humorously, a quiet notion surfaced in the chorus of calculations. A thought so simple, she nearly dismissed it. But then she paused. *Perhaps love was the answer.*

234

Silas was in a dream—one he'd envisioned many times before. The old house in the swamp. His mother, gone from morning till night, never alone, always with some mean-spirited asshole in tow. She never kept the house stocked with food. And little boys are always hungry. He and Elias were hungry all the time. Midnight hunger pangs were the worst. But their mother, she did love her animals. She fed them better than her own sons. There was always dog food and treats. And after one of her thrifty boyfriends had padlocked the fridge and freezer, dog food started looking like a decent option. Yes, it sounds insane. But when you're six years old and starving, logic takes a back seat.

Silas remembered the fancy brand. Bits that looked like cheese or chips. He was sitting in the pantry, the old walk-in with wooden shelves and peeling paint. Huddled on the floor, his fingers dug into the dog food bag. He listened for tires on gravel. If he heard a car pull up, he'd have to bolt out the back door. Run and hide. The rules were clear: when she wasn't home, they stayed outside. Hot, cold, or rain, it didn't matter. The dream started sinking deeper. The hopelessness thickened around him. And then came a familiar voice. "Silas." It was gentle yet strong. Alex. "What're you doing, man? You don't dwell here anymore." The voice echoed inside the pantry like sunlight piercing through the dark. "You never have to feel this fear again. You're not alone. You have me. You have a new mother now, one who will see to your every need. I will never leave you. I will never choose anyone over you. We are bonded for life."

Then Silas realized he was dreaming. He whispered back, "I go to this place to remember how far I've come."

"I get that," Alex said. "But you don't need to stay."

Silas nodded slowly. "In boot camp, I remember thinking I was lucky. No one hurt you there. And you weren't hungry. Hard work? I'd done harder work at six than any man in that camp." He smiled bitterly. But the smile didn't last. "She never told us she was proud, not once. Not when we graduated. Not when we were deployed. We received no letters, no visits, no welcome home." The dam broke. Tears spilled from Silas's eyes and poured down his cheeks. Then came the sobs—harsh, heavy, and full of grief. He clutched at his sides, crying like the little boy he used to be. And as he did, Alex's warm, furry head pressed tight against his ribs.

"It's okay, little brother," Alex whispered, his voice fierce and loving. "Let it go. I've got you now." He stayed like that, nuzzled close. A protective and steady presence. In all his years of guiding twins into becoming warriors, Alex had never met one so broken. His heart ached. Not just with empathy, but with rage. Pure, righteous fury. Who had done this? Who had shattered Silas so completely? He would find them. He would make them pay.

Alex made a decision in that moment. He wasn't just going to get even with the walking refuse heap that called herself a mother. He was going to get ahead. He would do everything in his power to make her feel the weight of what she had done to this man, this soul who carried such quiet goodness beneath all that trauma. And not just her. Every paramour she'd ever entertained—if they were still breathing—he would find them, too. He wouldn't need to harm a single hair on their heads. No, that wasn't his style. He could visit their dreams, just like he visited Silas's. But he wouldn't bring them comfort. He would bring a reckoning.

Alex blinked, shaking himself from the trance he'd slipped into. He had never felt anything like this before. The ever-expanding power of Silas's evolving mind was both frightening and wondrous. It crackled beneath the surface like a gathering storm, too vast to fully comprehend. At this rate, his mind might one day rival that of the great ship herself. Alex didn't know in that moment whether to be comforted or terrified by the prospect of what was to come. He pondered it for a heartbeat. And then he felt it—warmth spread through his body and wrapped around him like a blanket of certainty, quiet and powerful. It was compassion and loyalty. A fierce, unwavering moral compass radiated from Silas's core, and Alex knew then—no matter what changes came, Silas would never become something monstrous. He simply couldn't. Not with that heart. Elias, well, maybe they'd need to keep an eye on him. But Silas? He would be the glue that held them all together.

While Silas was wrestling his demons in silence, Elias was exorcising his in a very different way. The great ship, who now answered only to the name *Mother*, had molded her interior to suit her newly bonded crew. Like her sibling Valshar, she was an adaptive, living warship, and within her vast interior, she had created an elaborate array of training zones: combat arenas, weapon ranges, and sparring chambers.

Elias stood alone in a room that defied logic—a live-fire weapons range aboard a sentient ship floating in deep space. It should have been impossible. It *was* impossible. But then again, Elias and Silas were no ordinary twins. And *Mother* was no ordinary ship. In an array before him was an arsenal that would make even the most seasoned warlord weep with joy: sleek pistols with hissing plasma coils, elegant submachine guns that hovered slightly above their racks, and even what looked like anti-vehicle missile pods tucked away behind impact-shielded glass. He moved through the armory like a kid in a candy store, grinning as he examined each piece. Bigger was better and louder was glorious. The more earsplitting, the better. And then he saw them. Tucked neatly into a tiny velvet-lined compartment were small, dense, matte-black spheres, no larger than marbles. The warning above them read simply "Use with Caution." Elias grinned like a man who had just seen God. "Oh," he whispered to himself, eyes gleaming. "I am anything but cautious." Even he wasn't reckless enough to toss one inside a living ship. *Probably.*

Mother, of course, never allowed anything to happen aboard without being fully aware. This time, however, Max was a few seconds ahead of her—something that almost never happened. It was a true testament to just how closely bonded Alex and Max had become to the twins. While Elias was toying with one of the small but exceptionally powerful grenades in the ship's armory, Max casually sauntered into the room. Just as Elias began to wonder where on the indoor range he could set one off, Max gave him a quick nip on the right calf. Not hard enough to injure, just firm enough to get his point across. It was the kind of cuff a pack leader would give a pup, a warning that danger was near. Startled, Elias jumped. He hadn't heard Max approach. That alone shocked him—he didn't think anyone could sneak up on him.

"Well, aren't you the quiet one," Elias muttered aloud.

Max snorted and shook his head slowly, as if to say, *Really? I have to keep this close an eye on you? Your talent for doing stupid things is almost impressive.* Then, Max made a strange chuffing noise.

Elias squinted. "Are you laughing at me?" Max's tail wagged once, and Elias knew. He *was* laughing. Laughing at how absurd it was that Elias was seriously considering setting off a grenade inside a sentient ship. Elias looked down at the tiny explosive in his hand, sighed, and then glanced at Max with a wistful smirk. "I really wanted to see it go boom."

Max barked once and gave him a firm mental nudge. *Follow me.* Then he turned and padded out of the training room, leading Elias toward another part of the ship. Something waited there. Something Max believed would speak to Elias louder than any explosion ever could.

With a loud sigh, Elias turned and followed Max out of the live-fire range, padding down one of the long corridors within the ship's winding core. After a few minutes, they reached another door marked by a strange symbol. As Elias approached, it slid open silently like every other door on this strange ship. So far, not a single one had denied him access, giving him the impression that he and his brother had been granted full run of the place. Inside, the room resembled a sparring chamber. Standing near the center was Vaeril, working over what looked like an oversized punching bag. Each blow from his fists sent shudders through the bag, and Elias could swear he saw dust puffing from its seams. The old warrior hit like a freight train. Still,

Elias felt confident. The serum had rebuilt him, muscle on top of muscle. He was bigger, faster, and stronger. He'd always been a tough bastard—pound for pound, ounce for ounce—but now, he was something else. He hadn't met many people he couldn't at least bloody. And if nothing else, he could always deliver a solid ass-kicking.

Vaeril looked up mid-combo and arched an eyebrow. "Care for a few rounds?"

Elias grinned, the sarcasm automatic. "Well, old man, if you think you can hang, I'll jump in. But I should warn you, I don't want to break anything brittle. You're a couple thousand years old, right? Want me to take it easy on you?"

Vaeril just gave him a long, cold stare—his version of "bring it on." They stepped into the sparring square—no ropes, just a padded mat. Max trotted to the edge of the room, tail wagging as he settled in to watch.

"Any rules?" Elias asked. "Do we need pads?"

"Why would you fight with pads?" Vaeril replied. "You train like you fight. The more blood you lose in training, the less you'll lose in battle."

Elias rolled his eyes. "Wow, that's cliché. You been reading fortune cookies again?"

Vaeril smirked. "If it keeps you alive, you can call it whatever you want."

Without another word, they raised their hands and launched into it. Elias was immediately shocked by Vaeril's speed. For a big man, the old warrior moved like liquid steel. His body was hard as a wall—no give, no flinch, and no grunt. Punches landed, but Vaeril kept coming. And when he struck back, Elias felt it. His body, his face, nothing was spared. One brutal uppercut nearly put Elias flat on his back and stars exploded behind his eyes. After fifteen grueling minutes, Vaeril stepped back and raised a hand.

"Tired?" Elias taunted, catching his breath. "Have I worn you down with my rope-a-dope?"

"Rope-a-what?"

"Rope-a-dope," Elias said. "You know, float, dodge, let your opponent tire himself out …"

Vaeril just laughed. "I wasn't tired. I was going easy on you."

Elias blinked. That wasn't the best sign. They walked to the edge of the room.

"Next stop," Vaeril said, "the medical bay. It's time for your armor fitting."

"You mean you've been wearing armor this whole time?" Elias asked. "Is that why I couldn't hurt you?"

Vaeril nodded. "My armor never comes off. It's not gear, it's part of me now. You'll understand soon enough."

Elias chuckled. "You had me thinking you were just that tough. Hell yes, I'm ready. Let's get that second skin on me. I don't like bruises. I don't want to bleed. I want to be invincible."

Vaeril gave a rare grin. "It won't make you invincible. But it will make you a hell of a lot harder to kill." And with that, they exited the sparring room and headed toward the medical bay for the next transformation.

Elias stepped into the medical suite, uncertain of what to expect.

Vaeril remained in the hallway, glancing inside only long enough to say, "You won't need me for this part of your journey."

Max padded in beside Elias without hesitation. Elias looked down at the dog and muttered, "You getting armored up, too, boy?"

Vaeril smirked from the doorway. "Of course not, you moron. He was born with armor."

Elias grumbled under his breath, "How the hell am I supposed to know what comes standard on your garden-variety space dog? Could be an upgrade, for all I know."

To his surprise, Vaeril actually laughed, loudly. Shaking his head, he turned to leave, still chuckling. "Oh, and the old man will be in the sparring ring waiting for you," he said over his shoulder. "Just remember, I'm not going easy on you this time. The armor protects, but it doesn't numb. You'll still feel pain. Come ready."

Once he was alone, Elias turned toward the sleek medical suite. A tall, slender medical bot glided toward him, arms ending in an array of elegant but ominous attachments. Its voice was smooth and calm, almost musical. "What medical service can we provide for you today?"

Elias blinked. "Uh … I thought I was here for armor?"

"Armor," the bot confirmed. "A simple procedure. It will only take a few moments. Do you have any questions before we begin?"

Elias hesitated. "Yeah. Once this armor goes on, does it ever come off?"

"No," the bot said. "Once bonded, it becomes part of you. You've taken the serum, so your bones are strengthened, your muscles are denser, and your ligaments are reinforced. You are already far tougher than before. This procedure will enhance that further—your strength, reflexes, and endurance. All will be significantly improved."

Elias's grin grew wider by the second. He was practically vibrating with anticipation. But then, just as the bot began prepping its tools, a stray thought crossed his mind. "Wait, I have an odd question. Is this going to … you know … affect me with the ladies?" The bot hesitated. There was a long silence. Elias fidgeted. "I mean … with my perfor-mance? Or, uh … sensation?" Still silence.

Elias was just about to blurt it out again when the bot replied, "You could be referring to two separate concerns. One, functional performance. Two, sensory reduction."

Elias, for once in his life, turned beet red. "Y-you know what? Never mind. Let's just roll the dice and see how it goes."

Unbeknownst to him, Mother was listening. As the living ship monitored every system aboard, she caught every word, and she found it *hilarious*. The procedure wouldn't impact Elias's physical pleasures at all. But the fact that, in the middle of a cosmic war and bio-en-hancement surgery, he still had *women* on his mind? She adored him for that.

***

Silas stirred from his dream—a dark tangle of childhood memories—and woke to an unexpected feeling: comfort and strength. He blinked against the soft ambient light of the room, taking in the surroundings. It was as if someone had reached into the deepest recesses of his mind and pulled out every object, every arrangement, every color that brought him peace. The room was Spartan but perfect. A desk sat in the corner, exactly like the one back home. His old computer setup blinked to life beside it. And on the desk, of all things, sat his antique abacus—a hand-painted Asian artifact, lacquered and worn with age, a thing of beauty and memory. Then he realized his hand was resting on something warm. Alex. The dog's head was nestled under Silas's palm, his fur soft and grounding. This was no small thing—Silas had always struggled with physical touch. But this? This felt natural, right. It was healing. The chasm between him and Elias had always existed, wide and deep despite their closeness. But here with Alex, there was no distance. If Elias was his twin, Alex was his shadow. No, his anchor. For the first time in his life, Silas allowed himself to imagine what it might be like to share something this profound with someone else, someone not his brother. Someone like ... Grace.

And then, right on cue, Mother spoke. "I can help you with that. If you'll let me." Her voice was like music—gentle, wry, and knowing.

Silas wasn't startled. Normally, he would have recoiled and gone silent, his walls slammed into place. But the serum had done something to him. It strengthened his mind and calmed his instinct to defend. When he answered, it was not just with words, it was with vulnerability. "So, Mother," he said softly, reverently. "How do you think you can help me with that?"

"Well," she said with a grin in her tone, "I've already picked your prom date."

Silas actually laughed—out loud and full-bodied. He couldn't remember the last time that had happened. "Mom, I think I'm a little past prom age."

"Forty-five? Forty-six?" she teased. "Well, the serum reversed all that. You're young again. And maybe, just maybe, it's not too late for you to experience the things you were denied."

Silas swallowed hard. "You picked someone out already?"

"Oh, I don't think I have to. I think you've already chosen her."

He felt no violation, no alarm, just warmth and trust. He'd never let anyone in like this, not even Elias. But with Mother, it felt different. It felt safe. He'd opened every door and lowered every wall.

"You're stalling," she said, gently chiding him. "You like her. Don't worry, I'm sure you'll have the *Grace* to shoulder it."

Silas groaned at the pun but couldn't help smiling.

"Now," Mother continued, "it's time for you to put on your armor."

"Armor?" he asked.

"You'll see. Vaeril is on his way."

Just as the door slid open, Vaeril appeared. "Well, calmer twin," he said with a grin, "I see you're ready."

"What's this about armor?"

"It won't hurt. It applies quickly and never comes off. Don't worry, it doesn't interfere with your … physical sensations."

"What?"

"Oh, nothing," Vaeril said with a sly grin. "Just something your brother asked about. Loudly."

Silas sighed. Of course, it was Elias.

Right then, Elias stepped through the opposite door with Max by his side. "Hey! Look who's vertical. You good?"

"Better than ever," Silas replied.

"You sound … relaxed. That's weird."

"There's a first time for everything. You know how I am," Silas said, voice calm. "I take things as I can, when I can. But you know what? It's never when *you* need me to come to your rescue, whether it's from some random brothel or a jealous husband with a shotgun."

Elias tried to look shocked but couldn't keep a straight face. "Yeah, okay, you got me," he said, laughing. "But hey, you've got to check out my armor! Go ahead—*hit me.* Punch me right in the face. Don't hold back. This stuff is freaking unreal."

Silas didn't hesitate. He reared back and smacked Elias across the face with full force. It felt like hitting a cinderblock. The punch rocked Elias slightly—his new, denser frame absorbing most of it—but he didn't even flinch. So, in true Silas fashion, he followed it up with a swift kick to the one place Elias had always claimed was sacred. He got no response and Elias just grinned wider.

"That was *dirty,* man! I *respect* that! Didn't think you had it in you to fight dirty."

"I can be resourceful," Silas muttered.

Elias clapped him on the back hard enough to rattle his bones. "Didn't feel a thing," he said proudly. "This stuff is *insane.*" And just like that, with Max padding after him, Elias strutted off down the corridor.

Silas looked at the open door to the medical suite and sighed. "Show-off," he muttered, and stepped inside with Alex close behind. The med bay gleamed with soft light. A sleek medical bot waited on the other side of the table, arms poised with various attachments. Silas instinctively sized them up, thinking about edge geometry, blade length, and point-of-entry angles.

The robot, connected directly to Mother, picked up the thought instantly. "I don't have any scalpels or—what do you call them—*knives,*" the bot said in a crisp voice. "Crude instruments, abandoned long ago. What we do here is therapeutic. We promote healing, not butchery."

Silas actually paused, wondering if he'd offended the bot somehow.

Then, after a beat, he spoke again. "I am only jesting," the robot said, voice lifting slightly. "Your brother mentioned your sense of humor is legendary. Perhaps *I* am the true butt of the joke."

Silas raised a brow. "Don't feel bad. I think we both know Elias is just a few stops north of Moron-ville." To Silas's surprise, the robot let out a full-bodied laugh—a hearty sound, like a jolly old uncle chuckling at a family story.

"So," the robot said, recovering. "You're here for the armor, Silas?"

"Yeah," Silas said, stepping forward.

"Any questions about side effects?"

Silas narrowed his eyes. "Don't even start with me." Silas lay on the table as instructed, Alex seated loyally beside him.

Arche, the medical robot, regarded him with his usual efficient tone, but this time, there was something different behind the words. "Your companion may remain," Arche said, gesturing toward Alex. "Unlike your brother, I trust you won't ask if the dog is to be armored as well."

Silas chuckled quietly.

"You, of course, understand that Alex and Max were born with this armor. Yours will take only moments to install. You'll feel no pain and likely hear nothing." Arche hesitated. "I can offer you something I couldn't provide to your brother—an upgrade. Several options, in fact, based on your neural responses, fighting style, and data gathered by Mother and The Emissary. Or I could simply choose what's optimal."

"Hang on a sec," Silas interrupted, leaning up slightly. "What do I call you?"

The robot paused. In all its years aboard the great ship, no one had ever asked that. "Are you familiar with Greek?" Arche asked.

"I know enough to bluff my way through a myth," Silas replied. "Why?"

"In Greek, there is a word—*arche*. It means life source. Would that suffice?"

Silas smiled. "Then Arche you shall be." He realized, perhaps for the first time, that he was beginning to understand this whole compassion thing. Even in regard to the feelings of a so-called machine. "Well then, Arche," he said, "can I get racing stripes with this armor?"

"Sadly, no," Arche replied, voice almost amused. "That option is not available in this production cycle. Maybe next year." They both laughed. "Now," Arche said, shifting back to business, "here's what I've installed: enhanced vision—you'll see in the dark as if it were day. Underwater and in toxic environments—your eyes will remain unaffected. Though, I advise you to keep your mouth shut. I can't protect what you willingly let inside."

Silas nodded. "Fair."

"Enhanced muscle strength, faster reflexes, speed. And two final gifts. First, an upgrade to your traditional weapons—your knives are now integrated beneath the armor. Hidden, undetectable by Vorrhaxi tech. The garrotes, too."

"And the second?"

"A built-in medical AI. Arche Two. A part of me, traveling with you. It will stabilize you in the field, analyze food and water, and detect toxins. And it will even tell you which alien fruit won't kill you."

"That's damn impressive."

"I thought so," Arche replied modestly. "Elias would've gotten all of this, too, if he hadn't been worried it might interfere with his … appeal." They laughed again.

"So, how do I deploy the knives?"

"Think of the one you want. Touch the usual location. It will respond."

"And the AI?"

"Say or think 'Arche Two.' He will respond as I do." Silence followed. Then Arche said, "That's it. Don't swim or drink alcohol for five hours."

Silas gave him a deadpan look. "You're kidding, right?"

"Of course. Where would you swim? This is a starship."

Silas sat up, fully armored and newly enhanced.

"Take good care of yourself, and the galaxy," Arche said.

Silas winked. "You too, friend." With Alex at his side, he walked toward the door. Just before exiting, he turned, glanced back at Arche with a nod and a half smile, then disappeared into the corridor, an even more dangerous man than when he entered.

Almost as if expecting trouble, the moment he stepped through the door, Elias was immediately met by Silas and Vaeril. Vaeril, dry as ever, greeted him with a flat, "Well boys, I suppose it's time to get to the hard stuff."

Silas raised an eyebrow, a rare glint of amusement in his eyes. "The hard stuff, huh? That's going to be a challenge for Elias. Anything beyond coloring, drinking, brawling, or chasing skirts might be out of his league."

Elias feigned shock, though his grin betrayed him. "First off, I don't color … anymore. Because I can't stop eating the damn crayons." Vaeril gave him a long look but said nothing.

"And drinking?"

Elias gestured at Vaeril with mock offense. "Well, *he* screwed that up with his miracle juice. But" —he flexed an arm and admired the tight, corded muscle— "damn, I am jacked! Which means the ladies are going to have an even harder time resisting my obviously irresistible charm."

Silas rolled his eyes and turned away. "Let's just get on with it before Casanova here falls in love with his own reflection."

Elias threw up his hands. "Hey, if women are into tall, dark, humorless, and emotionally constipated, then *you* are their dreamboat, Silas."

"Boys, boys, boys," Vaeril said, finally deciding they'd veered too far off track. "Time is short, and we've got no time to lose."

The twins snapped back into focus. Their faces shifted, professionalism sliding into place like a well-worn mask.

Vaeril gave a small nod—things were back on track. "Alright," he said, motioning them forward. "Let's get to it. We'll start with a workout."

Silas and Elias shared a look that screamed *What the hell?*

"Whine less, work more," Vaeril growled, and then the fun began. The first exercise wasn't a sprint or a jog—but it sure as hell wasn't walking. They were moving fast. Faster than normal. The strangest part wasn't that they were running inside a spaceship—it was that the room itself seemed endless. The floor didn't move, but the walls stretched farther and farther the longer they ran, like reality itself was being rewritten under their feet. Even stranger? Alex, Max, and Vaeril kept the pace effortlessly. The dogs trotted alongside them with casual ease, and Vaeril looked like he was strolling through a garden. No effort and no sweat. He wasn't even breathing hard. On and on they ran. It felt like a marathon. Four hours passed before Vaeril finally called a halt.

The twins staggered to a stop, chests heaving, lungs burning. Despite the serum, despite their restored youth and power, they were absolutely gassed. Vaeril? Not even winded. The dogs? Wagging their tails like they'd just finished a nap.

Elias, hands on his knees, gasped out, "Dude … we just got smoked by an old-ass man. I mean, alien … or whatever the hell he is."

They both looked ready for a break, but Vaeril wasn't slowing down. "On to the weight room," he said.

Silas lit up the moment he walked into the space. "Now we're talking," he said with a sly grin, then gave Elias a wink and mouthed, *Now it's time to let the big dog eat.*

Elias was not amused. What followed was the most brutal workout either of them had ever endured. Vaeril put them through round after round of exhausting drills—strength, speed, reflexes, coordination—with no letup and no mercy.

Silas began to overheat. He could feel it, sweating through his armor, breathing hard. He hadn't even meant to, but suddenly he was accessing Arche Two instinctively.

A2 chimed in his ear with that same dry humor the med bot had used earlier. "Little hot under the collar, are we, Silas?"

Silas let out a sharp breath. "I don't know, what do *you* think?"

"Well," A2 said, "have you tried regulating your armor's cooling system?"

That stopped him cold. Silas blinked. *Wait a second.* "A2, what's my current armor temp set to?"

"Maximum heat," the bot replied cheerfully.

Silas groaned. "Damn you, Vaeril."

From across the room, Vaeril finally laughed. "Took you long enough. I guess we know which one is the smart one now."

Elias, still drenched and miserable, looked confused until Silas showed him how to adjust the temperature settings. After a short break and lots of water, the *real* training began. Endless hours of tactics, weapons handling, navigation, and coordination followed. Again and again. Movements were practiced until they blurred into instinct, until Silas and Elias weren't two warriors anymore. They were one seamless entity inside the great ship, flowing together, reading each other's thoughts, and reacting before the other could even speak. It was hard. But it was *working*.

CHAPTER ELEVEN

After six weeks of intense training, they were ready to take on the universe. Or at least, they believed they were. Both twins were enjoying a rare morning of sleeping in when Mother's voice stirred them gently from their beds. "Alright, my able-bodied warriors. Time to test the void."

They made their way to the control room, newly grown and shaped precisely for them. Every surface curved naturally beneath their fingers, every panel and couch had been formed with them in mind. As they strapped into their acceleration couches, each with their controls within perfect reach, Mother's voice echoed softly. "The void is unlike anything you've experienced. It is the space we enter when we need to travel great distances quickly. But it comes with strain. On the body, yes, but more so on the mind. We'll need to make several jumps in the coming days to acclimate you. Once battle begins, you must be able to slip into and out of the void without hesitation.

"Silas, you must keep your mind clear. Tactical thinking, precision, and reaction time—your focus will guide our movement. Elias, your instinct and speed must mesh with your brother's thoughts, integrating the weapons with his maneuvers. Strike before being struck. Move as one. Think as one."

She paused, almost contemplative. "With you two, something remarkable happens. Your minds—working together—are more capable than even my own vast systems. I am a powerful warship on my own. But with you, I become something else. Something more."

And with that, they began. The first ten jumps were brutal. Each exit from the void left them panting, their hearts racing. After the tenth, both lay gasping in their couches. A2 flickered to life, concerned. "Silas, your heart rate and blood pressure are elevated. Are you alright?"

Silas didn't need to speak aloud, but he did anyway, forcing a breathless grin. "I feel like I just ran ten marathons. But I'm fine."

"That's expected," A2 replied. "It's similar to experiencing multiple g-forces in a jet or being deep underwater with crushing pressure. Your body will adapt. Imagine how much worse it would be without armor."

That thought sobered Silas. The strain was enormous and they were protected. What kind of stress had Mother shielded them from? There was no time for reflection. The exercise resumed.

Over the next month, the twins trained relentlessly—diving in and out of the void, striking projected targets, and reacting faster each time. They didn't need to speak. Not anymore. Thoughts passed between them effortlessly, one mind guiding the ship's course and the other unleashing its fury. Silas moved through tactics like a composer at a symphony—each beat timed to perfection. Elias danced through fire with lethal grace—every shot an extension of himself. The integration was total. Mother watched it all with something bordering awe. *They might be the finest crew I've ever carried.*

***

Valshar was feeling better. Strange as that might sound for a living ship, it was true. In fact, he felt stronger now than at any time in memory. His crew was focused and hardened. They had come to the edge and survived. That experience had forged something new in them: not just skill, but unity. They had learned a new form of war, one that might yet free not only his people but countless others crushed beneath the emperor's heel for far too long. He felt fearsome.

With fresh energy, Valshar called out, his voice resonating through the corridors of his sleek hull. "Wake up, my charges. We are ready. I have been restored by the Ancient One's gifts, and now I will lend my strength to the great ship in this battle. Today, we take the fight to them."

Grace and the noble soldier were already rising, their bodies sore but their spirits burning with new fire. When they reached the control chamber, they noticed immediately that they were already in motion. The stars streaked around them in a blur as Valshar hurtled through the void, back toward Earth.

"Valshar!" Grace shouted, grabbing a support rail as she steadied herself. "Why the rush?"

Valshar's reply was immediate, almost urgent. "Because I can feel it. The great ship and the twins—something is coming. Whoever commands this fleet knows what they're doing. We must prepare, and we must strike before they reach Earth." What Valshar didn't yet know was that the great ship, and the twins, were racing toward him, too. Two forces hurtling toward one another. The clash, when it came, would shake the foundations of the galaxy for centuries to come.

***

Mother's voice came to them, not spoken aloud, but felt deep within. It echoed in their minds like a shared breath, and all who were aboard the ship understood it. The twins, the dogs, the bots, even Vaeril. A silent broadcast, a message felt rather than heard. *Attention, my crew. We are en route to intercept Valshar now. The enemy fleet we face is approximately one hundred forty ships strong. Between the two of us, we should be able to manage. However, if the situation becomes dire, the Ancient*

One is nearby and may intervene, though she will only act if the need is great. Her ways are mysterious, but her loyalty is without question.

Mother's tone sharpened slightly. *Valshar has already reported something different about this fleet. I believe they have a tactician with them.*

Silas stiffened. "What kind of tactician?"

A queen, Mother replied. The word dropped like a stone.

"A queen?" they all shouted—Silas, Elias, Vaeril, even the dogs reacted instinctively.

Yes, she continued. *If this is true, it's a rare chance. Capturing or eliminating a queen could yield crucial intelligence—on their command structure, fleet organization, even internal fractures in their hierarchy. This could give us a significant advantage.*

Silas leaned forward. "Then let's get to it."

Vaeril interjected, "Should I bring my ship into the fight? One more vessel in the fray couldn't hurt."

Yes, Mother answered. *But I will also be giving you a tactical enhancement. It won't replace your twin, but it may give you an edge.* She paused before adding, with a hint of amusement, *The Ancient One has gifted me a tactical AI—an autonomous battle unit stored in the hold. It has been activated and is already integrating with your ship's systems. You may find it colorful.*

Vaeril arched a brow, suspicious but curious. His sleek courier ship, already linked with Mother, accepted the tactical robot's systems. As the AI settled in, Vaeril couldn't shake the feeling that his quiet ride was about to get a lot louder.

Silas's thoughts began to drift. They circled around one name, one face. Grace. *I'm consumed with thoughts of her,* he admitted silently. *I just hope I cross her mind once in a while. Or hell, maybe even more than once. That would be nice.*

Strangely enough, light-years away, Grace was having the same thoughts. She sat quietly in Valshar's war room, a storm of fire and death raging just outside the hull, yet her mind was elsewhere. *I wonder if I ever cross his mind. Even just for a moment.* She could still feel the pressure of his hand on the small of her back—that gentle, instinctive touch to keep her from falling in the store. She hadn't been in real danger, not truly, but his reaction had been immediate—protective and pure. That moment had stayed with her. She had known loyalty in her life. Twisted, warped versions of it, bred from fear and manipulation. But simple, selfless *kindness*? That had been rare for her, maybe nonexistent. Until Silas. And now she wanted more. Not just any kindness, *his* kindness. Not from anyone else. Just him.

Vaeril was nervous. That was strange. He boarded his ship, the only place that had ever felt like home, and paused. For the first time in centuries, he wasn't sure what came next. This ship had been his sanctuary ever since the death of his twin. After the screaming had stopped. After the silence had grown too loud to bear. After the rage had burned away the grief and left him hollow. He had stopped lingering on planets. Stopped talking to people. He drifted between stars like a ghost in a tomb of steel, recruiting twins, fighting battles, and just … surviving. His anger had been his compass, his wrath, his companion. His revenge and his religion. But revenge, he'd learned, begins white-hot and pure. It sears and scars, but then it cools. And when it cools, it calcifies. It becomes cold—*ice-cold.*

He had destroyed everything in his path. But destruction only numbs the pain, it never erases it. Now, he had seen the twins rise after all they had suffered. He had seen something rare in Silas: restraint in the midst of wrath. And something rarer still in Elias: hope beneath all the chaos. Maybe he *could* be whole again. He didn't know how to talk about it, not even to an AI. He wasn't ready. He didn't trust his own voice yet. And solitude had become such a deep part of him that even a conversation felt like peeling back armor. But still … something stirred.

***

Varnak'Tal, High Executioner of the Vorrhaxi and the emperor's most ruthless and loyal fleet commander, stood silently in the throne hall. He had been summoned to the emperor's palace, though in truth, he would've come uninvited if necessary. Like Khar'Zul, he did not suffer fools, and the empire, in his view, was choking on them. He seethed at the reckless waste he saw unfolding across the galaxy. Resources—ships, warriors, entire colonies—were being squandered in petty internal skirmishes when they should have been driving the conquest forward. The emperor, once a towering figure of control, had allowed things to spiral. The queens had grown wild, indulging in power plays that had sparked a needless rebellion. And now the emperor, so desperate to send a message, had unleashed the lunatic Malvek on his own garrisons, slaughtering loyal warriors and innocent civilians alike.

Each queen once had her use. Now, only three of the original five remained. One had been butchered by Malvek. Another executed by the emperor's own hand. Of the remaining three, two had vanished into the black. Only Threxil remained visible—still at large, now joined with that ragtag fleet dispatched to deal with the "threat" the Spymaster had discovered. Shaskiel, the one commanding that mess of a fleet, was no fool. A capable commander. But the fleet he'd been given? Trash, mostly. A few proper warships surrounded his flagship, but the rest? Barely functional, with crews even worse. And yet, something out there was still managing to destroy them.

Varnak'Tal's informants had reported disturbing details: a single enemy ship, maybe two, had utterly annihilated the Reaver and his twenty-four-ship flotilla. The Reaver wasn't brilliant, but he wasn't soft, either. Fanatical, yes, but no amateur.

And before that? Sixteen other ships, stalked and destroyed, one by one. This wasn't just bad luck. Something powerful was out there—something dangerous. Varnak'Tal clenched a fist behind his back. The emperor needed to get off his damn throne of bones and start acting like the warlord he once was, before it was too late. Malvek had to be leashed and the queens brought to heel. And whatever was lurking in the void had to be met with every ounce of the Empire's remaining strength. Because if they didn't unite now, the waves crashing toward them would drown them all.

***

Roach awakened once again—a stranger in a stranger land. He was uncomfortable, but then again, he'd been uncomfortable his entire life unless he was in his own space. In that space, he was in control, merciful or merciless, however he pleased. He was the undisputed master of his own universe. He despised anything outside of it.

These past months, under the control of the Nillith, had been equal parts heaven and hell. When the Nillith stuffed him down into one of his tailored fantasies, it was bliss—his heaven. But when he was cast into *that* other place, he shuddered involuntarily. He didn't even like to think about it. He wouldn't, not yet. What the Nillith didn't seem to realize was that Roach was always testing the walls, always probing for weakness. He'd started to understand what irritated the Nillith just enough to get what he wanted—a shift in setting, a little freedom, or a better dream. It was a game now. A long one. What the Nillith didn't understand was that inch by inch, foot by foot, even if the journey was a million miles, Roach would move forward. Relentlessly and patiently, like a starving predator locked on the scent of prey.

Soon, I will take this body back. Then I will have the power. The power to return to Earth and make all those who wronged me, even slightly, pay a grievous and terrible price. Just as they deserve. For denying me what was mine, for denying me everything. Suddenly, the room faded. Roach was back inside one of his twisted mental playgrounds, acting out another revenge fantasy like a child breaking toys in the dark.

The Nillith chuckled to itself. *What a piece of clay I have in this Roach. Maybe I'll keep him after all. He keeps getting more interesting by the day.*

Defeating the Nillith, he mused, was like an ant facing off against a god. But a chilling thought slipped through the cracks of his smugness. *An ant can still bite, painfully so.* Still, he could handle an ant bite, or any bite, for that matter. He had been bitten before. Now wasn't the time to fear a minuscule sting. Now was the time to close in on his prey.

And speaking of predators, Malvek was basking in his own private carnival of slaughter. So much death. So much chaos. And he loved it with every blackened, rotting fiber of his being. His latest tactic? He took his victims one by one, leaving their comrades to stew in dread and paranoia. A few days later, the missing would reappear, macabrely displayed for all to see, posed like dolls in some twisted funeral diorama. The message was simple: *You are next.* They couldn't fight what they couldn't catch. Couldn't run from what they couldn't see. Couldn't protect their loved ones from a phantom with a butcher's heart. The feeling of dominance was euphoric. The terror in the air was thick as fog. Not the kind that burned off with morning sun—*this fog lingered.* But soon, very soon ... the tables would turn. And the predator would become the prey.

Darkness had fallen, and Malvek was on the hunt. He had already chosen his next victim—another soul to drag back to his lair of despair. As he crept forward to claim his prize, something strange happened. He felt a presence behind him. That alone was unusual. No one had ever dared stalk Malvek. No one had ever succeeded in sneaking up on him. Yet, the sensation was there, looming, just beyond the reach of his senses. Something was watching and waiting. It unsettled him. For the first time in his long life, Malvek—monster of a thousand massacres—felt something alien to him: fear. But the fear didn't last long. There was no time for it to fully bloom.

In the next instant, there was only darkness. Not the comfort of shadows he had known his whole life. No, this was deeper. A total absence of sensation. No sound, no feeling, no form. He couldn't move. He couldn't even scream. The great butcher of worlds was caught like a spider in a far older web. And his torment had only just begun. Soon, Malvek would pay for his sins, and his punishment would be so horrific, it would make the very stones weep.

***

Khar'Zul hurried back to her hidden lair, the air around her vibrating with anticipation. She had just received news of a potential game-changing advantage. The Spymaster, sniveling, treacherous vermin that he was, had finally uncovered something truly useful. The armada, it seemed, was in the midst of laying an audacious trap. Risky, yes, but undeniably clever. Threxil, the inconvenient warrior queen who had attached herself to Shaskiel's fleet, might yet serve a purpose, even if her greatest value ended up being her death. To Khar'Zul's mild surprise, the bumbling fool Shaskiel was displaying a flash of cunning she had never credited him with. His ploy was simple and vicious—use Threxil as bait to draw in the living ship for one final ambush. The capture of such a ship would be nothing short of a prize beyond imagining, a weapon that could shift the balance of the war.

But Khar'Zul suspected there was more at play, far more. The enemy would find this bait irresistible, and if they took it, she might finally discover whether the assassin and the noble soldier had truly turned traitor. Their ship had returned to the empire without them, an unprecedented act that hinted at something extraordinary. If they *had* been turned, she could spin it to her own advantage. She could turn their betrayal into a blade aimed directly at the emperor himself.

The question of how to aim this weapon at the emperor was, in truth, far simpler than it appeared. The Spymaster, who, for once, had proven himself to be more than a self-serving parasite, had woven a scheme so intricate that even Khar'Zul found it compelling. There were many *ifs* to account for, but the foundation was solid. First, Malvek had to be gone, either permanently, or at the very least, long enough to remove him as a variable. Second, the assassin and the noble soldier had to be confirmed turncoats. Third, Shaskiel's plan to use Threxil as bait in the coming assault on Earth had to unfold exactly as intended, tempting their enemies into the open. The tactical lure was undeniable. The capture of Threxil was an opportunity too delicious to ignore. True, there was the faint risk that Threxil might reveal secrets to the enemy, but in Khar'Zul's mind, the far likelier outcome was that Threxil would die in battle. And if, against all odds, she emerged victorious, then Khar'Zul would have a far greater prize: a living ship to dismantle, study, and replicate—building her own fleet of intelligent, unstoppable warships.

Yet, despite the ship's allure, Khar'Zul's eyes were fixed on an even greater prize. The noble soldier. If she could capture him, the rewards would be immediate and devastating. In her hands, he could become the spark that set the emperor's reign ablaze and reduced his legacy to ash. Oh yes, she had plans for him. And none of them ended with his survival.

"So, Spymaster," Khar'Zul purred, "how exactly are you going to make Malvek disappear for me?" If the Spymaster could have changed color, he would have. Instead, the air around him shifted. Khar'Zul caught the subtle change in scent—the acrid tang of fear, the stale shadow of death, and the bitter sting of torment—rolling off him in equal measure. Had he been able to speak, his reply would have come out in a stammering, broken mess. But he never got the chance. The chamber's shadows stirred, and someone unexpected stepped inside. Zev'Kala.

Her eyes found the Spymaster instantly, and her lip curled. She despised him—saw him as the simpering waste of flesh he was—and had never bothered to hide it. She spared him no more than a glance before turning to Khar'Zul. "I have news," she said, voice low and deliberate. "Important news. Relevant to our survival." Khar'Zul's eyes narrowed. Zev'Kala stepped closer, her tone sharpened to a blade's edge. "I have information about Malvek. While you've been weaving your webs, I've been spinning a few of my own."

The two queens exchanged a look heavy with calculation. Both had the same unspoken concern—since Malvek had already tasted the blood of one queen, would he now seek to wet his fangs and claws with the blood of others? And they both knew the emperor's decree: betrayal, imagined or real, carried only one punishment. A death sentence without reprieve.

Little did either queen know that Malvek had already been removed from the board. The Nillith was now the hidden hand behind the empire's inner workings. Malvek would pay for his sins many times over, not in retribution for his crimes, but because the Nillith fed on suffering. The darkness that had long embraced the empire was nothing compared to the blackness now circling just out of sight.

The Spymaster knew Malvek was gone, and the knowledge unsettled him. To think that something—or someone—could swat Malvek aside like a child, without struggle, was almost unthinkable. That was not mere strength, that was dominance. Whatever had done it, he was certain it would bring no benefit to him or to the empire.

Far away, the Nillith cackled to himself. The pieces were in play, though the exact shape of the game had yet to form. Chaos on an epic scale was inevitable. The suffering and fear Malvek had inspired would soon be as nothing—mere drops in an ocean compared to what the Nillith intended to unleash. If the Nillith had a physical mouth, it would have filled with saliva at the thought of the feast to come. It was okay, though, that's why he had Roach.

***

Malvek thrashed in the dark. He could see nothing, feel nothing, smell nothing. It had been lifetimes since he'd felt fear or helplessness, yet now, he'd tasted both twice within a single planetary rotation. What could have taken him so completely by surprise? Who dared to pull him from his fun? It didn't matter. Whoever it was, he would find them. He would make the blood flow like rivers and kill everything they loved.

Little did he know, what had him didn't love anyone or anything beyond the endless hunger it fed on. Suddenly, light—harsh and alien—broke through a sky choked with clouds. He was lying on his back in mud. Ramshackle old houses stretched in all directions, their walls stained with the soot of a fire long past. The place felt familiar, but the memory danced just beyond reach. Rough hands seized him, dragging him upright. Voices barked in a language that should have been familiar but felt strangely wrong. Blows rained down. He hit the ground, was hauled up, and beaten again. Instinctively, he looked for his talons, only to see soft, blunt flesh where they should have been. No armor. No claws. *What is this?*

They dragged him into a brick-and-metal building and hurled him into a cell. Every few hours they came, dragging him out for another merciless beating. They never asked a single question. *What the hell is this?*

The Nillith roared with laughter, savoring the sight of Malvek struggling to understand where—or when—he was. Such a delicious mind to unravel. So many lovely sins to choose from, each one a jagged shard the Nillith could twist to torment him. It was too easy, really. Punishing the evil with their own sins … it was almost poetic. It never once occurred to the Nillith to consider what might happen if the tables were ever turned.

Silently, in the background, Roach absorbed everything. The Nillith's new toy had given him another chance, another sliver of time to study the cracks in the entity's armor. One day, he would escape. Or at the very least, he would find a way to lock the Nillith out of his mind. The suffering had been so relentless that for the first time, Roach almost wanted to repent. To beg forgiveness from whatever merciful creator had brought him into existence. Surely, there was something greater out there. *What's wrong with me? Am I so broken*

I'm seeking repentance for the unforgivable? He tried to justify his crimes. He'd only killed those he'd been sent after. He had a code—there were no innocents on his list. But he couldn't deny the truth: he'd enjoyed it. Every kill. Every moment. All those who had hurt him in his youth had shaped him into the monster he'd become. And yet, there were no accidents, only choices.

The thought faltered as the mocking, maniacal laughter of the Nillith rose in the background. Once again, the bastard had steered his mind where it wanted, and once again, Roach found himself dancing on the puppet strings.

***

Vaeril stepped into his ship. It had never been named, sentient only in the barest sense, just enough to care for itself with minimal direction. Unlike Mother, Valshar, or the Ancient One, it had no discernible personality. If it had ever formed opinions, it had kept them to itself. Most ships were given female names, with Valshar as a rare exception—a unique character in every sense, at least according to Mother's stories. Truth be told, Vaeril had never thought much about it. But now, with a combat AI installed, things would be different.

Solitude had always been his refuge. He wasn't sure how it would feel to have someone—something—talking to him constantly. And not just any something, but an AI with the personality of a teenager, smarter than him by a factor of a million. Which, he mused, was what most teenagers thought anyway. Except in this case, it was true. And this "teenager" now controlled some of the most devastating ship-to-ship weapons in the galaxy, working in concert with other vessels whose arsenals might be even deadlier. Added to this was the fact that the fate of the universe was currently perched in his claws, and well, as humans liked to say, it was just another day at the office. Yeah, right.

Vaeril stalked onto the deck, each step striking the floor with deliberate weight. The sound wasn't accidental, it was a declaration, even if he hadn't yet decided exactly what he was declaring. Intent? Authority? Maybe both. What he *did* know was this: when dealing with new recruits—or teenagers, which wasn't much different—you had to come in hard from the start. Set the tone, establish authority immediately, and never let it slip. Start soft, and you'd never get it back. He'd seen too many twins fail over the years because no one had taken a firm enough hand early on. And here, there was no room for sympathy. No room for error.

So, he squared himself up, ready to treat this AI like any green recruit—sharp orders, no warmth, and no leniency. That turned out to be a mistake. Vaeril entered the control room of his courier warship without a word. He lowered himself into the command chair and sat in silence. Minutes passed, then an hour, then an hour and a half. *Stubborn. Alright, two can play at that game.* By the two-hour mark, a hint of impatience was creeping in. He wasn't sure why, it wasn't unusual for him to go days aboard a ship without speaking to anyone. He'd done it so often that when he finally did speak, his throat would croak like a rusted old hinge. *Still, we've got work to do.*

Finally, he broke the silence. "So, by what name are you called, AI?"

"Oh, so now we're speaking?" the AI replied, voice calm but carrying a subtle jab.

Vaeril bristled, unsure why it irritated him so much. "Yes, we're speaking now. I'm in command, and I'll decide when to speak and when not to speak."

The AI's tone sharpened—biting but with a trace of amusement. "Oh, *you're* in charge? Well, sir, I won't make a move without your command."

"What the hell is that supposed to mean?" Vaeril shot back.

The AI didn't miss a beat. "Well, Pops, let's just say there are missiles coming in and you're distracted. Maybe something to do with your *ancient* bodily functions not working the way they used to. Should I defend the ship, or let us be destroyed while you answer nature's call?" This comment landed like an atomic bomb.

Vaeril was on his feet in an instant, his fist slamming into the control panel hard enough to send a spray of sparks into the air. His voice, normally calm, collected, and deliberate, now thundered through the ship. "Why, you little shit! If you ever take that tone with me again, I will make it my life's mission to hunt down exactly where you reside in this ship and rip you out—wire by wire, circuit by circuit—until there's nothing left of you but the smell of ozone and melted nanotech!" The echoes of his outburst rolled through the corridors, lingering like the aftershock of a quake.

It was then that a phrase the AI had just used caught him off guard. It sounded familiar. He stood still for a long moment, searching his memory. Vaeril was easily bored, and during his long surveillance of the twins on Earth, he'd often sought ways to amuse himself. When they slept, or in Elias's case, when he spent long hours either with women or was passed out from too much of the hard stuff, Vaeril had watched something he'd found strangely captivating: Earth sitcoms. Especially the ones with snotty teenagers who seemed to think sarcasm was a martial art. He couldn't be certain, but he was fairly sure he'd heard something very much like the AI's remark from one of those shows.

He let the thought roll around a moment longer, then leaned in toward the console. "So, AI … how exactly did you learn to communicate with entities so unlike yourself?"

"Well," the AI began, "I learned to communicate the best way I could. I didn't really have anyone to talk to, so I tapped into the television broadcasts from the nearest inhabited planet. I didn't have access to anything from your home world, so I made do with what I found—Earth programming. I absorbed everything I could: sitcoms, war films, documentaries. There were a lot of war films. I used them to try to understand how to interact with someone like you—a soldier, battle-hardened, and cautious about trusting a new partner. Especially one you might be expected to lead into battle for the first time."

Vaeril let out a long breath. "I think I understand. So, what are you called?"

"I'm not really called anything," the AI admitted. "But if I'm allowed to choose …"

"Let's pick you a name, then," Vaeril said. "What do you most closely associate yourself with?"

The AI went silent, and for an AI, silence meant processing at a speed measured in trillions of calculations per second. Finally, it spoke, hesitant but certain. "If I can choose my own name … I think I'd like to be called Orrin."

Vaeril had never heard the name Orrin before, nor did he know its origin. In the interest of forging a better connection with the AI, he finally asked, "Tell me, what does Orrin mean?"

"It means green or leafy," the AI replied without hesitation. "It can also mean pale green, but the deeper meaning is 'like a tree.' A tree is the foundation, the living anchor from which all else grows. I would like to think of myself that way—rooted, steady, the base from which we move forward together. When you say my name, you'll know that I am the trunk and roots of our relationship."

Vaeril chuckled softly. "You're a bright one, Orrin. Well then," he said after a moment, "Orrin it is. I'm going to depend on you for my life, and more importantly, the twins and the other sentient ships will depend on us for theirs. We're well-armed," Vaeril continued, "not heavily armored, but fast and highly maneuverable. Our job is to scout and harass—make them bleed in a hundred little ways—until the other ships are in position for a decisive strike. Think you can come up with some strategies for that?"

Orrin's eyes would have lit up if he had actual eyes instead of just a million tiny connections to the ship's sensors. As proud as any teenager who sought the approval of his demanding but loving father, he launched into a rapid-fire stream of ideas—ambush patterns, feints to lure Vorrhaxi ships out of formation, strike angles that would cripple weapons arrays, and ways to shield each other while setting up kill shots.

Vaeril nodded as he listened. "I like it. But remember, if I think it, you think it. If you're thinking it, I'd better be thinking the same. We move like one mind, one purpose. Whatever we do multiplies the other's effort."

"I can do that," Orrin said without hesitation.

"Good." Vaeril keyed the controls. The engines roared to life, and in the next heartbeat, the ship slipped into the void. Vaeril, all the while, was nodding in approval just like any proud father would do. It was very strange how the little shit had turned the tides on him so quickly. Vaeril felt the sudden pressure pinning him back into his command chair, the familiar weight of acceleration wrapping around him like an old friend. The void had been calling to him for months, though he hadn't realized how much until now. All that time on Earth—watching the twins from the shadows above or in the thick of their chaos—had felt like a detour. This was home.

Soon, they would take the fight to the Vorrhaxi. Maybe it wouldn't be the last battle, but it could be the first step toward ending this war. The beginning of the end. A push to turn the galaxy back toward what it was meant to be. For the first time in years, he allowed himself hope. And that hope was enough to carry him forward. He glanced at the ship's consoles, the quiet hum of the AI beside him. Strange, how easily he found himself thinking of it as a friend. Stranger still, how in this universe, some of your truest companions weren't flesh and blood at all.

CHAPTER TWELVE

She's here. The thought slammed into Silas's mind without warning, yanking him from sleep. Alex lay at the foot of his bed, keeping watch, though it wasn't really necessary. Mother would never let anything get near him without warning. She was the kind of mother everyone needed: fiercely protective, endlessly loving, and smart enough to know her boys weren't always blameless but always redeemable. It was a miracle, really, how well they'd turned out considering the role models they'd had … or hadn't had.

But none of that mattered right now. Grace was here. Hours, maybe less, separated him from being in the presence of the woman he longed for, despite their very brief encounter. Stranger still, he knew she'd been sent to Earth to kill him. *How freaking weird is that?*

Alex chuckled in his mind, playfully projecting an image of himself being chased by a female pit bull clearly intent on mating.

"You're very funny, Alex," Silas muttered.

Oh really? Alex's voice echoed back, dripping amusement.

"Not funny. Not funny at all, Alex. Get out of my head, you pervert."

Nature is nature, man. I can't help you're naughty. Now Alex was doing the full-on doggy roll-on-the-floor laugh, and Silas did not find it amusing. With a huff, he stomped out of the room, rushing toward the main control deck, Alex trotting close behind.

Valshar and Mother eased toward each other, their hulls aligning with practiced precision. They had known each other for eons, but never had their connection been so frequent, so … intimate. Docking this often felt like clasping the hand of an old friend after decades apart—warm, familiar, and strangely comforting.

Mother's thoughts drifted, her mind lingering on that warmth, on how smooth and welcoming it felt. Then, abruptly, she caught herself. *What in the Ancient One am I thinking?* She knew the answer. Silas. His mind had grown so strong, his thoughts so potent, they were bleeding into her own. It was unsettling and astonishing. In her long life, she had met millions of sentients and knew of trillions more, yet none possessed the raw, natural force Silas now carried. The implications were staggering. She imagined, for a moment, the kind of children that might come from Silas and Grace, beings whose combined DNA might reshape the very balance of the universe. The thought was intoxicating and dangerous. Her mood sobered. Perhaps this was something best prevented before it began. The outcome could be overly dramatic, to put it mildly. It might even shake the foundations of existence itself. Still, a faint inner smile touched her mind. *Young love or old love. It's all the same in the end.* Then her tone shifted, her resolve hardening. Time to play the protective parent. Time to have *the talk.*

Elias caught up with Silas in the narrow passageway leading to the control room, where they'd be meeting with the others. The moment he saw him, Elias knew something was on his brother's mind. No mental link was needed—he was his brother, and that was enough. Even the AI managing Silas's armor had noticed. A2 had asked him three times in the past fifteen minutes if he was all alright. His heart rate and blood pressure were elevated, and he was sweating despite A2 lowering the armor's internal temperature twice.

Meanwhile, Alex and Max sat nearby with looks that could only be described as *mischievous dog humor*—the kind that usually meant they'd just shredded someone's favorite slippers.

Elias caught the thought instantly. *Oh, hell no. Nobody's putting anything in their mouth that's been near those smelly-ass feet. That stench would knock a maggot off a gut wagon, pal.*

Both dogs glanced at each other, looking seconds away from collapsing in a wheezing heap, the kind of laughter so hard it steals your breath.

Mother slowed the twins' progress just enough as they made their way toward the control room, giving herself time to speak privately with Grace before the twins met the empire's two newest warriors-turned-liberators.

When the assassin stepped into the airlock, the noble soldier, who normally insisted on leading whenever danger might be ahead, was strangely two or three feet behind her. It wasn't much, but enough to notice. Everything in his movement seemed just slightly delayed, though not in any way he could put a finger on.

Grace stepped through the hatch into Mother's entry chamber and the airtight door slammed shut behind her, locking with a final metallic clang. The noble soldier lunged forward, his internal alarms flaring, and grabbed for the controls. Before he could act, he felt Valshar's presence in his mind, a calm, steady reassurance. *Don't worry, my friend. Nothing will happen to Grace. Mother would never harm anyone entrusted to my care. I suspect she only wants a few moments alone with her to explain the finer points of caring for and handling a certain twin they both have an interest in.*

An interest? The soldier blinked, surprised. *Surely not.* But then again, he'd seen stranger things lately. With a reluctant nod to himself, he stepped back and waited for whatever was unfolding on the other side of that hatch.

Grace flinched as the hatch slammed shut behind her, the sound ringing in the narrow corridor. For an instant, she feared it had caught her escort, the shadow who had rarely been more than a step away from her in recent memory. She turned toward the next hatch, intending to keep moving, but it sealed with the same sudden violence. A spike of unease slid through her chest. Then something truly strange happened. Mother appeared. Not a voice in the air or the unseen presence Grace had come to know, but a physical form—a woman, perhaps in her late fifties, strikingly fit and poised. There was a disciplined elegance to her, the kind of strength that came from years of refusing to let the world wear you down. She addressed Grace in perfect Earth-standard, but also in a far older language—one of subtle gestures, faint pheromone traces, and luminous pulses where a Vorrhaxi crest might have been.

"Young woman," Mother said, her voice low and even, "I have one question for you. If your answer is not what I think it should be, I will open this airlock, and the frigid embrace of space will be the last thing you ever feel." She let the words hang in the silence, giving Grace a moment to feel the full weight of the threat before continuing. "We are about to engage in a battle—a battle that will ignite a war capable of consuming this system and many others. The Thal'Naari, the Vorrhaxi, and humanity are about to be locked in a death struggle. It will end one of two ways: with the emperor and all his lackeys overthrown, or with the final extinction of my kind and the destruction of every race aligned against the empire. I will need everyone in this struggle to be *all in*. No hesitation and no divided loyalties. If we are to be victorious, there can be no fractures in our resolve. This is our last chance to bring freedom to the universe. And know this—there are far worse things in the dark beyond the empire. The day may come when all free people must unite against something far deadlier."

"Oh, great ship, I am all in—there's no doubt, one hundred percent!" Grace's voice carried conviction.

"I'm glad to hear that," the ship replied. "You can call me *Mother* now. That is my chosen name." There was a pause. "However, that wasn't my question."

Grace tilted her head. "Then what was it?"

"My question," Mother said, her tone hardening, "is this: what are your intentions with my boy Silas? Don't answer right away, girl. Think before you speak because that space temperature I mentioned before isn't getting any warmer, if you take my meaning."

Grace's smile was faint. "Oh, Mother, is that all you need to know?"

"Yes," Mother said sharply, nearly losing patience.

"Then here it is: I intend to give him everything he will let me give. My strength and my loyalty. All that I am. As long as I breathe, I will defend him with every ounce of what I have, until I live no more."

"Well …" Mother's voice softened only slightly. "I suppose that will do. But be warned, if you don't … if you hurt him or if you break him, I will not be merciful. You've heard of my reputation among your kind?"

"Yes, Mother."

"Then you know I've burned worlds for merely *scaring* one of my charges. Silas is not just a charge, he is one of my children. Oh, he may not look like me, and I may not have birthed him like his birth mother, but I am his mother now. I will protect him as if I birthed him myself. Do you understand me?"

"Yes, Mother."

"Good. Then we won't need to bring this up with Silas. Agreed?"

"Agreed. A question, Mother—what about the other twin, Elias?"

"Oh, sweetie." Mother slipped into a slow, honeyed southern drawl. "That boy's a tomcat, and I actually feel sorry for the girl who manages to catch him for real."

The hatch opened, and the noble soldier stepped in, catching the faint look of amusement still on Grace's face as she turned and headed for the control room to meet the twins.

***

Varnak'Tal had been waiting outside the throne room for what felt like ages before he was finally summoned inside. The emperor was pacing when he entered, his massive form moving with restless energy. At the far end of the hall, the emperor turned, spotted the grand admiral, and without a word, dismissed the remaining courtiers and advisers with a single gesture and a sharp pheromone of banishment. The admiral was accustomed to these brief, almost wordless meetings. Normally, the emperor's communication came in fragments—gestures, a flash from the ridge of his crest, or the layered complexity of scents so strong they were almost overwhelming. Sometimes the orders didn't even come from the emperor directly; he would hand over sealed scent capsules to be opened later, away from the throne. Questions were never welcomed. Orders were given, and they were to be carried out, swiftly, and without hesitation, no matter how impossible the task might seem. The grand admiral had always delivered.

But today was different. The emperor's posture was less imposing, his movements lacking their usual certainty. The rapid back-and-forth that followed was strange, almost unsettling. For the first time in Varnak'Tal's memory, the emperor seemed unsure; his confidence was diminished and his presence somehow smaller. It was as if the unshakable force that had ruled for centuries had been hollowed out, leaving something hesitant in its place.

The emperor did not want him to act, only to watch and report. It was an unusual order, one he had never been given before. Normally, such a battle would have been beneath his notice, a flicker of conflict soon extinguished. But the Spymaster's warning had unsettled the emperor, and that alone was enough to make him curious. When the grand admiral learned of the assassin's failure and the noble soldier's defection, he had expected to be ordered to end the threat outright. Destroying Earth would have been trivial—a single task force could reduce that primitive, undefended backwater to ash. Instead, the emperor had left the matter in the hands of Shaskiel and now, the capable Threxil. It made no sense. Why entrust such a problem to a ragged fleet when overwhelming force was readily at hand?

He did not ask. It was not his place to ask. His duty was to obey, to carry out the emperor's wishes, and to see his plans realized exactly as ordered. Still … the directive gnawed at him. Something larger was in motion, something the emperor had not yet revealed. And though he could not yet put his claw on it, he knew the truth would show itself in time.

***

After putting his ship and the new AI, Orrin, through their paces, Vaeril swung the vessel back toward the sector where Mother and Valshar waited. The team was finally together again, gathered in the freshly formed war room aboard Mother.

Mother's voice filled the chamber, calm, yet carrying the weight of command. "The time has come for us to project our strength against those who would see us destroyed. We must send a message that this solar system is off-limits to the empire and to anyone else who would threaten it. This will be our fortress, our rallying ground. From here we will strike back, and from here we will endure. We will make this system and the space surrounding it so impenetrable that none will dare face us." She paused, and her eyes—if such a thing could be said of her—seemed to focus on each of them in turn. "Now, to the most immediate matter: the fleet approaching us. We will meet it far from this place. Earth is not ready to see what is about to happen. If they witness the battle, panic will spread across the planet, and unity will become impossible. It will already be difficult enough to bring Earth's fractured factions into alignment. We cannot afford to make that task harder than it already is." Her words left the room silent, the reality settling over them like the weight of a drawn blade. The battle was coming, sooner than anyone wanted, and the space between the stars was about to burn.

"First things first," Mother continued, her voice filling every corner of the command chamber. "We reduce the fleet in stages, set a series of traps. We'll pick them off one by one. If targets of opportunity present themselves, we strike without hesitation. But most importantly … it has been many years since we have faced the empire outright in open combat. Things will have changed. We must gather intelligence, everything we can, to make our strikes more effective. It will take time to rally ships and train crews. We must send a message to the empire that we are far stronger than they believe."

Vaeril opened his mouth to speak, but Grace cut in. "Mother, the last fleet we faced, though small, was destroyed handily by the Ancient One. Is there any chance she'll appear again? She alone could tear through the fleet like a human child swatting a fly."

For the first time, Mother called her *my child.* The title settled over the crew with unexpected weight. "She is fickle," Mother said. "She comes and goes as she pleases, answering to no one. If she believes our cause is righteous, she may come. The last time, she intervened because you were hopelessly outnumbered and the Ancient One hates a bully. Whether she joins us now depends entirely on her mood.

"So, to make a long story short, I don't know. We'll have to wait and see. But the most important thing we can do is fight our own battles. We must send the empire a message. If nothing else, they are cautious until they believe they can overwhelm their enemy. Grace and her companion know this all too well."

The Vorrhaxi soldier stepped forward without hesitation. *Yes, Mother. That is exactly our doctrine. We attack only when the numbers guarantee victory.*

Mother translated his words for the others, since only Grace understood his language of gestures, scents, and flashes of light. It was a barrier she knew she'd have to solve, eventually. But not today. Today, her mind pushed that problem aside and returned to the only thing that mattered now: planning the battle to come.

"So, Mother," Silas began, "when you're talking about intelligence we can gather, what exactly could give us the upper hand?"

Mother's voice came through, steady and confident. "Many things. Weapons designs, tactical doctrines, even a single live captain or engineer could be a boon. But if we were to capture the leader of the fleet" —she let the thought hang for a moment— "we could learn far more: how the fleet was formed, what its true mission is, and perhaps most importantly, the current state of the empire's inner politics. The empire has been quiet for some time. Expansion has slowed. That is not in their nature. Something is happening, and if we uncover it, we may find leverage."

Grace leaned forward. "Mother, I think you're right about something going on, though I'm not certain it will be the kind of leverage you mean. But I am certain there's another possibility. During the last battle, there was a presence in their fleet. An influence that hadn't been there before. I felt it guiding them, directing them. If I'm correct, a queen may be among their numbers." Her eyes hardened. "If we could capture her alive … the things we might learn could change the entire war."

Zareth'Kai. Mother's voice filled his mind, the sound of his own name echoing inside his head in a way that felt utterly alien. *I am going to ask your permission to do something for you,* she said. *It will make you more capable in the battle ahead, and it will benefit those around you. Will you accept for their sake?*

Being asked permission was strange enough. Stranger still was hearing his name spoken like this. He had always known it, of course, but never as something personal. Never as something that belonged only to him.

For the good of the many, he answered without hesitation, *and for the good of us all, I will do my duty, Mother.*

She was impressed. She could feel the truth in him, the quiet nobility beneath the armor. She had destroyed many Vorrhaxi ships, razed their worlds, and carried a deep hatred for what they had done across the galaxy. But never had she looked this closely at one of them. Now she did. And what she saw changed her perspective.

Zareth'Kai, she said, *go to the medical lab. The bot will be waiting. I am about to make you even more capable.*

Zareth'Kai stepped into the medical lab, guided by Mother's soothing voice in his mind. For the first time in longer than he could remember, he felt no fear, no wariness—strange sensations for a soldier of the empire. Those instincts had kept him alive all his life. In the Vorrhaxi ranks, the unwary were already dead.

Arche waited for him beside the medical table, silent but patient. The robot greeted him in Zareth'Kai's own native language—in gestures, pheromones, and brief pulses of light. The invitation to disarm was polite but firm. Slowly, he complied. One by one, blades and tools clattered to the deck, followed by plates of thick, battle-scarred armor. That armor had been a part of him since his first commission, only removed when wounds demanded intervention. In the empire, it was simpler to recover a warrior's memory sack than to heal him. When the last piece hit the floor, the weight he carried—over two hundred human kilograms—was gone. Without it, the noble soldier seemed taller, broader, and more human.

He lay back on the table. Arche's voice came again, calm and certain. *Can you hear me in your mind now, soldier?*

"Yes," Zareth'Kai replied, startled at the intimacy of the thought-voice.

"Good. From now on, your words will be spoken through the medical AI bonded to your new armor. You will no longer need the heavy plates on the floor. Your armor will become a second skin. Others will see no change, but your new shields will hold the weapons you carried in precisely the same hidden places. Imagine the weapon in your mind, touch the place it was stored, and it will appear in your hand. Stronger, lighter, and sealed against the void. Environmentally controlled and always ready."

Zareth'Kai's scarred hands flexed slightly at the thought.

"When you interact with your armor," Arche continued, "the AI, an extension of me, will speak to you as I do now. Welcome to the rebellion, noble soldier. Mother believes you are a kind and honest soul. I hope she is right, because we have just made you a hundred times deadlier than before."

"I understand," Zareth'Kai said aloud, his voice resonating strangely through the AI link.

"And I ask only one thing in return—protect this motley group of warriors. I have grown fond of them."

Zareth'Kai didn't hesitate. "I will. To my last breath."

A new voice spoke then, deep inside the link. *Well, here we go. What will you call me?*

He blinked. "I've never named anyone before. What do you want to be called?"

In keeping with your warrior traditions and the new path you have chosen, you can call me the Path Keeper. I will be your guide. Duty and honor will be our guiding stars.

Zareth'Kai smiled faintly. "Path Keeper it is."

As Zareth'Kai stepped out of the medical suite, there was a lightness in his stride he had never known before. The door slid open, and Grace appeared in the threshold. She didn't simply walk inside, she glided as effortlessly as an ice skater crossing untouched ice. She was beautiful in every form she chose to wear. Not in the way a man might look upon a woman with lust or longing. This was something else entirely. She was like a painting in a museum, or a finely sculpted statue, something that simply existed to be admired. Her presence stirred a quiet joy, welling up from deep within the soul. Their eyes met for only a heartbeat, yet the glance carried the weight of hours of conversation. In that instant, both understood they were committed to this path. Whatever the end might bring, they knew, perhaps for the first time in their lives, that they were doing the right thing.

The medical robot's head swiveled toward the doorway as Grace stepped into the suite. "Well," it said in a smooth, almost amused tone, "the lovely and deadly Grace finally graces our humble medical bay. Forgive my rather obvious pun, my dear. Regardless, I am *most* pleased to see you."

Grace raised an eyebrow but didn't comment.

"I suppose you're here for your armor," Arche continued, "in preparation for the battle ahead."

"Yes," Grace replied. "Mother insisted, in fact."

"Wise of her. You may call me Arche. I know Mother seems, well, *motherly*, but she just wants to make sure you're safe. She may not say it outright, but she's quite fond of you. And even more fond" —Arche's optics gleamed faintly— "of the way you've awakened hope in Silas's heart."

Grace would have blushed if she remembered how. Instead, her ears felt strangely warm, a sensation she wasn't used to.

"Well," Arche said briskly, "let's get to work. Lay your weapons on the table there. I'll handle the rest."

Grace obeyed, removing her sidearms and blades, setting them carefully beside the operating couch. She lay back without hesitation, something that was, in itself, bizarre. Complete trust was a foreign feeling to her, yet here she was, relaxed while under the care of a medical machine.

"This won't hurt a bit," Arche assured her, beginning the armor integration process. Layer by layer, the living alloy fused with her skin, bonding seamlessly. Grace's breathing slowed. She felt the strange warmth of the armor spreading over her body, not hostile but protective. Almost like a second presence.

"You're finished," Arche said at last.

The armor's voice came alive inside her mind—low, steady, and clear. *I understand you are called Grace. I am your armor's AI, and I will remain with you as long as the armor functions.*

"How long is that?" Grace asked.

A faint chuckle echoed in her thoughts. *As long as you do, Grace. As long as you do.*

She smiled faintly. "What shall I call you?"

I know my brother AI protects your friend Zareth'Kai. He calls himself Path Keeper—he has sworn to keep your friend on his destined road. I understand you have sworn to Mother that you would protect Silas with your life. I will help you, as my brother helps him. How do you feel about the name Oath Keeper?

Grace considered it. "That will do," she said. "Oath Keeper you are, and together, we'll make sure the oath is never broken."

Mother hadn't been wasting her time drifting around Earth, watching the twins. She had been preparing, practically from the moment she'd entered the solar system. The first step was laying a web of sensors, each one giving her early warning of any approach. Those sensors had done their job. The fleet had turned toward Earth at last, beginning the final leg of their journey to unleash the attack she had long anticipated. She had prepared other surprises, too. Traps weren't her preferred method—she liked to meet her enemies head-on—but since they had been courteous enough to bring so many of their friends, she was more than happy to accommodate them. Now it was time to gather the players and set the stage, to let them begin writing their own tale. Once, hers had been a story of loss and desperation. Now, it would become one of rebirth and redemption. She had waited so long for this moment she could scarcely believe it was finally here.

***

Shaskiel and Threxil sat together for one final meeting before beginning the last leg of their journey into Earth's solar system. In three days' time, they would arrive. This would be their last tactical discussion before the opening moves of what they both hoped would be the end of this backwater world and its reported overabundance of those damn insufferable twins. The reemergence of the old enemy, with its twin-based technology and sentient ships, stirred conflicting feelings in both commanders. It was a reminder of dangers best forgotten, but also a spark of nostalgia for the glory days, when the empire marched like a well-oiled legion, loyalty flowing only toward the emperor and his insatiable appetite for conquest.

If this battle went well, Shaskiel thought, it could be the beginning of those glory days once more. It could return him to the emperor's good graces, even to the favor of the grand admiral, exactly where he belonged.

Threxil's thoughts were much the same, though her ambitions ran deeper. If she could capture one of the sentient ships—or even the wreckage of one—she could bargain her way back into the emperor's favor. Perhaps she could win a place there for her reluctant ally, Zev'Kala, as well. She could already see herself returning to the throne room with the traitors in chains, dragging them before the emperor. Better them than her.

"Well, what plans have you for this battle?" Threxil asked, her tone guarded.

"As I'm sure you've already guessed," Shaskiel replied smoothly, "I want to lay a trap for these ships. They think they're clever—let's prove they're not. We'll dangle a target they can't resist, and when they come for it, they'll walk right into our web."

Threxil's crest shifted subtly, her body language betraying hesitation before she even spoke. She already knew what was coming—*she* was to be the bait. There was no more tempting lure than a queen. Finally, she released a faint pheromone of reluctant acceptance. She would play her part in the plan. But if this fool's trap failed, he had better hope she didn't survive. But the trap was already in motion. Soon, the two forces would collide.

***

Silas slipped back to his room with Alex close on his heels. He was feeling uneasy and more than a little uncomfortable. Mother had laid the plans out clearly. Everyone knew their part by heart. But waiting was always the hardest part. Harder now, with his mind spinning faster and faster, refusing to slow. So many possibilities lay ahead. Ten trillion missteps could lead to disaster. Only a precious few would keep them on the path to success. As he lay in his rack, staring at the ceiling, a gentle tapping came at his door. "Please, come in," he said, not looking away. The door slid open. She stood there in the frame, lithe, poised, eyes bright blue, and hair so dark it almost shone black.

"May I come in, Silas?"

His mouth went dry. He barely managed a croaked *yes*.

Alex got up, gave Grace a long stare, then glanced back at Silas with something like a sly dog's wink before slipping out between her and the door.

She stepped inside. The door closed behind her. Silas sat up in the bed.

Grace moved toward him slowly, her voice gentle, like a trainer soothing a wary animal. "I have been waiting so long to be here with you," she said, "even for just these stolen moments. I know we don't know each other well … but I feel so strongly about you. So connected." She reached out, fingers brushing his leg. Silas flinched, his reaction too fast. She saw it and pulled back.

He caught the expression on her face and spoke, not with that dry, hesitant voice, but with a confidence that startled them both. "I've imagined you sitting next to me since the first time I saw you in that store. I've longed to touch you again since the moment I put my hand on your back to keep you from falling. I wish there were more time. I have so much to say, and as a man of few words, it frightens me to feel this much all at once. I need time to catch up. It's not possible to feel so much when we've barely met. You're alien. You're dangerous. And I know you were sent here to … well, it doesn't matter."

Grace hesitated, then said, "All of that is true for me, too. I had never known kindness before I met you in that store. I have never had anyone act to protect me, and you did it without hesitation, even knowing I wasn't what I seemed. Why?"

Silas thought for a moment. "Because I liked your smell. Because I liked your walk. Because I knew there are only so many perfect moments in the world, and there have been so few for people like me. When I looked into your eyes for the first time, I think I experienced my very first one. I'm no romantic. I won't sweep you away and fill your life with joy. But I can promise one thing: my undying devotion. The only other person I've ever felt this bond with has drawn every breath with me. And now, my heart beats to a different rhythm than his. Because now … it beats with yours."

***

The admiral studied the faces of his bridge crew. Each was someone he trusted without question, veterans who had stood beside him through countless battles. Yet, as he looked at the fleet arrayed around him, he couldn't help but feel underwhelmed. This was no armada. It was barely an observation force, if that. In past campaigns, he'd traveled with enough warships to blot out the stars; this wouldn't have been enough to form his personal guard. A sour thought crept in—was the emperor setting him up for failure? Or something worse? It wouldn't surprise him. Still, he was no fool. If the coming fight offered no victory, then he would take something else from it—information. And if not even that could be gained, he would vanish into the dark, taking his most loyal with him. They had been at his side since the beginning, and emperor willing, they would be there until the end.

***

It was time for the teams to break up and head to their respective ships. The plans were laid, the traps were set, and at long last, it was time to take the fight to the enemy. No warrior ever fought harder than when their home was at their back, and nothing stood between the empire and their world but a handful of defenders. Each was lost in their own thoughts.

Silas's mind was only on Grace. He didn't worry about Elias. If an atomic bomb went off, Elias would probably be the one man to crawl out of the crater grinning. Many thought him unkillable, and so far, they'd been right.

Silas's face flushed as he remembered a reckless impulse. Passing Zareth'Kai in a corridor, he'd handed him a folded note for Grace, something he'd written on a whim. He never acted on whims. Now he was regretting it. Still, maybe it was time to start taking chances. It had worked out so far.

That, of course, was the exact moment Alex brushed against his leg, looking up with bright eyes. His voice came into Silas's mind, not whispering, but laughing. *Oh boy … she's got you trapped already, and you don't even feel the chains that bind you. That's okay, though, buddy. They're velvet chains. Best kind.*

Elias walked with purpose, Max pacing beside him, stride for stride. The two were locked in, amped and ready. Elias was buzzing, not with fear or doubt, but with anticipation. No thoughts of the future or ghosts from the past. Only the now. That was Elias's sweet spot—smack in the middle of chaos. He wasn't a planner. He was a storm, a wildman. A berserker with a cause. When Elias had a righteous target in his sights, there was no stopping him. Mercy didn't enter the equation. And he liked it that way. He didn't expect to survive this war, and honestly, that didn't bother him. Every breath he'd taken since the serum had been a blessing. Every morning, he woke up without a burning thirst for whiskey, without the bone-deep ache that used to define him, and that was enough. These empire bastards? They had it coming.

Vaeril entered his ship after bidding farewell to the twins and the others. It surprised him, how deeply he'd come to care for Grace and Zee. *Zee*, the nickname he'd started calling the Vorrhaxi soldier, still felt odd on his tongue. The man had once been an enemy, a believer in everything Vaeril had sworn to destroy. But now, he looked at him as a kinsman. A brother-in-arms. War made strange allies. Survival made family. And Grace? She was a breath of fresh air in the long corridors of his weary soul. He had never had children—it wasn't in the cards for someone like him. Truthfully, he still could, but the odds were slim. He'd be lucky to survive the battle ahead, let alone the war that was coming. Still, if there was one thing he knew with certainty, it was this: They might not win, but they were going to give them hell.

And the twins? He chuckled to himself. He had never seen anything like them, and he doubted he ever would again. They were forces of nature, blunt and razor, chaos and calculation. And they were ready.

As he stepped onto the deck, Orrin's voice greeted him cheerfully. "Welcome, old man. You ready to kick some Vorrhaxi ass?"

Vaeril grinned. "Hell yes, I am. Let's do this."

Orrin, still channeling that sitcom humor Vaeril had grown used to, quipped, "You sure you wouldn't rather be back on Earth, yelling at kids to get off your lawn?"

Vaeril burst out laughing, snorting as he doubled over slightly. "You little shit. Just be ready. You know our task. Let's not fail."

Orrin's voice, for once, turned serious. "No worries, sir. We've got this."

For the first time, the AI had spoken to him not as an assistant or a soldier, but with genuine *reverence*. Vaeril nodded slowly, heart pounding with something very close to hope. "Yes, my boy, we do. Yes, we do."

Zareth'Kai stepped aboard Valshar behind Grace, the echo of farewell still lingering from his last conversation with the others. Before leaving, he had even knelt beside the twin dogs—Alex and Max—stroking their fur with a gentle reverence. They were more intelligent than most soldiers he had known, but what struck him most was their calm, their warmth and their loyalty. And they expected nothing in return. Such a thing did not exist in the empire. Kindness had always come with a price, affection with hidden strings. But this felt different. Genuine and honest, something worth fighting for.

He thought of Silas and the way the quiet man looked at Grace. He didn't need words. It was real, undeniably so. Silas had pressed a small folded note into Zareth'Kai's hand before departure. It was warm, as if the emotions that birthed it still lingered in the ink. Zareth'Kai was surprised it hadn't ignited in his palm.

As he approached Grace in the corridor, their eyes met. A glance passed between them, heavy with meaning, unspoken but clearly understood. Without a word, he placed the note in her hand. Then he turned and walked to his station. The time for emotion had ended. The battle was about to begin.

Grace had said her farewells to the crew, brief and purposeful, but had lingered when it came to Silas. There was something about him that stirred questions she wasn't yet equipped to answer. She'd observed his inner war with a mix of awe and something warmer. His affection for her was like an endless well—quiet, unspoken, but unmistakably deep. He held himself back, always. When she reached for him, he flinched, as if her touch might unravel something carefully contained. It broke her heart. She could guess at the horrors that shaped him, but even her training hadn't prepared her for someone like Silas.

She had spent long hours discussing it with *Mother*, the ship's vast, knowing mind more maternal than any human she'd ever imagined.

Mother had shown her the unvarnished truth, explained his broken-ness with brutal compassion. Silas carried wounds few could fathom, and still, he stood. Still, he fought. He still *loved*. And Grace? She would love no other. She felt it in her bones, in her blood, and in her mind. As surely as Elias chased everything with a skirt, Grace had found her own reckless devotion. The thought almost made her laugh. Silas's dry humor was rubbing off on her, and somehow, she was okay with that. But there wasn't time to dwell. Battle loomed.

She glanced at the note Zee had given her, its edges still warm from her palm. She had planned to save it, wait until after the battle to read it. But what if there was no *after?* Her fingers trembled as she unfolded the paper and began to read words that reached her in a voice she had longed to hear: Silas's heart, laid bare.

Grace, I know I don't always express myself well—not the way you do with your beautiful gestures and those graceful pheromones that say so much with-out words. I wish I could. So, I wrote this for you instead. It comes from the only place I know how to speak from—my heart. I hope, in these words, you'll see even a small part of what I feel for you.

Sometimes I hurt, sometimes I'm lost. Sometimes the walls press in until I can't breathe. Sometimes I feel so hollow, I cut at my own heart, just to see if it still bleeds. The pain that takes root in me, the kind that doesn't scream but stays, has broken me into more pieces than I knew I had. But you are the light that banishes my darkness. You never flinch and you never leave. You just keep picking up the pieces, no matter how sharp they are, no matter how many times I fall apart. No love is stronger than the kind that drags someone back from the edge. No love means more than the kind that faces the monsters and doesn't run. You faced mine and stayed. For you, Grace, all that I have to give, I give to you.

***

Mother would have sighed if she could. But sentient ships weren't built with fear or anxiety. Those emotions belonged to flesh. But love and rage? Yes, she had those. Why her kind had been made to feel those two emotions she did not know. It one of the few mysteries she'd never solved, she mused with a trace of amusement. But the loyalty she felt for this ragtag band of misfits, these wounded warriors and lost souls … it was stronger than anything she had felt before.

She needed clarity. The battle ahead was treacherous. This was more than a skirmish, it was a message. One to the empire. And one, perhaps, to all those still watching from the shadows of broken worlds. Someone had to rise. Someone had to *fight back.*

She reached out, not to the twins, but to the two ancient minds always near her. *Alex. Max.*

They responded instantly. *We're here, Mother,* they said in unison. *We've got this. You can count on us.*

This time, Alex added, *we have the right team. The right moment.*

This time, Max continued, *we win.*

She felt something stir in her—a flicker she didn't recognize. *Was it fear?* Not for herself, but for *them,* her boys. She needed to be her best self. Her sharpest self.

Mother, Alex said gently, *do you think they'll fear us when they see our true form? We're dogs … kind of. But not in the way the twins think, not really.*

She responded softly, *They will never abandon you. Any more than you would abandon them.* The connection pulsed with warmth. *Now go,* she commanded. *Take your posts. Let's make the empire rue the day they ever crossed our path.*

Valshar did not need to consider whether he was ready. He *was* ready. He had already faced the Vorrhaxi once before and survived. With the Ancient One's mechanical helpers having restored his systems beyond their original design, he was stronger than ever. And with this new crew—tested under fire, wounded but unbroken—Valshar felt something he had not dared to feel in centuries: hope. For the first time, victory didn't feel like a fantasy. It felt possible. And more importantly, *survival* for his crew, these strange, beautiful, imperfect beings he had come to cherish, also felt within reach. There would be no more waiting. It was time to take the fight to the enemy.

***

Shaskiel, true to form, surged toward Earth—driven not by caution, but by raw impatience. He was pressing every crew member, pushing them to their limits. He and Queen Threxil had devised a plan—calculated, brutal, and razor-edged. At the end of this cycle, he would either stand victorious or become just another shattered husk drifting through the black tide of space.

Threxil, ever the tactician, played her part to perfection. She was the bait—subtle, sharp, and smiling. A wounded predator feigning helplessness. Her ship, on her orders, had been meticulously rigged by her engineers to appear mortally struck in the early moments of battle. It would drift aimlessly, flickering on enemy sensors like a lamb awaiting slaughter. But that lamb had teeth. Too late would they realize the goat tethered to the stake was not prey. It was the trap.

The first stage of the battle began before Shaskiel even knew what was happening. The enemy fleet had been divided into four groups. The first, forty reinforced scout ships, dropped out of the void three jumps from Earth. The void had many oddities, but one truth remained: only a limited number of exit points existed. And Mother, ever the strategist, knew exactly which one they'd use. Large groups, especially forty ships or more, couldn't simply scatter out into open space—they needed to emerge together. But that made them predictable. And predictability was death. The ships emerged into an ambush. Mother's ships struck instantly, moving like a coordinated fighter—a middleweight against a lumbering brute. The enemy was larger and stronger, but slow. Mother's vessels darted in and out like a phantom boxer, untouchable and unrelenting. The enemy fired. They missed, again. And again. The slaughter began. The Vorrhaxi doctrine dictated strength in numbers, even for scouting runs. But these weren't elite imperial fleets, they were a cobbled together, barely disciplined swarm. And they were following outdated tactics. Tactics Mother had studied for centuries.

Three ships—Valshar, the Ancient One, and Vaeril's shuttle—moved as one, shielding, striking and covering. It was surgical violence, calculated and elegant. It was carnage. The scout ships, likely considered expendable, died first. Their crews didn't inspire confidence with their deaths. They died with confusion written across their consoles, wondering where the enemy was located.

Inside the shuttle, Vaeril worked in seamless coordination with Orrin, the young AI gifted to him by the Ancient One. "Listen, boy!" Vaeril snapped for the tenth time in as many minutes. "You've got to stop taking so many damned chances. We're fast, sure. We hit hard. But it only takes one solid punch to knock us out of the fight."

Orrin didn't argue, but the shuttle still danced too close to death. They streaked through the enemy formation, sometimes missing blasts by centimeters. The hull glowed red-hot from repeated near misses. Vaeril grit his teeth. "Luck doesn't last forever." He was proud of the AI. The boy was flawless. But flawless or not, overconfidence killed.

The commander of the scout fleet was outmatched, overwhelmed, and clearly out of his depth. He continued barking orders to ships that had already been destroyed, vaporized before they could even act. In Earth terms, it was as if he were playing checkers while his enemy played chess. Desperation crept in. One gambit remained. They might not be able to defeat the enemy outright, but if they could seriously damage just one of the ships—maybe even cripple it—it might throw the others out of balance. It might buy them enough time to hold until the rest of the fleet arrived. There would be no retreat. No surrender. In Shaskiel's final war council, the orders had been clear: succeed or die. Nothing else was acceptable.

As a last-ditch strategy, the commander ordered not one but three of his remaining scout ships to overload their cores and self-destruct at the exact moment the courier-class vessel came in for another strafing run. Of the three enemy vessels, that small ship appeared the most reckless—constantly darting in and out, inflicting damage, weaving through chaos with insane precision. If they could just wound it badly enough to force it to withdraw, it might be enough.

The orders were confirmed. The trap was laid. All that remained was for that damned courier to make one more run across the heart of the formation. The commander's face split into a grin as the shuttle peeled off and began its attack vector. Right on cue. The vessel screamed across the void, aiming straight for one of the larger ships near the center of the group. And just as it drew perilously close, three ships ignited at once. The explosion was magnificent. A rolling inferno of metal, radiation, and fire. For a moment, it was blinding. And yet, that damned little ship survived. Battered and leaking vapor, it limped away under covering fire from the other two vessels. But it was still alive. And that meant the commander's gamble had failed.

The enemy commander believed he had failed but in truth he had done exactly what he needed to do. The courier ship had taken damage but it hadn't been destroyed. Instead, it limped away through the void, wounded but alive. Worse still, the other two ships had immediately broken off their attack and raced to aid their crippled companion. This gave the enemy the time it sorely needed to regain the advantage in the battle.

Aboard the courier, Vaeril fought to stay calm. Smoke filled the control chamber. He knelt, coughing, his armor shielding him from the worst of it, buying him hours of breathable air. But the damage from the scout ship's final sacrifice had crippled key systems. "Orrin!" he called again. No answer. The ship's AI had either been silenced or worse. Vaeril's voice trembled, not with fear, but something deeper. He wasn't worried about the ship. The nanites would eventually repair it. No, his thoughts were with the young soul who had become like a son to him. He reached out with his mind, connecting to Mother, the great ship. *"Mother, Orrin is hurt, or worse. Please, come to me.*

Help him." There was no pretense of command, no diplomatic poise, only the raw, heart-wrenching plea of a father terrified for his child.

The twins looked at one another. No words passed between them, but they *knew.* The time had come. Vaeril's anguish rang clearly in their minds, and though he said nothing aloud, the feeling struck hard. Orrin—the quirky, spunky AI they'd all come to care for—might have been critically damaged in the blast. The self-destruction of the Vorrhaxi ships wasn't bravery. It was cowardice. Hundreds of lives thrown away. Not for strategy. Not for honor. But to deny the enemy information. To waste life.

Silas felt a white-hot fury rise in him like never before. It boiled in his chest, and the heat of it fed a clarity he hadn't known he needed. He'd once heard that in every land ruled by tyrants, the people weren't necessarily bad, they were either too brainwashed to know better, or too terrified to resist. It was true here, too. Most just wanted to live, to survive, to protect their children, and find some kind of peace. The empire had turned that simple dream into a weapon.

Silas clenched his fists. He was ready to act. And this time, there would be no shadow. You could have heard a pin drop in Mother's control room when Elias and Silas spoke in perfect unison. "It's time." The words echoed like a final key turning in a lock.

The ship stilled, the lights dimmed for a breathless moment, and even the hum of her systems seemed to wait. Then, as if by ancient instinct, the twins added softly, "Mother, let us go."

Alex and Max turned to one another. No words were exchanged—none were needed. The bond between them was older than any language. Then they changed. Before the twins' eyes, the two loyal dogs transformed. Their bodies grew taller, broader, and more angular. What had once been fur was now a flexible mesh of armor. Their eyes glowed with fierce intelligence and shimmering energy pulsed beneath plates of radiant bio-steel. Along their backs rose sharp quills, vibrating with raw kinetic power. Still dogs, yet something more. Guardians ascended, perhaps. In perfect mimicry of their bonded humans, the newly revealed forms of Alex and Max said, "Mother, let us go. It is time for all of us to become what we were always meant to be—the hand of the righteous warrior who will strike down this evil, once and for all." And to the dogs' quiet astonishment, neither twin flinched at the transformation. They simply turned and nodded—acknowledging them, accepting them. Their ascension was no surprise. It was destiny.

EPILOGUE

VOIDRUNNER TWO | THE BATTLE BEGINS

The battle for the galaxy was only just beginning. The Vorrhaxi had no idea what they had truly unleashed when they went after the twins. Silas and Elias had been reborn into something new—something the galaxy had never seen before and might never see again. This was no war. This was ignition. This skirmish was a match struck against the dry, cracking forest of a galaxy ripe for a wildfire. What was coming would rage across star systems, consuming tyrants and turning empires to ash. The emperor, had he worn boots, might have quaked in them. But he didn't know, not yet. But he would. The regret of awakening these twins, of playing God without knowing the storm he'd called forth, would haunt him until his final breath. *And maybe not even then would his soul know peace.*

ABOUT THE AUTHORS

Daniel L. Watson and James D. Watson are identical twins born in Arkansas and raised with a deep respect for service, honor, and storytelling.

Daniel is a United States Marine Corps combat veteran of Operation Desert Storm, a retired chief of police, and a retired adjunct college professor. In addition to writing, he's an avid runner and golfer. He's also a passionate advocate for character, discipline, and resilience.

James is a retired Command Sergeant Major in the U.S. Army, a career Airborne Infantryman, and a veteran of numerous global operations, including Desert Storm, Mogadishu, Iraq, Afghanistan, Cuba, Haiti, Egypt, and Manas, Kyrgyzstan. His leadership across decades of deployments is the foundation for the moral and emotional depth of the worlds they create.

The Watsons are lifelong patriots and fierce supporters of all branches of the U.S. Armed Forces. They are also the creators of the Voidrunner series—a story of devotion forged in loyalty and written for all who have felt no hope remained, only to realize it was always within their reach.